Here's what four of America's favorite authors-about-town have to say about Ramble House's two Joel Townsley Rogers' collections, NIGHT OF HORROR and KILLING TIME—

"Rogers was the real deal, author of a true masterpiece, *The Red Right Hand,* and a pulp man who could, and did, do it all. If you want the strong heady thrill of genuine pulp — and not the pale imitation that came later — latch on to both of these collections immediately."

— Ed Gorman

"*Killing Time* collects six pulp novellas by Joel Townsley Rogers, including the original version of the classic *The Red Right Hand,* along with a story about a pulp writer and a story with a character named Captain Sparrow, whom I like to think is a distant cousin to the famous Pirate of the Caribbean. Highly recommended!"

— Bill Crider

"The six tales gathered here are among Joel Townsley Rogers' most accomplished pulp magazine contributions of the 30s and 40s — cleverly plotted, highly atmospheric, suspenseful, and dripping with menace. The original magazine version of his classic crime novel, *The Red Right Hand,* and Alfred Jan's insightful analyses of Rogers' work, are the highlights. *Killing Time* is a must for every connoisseur of vintage crime fiction."

— Bill Pronzini

"Ramble House has specialized in bringing neglected (and sometimes alternative) geniuses back into print. First came the great Harry Stephen Keeler, then the so-clever Norman Berrow. More recently Ramble House has been sparking the rehabilitation of Joel Townsley Rogers, a versatile and prolific author who seemed to be totally forgotten save for one novel, *The Red Right Hand. Killing Time* is the second Ramble House collection of Rogers's shorter fiction, and every story in it, from the 1934 'Murder of the Dead Man' to the 1947 title story, hits with a wallop and a sting. Bravo! Bravissimo!"

— Richard A. Lupoff

# KILLING TIME:

## And Other Stories

# KILLING TIME

## And Other Stories

**A COLLECTION OF SHORT FICTION**

**BY**

***JOEL TOWNSLEY ROGERS***

**WITH AN INTRODUCTION AND AFTERWORD BY**

To Loretta,

***Alfred Jan***

Happy scary reading!

**RAMBLE HOUSE**

ISBN 13: 978-1-60543-000-3

ISBN 10: 1-60543-000-5

Published: 2007 by Ramble House
Cover Art: Gavin L. O'Keefe
Preparation: Alfred Jan and Fender Tucker

*Table of Contents*

# Killing Time and Other Stories:

## A Sample of Joel Townsley Rogers' Mystery Novelettes

### Introduction by Alfred Jan

One of the most versatile authors of the pulp era, Joel Townsley Rogers appeared in magazines as diverse as *Wings*, *Snappy Stories, Adventure, Argosy, Detective Fiction Weekly,* and *Thrilling Wonder Stories*. Even within the mystery genre, Rogers did not adhere to one formula, as this collection will show. Regarding my previously published essay on imminent menace, I made it an Afterword, because I analyzed plots and revealed endings in "The Red Right Hand", "Killing Time", and "The Hiding Horror", so readers who want the thrill of discovery should attend to the stories before the Afterword. The remaining story discussed, "The Murderer", can be found in *Night of Horror and Other Stories*, the first Ramble House Rogers collection edited by Barry Warren.

I included the original pulp version of his masterpiece *The Red Right Hand,* because while the novel has been reprinted numerous times since its 1945 release, the pulp novelette upon which it was based has never been reprinted to my knowledge. Both exude identical degrees of horror and tension despite length difference. "Murder of the Dead Man", a traditional murder mystery taking place in a resort hotel reprised the venomous snake theme Rogers used in the supernatural yarn "Hark! The Rattle!" which was honored by its appearance in the first issue of *Weird Tales*, March 1923. "The Crimson Vampire" combined his interest in aviation (which he taught to recruits near the end of World War I) with the standard weird menace plot found in pulps like *Horror Stories*, *Terror Tales, Dime Mystery.* "The Hiding Horror", with its creepy old house and eccentric inhabitants, employs devices anticipating those in "The Red Right Hand", but also contains social/political commentary usually missing from his stories. "My Friend Death" allows us access to the mental deterioration of a psychopath whose defenses crumble before our eyes.

The most amazing connections, however, occurred between "Killing Time" and Cornell Woolrich's "The Penny-A-Worder" from Ellery Queen's Mystery Magazine, September 1958. Self-referentially, both used pulp magazine writers as main characters, and the act of writing, along with its chief tool the typewriter played prominent roles in their plots. Furthermore, Rogers' title mirrors Woolrich's fictional story title, "Killing Time" used for the story by his character Dan Moody for a detective pulp called Startling Stories! But Rogers also wrote "The Night the World Turned Over" for the real Startling Stories, a science fiction pulp dated November 1952! The chances of the reclusive Woolrich contacting his contemporary were probably nil, making these parallels very unusual.

Despite plot diversity, Rogers maintains thematic unity of expressionistic evocative concepts such as touches of Grand Guignol, psychopathology, fluidity of identity, and the banality of evil represented by horrific acts committed by milquetoast men. The double meaning of "killing time" collapses temporality by alluding to instantaneous murder and the long build up preceding it. Roger's atmospheric style approaches, but is distinct from Cornell Woolrich's, which may render the previously described coincidences less shocking. As I wrote in my published essay, Joel Townsley Rogers remains under-appreciated today, but Ramble House is doing its best to remedy this situation.

# KILLING TIME

## CHAPTER ONE

## YOURS FOR MURDER

"THE MURDERER—" Tiny Little read over again the sentence on his typewriter—"was lurking just beyond the door, I realized."

He rested his elbows on his pajama-clad thighs, meditatively wiping the sweat from his naked chest and brown, golden-haired forearms with his palms, while he considered it. *Semper Fidelis* said a tattooed inscription on his right forearm, beneath a design of a globe and anchor. *Death Before Dishonor* said a tattooed ribbon on his left forearm, wound around a tattooed dagger from which dripped drops of blood. *Atom Baby* said an inscription on his chest, beneath a picture of a well-developed young person, obviously of the female sex, and apparently a native of the tropics, since she had no clothes on. Or, practically none.

The New York summer day was hot. The air in Tiny's furnished rear bedroom-and-bath was stale and windless. The fabric of his pajama pants stuck to the varnished wooden seat of his rocking chair. He sweated; and the Atom Baby sweated, and she jiggled when he breathed.

The line upon his typewriter was a simple direct statement of fact. It was grammatically correct, easily understandable by even the most elementary intelligence. Still, he wasn't quite sure whether he was completely satisfied with it. It might not be sufficiently interesting and exciting. "So what?" he supposed anybody might say on reading it, and toss it down again.

Rule three of "Five Fundamental Rules for Writing Murder Stories, by Richard C. Morgelhead: *Start your story with a high-tension situation which hangs over the reader like a rat-trap about to snap.*

Well, Tiny thought defensively, if a murderer lurking just beyond the door wasn't enough to interest anybody, he didn't know what was. It would interest him.

He lifted up his right fist, and jabbed the index finger of it down.

"W-i-t-h a-p-p-r-e-h-e-n-s-i-o-n," he plunked down upon the keys, with the slow and solid force of a pile-driver.

The murderer was lurking just beyond the door, I realized with apprehension. . . .

That was in accordance with rule four of the Five Rules: *Put feeling into your story.* Apprehension was what a man would feel in such a situation, naturally. Perhaps he should make it "terror." But apprehension, at the least.

So far, so good. He had already followed rule two—*Give your story an interesting title, and tell whom it's by*—in the lines above which read:

MURDER WILL IN
By Reginald Meice Little

It was an interesting title, since it could be about practically anything. Rule one, of course—*Put your address at upper right hand corner of first page*—he had obeyed in the prescribed place.

Only rule five remained to follow. Rule Five: *Narrate the various happenings of your story, and end it with a bang—the trap which you set up in your opening sentence has snapped.*

It was really rather simple. The only difficulty was that he didn't know just what was going to happen. He had a murderer at the door. But he didn't even know his name. He didn't know what he looked like, or why he was there, or what had made him a murderer in the first place, anyway.

Tiny focused his straw-lashed guileless, sky-blue gaze on the door of his room, facing him across the rickety little book-end table which served him as a typewriter-stand. He stared at it with an unwinking intensity.

It was a rectangular-shaped door, with a top, a bottom, and two sides. It had a white china doorknob and a black-japanned lock-case, and was hung on three tarnished brass butt hinges. It was divided into two panels, an upper and a lower. It was painted a dark red imitation mahogany, much scuffed and scarred.

Its top panel had a split down its middle, through which a hairline of light, he recalled, was visible at times—at night, for instance, when the hall light was on, after he had turned his own lights out; or at times during the day when possibly there was bright sunlight out in the hall. However, there was no light visible through the crack now.

Some previous tenant, obviously an artist, had scratched a setter dog on the panel, and some other artist—or the same—a woman's bust and hips. There were telephone numbers and triangles scratched. Someone had scratched a large crude heart, inscribed with initials and a date: "R.M. loves D.D., 12/15/44." It was a record of departed love which had a mildly nostalgic quality to Tiny, since his own two first initials were

R.M.; and on the date recorded he had still been on Adalak, where Captain D.D. Smith, known unofficially as Desperate Desmond, had been the battalion adjutant, whom nobody had loved, not even the booby gulls.

The bottom panel was scuffed with shoe marks, but otherwise unadorned. The door was somewhat warped, or else the floor of the old rookery had sagged, leaving an inch-wide gap between the door bottom and the worn threshold, through which at times he was aware of the shadowed feet of other tenants on the floor, or on the floor above, as they passed along the worn hall carpet towards the stairs, or perhaps paused for a moment outside, feeling for their keys, before approaching their own doors. There was some shadow out there now in the hall, just beyond his threshold—probably a trashcan or carpet-sweeper that Mrs. Yussup, the building superintendent's wife, had placed there during her daily morning task of spreading around the dirt, and not a pair of feet.

Tiny wiped the sweat from his pectoral muscles again. He pulled his eyes away. His alarm clock, standing on the bureau beside the bottle with the red satin ribbon around it—a bottle of one hundred proof Clover Dew which he had bought to celebrate with when he should have sold his first story—said hour 1404. Actually it said four minutes after two, civilian time.

He had piled out of bed an hour ago and planted himself down at his machine, without dressing or even having yet had his bath. It was a good hour for concentration, or should be. The midday noises of Gruber Street out front came to him only in muted tones here in the rear. Most of the other tenants in the building were job-holders—the poets employed in advertising agencies, the artists in comic-book publishing houses—and had left for their offices hours ago, as if they were no more than ordinary white-collar workers from the Bronx. Down in the basement Mrs. Yussup was taking her siesta. The Atom Baby in the apartment above his had not yet begun to shake the ceiling with her tap-dancing exercises.

The Atom Baby—the big, smooth-limbed, red-haired model who lived up in 4D. She was not related to the tattooed lady on Tiny's chest, who had merely come out of the needle artist's brain. She called herself Miss Dolores Delarte, and had probably been born Mildred Kluntz, but Tiny thought of her as the Atom Baby. It was about time now for her to be arising to a new day and night. Since she had been having a party up in her place till five o'clock or after this morning, that Tiny knew of, it might be a little later yet before she waked.

Yet with all the quietness about him, during the hour he had done no more than write a title for a story, without any story in mind, and that one sentence as a starter on it. A murderer was at the door. Beyond that his brain was a blank.

He picked up a squeezed half lemon from a saucer of sugar beside his typewriter, and sucked it moodily. If at first you don't succeed, suck lemons.

In three weeks of being a Greenwich Village author, he had written eighteen stories—nineteen, counting the one he had done last night and sent off this morning. He had eighteen rejection slips from *Banner Murder Stories* to prove he was a writer.

Last night's story hadn't yet had time to come back.

One of his handicaps in writing murder stories, perhaps, was that he had never known a murderer. He had seen men killed, of course. There had been that night on Adalak when he had waked up in barracks with the roar of a .45 hammering in his eardrums, and shouts and screams, and flashes in the blackness. And had rolled from his bunk, and crawled, and leaped upon that dark figure standing in the doorway shooting and laughing, bringing it to the deck. But it had been only poor Captain Desperate Desmond Smith, lean, blond, and shaking, and gone quite crazy. And though Desperate Desmond had killed three sleeping gyrines before Tiny brought him down, that hadn't been murder. It had just been Adalak.

Again there had been the maniac Jap who had been still holed up in a cave on Saipan when he had got there, a year after the island had been taken. He had used to creep out at night and cut throats in native huts, white soldiers' and brown girls', and do a little vampire-drinking of their blood, until he had finally been located in his stinking hole and blasted to an end. But he had been only an animal, not even human. And an animal may be a tiger or a vampire, but it can't be called a murderer.

Or the big shaven-skulled Russky sergeant in Tokio who had carried grenades around in his pockets, which he had liked to heave into passing *Amerikanski* jeeps, and run. He had carried two pistols, too, and a curved Cossack knife; and on the night when he had heaved a grenade beneath the wheels of the car that Tiny had been driving, and had made the tactical error of running away down a blind alley which had proved a cul-de-sac, he had used both guns and knife, as well, against the M P.'s and the little wooden-faced Jap cops who had helped Tiny corner him. They had had to break a tommygun butt on his head before they had hammered peace into him.

But he had been just a great big boy with an overgrown sense of humor, as the Russian Tokio command had realized when he had been turned over to them, finding it sufficient to give him a reprimand and send him home—Tiny had heard that in the hospital, while he had been getting himself measured for a metal foot to replace the five-toed pink one which the big Slavic humorist had blown off. He didn't have any hard feelings about it. The Russkies were good-natured, and liked to play. They just played rough.

To be a real murderer, a man has to have brains, and has to kill secretly, for some purpose useful to him. And Tiny had never met any in his life.

Maybe his name was against him, too, as a murder author—Reginald. Still he couldn't part it on the side, and call himself R. Meice Little. It sounded like a question about the size of household rodents. His nickname of Tiny Little was no better. The inevitable picture which it conjured up, of a six-foot two, two hundred and ten pound straw-headed giant who could pick up a jeep by its rear end out of hub-deep Adalak mud and spank its behind before setting it on the road again, and heave ammunition cases around like bricks and lob forty-pound mortar shells like tennis balls, hardly seemed dignified for a some-day-to-be (he hoped) world-famous author.

Yet in spite of his handicaps of name and of non-acquaintance with murderers, he would make out eventually. He was twenty-one years old, which isn't the end of the road yet. He was a high-school graduate and knew several thousand words. He knew the approximate location of most of the keys on a typewriter, too, and could manage to hit the one he wanted nine times out of ten, when he took good aim. He had beef, persistence, and an inquiring mind.

Beyond those qualities and abilities, he had some promise of eventually becoming a writer because, unlike a million and a half other aspiring novices and beginners, he didn't send his scripts to the *Saturday Evening Post,* which gets a freight car load every day, more than ten thousand readers could read if they read around the clock; but had fixed his aim, more realistically and objectively, on *Banner Murder Stories,* which didn't cover quite so wide a field, and had more measurable and definite editorial demands.

He had fixed his sights on that particular market in part because a packing case containing all the old issues of *Banner Murders* for fifteen or twenty years back had been, by chance, the principal component of the recreational library which had been put ashore at Adalak when the station had been established, contributed by the SPREAFFS, the Society for the Providing of Reading Entertainment to American Forces on Foreign Service. If he had been at some other station, it might have been a box of old *Lifes, Farmer's Almanacs,* Sears-Roebuck catalogs, or copies of *Compact, the Magazine of Feminine Hygiene and Charm;* in which case his life might conceivably have been altered. During the two years he had been on Adalak he had read the stacks of them as some men read Shakespeare or the Bible, starting at the beginning and going right through, and then starting all over again, till he had practically memorized verbatim every story in every issue. *Banner Murder Stories* had been his anchor-chain to the world of reality and stateside life, the world of city streets, girls, lights, movies, cops, fights, and normal human impulses, amidst all that fantastic nightmare of fog and mud and willawaw-driven rain. Perhaps if poor old Desperate Desmond had read murder stories himself, he wouldn't have gone crazy.

But perhaps the chief reason that he had picked on *Banner Murder Stories* as his goal to shoot at was because he had discovered, on getting hold of a current issue after his return to the States, that Richard C. Morgelhead himself was now the editor of it.

He was one of Richard C. Morgelhead's followers and devotees. And it had seemed to him that Richard C. Morgelhead would recognize by instinct and at sight the work of one of his own pupils when it arrived in the editorial offices of *Banner Murder Stories,* and would read it with extra loving attention—that if any editor in the world would buy his stories, that one was Richard C Morgelhead. And yet he had written and sent to *Banner Murders* eighteen hopeful contributions—nineteen, counting last night's—and had received them back with eighteen printed rejection slips, typographically attractive, but not varying by a comma in the cold impersonality of their regrets.

Perhaps Richard C. Morgelhead had never got to see them. Perhaps they had been opened by some fluff-brained eighteen-year-old typist or telephone girl who wouldn't know a murderer if he put a noose about her fair white throat, and who had a natural antipathy towards all writers just on general principles, like his neighbor Miss Dolores Delarte, the Atom Baby upstairs, and who had sent them back unread.

With the hope that that might be the explanation, in sending off his story this morning—THE BODY IN THE BATHTUB, by Reginald Meice Little, twenty-eight pages of double-spaced typescript, about nine thousand words, return if unavailable to R. M. Little, Apartment 3D, 99 Gruber St., Greenwich Village, New York City—he had ventured to enclose, at the last moment, a little note of a few hastily scrawled words, cheerfully and informally calling the story to Richard C. Morgelhead's attention:

> Here you are, Mr. Morgelhead! Surprise, surprise, from one of your unknown followers! Will be interested in obtaining your reaction to my little detective effort.
>
> Yours for quieter and more diabolic murders,
>
> Richard Meice Little,

It had been an effort to establish what had been called, in the high-school salesmanship course which Tiny had taken his senior year, "the personal touch."

## CHAPTER TWO

## UP AN ATOM

THE STORY WHICH he had written last night and sent off this morning had been inspired by Miss Delarte, the Atom Baby in the apartment above him. Miss Delarte would probably have been surprised, and perhaps insulted, to learn that she had been a literary inspiration, even for a murder story. She was definitely not the intellectual type herself. It was possible that, at one time in her life, she had been compelled to go through the first grade, and even grades three and four, and had learned to spell c-a-t and a minimum of other words—if so, she must have heartily resented it. But she was hardly literary, or even literate. Her sole reading now consisted of the sign, LADIES ROOM, in night clubs, when she wanted to powder her nose after the fourth or fifth highball; and, of course, the figures on folding money. Her purpose in life was to be a delight to the eye and an excitement to the senses.

Tiny didn't know the Atom Baby very intimately. He had met her first one morning a couple of days after he had taken his apartment, when he had had to complain to her about her tub which had overflowed.

He had been lying, luxuriating, in his own hot bath at eight o'clock, when the first drop had hit him between the eyes. He had blinked and turned his gaze upwards, just as another had come *splopping* down.

A seepage of water was spreading across his bathroom ceiling. It gathered slowly to a point directly over him, and when it reached drop size, it dropped; while another gathered. *Splop! Splop! Splop!* Chill, dismal, dirty with the woodbeams and laths and plaster and rusty nails through which it had seeped its way, immitigable and endless, the water oozed and gathered on the ceiling, coalescing its molecules, and hesitated over him; then let go, descending. Between his eyes again—*splop!*

More than a little mad, he had wallowed up out of his tub, and given himself a flick of his towel and jerked on pants and shirt. Strapping on his aluminum foot, already shod, and kicking on another shoe, he had grabbed up his cane, and had gone upstairs to knock on the door of 4D above,

The Atom Baby, clad in a green silk couch cover or luncheon cloth thrown casually and loosely about her splendid torso, had opened the door in person, her dark red hair tousled, her eyes the smoky lava-grey of slumbering volcanoes.

"Oh!" she said, with her gaze slowly awakening as it moved from his unbuttoned shirt front up to his face and over it. "I thought you were just my hubby. Wait till I put on some lipstick. I don't feel dressed without it."

"That's all right," he said. "My name's Little. I live in the apartment below you. There's water dripping from your bathroom onto me."

"Oh!" she said. "I remember I started to draw a bath when I came in. I must have dropped the body down while I was waiting for it, and tumbled off. What time is it?"

"It's eight o'clock," he said patiently.

"It can't be," she said. "We didn't leave the Dutchman's till almost eight. And after that there was Jerry's place, where I met that fella George. I was stinko. I remember now, it was eleven when George brought me home. I thought I'd have a cold bath."

She rubbed her beautiful face with her fist, as if it were no more than any common face.

"Oh, eight o'clock in the morning, you mean. Has it been dripping on you long?"

"No, it just started dripping."

"I must have tumbled off," she repeated. "You're in three-D?" she added. "There used to be an artist. He had wild parties down there. That's where I met my hubby. His name was Charlie Baltz or Billy Merkey, but then he lost his money and they sent him to jail or something, or maybe Indiana. Oh!" she exclaimed, hitching her casual covering more closely about her. "You must be the writer! Mrs. Yussup told me there was a writer moving in three-D. God, how I hate writers!"

Her smoky gaze slid from his face down to his chest, and on down to the ashwood cane he leaned on to his feet motionless at the threshold. Standing on one hip, with her beautiful thighs and calves posed like a marble Venus, with a drooping mouth.

"What's the idea of the cane?" she said. "You got a gimp?"

"I've lost a foot," he explained. "It helps to use a cane, till I get more used to it."

"Lost it!" she exclaimed, with a visible shudder. "My God, you mean you've got a foot off? How horrible!"

Her mouth was curled downward. Her sultry eyes were full of scorn.

" 'S too bad," she said, with an effort at graciousness. "It's not your fault, I guess. What do you wear—one of these gumpus things? I suppose you were a sojer. You get it shot off?"

"No," he said wearily. "I put it in my mouth and bit it off. You'll turn the water off in your tub, will you? Thanks."

She was a beautiful Polynesian savage with a white skin. She was something that belonged in an art museum, on a marble pedestal. She didn't have a brain in her head or a heart in her breast, but she could drive any man's brain crazy and burst his heart, just looking at her. . . Tiny had wheeled on his good foot, with a wry, grinning nod, and had descended the stairs again carefully with his cane.

The ceiling in the bathroom had continued dripping all day, though she must have turned the water off, with an accumulation in the beams and plaster. He couldn't forget her.

He had seen her again four or five days later, around six in the afternoon, when he had been going out with the manuscript of a story which he had been working on furiously all day—a story about a mad scientist, who shot hypos of nuclear-fission material into unsuspecting victims whom he lured to his lair—on his way to mail it to *Banner Murders* and have dinner at the Italian restaurant down at the corner. Just as he had been starting out the front door of the apartment house, she had come charging in, with her arms embracing a load of bottles, from off the bright sunlit street.

She had hit him headlong, knocking him back against the wall of the hall with the force of her charge, jolting the manuscript out from beneath his arm and his cane out of his grip. He had sprawled, with his shoulders sliding on the wall, off-balance, trying to get his stance again on his good foot and his other foot which wasn't there. She had paused breathlessly to glare at him, beautifully and fragrantly perspiring, with a healthy young animal warmth, her dark red hair in damp tendrils about her broad, low brow, her wide crimson mouth melting, a smoky look in her eyes—clad in some diaphanous knee-length frock of pale-green silk, cradling her dozen bottles lovingly in her arms.

"Oh, hello, Mr. Gimpus!" she said brightly. "That's all right. I know you didn't mean to bump into me. Gee, you look a scream, staggering that way, like you had a load on. Did anyone come to see me while I was out?"

"There was some man upstairs knocking at your door as I came down, I think," said Tiny, reaching carefully down to the floor for his manuscript and cane.

"What kind of a looking fella?" she said. "Was he kind of reaching his right hand over and pulling his left ear-lobe while he was standing there?"

"I didn't see what he looked like. Just someone at your door, up through the banisters."

"It was probably my great big sweet hubby," she said with a bright, sharp laugh. "It had better be. He's ten days late with my maintenance, and I phoned his secretary this morning that he'd better come across today, or else. He always jerks his left ear with his right hand like he was milking it when he's agitated, and he's always agitated when he thinks of me. That's why I asked. I said I'd wait in for him, but I had to run out a minute to get some refreshments for a poker party I'm having tonight."

"Well, he must be still up there," Tiny said. "You haven't missed him."

"A hundred and fifty lousy bucks a month," she said. "And I've got practically to tear the town apart every time to get it. If I didn't have friends, I don't know how I'd live. Would you like to come up and join the party this evening, Mr. Gimp?"

"I'm sorry," said Tiny. "I have a previous date."

"Well, some other time," she said. "Table stakes, dealer's choice and we generally play stud. When anybody's lost the pile he brought, we play strip for fun."

"It must be fun," said Tiny.

After finishing dinner, Tiny had gone up to Times Square for a couple of long and late movies, though he hadn't intended to. When he had returned home, after two o'clock, by the raucous noises upstairs the party was still going on. For sleepless hours, it had seemed to him. Though perhaps a part of it was mingled with his dreams.

There had been other parties upstairs, about twice a week. And every afternoon when the Atom Baby wasn't off on one of her long week-ends there had been the tap of feet overhead and the vibrating of the ceiling which announced that she had aroused to a new glorious day and night, as she practiced gymnastic dances, not more than twelve feet away from him, as the moth flies and the wood-worm bores. If he had been a termite.

But Tiny had shunned seeing her again, or any of her friends and party guests, timing his comings and goings to avoid hours when she or they might be passing up or down the hall and stairs. A beautiful animal in woman's shape, he reiterated to himself, without a brain or heart. No more than a potato. He felt almost grateful, in a way, to the humorous Russky prankster who had blown up his speeding jeep with such hilarious surprise and run laughing from him down the alley, while he had crawled out, and crawled after him, bloodily and grimly, with his foot hanging by a thread. For except for his maiming, which made her think of him as Mr. Gimpus, a mutilated man abhorrent to the perfectly healthy animal that she was, she might have made a play for him; and he might have let himself be as gone over her, and sunk as deep with her, as hell.

A writer's life, he told himself, is to observe and write about life, not necessarily to live it. Certainly not with any Atom Baby. He had seen her and spoken to her twice, and that was all. He knew nothing of her past, and little of her present; he didn't know any of her friends, he didn't even know her name, beyond her improbable art one. He knew nothing about her, really.

Still he had got something out of her last night—the story he had done. Probably the first time that any man had ever got anything out of her without her knowing it, and for free, in all her twenty-odd years of rich abundant and carefree life.

It wasn't anything that he had planned at all. It had just come to him. He had been trying to start a story after dinner about a hashish-eating assassin, when in her apartment overhead another party had begun.

It had started strong, and had given promise of keeping up strong, the biggest and most hilarious yet. A dancing or stomping party, and not strip-poker tonight, it seemed, mingled with whoops, howling laughter, and bellowing off-key songs. Even a hashish-eating assassin couldn't keep his mind on business during that. Grimly Tiny had pulled out the page on his machine which he had wrecked and mangled, and crumpled it on the floor. He had inserted a fresh sheet, plunking out again his name and address at the upper right hand corner. And had sat rocking himself quietly and grimly in his hardwood rocker at his typing table, sucking a lemon.

He had tried to concentrate on his assassin. But instead, the noise upstairs, the thought of the Atom Baby's sculptured limbs, of her smoky eyes and melting cherry mouth, and all the little things about her—her turning on of her bath-water and leaving it to overflow, till, hours later, it had seeped through the floor and ceiling and begun its slow *splop* down on him; her great big sweet hubby who always got agitated when he thought of her (and who could blame him?); the mysterious weekend parties she went off on and her nameless friends—had all mingled together in his mind and coalesced, like the molecules of water on the ceiling, to form a story about her, which had dropped down on his head.

THE BODY IN THE BATHTUB

He had plunked out the letters of the title.

By Reginald Meice Little

And had swung the carriage to the next line, to begin it.

She was full of life, but she was doomed to die, the beautiful playgirl who lived in the apartment overhead. . .

Some time later—about fourteen pages and one body later—he had paused to rest his fingers, looking up from his machine. The clock on his bureau said hour 3:30. The party above seemed to be dwindling away. There were drunken voices and laughter passing along out in the hall beyond his door—some of the happy throng, anyway, were departing. He had put another sheet in his machine and had pile-driven on.

In the middle of page 23—and getting towards the end of the story—he had paused to rub and wring his fingers again. He had picked up the half lemon from beside his machine and treated himself to a suck of it. The hour was almost five, daylight saving time. There was a smokiness of the dawn outside his rear window, looking out over the backyards of the Village. He had a subconscious feeling that the merrymaking in the Atom Baby's apartment above had at last come to an end—that the party had for some time been over.

But not completely, it seemed, even yet. He heard, within the stopped silence of his typewriter, within the utter silence all through the sleeping rookery, within the silence of the fading night and city, a murmur of voices overhead. And suddenly one of them rising sharp and loud, the Atom Baby's own husky contralto voice, with a twang in it like wires.

"Why, you wouldn't dare!"

And then a thud upon the floor above, like the overturning of a table or a chair.

He heard, after that, a silence. The silence hummed. The silence rang and whispered. The silence was very loud. He heard the silence overhead like the silence of a cave.

He pressed the capital key of his machine with his left thumb. He lifted up his right fist above the keyboard, and plunked the index finger of it down upon the "h."

He stood looking at her. A long time he stood looking at her. She was very beautiful. But she was dead. . .

He finished it, the last word of it, page 28, as his clock stood dead on six. He typed a dash-o-dash-o-dash-o-dash, and pulled the page from the machine. He stacked the pages all together—his eyes blurred, his skin and nerves dead and numb—with tired numb hands. He got up and hobbled to his bureau, pulling out a manila envelope from the bottom drawer. He leaned upon his bureau top and addressed it with his fountain pen: "The Editor of Banner Murder Stories, 513 Eighth Avenue. New York City." He inserted the manuscript. He pulled four purple three-cent stamps out of his stamp book on the bureau top, and licked them, and slapped them on the envelope. No—six pages to an ounce, and twenty-eight pages, he had better make it five. He thrust the same number of stamps inside the envelope, on top of the script, for return postage.

He fished around in the back of his stamp-book then, and found a pale-blue 13c special delivery, which he affixed on the envelope in addition. He had four more stamps and fifty cents, and his government check would be coming in in a few days, so he might as well go whole hog about it. He licked the flap of the envelope to seal it. Then he thought that he had postage enough on it for another sheet, and he might as well add a personal touch by addressing a little note to Richard C. Morgelhead, light and casual in tone, insouciant and debonair, requesting his opinion of the story. To get it past the hands of the fluff-brained typist or telephone-girl in the outer office who hated authors, and wouldn't know a murderer if his hands were about her throat, and who always sent them back with a rejection slip. To make sure that Richard C. Morgelhead really read it.

So he hobbled back to his typing stand again, and picked up a sheet of paper from the ream on the floor, returned to the bureau, and scrawled his little note, and put it in with his story, and sealed down the envelope flap. Of course, it might come back still with just a rejection slip. Perhaps Richard C. Morgelhead had read all the others, too, and it had been he who had sent them back with rejection slips, not any fluff-brained girl. But he might as well know.

He buttoned up his shirt collar and slipped on a tie. He might as well go down and mail it at the box on the corner, before hitting the sack.

He tied his tie at his bureau mirror. It was ten minutes after six. The city had awakened a little, with early morning news trucks and milk trucks out on Gruber Street in front; but the old rookery itself was still asleep. The comic-paper artists and the advertising agency odists were deep and dead in their last hour of nightmares before their alarm clocks rang. The Atom Baby's party was long over. The silence above was as profound as everywhere. Her last visitor must have gone an hour ago. She must be asleep herself.

The silence lay. The silence slept. The silence did not stir. A faint occasional rumble from Gruber Street out front in the arising dawn. But in the house here, silence.

It was, Tiny thought as he tied his tie, like the silence in the black breathless cave on Saipan when he had gone crawling in to lay the dynamite to blast that stinking little yellow fox. The darkness had been so still, so still. Yet there had been something in it alive and breathing. . . It made him a little wet with sweat still to think about it. He had always been a fool for volunteering. It was a wonder he still had his head on his shoulders.

Silence. He drew the knot of his tie tight. From the edges of his eyes he saw, beneath his door, the shadow of feet creeping silently along the hall, towards the descending stairs.

Someone must have an early job, earlier than comic-paper publishing houses or advertising agencies. He hadn't heard any door open or close, whatever apartment they had come out of. Nice of them to go out so quietly. Or maybe it was some girl's boy friend, or some boy's girl friend, and they didn't want to be spotted. Well, he wasn't a snoop. Live and let live—a man learns that in war. He would wait till they were down the stairs. He didn't want to see who it was.

He waited till there had been time enough for anybody to have descended to the first floor and gone out the front door. He left his room then, with his manuscript under his arm, and went down the stairs, using his cane. There was pale lemon sunlight out on Gruber Street. A milk truck was parked in front of the next house; the white-coated milkman, weighted with his tray of bottles, was scurrying op the stoop like an eager beetle. An early morning beer truck came rumbling along the cobbles. A blue-clad patrolman was coming around the corner of Barrow Street from the east, from the direction of the sun, swinging his stick and yawning. To the west, in the direction of the shadows, down at the corner where the mailbox stood, in front of Joe's restaurant and bar, a black car was getting under way.

Tiny Little walked slowly down that way, planting down his aluminum foot with care, leaning on his cane. His shadow stretched before him. Six feet two of him, straw-headed, brown of skin and blue of eye. But his shadow was all grey, and longer. It stretched out long and stalking, in front of him down the sidewalk, reaching towards the corner.

He reached the corner. He pulled open the lid of the box and inserted his manuscript with care—a close fit—sliding it in sidewise. He *thunked* the lid two or three times to be sure the envelope was down.

The black car which had been getting under way when he emerged from 99 had vanished, of course. It had turned the corner almost immediately.

He had gone back home, and up to his room again. He had peeled off his clothes, and taken off his pedal contraption. He had put on a pair of pajama pants and got into bed at half past six, and slept through nightmare dreams of running water. . . .

## CHAPTER THREE

## MURDER WILL IN

HE SET DOWN his lemon skin. He lifted up his right fist heavily, and plunked down his index finger on the "I."

I d-i-d-n-'-t k-n-o-w w-h-a-t t-o d-o.

Well, that certainly was dumb. The "I" who was telling the story must be a hero, or he wouldn't be alive to tell it. All heroes lived, all murderers finally died, in stories. And it was a hell of a hero who didn't know what to do in any circumstances. *So I didn't do anything,* suppose he wrote. *I just sat there while he came in and murdered me. And that's the end of my story.*

He felt like it. Just ending the thing right there.

He was overtired, and his brain was drained; that was the trouble with him. Six and a half hours sleep, after pounding away all night on his story of the bathtub murder. (And Miss Dolores Delarte, the Atom Baby, would have been surprised to know that he had murdered her; and quite possibly enraged.) He hadn't given his imagination time enough to renew itself. He couldn't think of a story. He couldn't think of what would happen next.

He tore the page off the machine, with that silly last sentence he had written, and crumpled it. He inserted a fresh sheet, typed his address again.

MURDER WILL IN
By Reginald Meice Little

Just beyond the door, breathing quietly and watching me through the crack, the murderer was lurking. . .

Why, there *was* someone outside his door! At this hour of middle day there must be plenty of sunlight in the hall from the skylight well that shone down from the fourth floor, and he would be able to see a thin line of it through the crack if someone weren't standing just outside. And that shadow beneath the door *was* a pair of feet.

The hackles which had arisen on his neck subsided. He laughed to himself, it couldn't be anyone wanting to murder him. Maybe it was the electric man—the meter was in his closet, and the meter reader would be around once a month to look at it, Mrs. Yussup had told him when he took the room. Maybe it was some messenger boy with a wire from Uncle John out in Shaumee, saying that Gertie, his prize brood-sow, had the mumps, and he needed him to come home and take care of her, now that he had had his fling of this story-writing business, because he had always had a way with animals. Maybe it was Richard C. Morgelhead in person, coming to tell him that his BODY IN THE BATHTUB was the most stupendous and colossal story that had ever appeared in the offices of *Banner Murder Stories,* and hailing him as the new Mary Roberts Rinehart and Agatha Christie.

Oh, unquestionably it was Richard C. Morgelhead in person. Tiny gazed at the door with his quiet smile, letting his mind float. He pictured to himself what Richard C. Morgelhead would look like. He would be a lean, ironic man, wearing eyeglasses on a black cord, speaking with a lofty Harvard accent. He would be a brisk, alert, stocky, cigar-chewing man, bursting with energy and vitality, making quick jabbing gestures with his arms as he expressed his opinions about literature, politics, and philosophy in a rapid voice which couldn't keep up with the speed of his brain. He would be a big, slow, lazy friendly man with a western drawl, full of kindly human understanding, like the editor that Joel McCrea had played. He would be like that other editor with the wild dark rolling eyes, in that other picture, the one portrayed by Orson Welles.

He would be—any editor would be—like almost any other sort of man, Tiny realized. There wasn't any editorial type, any more than there was a banker, dentist, streetcar conductor, or soldier type. There would be nothing to set him apart out upon the street.

It wasn't Richard C. Morgelhead, of course, and it wasn't a murderer, either. But it was somebody.

"Come in," said Tiny. "The door's unlocked."

The door opened, and the man outside came in, closing it behind him.

Tiny eyed him politely.

He was a small man, about five feet four. He was a harassed-looking little man, with stooped shoulders and a deep frown. He had a mop of fuzzy leonine grey hair, with a shiny bald pate in the middle of it, like a pink lake among grey bulrushes. His coat fitted him very badly about the collar, one of his socks had a large hole in it, and his shirt was frayed. He had a briefcase under his arm.

He peered towards the bathroom door with a look of rabbity inquiry as he came in. He half twisted about on his heels as he closed it behind him, with an alarmed glance at the scratched panel, as if afraid that someone was following him through it. He looked at Tiny Little with eyes like a dazed rabbit.

"Mr. Little?" he said.

"Correct," said Tiny, wiping the sweat from his chest, amused by his chittery manner. "What can I do for you?"

"Reginald Meice Little?"

"Why, yes," said Tiny, widening his eyes.

He swallowed. Reginald Meice Little was his writing name. He had never actually heard it spoken in his life before, it was a little solemn, like reading it upon a tombstone. *Reginald Meice Little, Author, 1925-1946. His Fame Is Not Forgotten.*

He made a half gesture to arise out of his Boston rocker. But his knees were crowded beneath his typewriting table, and he didn't have his foot strapped on. He subsided, with an invitation of his hand towards a chair. There was something about the elfish little man or the quiet afternoon, or the tiredness in his brain, which seemed a good deal like a dream.

"Won't you sit down," he said, "Mr.—"

The little man leaned back against the wall beside the bureau, holding his briefcase against his small round stomach. He pulled a watch on a lapel fob out of his breast pocket and glanced at it automatically. He forced a stiff smile at Tiny, with his grey face and bloodless little manner, with his worried frown.

"Two-ten." he said a little breathlessly. "You haven't had lunch yet, have you? Could you hurry up and get dressed and come out with me; and we can talk it over. How would it be if I offered you two hundred for all rights, Mr. Little?"

"Two hundred?" said Tiny.

The little man swooped his hand automatically towards the bottle on the bureau with the red ribbon around it. He picked it up and looked at it. Clover Dew, 100-proof.

"I can make it four," he said, with a hurried, anxious smile, setting the bottle down again with a hand that shook. "That's twice the regular rate. I'll give you a check right now and take you around to the bank to cash it. If you hurry up we can get there before two-thirty. It doesn't close till three."

"You're from *Banner Murder Stories,* and you're offering to buy my story?" said Tiny dazedly. "My 'Body in the Bathtub,' that I just wrote last night?"

It was, of course, a dream.

"I'm sorry I couldn't get here sooner, Mr. Little," said the little man placatingly. "It was nearly noon when it reached my desk, though, and it took me a little time to read it over. The publisher grabbed me into a conference that was scheduled just as I started out to see you, and I couldn't tear myself away. But put your clothes on and come on out, and we can talk it over. How much did you expect me to pay for it?"

"You want to buy my story," repeated Tiny dazedly. "Are you Richard C. Morgelhead, the world-famous editor, formerly of the staffs of *Carper's Pre-Digest, Magnificent,* and other magazines too numerous to mention, the author of 'Five Fundamental Rules for Writing Murder Stories,' himself, by any chance?"

The little man, of course, would say yes, and vanish like a dream.

"I tried that racket for a couple of months, two or three years ago," said the little man, swooping his hand towards the bottle again, a little haggardly. "I thought there might be dough in it, but there wasn't much. Why bring that up?"

"I've sold a story!" said Tiny dazedly. 'You're Richard C. Morgelhead himself, and you're buying my story. Mr. Morgelhead, there are two glasses in the top bureau drawer. Do you mind opening that bottle and pouring us both a drink—or do you drink?"

"A man doesn't get fired from fourteen editorial jobs in nine years unless he does, in this man's town," said Richard C. Morgelhead with defiant pride. "I'll have a quick one, thanks, while you get dressed."

He pulled the seal from the bottle with a hand that had begun to shake anticipatorily, glancing at the clock on the bureau as he did so. He poured out liquor into one of the glasses saying, "Say when." And when Tiny had said it, at the inch and a half mark, he filled the other up halfway to the brim.

"There's water in the bathroom," said Tiny in a dream, seeing the little man glance towards the bathroom door. "Don't bother, though," he added, as the little man reached his glass shakily to him and hoisted his own without more preliminaries and delay. "If you're taking your own straight, I'll do the same. Here's looking at you, Mr. Morgelhead. To quieter and more diabolic murders."

He touched the liquor to his lips. He tasted it; so it couldn't be a dream.

"Down it and get dressed, Mr. Little," said Richard C. Morgelhead urgently, gulping his own with a shaking hand, with a glance at the bureau clock again. "I know a bar where we can talk. There's something else I have in mind for you, that I'd like to discuss with you after we get out of here. Have you ever wanted to take a trip to Mexico, Mr. Little?"

"Take a trip to Mexico?"

"Or Peru," said Richard C. Morgelhead, pouring himself another drink with a hand that still shook a little. "A two-months trip to Peru or Chile with all expenses paid, to get some local color. How does that sound to you, Mr. Little? I've always dreamed of going there myself. You might throw some clothes into a bag to take along with you when we go out, so you won't need to come back: You could catch a train for New Orleans this afternoon, as soon as we've got some money from the bank."

He had glanced again towards the bathroom door after pouring his second drink, but again he hadn't bothered to step in and mix it with water; he was taking it straight. He sounded so ardent, he looked so frowning and bloodless, as he downed it. Perhaps the idea of sending Tiny to Mexico or Peru was an idea that had just occurred to him—it sounded a little vague—but he was all intent on it. Maybe he meant to pay for it with his own money—*Banner Murder Stories* would hardly need any South American correspondents. And he didn't look as if he had too much. An impulsive and generous little man, somewhat erratic, full of little oddities. But geniuses are that way. Of course he, and all about him, might still turn out to be just a dream of a tired brain.

"I haven't any yen for traveling, Mr. Morgelhead," said Tiny appreciatively. "I had a lot of it with the United States Marines. But much obliged. What about my story struck you most, if I may ask?" he added, turning his glass in his hand with a blank grin and wiping the sweat from his chest. "The characters or the incident? I'm still a little dazed, and half expect to see you blow away in smoke. I didn't think it was quite so good myself as some of the others I have done. But one never knows, I suppose. If I knew what hit you most, maybe I could do another."

Richard C. Morgelhead hoisted before his eyes the third drink that he had poured himself, admiring its amber light. His grey face, with its worried little frown, was still sweatless and bloodless, but his hand had ceased to shake. The two drinks he had had had taken hold. There had come a definite slackening of the tension of his manner, and he smiled with an authentic air of ease. He downed his third drink more slowly, taking pleasure in it, beyond the mere imperative fulfilling of a craving and a need.

" 'To quieter and more diabolical murders,' " he said with a dry giggle, echoing Tiny's toast belatedly. "You used the same phrase in your note. No doubt it's a cliché of yours. All writers have clichés. 'Surprise, surprise, from one of your unknown followers!' You only meant you were one of the birds who had bitten on my rules when I was trying that racket, I suppose. I didn't know whether you mean you were some gumshoe who had been tailing me—I didn't know what in hell you meant. 'Will be interested in obtaining your reaction.' My God! But you're just a writer who wrote a story, and wanted to sell it. That's what I really thought. I needed a drink, I guess. But that's done it. No more."

He set his emptied glass down with steady and precise care on the bureau top. His knees folded with a sudden jerk beneath him. He sat down somewhat abruptly on the straightback chair beside the bureau, with the bottle in his hand.

"Let's go," he said, stretching out his legs at ease. "Let's get out of here. I'll take just a swallow while you get dressed. We haven't got all day. I never like to take the stuff straight, but you'd never notice this. You never knew Charlie Semple, the artist, did you? He used to live in this joint. We used to have wild times. The rules. I'll pay you back the two bucks you spent for them, and no hard feelings. What the hell did they say, anyway? I wrote them on the back of a bar menu one afternoon while I was drunk. Meant to write a whole string of them, write a hell of a lot about everything, get a book published. But I couldn't think of it. Had some rules, anyway; had 'em mimeographed; bought some ads. Thought I'd make a lot of money out of them. A lot of money. You get married and you need a lot of money. But only two hundred and twenty-three responses, and the ads had cost three C's. Too many in the game. And all you are is just a writer. Reginald Meice Little. God, you're big. You're a writer, and you wrote a story. Where the hell did you get the idea of it, anyway? The bathtub overflowing. This character who always pulled his ear."

He frowned. He reached for his briefcase from the bureau top and laid it on his knees. He unzipped it with a jerk, thrusting his hand inside.

"We'll take the bottle with us," he said. "Must have been only half full. Not much left. But every little bit helps. Are you dressed yet? Got to get out of here."

Tiny Little wiped the sweat from his chest. He was sorry to see the mind of the great Richard C. Morgelhead grow slightly confused with drink. He didn't drink himself, not more than a taste. But perhaps all great editors were that way. They had so much to read, that perhaps their minds grew tired. In his daydreams he had often imagined having a literary discussion with Richard C. Morgelhead, conducted on a high intellectual plane, with brilliant epigrams, and elevated references to books and authors, and analyses of theories of literary creation, all expressed in the choicest and most correct English prose; and there had been none of that. Just tense and scatterbrained phrases, and incoherent thoughts. But his question now of where Tiny had got the idea of his story seemed a serious and important question, and one well worth going into fully. Tiny wouldn't have been even an aspiring writer if he hadn't felt the urge to discuss his writing fully and to the smallest detail, with any excuse, or little, or even none. He clasped his hands together around his glass upon his diaphragm, leaning forward in his chair.

"Why, you just get little incidents from here and there, Mr. Morgelhead, and you churn them around in your mind, and put them together," he explained earnestly. "And all at once you find you've got a story. That's the way it works, I guess. Now this bathtub thing that you asked about in my story, where he has killed her and is worrying that maybe he will be suspected when they find her, and so he figures on putting her in a cold tub that will delay rigor mortis and make it seem as if she had died later than she did, when he will have an alibi; and that maybe will make it seem, too, that she had just accidentally slipped and bumped her head on the tub when she was getting into it, and had just drowned; only the tub overflows and spills down on the guy who lives below, telling him at what hour she was really killed—why, I got the idea of that little particular piece of business from the girl who lives upstairs, in four-D over me, I guess."

"You did?" said Richard C. Morgelhead.

## CHAPTER FOUR

## THIS WILL KILL YOU

HE SAT WITH his legs stretched out stiffly before him. He had one hand inside his briefcase, and the bottle in his other hand. His hands were steady, but his eyes had a little waver in their depths. Tiny wasn't quite sure whether he had been following his rather complicated exposition of the bathtub incident in the plot. Still, he must have. His eyes steadied now. He sat looking at Tiny, with his face sweatless and bloodless, in a drunken calm.

"You got the idea from the girl upstairs," he said. "Well, well."

"That's right," explained Tiny earnestly. "You see, one time her bathtub overflowed down through the ceiling of my bathroom, and began to *splop* into my tub. You see, the plumbing in the house is pretty old, and the pipes are rusted, and the water runs in kind of slow. That was why she had fallen asleep the night before, waiting for it to fill up. But the overflow outlet in her tub is rusted up, too. And so, no matter how slowly the water runs in, it runs out of the overflow a little slower; and when it gets up to the top of the tub it begins to creep over the edge. And since it was eight o'clock in the morning when I first noticed it, by learning from her what time she had started to run her bath, at eleven o'clock the night before, I could figure that it had taken just exactly nine hours for the water to start dribbling over the edge, and for the dribble to work down through the floor and beams and plaster, and gather on my bathroom ceiling, and begin to splop down into my tub.

"In my story, of course, I changed the times around, and had it six o'clock in the morning when the murderer puts her in the tub and starts the water running. He figures the cold water will make it look like she had died at around not earlier than eleven o'clock or noon, when they find her that evening, and he makes himself an alibi for that time. But the tub overflows and starts to drip on this guy below at three o'clock of the afternoon; and that means it must have been turned on at six o'clock in the morning. And the murderer's alibi isn't any good, and he gets it in the neck. They always have to get it, don't they, in stories.

"But it wouldn't have worked, anyway, as I guess you know, Mr. Morgelhead," he went on a little hastily, as Richard C. Morgelhead, with a sidewise sliding of his worried little eyes, glanced at the clock upon the bureau, which said 2:19. "If she was dead before he put her in the tub, there wouldn't be any water in her lungs when they made the autopsy, and so she couldn't have just drowned. See 'The Case of the Drowned Cat', by Ergell Morton. *Banner Murder Stories,* Volume 31, Number 9, issue of March 18, 1933. The blow that he had used to kill her was too vicious and bloody, too, to have come from just a bump upon the tub. See 'The Deadly Blow', by William James Amson, *Banner Murder Stories,* Volume 17, Number 8, issue of July 5, 1929. They would find traces of her blood on the bronze elephant he had killed her with, for a third thing, no matter how much he had rinsed it off and scrubbed it, when they used the spectroscope. 'The Mark of Crimson', by Ermin Brailey, *Banner Murder Stories,* Volume 40, Number 6, issue of February 29, 1936. He certainly didn't know anything about murder stories, not to think of any of those things.

"And he was all loose about that business of a delayed rigor mortis giving him an alibi, too, Mr. Morgelhead, as you know," he added with an earnest grin, wiping the sweat off his broad forehead beneath his shock of straw hair, and wiping the little lady on his chest. "Putting her in a cold tub probably would have delayed it some, particularly in hot weather like today. But not enough so that any medical examiner would make a dumb mistake and say bull-headedly that she couldn't have died earlier than around eleven o'clock or noon, when he was at his office and had his alibi, instead of maybe as early as five or six o'clock, when she had died.

"Rigor mortis works at different rates in different cases," he explained. "It depends on how quick a person was killed, and how tired or tensed up he was when he got it, and a lot of other things. Maybe in some cases it's twelve hours. Maybe in some, not even two. In the war, for instance, men would be in action, and get it; and they'd be stiff before the second wave. On Saipan, for instance, why, there was a little yellow fox, a crazy banzai fox; he crept around at night and cut girls' and soldiers' throats and drank the living blood. And we ran him down to the stinking hole he hid in, and so someone had to go in and get him—the way the cave was shaped, you couldn't reach him with dynamite on poles, and there were too many openings to use gas; and if you sat down and waited a week, trying to starve him out, there might be some other exit that he would be out of. So someone had to go in and get him.

"And there he was, somewhere in the blackness, all muscles, all tensed up and wires; and you could smell him, you could feel him all through your skin, breathing and creeping, with his razor-sharp knife, and maybe with fox eyes that were better in the blackness than yours were, trying to find your throat. And then you blew the charge off, with your head buried beneath your arms. And the pieces of him were stiff as rock when they dug him and you out of the rubble ten minutes later. He had been only ten feet from you."

Tiny stopped, suddenly realizing that he had been carried away. That hadn't been a story.

Tiny wiped his palm across his forehead again, nursing his glass. He wiped the Atom Baby on his chest, whose name he had given to the big-limbed, warm, curvaceous, lava-eyed, human and living Atom Baby in four-D above. Changing his glass from one hand to the other, he wiped the hawser-like muscles of his forearms, the Marine Corps *Semper Fidelis* with the globe and anchor, the dagger, *Death Before Dishonor,* dripping blood. He wiped the sweat off him, but he was still sweating: and there was a curious horror in his bones.

It came from remembering the feeling of that little yellow murderer in the cave blackness, he thought. In war, a man gets so he can smell a murderer. Maybe all men are born with that blood-instinct, like animals; and it is only civilization, books and education, the crowds and noises and machines and confusion of cities, which dulls the inborn sense. But now, as though he were still within the blackness of the cave upon Saipan, and the creeping death so near to him, he had a horror in his bones.

"What I mean," he explained earnestly and brightly—feeling that his story had to be justified in detail, since *Banner Murder Stories'* editorial standards, its old and high prestige, required that its stories be accurate in detail—"what I mean is that in this particular story of mine, of course, the overflow of the tub pins the time when she was put into it down almost to the minute: three P.M. on the dot when the drip starts; nine hours before that equals six o'clock. But even if it hadn't overflowed he wouldn't have been alibied absolutely, just because rigor mortis had been delayed by a few hours. See 'The Hour of Death', by Charles Preston Downey, *Banner Murder Stories,* Volume 19, Number 12. issue of September first, 1924. See also 'Sleep, My Sweet,' by Alston Means. *Banner Murder Stories,* Volume 51. August 8, 1943. And there's a story right in the current issue, 'The Sickle's Blade', by Harvey P. Breeg, which I understand is just another name for Justin Code.

"Gee, it makes a guy feel that he's stepping out into fast company, to have a story of his lined up with the work of men like that! But you know, I didn't mean to bore you. I guess you know every story they ever wrote, including a lot that I have missed. I'm wasting your time. I guess you know all that."

Richard C. Morgelhead sat stiffly, with motionless hands and eyes. "Lord!" he said.

He slid his eyes to the clock upon the bureau. It said 2:22. He lifted up the bottle he held in his left hand, and tilted it to his lips.

"Lord!" he said. "What do you think assistant editors are for? Do you think I read the dam stuff myself? I'm Richard C. Morgelhead of *Peek.* I'm Richard C. Morgelhead of *Magnificent, The Pacific, Tide.* I'm Richard C. Morgelhead of the *Pre-Digest* in person, and to hell with all of you."

He shook the bottle upside down, carefully, above his lap. He set it down carefully on the floor beside him. His hands were steady—his left hand that set the bottle down, his right hand inside his briefcase on his lap. His face was bloodless and pale and without sweat. The liquor, within the hot and burning day, had given him no heat. He laughed.

"Lord!" he said. "What would I be doing reading the illiterate tripe in a lousy murder book? You're a writer. Writer. Meginald Leice Rittle. Leginald Reice Mittle. Your lousy whodunit was the first one in my life I ever read. It was that note of yours that got me. 'Here you are, Mr. Morgelhead!' And your lousy story with it, 'The Body in the Bathtub'. To hell with you. You're just a dumb pulp writer. You're just a lousy writer, 's all you are. 'Following in my footsteps.' I didn't know what you meant. But you were just sitting here pounding at your keys all the time, and dreaming up a story. Wait a minute! Why did you have him hit her with a bronze elephant? Why did you pick on that?"

Tiny wiped his sweating chest.

"She has one on her table," he explained earnestly. "I saw it the morning I came to her door. It seemed a natural and convenient weapon to have him use."

"Why did you have this murderer a man who pulled his left earlobe?" said Richard C. Morgelhead.

"She has a husband who does that whenever he's agitated," explained Tiny earnestly. "She told me. It seemed a rather individual thing to have the murderer do, since he's her husband in the story."

Richard C. Morgelhead sat looking at Tiny with motionless eyes. He was a little man. So little. A little man, and comical. With his bald scalp and sprouting fringe of hair, like a pink pond among grey bulrushes. As little as a Jap. His right hand was motionless in his briefcase on his lap.

Tiny Little wiped his sweating chest. He lifted his glass and took another sip of it. It was too hot to drink in haste. Straight liquor. Richard C. Morgelhead had not bothered—he had refused—to go into the bathroom and fill it up with water. Tiny hadn't finished his one drink yet, and even so his heart was pounding sluggishly, and he was all sweat. But Richard C. Morgelhead, who had finished the bottle, was sweatless and dry as ice.

How did men keep that way, so cool? Tiny had a headache. The house so quiet and empty. Only Mrs. Yussup taking her midday siesta down in the basement. The Atom Baby had not yet awakened.

So quiet. This little comical man. Richard C. Morgelhead. Richard C. Morgelhead in person who had come to see him about his story. But there hadn't been the high literary talk that he had dreamed of. Richard C. Morgelhead wasn't even interested in murder stories.

"Let's go!" said Richard C. Morgelhead with a sigh, straightening carefully in his chair, planting down his feet. "It'll be three o'clock in little more than half an hour. Got to get to the bank. Banks close. Pay you your money. Aren't you dressed yet? Get your clothes on. We'll put you on a train for New Orleans, couple of hundred dollars in your pocket. I've got that much. Maybe three or four."

"I haven't any yen for traveling." repeated Tiny.

*Splop!*

Tiny Little rubbed his sweating chest confusedly. He had a headache, that was confusing reality with his story. Perhaps it was all a dream.

He sipped his glass, swallowing the rest of his liquor. To the right of Richard C. Morgelhead, seated motionless on his chair beside the bureau against the wall, he saw the scratched panel of the door, facing him. The Atom Baby had said that she used to know the artist who lived in this apartment. Richard C. Morgelhead had said he had known him, too. Tiny wondered if she had been the model for the sketch of the woman's bust and hips on the panel.

It couldn't have been any artist, though, who had drawn that heart with the initials in it. Some guest of his at some drunken party. It was too amateurish and crude. A little pathetic, too. *R.M. loves D. D.* And a date two or three years ago.

A pledge of love, commemorating two nameless lovers. A man must be something of a sentimental sap. and a good deal gone over a girl, to draw a juvenile thing like that, even drunk, even pretending it was a joke. *R. M. loves D. D.* And there it remained, longer than most Greenwich Village love.

*D. D.*—Dolores Delarte, thought Tiny, with sudden idle recognition. The initials had reminded him only of Captain D. D. Smith of Adalak, seeing them before. A man's own experiences are the most important in his own mind. Dolores Delarte, the Atom Baby, though, those initials stood for, and some man with the initials "R. M." who had loved her. He had thought of his own two first initials in connection with them before, and of Desperate Desmond trying to blast him with that roaring .45 at midnight in barracks, with little love. It had seemed a little comical. But they weren't comical. Love between a man and woman is never that.

R. M. loved Dolores Delarte, the great big dark red-haired model, with her wide wet crimson mouth and splendid limbs and smoky lava eyes. R. M. had loved her, and who could blame him? Love's a curious thing.

*Splop!*

That was a dripping in the bathroom. Tiny turned his gaze towards Richard C. Morgelhead. Richard C. Morgelhead had his head bent towards the bathroom door, from which came that slow *splopping* sound. Richard C. Morgelhead had taken his right hand out of his briefcase on his lap, where he had been holding it taut and clenched. He had reached it across his meager chest, and was pulling the lobe of his left ear.

Cool. Cool as ice, he had been. Too cool to sweat. The cool and icy skin of him who has done murder. It is not the guilty man who sweats prodigally and freely. The guilty man must remember, drunk or sober, to be cool and not to sweat. But there had come a limit, a snapping point, to the coolness of Richard C. Morgelhead. That slow dripping sound, like the Chinese water torture, had broken something in him. Richard C. Morgelhead was agitated, as the thought of Dolores Delarte had always made him agitated. He had removed his clenched and hidden band, and was pulling his left ear.

*Splop!*

Looking at the little man with widened eyes, Tiny Little understood. He felt very sorry for him. He felt sorry for the Atom Baby, too.

"I forgot to figure a body in the tub, Mr. Morgelhead, I guess,'' he said unhappily. "With it, it wouldn't take so long for the tub to fill up and begin to overflow. If the murderer put her in at six o'clock, and left the water running while he crept quietly down the stairs, I should have had my guy in the apartment below, in 'Body in the Bathtub', begin to hear the *splops,* it seems, at twenty-five after two, not three o'clock. But I suppose the assistant editors can correct that. . .

"You were her great big sweet hubby, were you? And she had hooked you for separate maintenance, not leaving you enough for booze, and was always calling you at your office and hounding you and threatening to get you fired when you were late with her dough. And you came up to see her at four or five this morning, after her party guests had left—or maybe you were one of them, who came back. And you had an argument, and you got mad and hit her with the bronze elephant, and she was dead. And you tried to think what to do.

"I never had an idea of it until this moment. I never had an idea that it was really happening while I wrote it. I'm very sorry that I did."

Richard C. Morgelhead looked at him with dead eyes. Richard C. Morgelhead had released his left earlobe. His hand dived into his open briefcase, and came out with the gun that was there. And though he was a little man, the gun was big and deadly.

A small comical man with a worried look, with rabbit's eyes, with a pink bald tonsure tike a baboon's rump in his comical wild grey mane. A little man, a white collar man, a blue-pencil and scissors editor. But he had killed the beautiful woman whom he had loved, he had killed his wife, he had killed Dolores Delarte with her lava eyes and great warm cherry mouth, with her perfect limbs and body. And any lesser killings would be nothing to him, nor the death of the whole world.

*The smell of the murderer!* thought Tiny Little. He had had the smell of it ever since the little man came in. Yes, before, at the door. There had been a horror in his bones. But he couldn't believe it. He had been so entranced by the name of Richard C. Morgelhead.

Who could have figured that she was dead upstairs? That she was dead or dying while he wrote it. Who could have figured that she had been married to Richard C. Morgelhead; that she would ever have looked at the little bald, grey, comical man at all, much less have ever been in love with him?

She had never been, of course. He had given her the name and status of a married woman. Maybe she had thought he had a lot of money,

Richard C. Morgelhead, formerly of *Magnificent* and *Tide.* But what he had made in his good days, he had drunk away; and the money that even famous editors make is not much compared to head waiters and accountants and Hollywood office boys. He had tried to make money, he had tried to become a successful business man for her, with his "Five Fundamental Rules for Writing Murder Stories." A married man needs a lot of money, he had said. Drunken dreams of a fortune rolling in from a million would-be murder writers, at a dollar and ninety-eight cents each. To keep Dolores Delarte for his very own, with her sultry lava eyes.

Richard C. Morgelhead, the world-famous editor, formerly of the staffs of *Pre-Digest, Carper's, Peek* and *Tide,* and so on and so on. Formerly of too many magazine offices that couldn't stand a drunk, but he didn't need to say it. Even though he had never read a whodunit, why shouldn't he be able to tell them how they were done? But there hadn't been the response. Too many others in the game. And he hadn't much more than cleared the cost of the ads which he had written with such hope.

And so that dream had gone. And she had gone from him, with its fading.

A tired grey little man. A comical little man, and somewhat crazy. No littler than that little yellow fox in the cave on Saipan, though. No more comical than the big shaven-skulled Russky sergeant heaving his grenade with his bellowing scream of *'Amerikanski! Smerd!"* No crazier than poor old gibbering D. D. Smith. And Tiny knew that, no matter how little a killer is, or how comical, or how crazy, he is still a killer, and he deals death.

He had met three, and he was mighty lucky to be alive. Such luck doesn't last forever.

A comical, crazy little man with a great big gun. And he had killed the beautiful thing he loved. And all other deaths were nothing to him.

"You're just a writer," said Richard C. Morgelhead, with his dead motionless eyes in his sweatless and bloodless face, with his drink-steadied hand. "Just a damned murder writer. I heard you clicking and clicking and clicking when I came up the stairs and passed your door, though everyone else in the house was asleep and it was almost five A.M. I heard you clicking and clicking down below after I had hit her, and she lay on the floor looking up at me, and the blood was coming out of her head and she was dead, and I didn't know what to do.

"Clicking and clicking, a damned murder writer. But when I came down the stairs again, after I had thought of putting her in the tub, you'd stopped. And you followed me down and out the front door, and down the street while I was trying to start my car. The milkman hadn't seen me creeping out, the policeman hadn't come around the corner yet; but I saw your shadow walking towards me, walking towards me, and reaching out and touching me as I got it started and shot around the corner. And then I got your damned story just at noon, about the time they would believe she had died, I thought, after she should be found. But the bathroom ceiling would drip at three o'clock, you said, and so you would know she had been dead at six o'clock.

"Clicking and clicking. Clicking your damned murders. Rigor mortis and spectroscopes, and what happened in all the murder stories ever published. Do you think I read the things myself? But I had to read yours when it came. 'The Body in the Bathtub'. Here you are, Mr. Morgelhead! Yours for quieter murders. From an unknown follower. How do you like my little detective effort?' Damn you! Just a murder story by a murder writer. But I had to buy it quick, I couldn't let it be published, I couldn't let it be read after she had been found. I thought if I could get around to you soon enough, and get you out of here before three o'clock, and maybe get you out of town for a week or two, till after the autopsy was over, it would be all right. After all, maybe the cops themselves don't read murder stories. Maybe they would think she had just slipped and bumped her head and been drowned about noon, when I was at my office. Maybe they don't know what Jehosaphat Blat wrote in *Banner Murder Stories* in 1903. They aren't damned murder writers. Maybe they'll think, too, that you just blew off your own head with this gun."

Little man with a big gun. Tiny didn't doubt that it was loaded. He didn't doubt that Richard C. Morgelhead didn't know how to shoot it, either, which made it much more dreadful. For a man who knows how to shoot a gun keeps the safety catch on till he brings it down with a snap of his thumb in the instant that he squeezes it; and there may be time to parley with him, to reason and expostulate, and discover if perhaps you both haven't cousins living in Kalamazoo. But Richard C. Morgelhead had the safety catch off, and the slightest squeeze of his cold, sweatless, bloodless, drink-steadied hand would start it to racketing like a kennel full of all the dogs of hell.

It was a wonder it hadn't gone off before. It was a wonder it hadn't gone off in his briefcase on the way here. Except for the luck that protects fools and murderers—in life, if not in stories. But it was going off now.

What was Rule Five of the "Five Fundamentals?" *Now end your story with a bang—the trap which you have set in the beginning has sprung.*

A bang was right. That great big gun. *The murderer was lurking just beyond the door,* thought Tiny, *and I didn't know what to do about it, so*

*I didn't do anything. And he came in and murdered me, and that's the end of my story.*

Well, he was pretty tired. His brain was drained. It seemed all a dream, in the quiet sweating afternoon. But he couldn't let it go that way, by default. Not a man who had *Semper Fidelis* tattooed on his good right arm and *Death Before Dishonor* on his left. Not to speak of an Atom Baby on his chest. It wouldn't be right to the little lady to let her be blown to hell.

The hand of the little man with the bald head like a baboon's rump and the wild and woolly mane was very steady, cold as ice. But perhaps the depths of his eyes weren't steady, quite. *Splop!* From the bathroom. *Splop!* Dripping down from where her big beautiful ice-cold body was lying in her bath. Oh, his eyes weren't steady, quite. Looking at Tiny, but listening to that sound. Little comical grey man, quite crazy, with a gun. But he had never been to war.

Tiny heaved the glass in his hand, straight from his navel. Richard C. Morgelhead ducked instinctively as it came hurtling at him. The gun in his hand roared and bucked. The shot from it went somewhere, Tiny thought, in the direction of Canopus or the Pleiades, through the floor and all the other floors and the round globe of the earth that lay between. Tiny was jammed behind his typewriter table, and he had only one foot. He lifted up his typewriter above his head and lobbed it like a basketball. It was lighter than a mortar shell. It didn't weigh thirty pounds.

It slammed into the wall above Richard C. Morgelhead's chairback, breaking seven dollars worth of plaster. Richard C. Morgelhead had seen it coming, and had ducked. He was the little man who again wasn't there.

He was the little man upon the floor. The hurtling machine had grazed him across his bald pink skull, with all the letters of the alphabet upon it, with all the potentialities in it of all the words men ever wrote, excluding the Chinese. He had been hit by all the murder stories ever written, and to be written.

Tiny had pushed his table from in front of him. He hopped, and knelt beside the little man, picking up his gun. The skin was broken across the top of his skull, and he was groaning, with his rabbit eyes rolling his head. No doubt it would have been better for him if he had been brained.

*Splop!* from the bathroom. *Splop!* It would keep up for a long time.

"I loved her so much!" sobbed Richard C. Morgelhead. "She was so beautiful. If I hadn't loved her so much, I wouldn't have killed her. She didn't have a heart or brain, and was as cold as ice. But she was beautiful."

Tiny felt sorry for him, though he felt sorry for the Atom Baby, too. What could be done with him? They wouldn't burn him, probably.

Twenty years; and some time during it, a little grey man within his cell, he'd die. But the worst evil that could be done to him had been done long ago, and by himself. As is perhaps true of all men.

It was fun, thought Tiny, to write murder stories and to read them. But living them wasn't fun.

# THE RED RIGHT HAND

## CHAPTER ONE

## THE MISSING HAND

THERE IS ONE THING that puzzles me most, in all the dark and bloody mystery of tonight, and that is how that ugly little auburn-haired, red-eyed man, with his torn ear and tusklike yellow teeth, could have got away and vanished so completely from the face of the countryside after he killed Inis St. Erme.

That is point one of the whole problem. Point two is the question of what he did with St. Erme's right hand, if the state troopers and the posse of neighboring farmers haven't found it yet down on the Swamp Road, along with the rest of the murdered young millionaire bridegroom's body. For St. Erme had a right hand, that much is evident. And it must be found.

And yet, hardly less inexplicable, to me personally, is the puzzle, from the beginning, of how that smoke-grey touring car, with its blood-red upholstery and high-pitched, wailing horn, could have passed by me unnoticed while I was at the entrance to the Swamp Road just before twilight, with St. Erme in it, dying or dead already, and that grinning little hobo murderer driving it like a fiend.

Was I, Harry Riddle, Dr. Henry N. Riddle, Jr., of St. John's Medical and New York S. & D.—observant and level-headed, pragmatic and self-contained surgeon that I like to think myself—asleep with my eyes open? For certainly I missed it.

It is possible, of course, that I place an undue amount of emphasis on the matter in my own mind. Still, it continues to bother me my failure to see that murder car—because it involves the validity of my own sense perceptions and mental operations, which I have never felt it necessary to certify to myself before.

The question is set down, I find, in Lieutenant Rosenblatt's thick, cardboard-covered notebook, in which he painstakingly recorded all his inquiries earlier in the night, and which he left behind him on the table in MacComerou's living room here when he last went out.

Q. (To Dr. Riddle) And you were at the Swamp Road entrance all during the murder hour, Dr. Riddle?

A. I was.

Q. And you did not see the car pass by at all?

A. I did not see it.

Q. You have heard the detailed description of the killer, doctor, as given by Miss Darrie here, Mr. St. Erme's fiancée, and by others who saw him. But you did not see him yourself?

A. I did not see him. To the best of my knowledge, I have never seen him.

Q. You'll stand on that?

A. I'll stand on that . . .

And so I will.

In the larger view, of course, it makes no actual difference whether or not I, individually, saw the murder car go by, since obviously it did go by. Other men saw it all the way along the road, all the way from Dead Bridegroom's Pond to just before it reached me, and to them it was not invisible nor a phantom. It struck big shambling John Flail as he was walking homeward just around the bend of the road from me, and to him, for one dreadful moment—as he tried to spring out of its way with a bleating cry, hearing that demon at the wheel laughing, and feeling the iron blow smash the bones within his flesh like glass—it could certainly have been no phantom. Professor MacComerou himself saw it pass his place while he was digging in his garden, and recognized St. Erme as the stricken man in it, if not the little demon at the wheel. And Elinor Darrie, previously in the day, had driven it a hundred miles up from New York City, on her wedding trip with her handsome, black-eyed lover, before Yellow Fang took over.

They have found it now, moreover, down on the Swamp Road where the killer abandoned it after he had passed me by, with its engine still warm and its cushions blood-stained—a grey Cadillac eight-cylinder sport touring, last of production '42, made of steel and aluminum, leather, rubber, glass, and all the other ordinary, solid, visible materials, with its engine and chassis numbers that were stamped on it in the factory, and its federal tax and gas stickers on its windshield, and its license plate XL 465-297 N. Y. '44, together with the coupon books and registration of its owner in its glove compartment: A. M. Dexter of Dexter's Day-and-Nite Garage, 619 West 14th Street, New York City, who has confirmed by long distance that he lent it to St. Erme. A car worth three thousand dollars or more on the market anywhere today, and certainly no phantom.

They have found poor Inis St. Erme's body, too, so that he was not a phantom, either. Only the little man with the red eyes and the accordion legs—the man in the blue saw-tooth hat, the man who had no name—him they haven't yet quite found.

And so that aspect of the problem—the puzzle of the murder car's singular and specific invisibility to me, and to me alone—must be set aside, for the time being, anyway. Whether to be answered finally, or never answered, makes no difference now.

The thing that I have to consider now without delay—the thing that I have to consider most intensely, and with all my mind, and now *(now, sitting here at the desk in Professor MacComerou's dusty old-fashioned country living-room, with St. Erme's young bride asleep on the old horsehair sofa beside me, and the hot moonless night still black out of doors, though the dawn must break eventually; now, with the lanterns and flashlights moving out in the darkness, and the voices of the troopers and posse men near and far off, calling to each other with the thin empty sound which men's voices have in the night; and some of them dropping back a while ago to get hot coffee from the pot left brewing on the kitchen range, with their grim tired faces swollen from mosquito bites and their legs covered to the knees with swamp muck and damp sawdust from the sawmill pits, glancing in at me and the sleeping girl through the kitchen doorway only briefly while they gulped their drink in deep draughts to keep their brains awake, shaking their heads in answer to my silent questions to indicate they had found no trace yet, and then out again on farther trails, with an empty slam of the screen door behind them; and now the lanterns moving farther off through the woods and swamps, over the hills and down into the hollows; and now the distant baying of the hounds that have been brought in from somewhere; and armed men in pairs and squads patrolling every road for miles around, ready to shoot down at the rustle of a leaf that crazy little killer with his bloody saw-tooth knife and fanged grin, creeping so cunningly and red-handed through the dark)*—the thing that I have to consider here and without delay, in this deep darkness at the end of night, is this thing, and this thing only:

*Where is the killer now?*

For I have a cold and dismal feeling that he is somewhere near me, no matter how far off the lanterns move and the voices call and the far hounds bay. And near the sleeping girl beside me, his victim's young wife to be. A feeling that he will strike again. That he knows I am somehow dangerous to him. Though how, I cannot yet perceive.

Somewhere in the darkness outside the window. Watching me from the black garden.

I am not a policeman or a bloodhound. Yet as a surgeon I am, I trust, reasonably well disciplined in the scientific method, with a basic instinct for looking at facts objectively. And out of all those details which I have casually noted during the past few hours, it is possible that I may be able to arrive at some rational and unsupernatural explanation of where the killer is.

Let the others continue to hunt him through the darkness. Let them find more bodies of his dead. They have done that, too—I seem to have heard them shouting, back and forth, a little while ago, far off. With the hounds howling. But they haven't found *him* yet. And why not?

There is some item missing from the puzzle, or there is some item too many. I must assemble all the pieces, and work it out, to find the answer to that dead man I saw walking. And to where Yellow Fang is now—the ragged man, the little sawed-off man, the grinning, dirty man with the matted auburn hair who had a voice so strangely like my own.

For that is something which I must answer, too. It is an item never to forget.

Perhaps, if I could only see it, the answer lies before my eyes. Very well. I am here. I will start here.

I am sitting at the battered secretary-desk in the living room of the summer home of the late Professor Adam MacComerou, professor-emeritus of psychiatry at Harvard, on the Whippleville-Stony Falls road, in the northern Connecticut hills, a hundred miles from New York. The hour is half past three of the morning, of Thursday, August 9.

There is a quire of yellow work paper and a sheaf of sharpened pencils on the desk. In the glass doors of the secretary I can see my reflection when I glance up, and the room behind me to the farthest limits of the light. That man with the round head covered with close-clipped reddish hair, with the red-brown eyes and the brown, thickly freckled face, is myself, Dr. Henry Riddle, Jr. That's me, myself. The self that I have always known, for twenty-seven years.

In the desk's pigeonholes there are sheaves of papers—rough clinical notes and case-histories; jottings, apparently, for some sequel which the old man intended writing to his previous works.

The case of A, of good family, well-educated, colossally conceited of his own mental powers, who at 45, unsuccessful in any undertaking and greedy for money, plots uncle's death so as to inherit.

So one paper reads. But whether A succeeded in his plot is not told. It is a story not completed, for a book that will never be written.

Besides the work paper on the desk, then is a small memo pad with jottings on it:

Call lawyers, By 9-6400 after lunch—
Notify P. O. forward mail—
Have John Flail prune syringa & transplant roses—
Sugar, matches, potatoes, strawberries, bread—

A folded newspaper lies beside the lamp, a copy of the *Danbury Evening Star,* dated August 8, yesterday afternoon, with big headlines on it about some great naval action in the Pacific, it seems. "Tojo Hit by Truk!" No one has opened the newspaper to read it since it was laid there. No one has had time to read it. Nor will anyone read it now.

In addition, on the desk I have Lieutenant Rosenblatt's fat pulp-paper notebook, which he left behind him when he went surging out at old MacComerou's last death cry from near John Flail's.

More than an hour ago, and Rosenblatt has not been back since.

Through the open window at my left hand the odor of yellow roses and damp night grass and rich, black garden earth comes in. Moths are fluttering against the copper screen, with soft bumpings of their white dusty bodies.

At my right, on the sofa against the wall, St. Erme's young bride is sleeping deeply still, dreaming it all away now for a little while, with the recuperative powers of nineteen. The tautness has slipped away from her. Her breathing is quiet and cataleptic, without a stirring of her breast. Her slight body, in her periwinkle blue gown and thin white summer coat with the little rabbit's fur at the collar, is lying with knees bent sidewards, with her face turned away from me and the light. Her dark blue eyes, with their enormous pupils, which were so full of terror at first sight of me, are closed beneath a sweep of lashes. Her left arm has slipped down off the sofa's edge, with fingers trailing loosely to the floor. The big sapphire engagement ring given her by St. Erme, too large for her finger, seems in danger of slipping off. Yet it might disturb her if I tried to remove it for safekeeping.

She has turned her head just now on the sofa's headrest, and her face is towards me. A faint sweat is on her forehead and short upper lip, from the still heat of the night. A strand of dark curl is plastered to her temples. Her lips are a little parted, breathing more deeply now. The edge of the lamplight falls on her breast and the lower part of her face; but by propping up the newspaper in a kind of screen I have succeeded in shielding it from her eyelids. So there is a shadow on her look, a memory of tonight's terror. But none, I hope, in her dreams.

She was told that St. Erme's body had been found, but she was told nothing more. Perhaps it will not be necessary for her ever to be told anything more.

The voices of the men out in the night have gone beyond earshot now. The fragile beating of the insects at the screen will not disturb her.

My pencil moving on the page . . . I have a feeling that the answer to the killer lies in something before my eyes. And still I do not see it.

The *Banbury Evening Star,* August 8, 1944—it was outside Danbury, fifty or sixty miles away, that she and St. Erme first met Yellow Fang, on the main highway, as they came along it in their grey car in the sunset. It was about three hours later, and the twilight had become night, when I myself first came upon her, stumbling along the stony road from the lake shore eight miles below here, bewildered, terrified, and lost.

I was trying to make up time in my old coupe, after the lost time while I had been stalled, and hoped to strike the main highway soon, to get down to New York.

But it was still a nightmare road, narrow and rocky, winding between steep wooded slopes and big boulders which pressed out on the road shoulders on either side, as it had been from the beginning. Rounding a sharp rocky road, I saw her white figure pressed back at the right side of the road in my headlights. Like a pale Belle Dame Sans Merci from some Keatsian poem, gesturing imploringly to me.

Her eyes were enormous and dark in her pale face. There were scratches and dirt streaks on her cheeks, and dead leaves in her dark hair. Clusters of burrs had caught on her white coat. Her white pumps were muddy, and from one of them she had lost a heel.

She had nothing in her hands, not even a pocketbook—hers had been in the car, along with everything else, and was still in it when it was found down on the Swamp Road, though emptied of the fifty-dollar bill which St. Erme had given her at the bank that morning, and even of its small change. She was breathing hard from her scrambling and her running, and was near exhaustion, as I stopped beside her.

"Please!" she gasped. "He drove off with my fiancé in the car! Can you give me a lift somewhere? There is no one who seems to live around here! The police should be notified—I'm afraid something terrible may have happened!"

"Get in," I said, opening the door beside her. "Who was it?"

"O God!" she gasped. "You!"

She recoiled, with that frantic gasp. The car door, swung open against the roadside rock wall, blocked her from slipping past. She started to run towards the front, down the road ahead.

"Wait a minute!" I said. "Damn it, what's the matter with you?"

There is only one thing to do with hysteria, and that's to jump on it. Whatever had caused her terror and excitement, she had to be stopped before she hurt herself. I opened the door beside me, and was out after her in a leap. She tripped on her pump heel, and fell sprawling on the road in half a dozen steps. I got her beneath the armpits, lifting her to her feet.

"Stand up!" I said. "Nothing has got you. I'm not the bogey man. You're all right."

Her palms and knees were scraped from where she had fallen previously like that. But I had hold of her by the arm, and she couldn't run again. She stood swaying, staring at me in the headlights. Her dilated pupils went over each feature of my face almost incredulously. Her frozen look relaxed, and a deep, shuddering sigh went through her.

"Why, you aren't!" she said. "Are you? He was smaller, and his hair was matted. But I am a little near-sighted in the dark. And when you spoke to me, your voice sounded just like his—I thought he had come back. He attacked my fiancé, and stole our car—"

A little near-sighted. She was probably damned myopic.

"I am Dr. Riddle," I said. "Dr. Henry N. Riddle, Jr., of New York. Was your car a grey Cadillac phaeton with red cushions, and a license plate XL something?"

"Yes!" she said. "That was it! You noticed it as it passed?"

"Was your fiancé a man named Inis St. Erme—tall, with a black mustache?" I said.

"Yes!" she said, still a little incoherently. "Do you know Inis? I am Elinor Darrie. We were on our way to Vermont to be married. How did you know me? We picked up this terrible little man just out of Danbury, the most horrible looking little man you could imagine—"

"A tramp with red eyes and matted auburn hair?" I said. "With long yellow teeth and a torn left ear? Dressed in a checked black and white sport coat, a green shirt, and a light blue felt hat with the brim cut away in scallops all around?"

"That was the man!" she said. "Have they caught him? Is Inis hurt badly? Please tell me! Where is he?"

"I don't know," I said. "I didn't see him."

"He wasn't in the car any longer when it passed you? That must mean—"

"I don't know," I said. "I didn't see your car."

"You didn't see it—"

"No," I said. "But it went up the road I just came down, apparently. I'll turn around. There's a phone back a few miles up the road, if no place nearer. We'll get the police to send out an alarm."

I got her into my coupe, and went on down the road with her looking for a place wide enough to turn around, while she told me, a little more coherently, what had happened, so far as she knew, in answer to my questions.

She and her fiancé had motored up from New York this morning. They had picked up the hitch-hiker about sunset. They had turned off on this lonely side road to have a picnic supper by a lake a little distance down. They had left him in the car with their baggage and provisions, while they had gone down through woods to the lake side to see if the site was suitable.

The tramp had secretly followed them. She had looked up, and seen him peering over a rock ledge above them when they had reached the lake. Apparently he was only spying on them out of curiosity. But St. Erme had been angry and had gone after the fellow.

He had pursued him back up towards the road where their car was parked. She had heard him scream from there, as she followed up the hill slope after, and then a gurgling and a moaning, and a burst of ghastly laughter.

She had been terrified, and had hidden in the bushes. Presently the tramp had come stalking her again. For a long time, for an hour it seemed to her, in desperate fright she had silently crept and hidden from him in the darkening twilight woods, till he gave up trying to find her, and went back to the car. She had been near enough to the road to see St. Erme sprawled silently in the seat beside him, with his head on the car door, as the tramp took the wheel and drove away.

It was a simple enough story—yet made a little nightmarish by her terror. The terror that was still in her of her pursuit by Yellow Fang through the darkening woods.

A half mile down the road I found a place to turn around, where twelve or fifteen feet of level ground extended beyond the road edge, covered with grasses and black-eyed Susans, bordered by a deep sloping woods on the other side, with a glimpse of dark, starlit water down through trees.

"This is where we were parked!" she told me. "We were down there by the lake when I saw him spying on us and screamed. Inis ran after him up here."

I got out with my flashlight, after I had turned around, and looked the ground over. I could still see the tracks in the flattened grasses where the big car had been driven off the road, and had then gone on again.

There was some dark wetness on the ground beside the tire imprints. I stooped and felt it with my palm. It wasn't crankcase oil. It was a larger quantity of blood than a man could lose from a nosebleed or a cracked head. It was more blood than he could lose unless the ventricles of his heart were severed, and spurting out.

For a moment, squatting on my haunches, I held my palm before me, away from my knees, thinking of that other moment, in the twilight an hour before, when I had heard the croaking in the weeds beside the road, and had found the blue hat with the saw-tooth brim. I wiped my hand on clean grass. But it was more than my hand, I felt, that I had put in murder. It was all around me. Up to my neck.

I got into my little car again, and brought her here.

It was an ordinary and obvious crime, on the face of it, fitting an almost tediously commonplace police pattern, as I understand it—that first murder of the demon. A moronic hitch-hiker, having been picked up on the road, yields to sudden impulse and steals his driver's car and baggage, with murder as a casual incident, not realizing the certainty of his being caught after a few miles, or a few hundreds.

Every year, in almost every state, during ordinary times, men go to the chair or the gas chamber for crimes as stupid and meaningless. There is nothing to differentiate Yellow Fang from any other such casual moronic killer except that, afterwards, he made a supernormally cunning effort to conceal his crime. And when he did not succeed in that completely, he struck again. And he hasn't yet been caught.

From the beginning, I don't believe that Lieutenant Rosenblatt was quite satisfied, from the questions that he asked. A slow man, and a little dull, but patient and persistent. I can see him yet, sitting at the table in the living room here, with his wrinkled pugdog face, with his burly little shoulders, making his inquiries and putting down the answers that he got, in his small round precise handwriting, in his fat dog-eared notebook. Going back into Elinor Darrie's life, and into St. Erme's, to try to find a previous trace of that fantastic killer.

Q. (To Miss Darrie) Tell me all about yourself, Miss Darrie. Where you came from. How long you and Mr. St. Erme have known each other. How you happened to be here.

A. My name is Elinor Darrie. I am nineteen years old. I come from Spardersburg, Pennsylvania. I work in the Liberty Mutual Insurance agency in New York. I live on West 11th. . . .

## CHAPTER TWO

## THE RAISED CURTAIN

SHE MET INIS ST. ERME a couple of months ago when he dropped in to obtain some business insurance at the office where she was employed. He was a tall, black-eyed man, thirty-three years old, with dark wavy hair and a white, diffident smile, well-dressed, and a little shy.

He came from Oklahoma, the son of a wild-catting oil man, she learned after she had known him, who had made pots of money, and had spent and tossed them away, and had made pots more; and who had had the good luck to die, so far as his son was concerned, at a time when the pots were full. On his mother's side he had some Indian blood.

Like her, he had not been in New York long. His only acquaintances were his lawyers and brokers, and a few other business associates. His business was that of an entrepreneur and investor, and playing the market. He had never gone out with women. He had always felt a little afraid of them. His interests were mostly business. He had little interest in literature or books. His eyes would probably have kept him from much reading, even if he had cared for it.

He had never had any serious illnesses, according to the data he gave the insurance company. His only physical defect was in vision. It was a handicap not easily discernible, however, since he wore contact lenses, and had learned how to get around. It was something he never mentioned.

She had known him three or four weeks before she realized that he wore glasses at all. A glint of candlelight in a restaurant, catching his eyes at an angle, and turning them for an instant to shiny blankness, had been what had told her. She remembered then that once or twice she had noticed him stumbling over small, unexpected obstacles, such as a street curb which was a little high, or a hassock which might have been moved out of its customary place in her living room. She never spoke to him about his eyes, however. She suffered from her own near-sightedness, though it was far smaller in comparison. But she was more thoughtful to him because of it.

It would seem to indicate a somewhat juvenile vanity in him, his attempt to conceal that his eyes were not normal, which does not fit in with the other details of him as a mature, unegotistical, and unpretentious man. Yet some men are vain about one small particular thing and nothing else.

The business for which St. Erme wanted to insure his life was a small inventing business which he had been subsidizing as a side line. He had discovered a garage man by the name of Dexter who was one of these gadget-makers and mechanical geniuses, and had formed a grub-staking partnership with him to develop and exploit some of his inventions.

This Dexter was just a puttering, bald-headed, grease-stained, middle-aged mechanic who liked to tinker with odd devices for the fun of it—a failure, on the perpetual edge of bankruptcy. Yet in his shop, when St. Erme looked it over, he had on the ways a half dozen or more devices of great promise, including an adaptation of the radar principle for perceiving objects under water, a television walkie-talkie, and a method for producing a rubber substitute from coal-mine refuse culm.

St. Erme was not a technical man. Yet it required no great mechanical understanding to see that if even one of these inventions were perfected, and proved practicable, it would be worth an immense sum, quite apart from the importance to the nation at war of some of the military devices. At the worst, if they were all only a gadget-maker's dreams, he could not lose very much. He had signed partnership papers with Dexter and had put him on a drawing account, with regulated and businesslike methods of work. He wanted to insure that Dexter would be able to continue, in case of his own death.

Dexter did not know that St. Erme had taken out insurance in his favor, it would seem from his conversation, when Professor MacComerou called him up at dusk.

He did not even seem to know a great deal about St. Erme in any way. He did not know where St. Erme lived in New York. He did not know that St. Erme was being married. He had even forgotten that St. Erme had borrowed his car, until reminded. He was working on an invention, and could not be bothered.

"Young St. Erme?" I can hear him saying yet, in his dry rasping voice. "Certainly I know him. He's my partner. He's got buckets of money. Going to make a million dollars for us both, he says, when I get a gadget finished that I'm working on. . . No, I haven't seen him today, that I can remember. He lives at some hotel—I've forgotten the name of it. He has a girl—she ought to know. He called me up last night to borrow my sport touring job for a few days, come to think of it. He wanted to go some place in it with his girl.

"Where did you say you're calling from? Up in the Berkshires in north Connecticut? That does sound like my job you saw go by. XL 465-

297's the license number, if you got a look at it. I gave him the loan of it. His girl was going to drive. That's all I know about it. Excuse me, I've got something boiling on the stove now that's liable to blow on me, if I don't watch it. Call me up some other time."

And click! A hundred miles away down in New York, Inis St. Erme's partner hung up dryly.

That was within the hour of St. Erme's murder. Before it was more than a shadowy and intangible projection that something dark might have happened to him.

That scene keeps coming back to me—that scene at twilight when I first came here, looking for assistance, with my car stalled at the entrance to the Swamp Road. The voice of the locusts comes back to me, and the sound like a great frog croaking in the weedy ditch as I came down the road, and the hat that I had found, that damned remembered blue mutilated hat. There was something that troubled old MacComerou. There was something in all of it that he knew could not be right.

There were only the two of us around the place here. No one knew yet that murder had been done. St. Erme wasn't even a name to me, Yellow Fang not even a phantom. But MacComerou had seen the grey car going by, and I had not. And he knew the picture wasn't right.

The question is, what train of thought had started in his keen old brain, which impelled him to call up Dexter? There was something about that car which he wanted answered. I can see him yet, standing at the wall-telephone in the kitchen, in his gardening shorts and moccasins, gaunt and bent-shouldered, with a grey furze on his pale chest, thumbing through his black book for Dexter's number, laying a big silver watch down on the slanting phone-box ledge beneath the mouthpiece, then ringing the crank with a long white arm like a celery stalk, and asking for long distance. Putting his questions to Dexter, when he had got him, with meditative deliberation, still thumbing through his black book, with his big brain working beneath his bald skull, and his shrewd faded blue eyes that knew too much of murder.

Whatever the thought in his mind, I missed it. He may have just been searching every remotest angle, that was all. He seemed satisfied, anyway. There is nothing in the picture that I can see, myself—nothing whatever, to connect St. Erme's doodling garage man partner with Yellow Fang.

There is nothing to connect anyone with him. The problem must be approached from the beginning, to trace back his first appearance —the red-eyed wedding guest.

Q. (To Miss Darrie) When did you and Mr. St. Erme first decide on your marriage trip, Miss Darrie? How much money did he have with him? Who knew where you were going?

A. We decided to get married only yesterday at lunch. I don't know just how much money Inis had, but it was at least twenty-five hundred dollars. We stopped at the bank this morning before we started, and he cashed a check. No one knew where we were going. We didn't just know ourselves. . . .

He had said to her on Tuesday, "Let's get married." They had been at lunch together at a little place near her office. A place where one ate outdoors, in a Spanish patio beside a fountain, with caged birds singing; and it was a bright, sunshiny day, and they had known each other two months.

They were both alone in New York and the world, and only themselves mattered. They hadn't talked of marriage before. But they had had dinners together and gone to shows and movies. He had learned about her all that there was to know, perhaps; and she about him all that she would ever know. And so it might as well be now. He had set down his demitasse and tossed his crumpled napkin on the table.

"Let's get married today," he had said to her, smiling at her with his diffident white smile; his eyes crinkled.

All that she would ever know. But as much, perhaps, as most women know about the man they marry. She must take the unread pages on faith, or the whole thing is nothing.

"Why not?" she had replied, her heart beating.

And that's the way it was agreed, after luncheon on a bright summer day, in a patio with birds singing and a fountain playing and only the two of them in the whole world, and wanting life to be like this moment always. They had stopped at a telephone booth, where she had called up her office, saying she would not be back that afternoon. Without any more plans than that, they had gone down to City Hall.

But New York state had a three-day law, they found. They had thought, then, of Connecticut. It is a common belief among New Yorkers all their lives, that Connecticut is a marrying paradise, and that all one needs to do is to go over the line to the first lunch-wagon proprietor or gas-station attendant. The reason, perhaps, is that Greenwich is the first Connecticut town down on the Sound, and people may confuse its name with Gretna Green. As a matter of fact, Connecticut has had a five-day law much longer than New York.

But they didn't know that. When they found out about New York, they thought they would go to Connecticut. It was too late by then to do it that day, however; and so they had to put it off till the next day, yesterday. St. Erme thought that they might go by car, and they could then drive on up, making a honeymoon of it, to Maine or Montreal.

He didn't have a car himself, he didn't drive; but he might get a car from Dexter, and she could drive it. She had used to drive her grandmother's car for her.

A colored boy from the garage delivered it at her apartment door the next morning, driving around the block with her a few times until she had got the feel of it.

"I'd like to have Mr. Dexter pass on me himself as a competent driver, if he's around," she said, when she had returned the boy to the garage, a few blocks away. "It's a beautiful car. I know he must think a great deal of it. I wouldn't want him to be afraid anything might happen to it."

"Mr. Dexter ain't around," the boy said.

"Should I give you a receipt," she said, "or is Mr. St. Erme's name sufficient?"

The boy shook his head dubiously.

"Don't know him," he said. "Mr. Dexter just told the night man to deliver it to you-all. He didn't say anything about a receipt. I reckon you ain't going to steal it. I reckon nobody's going to try to steal it," he added, with a brown grin. "They wouldn't get nowhere very far with her if they did. She's a grey fire-engine coming down the road. Just remember that your gear-shift's on the steering post, and don't keep reaching down beside your knee. I reckon you're all right."

She picked up St. Erme at his hotel. He lived at the Molton in midtown, not far from her office. They stopped in the neighborhood at his bank, which was also hers, for him to get a check cashed for expenses; and at the same time she wanted to draw out twenty dollars herself—she had only a little silver in her purse, as always.

She gave him her check to cash with his while she watched their bags in the car out front. She hadn't seen how much his own check was for at the time he was making it out beside her at the counter. But when he, in his line, had reached the teller's window, she had seen him smiling at her over his shoulder. She had thought that perhaps he was summoning her, and she went back.

He hadn't been summoning her. It was just a smile. But she had seen the teller riffling out a sheaf of fifty-dollar bills as she came up.

"You know Miss Darrie, don't you?" Inis had said to him, smiling at her.

The teller—a sandy young man with hangdog eyes who had tried once or twice, she thought, to make a flirtatious approach to her when she had come in with her firm's deposits—nodded moodily.

"Fifty-fifties," he said. "Good morning, Miss Darrie. A big event is in the offing, I take it."

She felt herself blush warmly. She walked away with her hand in Inis's arm, out to the car.

"Why do people always leer at you when you're going to get married?" she said. "Why did you have to tell him?"

Inis smiled happily. "I didn't tell him anything," he said. "He probably just read it in our faces. But he wasn't leering. Just plain masculine jealousy." He passed her a bill as he put his bulging wallet away. "I tore up your silly little check," he said. "Your money's no good any more."

"Fifty dollars!" she said. "Why, what would I do with all that money?"

"All that money," he smiled at her. "I don't know. What can you do with fifty dollars? Buy yourself a lunch, some time, or a crazy little hat. Or how much do they cost?"

For a moment they stood smiling at each other, out of happiness over nothing.

It was only after they had got into the car and she had started to drive off, that she realized, with a belated mental arithmetic, how much money Inis had drawn. It seemed an appalling sum to her, just to carry around in one's pocket for day by day expenditures. It was as much as all the money she had in this world, from her grandmother's legacy. But his standards of money weren't hers, of course. She would have to get used to many different values than the small and narrow ones she had always known.

She had already phoned her office, earlier in the morning, that she was taking her vacation without pay now—which had been offered her—without saying where she was going, or the occasion. There had been that disappointment the previous afternoon at City Hall, and she was glad she had not told anyone. Perhaps there was some subconscious uncertainty, some shadowy inquietude in her mind, that some unforeseen event might again occur. A presentiment, however, formless and dim, of some dark opposing hand rising up against them.

They had no itinerary. They just started rolling, up the Grand Concourse, and out along the Bronx River parkway; and then taking this road and that bearing in the general directions east and north, knowing they would find Connecticut in the end, just where God had planted it, by and by.

It was after half past three when they reached Danbury, over the line in Connecticut.

They learned about the five-day law there, and learned also that Massachusetts, to the north, had a three-day law; and that the nearest place where they could get married without delay was Vermont.

They sat down in a booth in a little stationery and ice-cream store, and talked it over. It was too late to get to Vermont that day. It seemed to them both that there was some malignant fate opposing them. That an invisible hand had risen up against them, blocking them off.

If they went back, it would take the bloom off the whole thing. The hour, the mood, might never come again. Never the time and the place. There would always be between them a sense of frustration and retreat—of postponement for a few days more, and a few weeks, and perhaps forever. Yet to go on, stopping at some hotel or roadside tourist camp, even with circumspection, even though being married tomorrow, was something of which she could not conceive. Behind her was her old Amish grandmother, and all the strict training and deep instincts of her life.

Inis had not liked the thought particularly, either. He had his own sense of reticence, his distaste of being a common show—going to a hotel desk and registering, either as man and wife or under their own names, demanding separate rooms, before the eyes of the lobby loungers and the bellboys' curious smirks, while the clerk turned the book around, and read it with a slow fish eye. He had sat brooding, drumming his brown fingers on the booth table, a little dispirited that she should have suggested going back, and trying to think it out.

He had brightened, then, with his white smile flashing, suddenly remembering old John R. Buchanan, the steel king, one of the great men of the country, whose big summer estate was up near Burlington, just over the border in Vermont. Old John R. Buchanan had been his father's closest friend, and would be glad to put them up.

It was too late to reach there tonight. But if they made it at a leisurely pace, taking a good time out for supper, and stopping for coffee at lunch-wagons in Pittsfield and other towns en route, they could reach Buchanan's place about six or seven in the morning, when the house servants would be up. They could get a belated sleep there, and be on hand when the license office opened.

He had a road map in his pocket, and they had sat there in the booth picking out the route on it, counting up the distances between towns. And it didn't seem too long and tiresome, taking it at a leisurely pace, with plenty of stop-offs, and bed at the end. She had felt gay again, infected by his enthusiasm. The way seemed suddenly now clear, and there was now a definite shape and plan to what had all been rather planless and shapeless before their wedding trip. She put from her mind the disquieting thoughts she had had of turning back.

They would make an adventure of it. They would get picnic supplies here in Danbury, and stop at some pretty spot along the way for supper, perhaps beside a secluded lake where they could have a swim, building a fire afterwards and watching the shadows of the flames while the night deepened and grew late, until the embers died, and then going on, drifting up through the hills in the warm starlit darkness, with those stops at the lunch-wagons in the little sleeping towns, and on again, while the night faded, and the pearl dawn came, and the pink dawn. And so they would be there at the end, ready for buckwheat cakes and Vermont syrup and sausages and bed; and tomorrow they would be married in the great Buchanan drawing room, with flowers and organ music and a wedding cake, and perhaps an heirloom wedding gown lent by Mrs. Buchanan, and would go up to that paradisical lakeside cabin in the hills. And so their honeymoon life together would begin, and go on and on. With never a dark invisible hand rising up against them. . .

St. Erme did not know, of course. It was just a macabre coincidence that he should have suddenly remembered that old John R. Buchanan had his summer place near Burlington. But it is a little gruesome to think that he had planned to take his young bride to a dead man's house.

For at that precise hour, yesterday afternoon—though that is quite apart—at his estate in Burlington, on a white table in a quiet room, old John Buchanan was dying beneath my knife.

Yellow Fang may have been in the dark little stationery and ice-cream store while they had been laying out their route on the map and calculating their time schedule. He may have been in the next booth, eating a dish of chocolate ice cream, with little red blinking eyes upon his spoon, with slow lickings of his stubbly lips, pulling at his torn ear at times. There is nothing in the picture of him to indicate he was a man who would not like ice cream.

They saw him first on the road a little outside of Danbury. He was standing by the roadside, thumbing to go their way. That was the first moment—the very first moment, so far as I can see—when he was visible. When he made an appearance. When a finger could be laid on him at all.

He was a man about forty-five years old. He was a man about five feet, three inches tall. He had a dirty, seamy complexion, with a stubble of bristles growing up to his eyes.

His nose was nondescript—small, and rather flat. He had long unkempt hair that was tipped with grey, like the bristles of a badger shaving brush, and raggedly cut about his ears and across the back of his neck, as if with a pair of dull shears ineptly handled. His left ear lobe had been torn or bitten off, giving his face a lopsided look seen from the front—a look a little baffling, of something inexplicably missing, until one realized what it was. He had four long yellow teeth in his upper jaw when he grinned.

He wore a filthy old blue hat, with a brim cut away in sawtooth scallops. He wore a dirty black and white checked sport jacket with a belted back, of shoddy material, with torn elbows, and without buttons, as if it might have been passed on to him by some thrifty housewife who had first cut the buttons off.

He wore a faded green polo shirt, with almost all the coloring washed out of it, unbuttoned at the throat. He wore a garish green and red necktie loosely knotted, with the knot hanging down on his second shirt button—it was the only item of his clothing which seemed new or clean. His heavy corduroy pants were too large for him, and were gathered in folds about his waist with a broken black trunk strap. They were too long for him, as well, so that the pants legs wobbled down their length like the bellows of an accordion, giving an uneven silhouette to the lower half of him, like a man with corkscrew legs.

He might be called Red Eyes, or Clipped Ear, or Corkscrew Legs just as well, then, from his appearance. But it was because of those long inhuman teeth of his that Lieutenant Rosenblatt had named him Yellow Fang.

The late afternoon sun was at his back. He had some small grey things in his arm, which they didn't see till they were almost on him. He had nothing else, no bag, no bundle.

He lifted up his thumb with a grin as they came on. He was the little man who was there. The curtain was lifted on his brief but terrible appearance.

Repulsive—that was the feeling Elinor Darrie had about him at first sight. A distaste of his sheer dirtiness. A crawling in her skin. But not fear, at first. She hadn't thought of it as fear, anyway.

"Do you see what I see, Inis?" she said. "That extraordinary little man on the road ahead!"

Inis peered idly from beneath his flapping hat brim.

"What's so extraordinary about him?" he said. "He looks like just a tramp."

"Everything about him!" she said with vehemence. "He's a tramp to end all tramps. Why, he's grinning at us and thumbing us! How ridiculous. He looks as if he actually believed he's going to make us stop and pick him up."

"Maybe he's advertising something." Inis said. "He does look damned odd, doesn't he? He's got something in his arm, it looks like—like some kind of a dirty grey rag he's fondling."

"Why, it's a kitten!" she said. "It's a little grey kitten, with a red—"

She had taken her foot off the accelerator. She did not consciously intend to stop. But the thing which Yellow Fang was holding in his arms had snared her attention, with a queer sense of horror.

"Oh, how dreadful! It's been hurt!" she cried.

St. Erme put his hand forth and turned the ignition off. She had stalled the engine, anyway.

There, beside grinning Yellow Fang.

## CHAPTER THREE

## YELLOW FANG

HE WAS NO ONE whom St. Erme recognized, it was evident. No one whom, so far as St. Erme had the slightest idea in his mind, he had ever seen before. He was just a tramp on the road, thumbing a ride.

Not all the details of him so soon. But even if St. Erme had seen all the details, it is improbable that he would have been afraid. He was not a man who had ever had occasion to feel any particular fear of anything. A simple lack of fear is quite the opposite, of course, from courage. From the desperate, shivering, gut-vomiting courage which makes a man who has it fight with tooth and claw for his life, and fight even when he's half cut in two, and till death, and past it.

"Looking for a lift?" he said. "What the devil happened to your cat?"

Yellow Fang held the grey kitten in the crook of his left arm, against his dirty black-and-white jacket. He was poking at its fur softly and tentatively with his finger, while he grinned at them with his four yellow teeth. It was a fluffy kitten, not many weeks old. Its eyes were still watery. It must have been a pretty little thing once, as most kittens are—as are most young living animals. But it was filthy now, as filthy as Yellow Fang himself; and there was blood and froth on its muzzle. One of its front paws had been torn off at the shoulder socket, like the leg of a fly, and its head was mangled.

"What's happened to it?" Elinor echoed. "Oh, what's happened to it?"

"Found it on the road," said Yellow Fang in a soft quiet voice. "Truck must have run over it, poor little thing."

"Is it dead?"

"It's dead," he said. "End of its troubles."

He lifted it by the scruff. For a moment he held it aloft, looking at it with his small, inflamed eyes. It had lived out the destiny for which it had been made. He dropped it into the weed-lined ditch beside the road. With a brush of his hands, he opened the tonneau door and stepped in.

"Thanks for stopping," he said. "I always used to have Cadillacs myself. I wouldn't ride in anything else if you gave it to me today. I'm a little fussy, I suppose."

Elinor looked at Inis. But he seemed hypnotized by the quiet voice, or the red eyes.

"Where are you headed for?" he asked with a slight stammer, his own voice a little thin.

"Anywheres," said Yellow Fang.

He had ensconced himself among the groceries. Perhaps he had mesmerized them both with his red eyes and his quiet voice, with his mangled, dead, grey, kitten, thought Elinor Darrie.

All right, he had that soft quiet voice. It was one chief thing she remembered. Its incongruity with his appearance may have emphasized it on her mind. She thought of it as an educated voice, particularly.

He may have been a college man, or even a former professional man, she thought. There is quite possibly the same proportion of professional men as of any other stratum among hoboes and derelicts, in penitentiaries, and among the damned. It isn't education only which keeps a man from going down. What made her think he was an educated man was a quotation she thought she heard him make.

It was at sunset, when he had been riding with them for an hour. Unobtrusively enough, in the back seat. He hadn't thrust his conversation on them. Still he was there. They couldn't converse so freely between themselves, and must speak a word back to him once or twice. She had asked him if the breeze was too much, if he would like to put up the rear windshield, and he had said no. St. Erme had asked him what part of the country he came from, and he had said nowhere in particular. She had asked him a little later if he was hungry, and he had said yes. She told him that he could help himself to some crackers and fruit, or whatever else appealed to him, and that when they stopped for supper they would give him something more, if he was still with them; though perhaps by that time he would have wanted out. And he had said that he enjoyed riding with them, and would keep on. He offered to take the wheel if they wanted him to, later on.

They came over the crest of a hill, where the winding highway was headed west at the moment; and far beyond the Catskills more than a hundred miles away the red sun was going down.

Elinor slowed on the hillcrest, almost to a stop.

"The sun!" she said, with the tight feeling in her throat which sunset had always given her, from childhood. "It's going down."

She had forgotten for the moment his existence in the back seat. She had even forgotten Inis beside her. That feeling of an intolerable desolation had hold of her throat. Perhaps connected with the death of her young parents, killed in a theater fire in New York, or of their funeral at a red sunset hour, when she had been little more than a baby. The sun going down.

*"Soles occidere et redire possunt—"* she thought she heard him quietly murmur.

*Suns may sink and rise again*—She turned her head around.

*"Nobis cum semel occidit brevis lux—"* she added to it.

*For us, when our brief light goes out—*

And thought she heard the whisper of him finishing it, where he sat, red-eyed, behind her:

*"Nox est perpetua una dormienda."*

*There is one eternal night for sleeping.*

How few people know their Latin now! Catullus's lines to Lesbia. One would not have expected her to recognize them, with her young face, a word in a dead tongue. But not so long out of high school, and filled with books, she had. . .

Whatever kind of voice he had, it was a voice to be noticed and remembered. She remembered it. But that is all there is about his voice. There is no one else who heard him speak. No one who is now alive.

He did not tell them his name was Yellow Fang, of course. He told them to call him Doc.

I have been looking over Rosenblatt's notebook, his notes on Yellow Fang. There is the significant question of his height.

Q. (To Miss Darrie) You say that he was small, Miss Darrie. A small man. Do you mean that he was frail?

A. No, not frail. His torso and shoulders seemed normal in size, his arms rather long, with heavy wrists and hands. It was more that he was just sawed off. His legs seemed short for his body. He was only about five feet, three inches tall.

Q. His legs seemed corkscrewed, his knees bent, as if he were crouching?

A. It was the baggy pants he wore, I think.

Q. If he had been crouching, and had straightened up, then he would have been a tall man?

A. No, not very tall. He could not have been as tall as Mr. Quelch here or Inis.

Q. About as tall as Dr. Riddle here, perhaps?

A. Yes, about that tall, he might have been, if he had been taller.

Q. That would be about five feet, seven and a half.

A. (By Dr. Riddle) A good guess, Lieutenant. I am just five feet eight. . .

There is the question of the color of his eyes, also, an important item.

Q. (To Miss Darrie) His eyes were red, you say? You mean pink like an albino's?

A. No, the irises of his eyes were blue. A medium blue or grey. But his eyeballs, the whites of them, were inflamed and red, and even in the irises the red seemed to shine through. You noticed it at once.

Q. (To Dr. Riddle) What might that be?

A. It sounds a bit as thought it might have been chronic blepharitis.

Q. What's that, Doctor?

A. It's a condition of disease. However, I would not care to make any positive statement without having seen him.

Q. You never saw him at all?

A. I have never seen him.

Q. If he knew something about medicine, there would be some things he could do to his eyes to make them look red, without having a disease, I suppose?

A. He would not necessarily have to know anything about medicine.

There is also the matter of his torn ear, since the ear is one of the most significant indices of identity according to the Bertilon system, as I understand it. And while the ordinary, untrained observer does not pay attention to the shape of a man's ears, any great deviation from the normal in them does stand out. The question comes up in the inquiry of Quelch, the somewhat garrulous postmaster at Whippleville, who was the last man to see Yellow Fang before they reached Dead Bridegroom's Pond.

Q. (To Mr. Quelch) You are the postmaster at Whippleville, Mr. Quelch? And you saw this man called Doc in the back seat of Mr. St. Erme's and Miss Darrie's car, when they stopped at the post office in Whippleville about seven-thirty, to inquire about some place where they might have a picnic supper?

A. Yes. I was standing on the front porch, just closing up, when this big grey car drove up, with that fellow in the back. It was going on 7:36, nearer than 7:30, and the afternoon mail from Pittsfield had been distributed more than an hour ago, and there wasn't anything more till the mail truck at six o'clock tomorrow morning with the Danbury papers. Miss Darrie was driving, and a pretty picture she was, too, with her curly hair and her pink cheeks, and those blue-rimmed glasses she was wearing. And Mr. St. Erme said they were on their way to Vermont to get married, they were planning to picnic and were there any pretty places where they wouldn't be trespassing on anybody's front yard? And he said how about that road back there a couple of hundred feet, that road off to the side that they'd just passed, were there any pretty places on it? And I said that's the Stony Falls road and it's a bumpy stony road and nobody lives on it but Old Man Hinterzee and John Wiggens that raises bees and has a cider mill, and two or three artists and old college professors that have their places they live at in the summers, but there are plenty of woods along it, and there's a lake up the road about a mile, about a mile this side of Old Man Hinterzee's, that doesn't belong to anybody, and it has woods and rocks around it, and he and his lady could have a picnic there, I guess, and it's a kind of pretty lake, only it's mighty black and deep, and some call it Lake Tagore, only most call it Dead Bridegroom's Pond, because a man named Bridegroom used to live on it who's been dead a hundred years. And he said thanks, they might try it, and after they have had their supper and are ready to go on, should they keep going up that road and find some other road off it to get them to Vermont, or should they come on back? And I said there's no road off it at all except the Swamp Road about ten miles long, that all the swamp-rat Flails that is three-quarters Indian used to live on and raise so much hell, though there isn't any more of them than John Flail now, with Two-finger Pete in the pen for murder and the rest of them all dead; and the Swamp Road didn't go nowhere, anyway, except to the old sawmill. And he says thanks, they'll come back after they have had their picnic, and his lady smiles at me, and they back and turn around, and go back down to the Stony Falls road, and go on up it.

Q. You have given your Conversation with Mr. St. Erme in great detail, Mr. Quelch, and I thank you for it. I am sure, that you gave him complete directions. The question, however, is about this man who was with him and Miss Darrie, this tramp referred to as Yellow Fang, who called himself Doc. You saw him?

A. Yes. I couldn't help but see him. They were stopped there talking to me about eight minutes and a half, more or less. I seen this fellow there in the back seat. I didn't look at him so closely, maybe. I was looking more at Miss Darrie setting at the wheel, she looked so young and pretty, she was pretty enough to be a chorus girl, she was pretty enough to eat. More than that fellow in the back. I didn't pay any particular attention to him, except that he must have been a tramp they had picked up. I did notice he was wearing a coat with big black and white squares, and a light-blue hat with its brim cut saw-tooth all around, and he looked un-shove and dirty; and his eyes were red and he had yellow teeth. But I didn't notice how tall or short he was, setting down. He did have kind of reddish hair, come to think of it.

Q. What do you mean by red? Like Dr. Riddle's here?

A. Well, more auburn, maybe. More pink and brown, not so dark red, quite.

Q. Could it have been a wig?

A. They make wigs better'n that. I used to do bartering in Hartford, and—

Q. Did you notice his torn left ear, which Miss Darrie has described?

A. He was setting with his right side to me. He was kind of holding and pulling at his left ear, I think, now that you mention it. Maybe it was tore.

Q. Do you remember what his voice sounded like?

A. He didn't say anything. He just sat there on the back seat among the groceries.

Q. Have you seen him again since? I want you to think carefully before you answer me.

(Mr. Quelch, after deliberation, and after surveying a man present, states that he does not believe so.)

Q. (To Dr. Riddle) And you have not seen him since, either, doctor?

A. I have never seen him at all.

He must have been real. He was a man, and not a phantom. Not merely she and St. Erme saw him, and Postmaster Quelch, but old Hinterzee as well, and everyone along the road from Dead Bridegroom's Pond as he raced in his laughing getaway.

There is old Hinterzee, gnarled and bow-legged, with a broken nose.

Q. (To Mr. Hinterzee) You were homeward-bound from the Whippleville post office up the Stony Falls road, about a quarter of eight, and this grey car overtook and passed you, Mr. Hinterzee, with Miss Darrie and Mr. St. Erme in front, and this Doc, or Yellow Fang, in the rear seat?

A. Yah.

Q. Miss Darrie has stated that she did not see you.

A. I was down in ditch beside road. Tall grasses. I was looking for half dollar I lose last spring. Always when I go by, I stop and look for it. But I see them, yah. They come by.

Q. Describe this man we are referring to as Yellow Fang.

A. He has black and white coat, funny cut blue hat, dirty face.

Q. A torn ear?

A. I did not notice.

Q. And you saw the car again, and him and Miss Darrie and Mr. St. Erme, about half a mile farther along where it had parked off the road beside the woods leading down to Dead Bridegroom's Pond? Miss Darrie and Mr. St. Erme had got out of it, and were going down through the woods towards the lake, and you saw Yellow Fang slipping out of it, and slipping after them?

A. Yah.

Q. Describe how he was going.

A. Creepy.

Q. Can you illustrate? (Mr. Hinterzee crouches, makes a demonstration of a man stalking, lifting his feet carefully, parting bushes, with shoulders hunched.)

Q. Did he have a knife in his hand? A bread-knife?

A. I did not see.

Q. What did you see?

A. They just going down through woods to lake, maybe have swim, maybe pick wild flowers. This fellow goes creeping after them. I go on.

Q. And you saw him again, about forty minutes later, when you had reached your own house a mile beyond, and were sitting on your front porch beside the road? He was driving the car, with Mr. St. Erme sitting slumped beside him with his head on the car door, one arm dangling overside, and Miss Darrie wasn't in it any more? And as he passed he howled his horn and laughed?

A. Yah.

Q. How did he laugh?

A. Like a horse.

Q. Can you illustrate? (Mr. Hinterzee puts his head sideways on his shoulder and utters a loud whinnying laugh.)

Q. What did you do?

A. I thought he was crazy.

Q And Mr. St. Erme beside him did not move?

A. His arm moved. Over the side of the door, swinging. His head lying on the door. The car goes by fast.

Q. (By Dr. Riddle) Excuse me, Lieutenant. His right arm, Mr. Hinterzee?

A. Yah.

Q. (By Dr. Riddle) And he had a hand at the end of it?

A. I did not notice. But yah. He must have. If he did not have, I notice. . ."

Obviously. St. Erme had a right hand. That is definite.

And I do not know just why I feel it, but I feel it must be found.

There he is, Yellow Fang, beside the road. He lured them to stop and pick him up with a dead mangled kitten, with his red eyes, with his quiet voice. St. Erme acted like a man in a dream, and even she seemed half bewitched. When they stopped on a lonely road, and went down through the woods, he stalked them. Simple curiosity? Or to murder both of them by the lakeside, who knows? But she saw him, and screamed. And St. Erme awoke out of his hypnosis, out of his deadly dream.

Suddenly he realized that that contemptible, negligible little man was dangerous. Suddenly he saw him as more than just a rotten harmless tramp. But not enough. Not enough. Not with a mortal fear in him, for his own life, and for the girl's he loved. He was only enraged, with a lordly anger. Lordly, he pursued him, perhaps to catch him and shake him and rattle his bones a little, showing off his male courage, telling her to wait there.

Who was he to be afraid of anything? And Yellow Fang lured him back up towards the car, with the trick of the broken partridge wing.

The car keys, is the answer to what he wanted, quite likely. Elinor didn't have them; she hadn't taken them out. Yellow Fang may have seen St. Erme removing them, and not been sure whether St. Erme had pocketed them, or dropped them for hiding in the car in the grass. So he plays the partridge with the broken wing, while St. Erme, angry, follows. And then at the car he turns with the knife: "Where are the keys!" And the girl, following up through the woods, screams. So she has seen him do it, her scream says. He must get rid of her, too. Through the twilight woods, stalking her. Silently, terribly, wasting no breath. With the knife. With his red eyes. Only the deepening darkness saves her. Only that she had hidden from him, lying quietly like a bird.

A sawed-off nameless tramp beside the road, with yellow fangs, with a torn ear, and he seizes his opportunity for theft on a lonely road, and incidentally does murder. A common story to the police. But Rosenblatt from the beginning was not quite satisfied. And I have a feeling, myself also, that St. Erme's murder, and hers as well, were planned long ago.

He was not a phantom, anyway—Yellow Fang.

There were she and St. Erme and Quelch and Hinterzee who saw him, briefly or more at length. There was John Wiggens the beekeeper, two miles farther on from Hinterzee's, whose big, sluggish, amiable St. Bernard dog he deliberately veered and struck, with his hideous laughter, as it stood wagging its tail beside the road, in sight of Wiggens and his wife and their three children; and they ran out and gathered around the dying dog with tear-blind eyes and breaking breasts, poor simple people, not knowing there could be a fiend like that.

There was the refugee hermit-painter-musician, Unistaire, half monkey and half faun, who was in his studio a mile and a half farther down the road, devising a surrealistic dance before his mirror to a composition of his own upon the phonograph, dressed in a leopard skin, a chiffon nightgown, and a feather duster, when Yellow Fang drove that grey car in off the road, apparently mistaking Unistaire's entrance for a side road, and around the circular drive beside the studio with a rush of tires and a squeal of brakes, crashing down the wooden easel frames on the drive on which Unistaire had set his paintings out—to be impregnated with twilight dew, as part of some art theory that he had—and shooting back out onto the road again, with a blare of high-pitched wailing horn, as Unistaire went rushing out to see. There was Professor MacComerou, with his shrewd, keen mind, three miles farther on, who saw the murder car go rushing by his place and heard that demon laughing, and caught a glimpse of the ghastly look of St. Erme's face beside him, with eyes staring and lips moving in a kind of dreadful prayer, as if St. Erme in that moment was still alive. There was big shambling John Flail, whom he ran down on the road just before he reached me—and John Flail must have seen him, too, for one terrible moment, as he tried to leap out of the way with a bleating cry, feeling the iron blow smash him.

They all saw him, all the way along the road. He was not invisible. He must have passed me by. He went down the Swamp Road. They've found the car now where he abandoned it, after he had passed me by. And yet I did not see him.

Q. (To Dr. Riddle) And you are sure you were at the Swamp Road entrance all the time, Dr. Riddle?

A. I am quite sure of it.

Q. And you did not see the murder car go by at all?

A. I did not see it.

Q. And you did not see this man we are speaking of as Yellow Fang, this nameless tramp called Doc?

A. I did not see him. I have never seen him.

Q. You'll stand on that?

A. I will.

And so I must.

## CHAPTER FOUR

## THE GREY CAT

IT WAS ABOUT sunset when I turned off onto this hill country road, to get over from Route 49A to Route 7, on my way back to New York from John R. Buchanan's place in Vermont, where I had been summoned to operate on him for the brain malignancy of which he had been dying.

It had been a foredoomed failure. A hundred per cent against it. At his age, seventy-nine. He was dead before I could begin the operation. Still my failure depressed me. It was, perhaps, in a kind of subconscious flight or escape that I turned off from the highway.

The place where I turned off was at a little hamlet called Stony Falls. The road ran over to another hamlet called Whippleville on the map. It was a good deal shorter in miles, but was a terrible up-and-down, narrow, winding, and stony road, I found when I had got on it.

I kept on, hoping it would improve. But it didn't. It was practically an abandoned road. There were only two or three dilapidated farmhouses that I passed, and none of them appeared occupied. On both sides the road was lined with old stone fences, overgrown with great ropy poison ivy vines with glistening warty leaves a hundred years old. Beyond were only woods, deserted fields, boulder-strewn hillsides, and more woods. It was the kind of road one drives along in a nightmare. I had been going along it for about half an hour when my engine stalled.

My town sedan had been in the shop for an overhaul when I received the call to Vermont, and I had driven up in my old coupe. It was a car I had bought second-hand when I first started practice, and was more than ten years old. It was battered and not much to look at, but it would carry me along, and that was all I cared about. Only now its engine had quit, and in a few yards more it had rolled to a stop.

The place where it had stopped was right at the junction of a side road going off to the left. A half-rotted signpost with three arms stood beside me, with old hand-molded lead letters on it and lead pointers shaped like hands, which might have dated from Revolutionary days, when all this country had been more populated than it is now. One of the arms pointed back the way I had come, saying "Stony Fa 9 M", and one down the road ahead, saying "Whipl'vle 10 M", and one down the road beside me, saying "Swamp Rd., 1 $^{7}/_{8}$ M to Flail's Sawmill".

It was only the shadow of an old wagon-road, with deep grass-grown ruts and purple asters and yellow daisies and other weeds, and didn't look as if a wheel had passed over it for forty years. It was the first side road of any kind, though, that there had been since I left Stony Falls. It went along for about a hundred yards in sight, and then was lost in deep hemlock woods.

I thought I saw the figure of a man walking, away from me down near where the road vanished, as I stopped. He was a man with black hair, without a hat, wearing old khaki pants and a blue cambray shirt that was dark with sweat in the back, and he carried his coat slung over his shoulder. He seemed to be a powerfully built man, above medium height, and he was walking with a soft shambling stride, flat-footed, like an Indian. He didn't turn around when I began grinding the starter. He just went shambling on, and in a moment had vanished among the trees.

It is possible, I acknowledge, that he did not exist. That he was only an hallucination. Yet the problem is not of a phantasm which I saw, but of the grey car which I did not.

I stepped on my starter again, and the engine caught. But when I threw my clutch in, it died once more. It caught again, and stopped.

It was one of those teasing and exasperating things, where every moment you think you almost have it, and so keep on. I had half a tank of gas yet, so it couldn't be that. I wore down my battery, and then got out and cranked.

I'm pretty obstinate, as most red-headed men are, and I don't like to be licked. I would cut the switch, and swing the crank over half a dozen times to suck a charge in, and go back to the instrument board and turn the switch on, and back to the crank and snap it over hard. Each time the engine would catch, and then after a couple of kicks would sputter and die away; and I would have to do the same thing all over. By the tenth or fifteenth try I had grown a little careless, and didn't have the crank engaged properly. It flew out and went whirling past my head. If I hadn't ducked, it would have brained me. It nicked the lobe of my left ear was all, luckily, drawing a little blood. But the cartilage didn't seem torn, when I felt it, and the bleeding soon stopped.

I must have tried it twenty times or more, till I was sweaty and dirty and red-eyed. I'm not a truck-driver in build—five feet eight and a hundred and thirty-seven pounds—but my arms are pretty wiry, and I have strong hands, as a surgeon has to have. Still I got played out at last, with a ripping headache down my skull.

The evening was so hot and still. Even after the sun had disappeared and the twilight shadows were gathering, the stones of the road still gave forth their stored-up heat. If it had been midday I might have got a sunstroke, and in that case could have drawn a blank for a few minutes without knowing it, perhaps. But the sun had gone down. A mild heat prostration was what I had, with a bad headache, but not any blackout.

I remember thinking in the back of my head that I ought to push my car off the middle of the road, if anybody should come along, because I was probably blocking it. But I didn't bother to, because nobody came along.

Once while I was cranking I did think I heard the wail of a far-off, eerie horn behind me, and the hum of a car coming up the road. I stopped and looked around, wiping the sweat from my face. But nothing came up the road. It might have been only a railroad train off in some valley.

A kind of whirling little heat gust came spinning up the road as I stood there looking. It brushed against me, and went rushing on. I could watch how it went, though I couldn't see it. It veered away, after brushing me, and went off down the Swamp Road, bending the weeds and grasses and turning the undersides of them to silver, and skirling up a little sandy dust in the ruts like the smoke of a car going fast. But it wasn't a car. It was just a little whirl of air in motion.

It was while I was following it with my gaze that I saw the yellow rattlesnake. It was lying in one of the ruts of the Swamp Road about twenty feet away from me, staring at me with motionless eyes in its flat head.

A timber rattler, about four feet long, the color of dead grass, with pale milk-chocolate markings—a female, if it's true, as is sometimes said, that the lighter-colored ones are females. I don't know how long it had been there when I saw it. But the probability would be that it had been there all the time, or I would have seen it crawling. A moving snake catches the eye; and this one was lying yellow and still, mingled with the yellow roots of the wheel-rut grasses.

There was nothing strange in a rattler there on the old dead road. There are plenty of them in the hills all the time, and particularly out on old roads in August. They like to lie in the heat of the sun-baked dust and stones to shed their skins. They are apt to be more or less blind at that time, and anything that comes along may run them over. The only thing at all unusual about this particular yellow snake that I noticed was the color of its eyes. Most rattlers have mottled golden eyes. But this one's were red as fire. That may have been due to some last shred of sunset still burning in the sky, which was reflected on its hard, lidless eyeballs, giving them that burning color.

I wasn't sure but that it was dead. It might have been run over. But I jerked out the crank handle and hurled it at it. The iron hit the stony ruts with a whirling thud, right where that broad motionless, fanged head had been. But there was nothing there now. It had not been dead or blind. All the time lying there, maybe hours, maybe days, but still chip-quick at the flash of danger. At my gesture it had slid instantly, and was gone.

That figure of a man vanishing down Swamp Road, and the whirling gust of wind that went brushing by and the yellow rattlesnake, were the only things I saw at all during the time I was stalled there at the entrance to the Swamp Road.

I didn't clock the time, but I was there from about sunset till twilight was falling, a period of a good hour, at least. I was miles away from Dead Bridegroom's Pond.

That crank I had hurled had bounced off into the tall grass at the edge of the old wagon-road. I didn't bother to go and retrieve it. It wouldn't do me any good if I kept cranking all night, unless I located what the trouble was. I lifted up the hood, trying to figure out where the difficulty might lie.

I'm not an expert mechanic, by any means, but a car's internal machinery shouldn't be any more complicated than a man's, I told myself. There are just so many different organs, and just so many ways in which they can go wrong. The engine did look complicated. But maybe a cadaver would look just as complicated to a garage repairman who was trying to do an anatomical section for the first time. Still he ought to be able to figure out how the tissues were put together, after a fashion, just by using his common sense; and I ought to be able to figure this engine out.

It must be some dirt that had got in the intake feed-line of the vacuum, I figured it. That was why it kept choking off that way. It couldn't be anything else. I had had the same trouble with the old car once before, I remembered; only there had been a mechanic handy on that occasion to diagnose the difficulty and straighten it out for me.

It wasn't a very complicated mechanical operation, as I recalled it. All I needed to do was unscrew a little hexagonal nut and disconnect the line, suck out the dirt with my mouth till the gas flowed clear, clean out a little filter screen, and then tighten the nut up again. The thing oughtn't to take more than five minutes, with a small wrench. I should have tried to find the trouble in the first place, instead of wasting all that time. I would have saved myself a ripping headache, if I had. And perhaps more.

I rummaged around for tools under the car seat, but all I could find was a jack without a handle, a lug-wrench for changing tires, and a bunch of rusty chains. It was damned silly. All I needed was almost any kind of a small wrench, or even a pair of ordinary pliers; but I couldn't do it with my fingers or my teeth. I looked in the trunk compartment in the back, but there weren't any tools of any kind there, only my traveling bag and my kit of surgical instruments. And there was nothing in the latter which would be of any use. I closed the lid down again.

There hadn't been any house that had looked occupied, where I might borrow a wrench, since I had turned off at Stony Falls. That shambling figure which had vanished down the Swamp Road, and the rutted way itself, didn't look very promising. I decided to go on down the road ahead to see if I could find a house.

I left my coat on the car seat, and the keys in the ignition lock. It didn't seem likely that anyone would come along that God-forsaken road while I was away.

I had gone about a quarter mile when I saw an old shingled farmhouse at my right, a hundred feet off the road among tall weeds and a furze of second growth. I slowed when I came abreast of it, but the windows were eyeless, the chimney stones were fallen in a heap of rubble, and the roof was only a skeleton of ridge pole and naked rafters in the silver air. The gap in the stone fence where the entrance gate had been was filled with thick, high weeds, and the road that had gone in could no longer be made out.

I had veered just a couple of feet off the high crown of the road, before seeing that the place was abandoned. My foot struck something soft as I started on. It was a man's blue felt hat, or the remnants of one, lying on the road.

Its brim had been cut away in saw-tooth scallops all around, and crescent and star-shaped holes had been cut in its crown, in the way boys and boy-witted men sometimes do to old hats. It was just lying there, shapeless and dirty, with no one around it might belong to, while in the woods and weedy fields on either side insects creaked and sang.

I don't know just what impelled me to pick it up. Perhaps its color. It was filthy with ingrained dirt and grease. But it was—or had been once—of a soft lovat-blue color. I have always been partial to lovat-blue hats, though they're not always obtainable. I had bought my last one during my final year in medical school, and had worn it four or five years, and might be wearing it yet if my secretary hadn't protested. I still had it, the same way most men keep old loved hats, on a shelf of my closet at home.

This cut-up hat had the texture of what had once been a good piece of felt, in spite of its dirt. It had come from Haxler's, on Fifth Avenue, no wonder. I pulled down the sweat-band—a size 7 $^{3}/_{8}$. It was just my size, and if I put it on, I would look a beauty. . . Looking more closely, I could see where paper initials had formerly been pasted on the band. They had peeled off; but the stained leather was still a little lighter where they had been, and I could make out their shape: "H. N. R., Jr."

It was my old hat. When had I last seen it on my closet shelf? Last week, or last month? A man puts something away, and thinks of it as being still just where he put it. Its image is in his mind. Yet it might have been as much as six months or longer ago since I had last actually seen that hat on my shelf. Maybe as far back as last fall my landlady had given it to the janitor or the Salvation Army, in a fit of cleaning out, without bothering to tell me.

It gave me a queer sense of I don't know what to find it there on the deserted road in the twilight, a hundred miles from home, filthy and mutilated, but still something that had once been an integral part of my appearance and personality. A hat is more intimate than a pair of shoes. It's a kind of badge a man wears. King's crown or soldier's cap, banker's homburg or cowboy's sombrero, it marks a man's rank and sets his style. This had been my hat, and I had always worn it a little at an angle. Cut in the shape of a clown's hat now.

I had probably got fifty different species of bacteria and crawling protozoa on my fingertips, examining it. I tossed it into the deep weeds beside the road.

There was a crushed grasshopper on the road which had been beneath the hat when I picked it up. I took the insect up between my thumb and forefinger. A grey stone dust was ground into its body, from a car tire or a heel. It had been crushed before the hat had been dropped on the road on top of it.

The insect's feelers were still stirring, and brown saliva was still oozing from its mandibles. Its black eyes were still alive. I don't know just how long crushed insects take to die. But probably not long. The hat had probably not been there long. Perhaps the man or boy who had lost it would come back looking for it. I should have left it where I found it.

I crushed the insect's thorax in my fingers, and tossed it, too, into the weeds.

The eyeless old house with its skeleton roof stared at me across the high weeds in the silver twilight, and cheepers throbbed, and cicadas shrilled. I heard a croaking in the ditch beside me, like a bull-throated frog.

"Awg!" And then again, "Awg!" Slow, with long seconds in between, as if pausing for a tremendous breath.

There was a faint stirring in the dusty weeds of the ditch as I went on, though no more than a frog might make. Yet no doubt I should have regarded it as significant that I subconsciously thought of that slow croak from the weedy ditch as inhuman, as it caught my ear. Significant— because one does not think of a frog's croak as inhuman. It is the croak of a frog. One only thinks of something as inhuman which should be human. And perhaps is, in part.

A half mile or three-quarters on I began to come to the first indications of inhabited civilization since I had turned off on this nightmare way at Stony Falls. There was a red roof ahead, beyond a hedge, and the glimpse of a white cottage gable.

A hundred feet along the privet hedge I came to the entrance of a graveled, suburban-looking driveway, with tire tracks in it. The red-roofed cottage was only fifty feet inside. It was a story-and-a-half Berkshire colonial, of good original lines, painted white with red shutters, with a mass of Paul's Scarlet Climbers covering one side. In front of it, and across the drive which went up past it, a lawn of long grass was growing, and there was a glimpse of a flower garden in the back.

Beyond, another fifty feet or so, at the end of the drive, there was a big, substantial barn, also red-roofed and painted white, with a white-shuttered cupola rising from the center of its roof ridge, topped by a brass grasshopper weathervane, like the famous weather-vane on Fanueil Hall in Boston. A station-wagon stood in front of it, out on the drive, headed towards the barn doors. Beyond the barn was a windmill and a water-tank, and rock-strewn fields and evergreen copses back to a line of woods.

It was the kind of civilized rural place on which its owner had spent money, care, and intelligence. The barn itself was probably modern, but the house, with its old fanlight and tiny attic windows, was undoubtedly an eighteenth century original, restored to its pristine simple lines from whatever gingerbread decorations had been added by intervening fancy-loving generations. It was the summer home of some cultivated man of simple tastes.

There was a mailbox stuck on a five-foot pole at the edge of the road, beside the drive. "A. MacComerou" was the name on it, in black letters.

The name, somewhat unusual, rang a bell in my mind. For a moment I didn't place it. It couldn't be the name of anyone in the medical profession, for medical doctors are always particular about advertising their degrees. They would sooner appear without a shirt and tie than without their Dr. or M.D. I was reminded, though, of medical school. Then it clicked. MacComerou's *Homicidal Psychopathology,* which had been our textbook in Med Psych 12 during my senior year.

Was there ever a textbook like it? I could still feel the weight of it, just to lift it, and see again before my eyes its twelve hundred and eighty-seven pages of fact-packed type, with notes and indices. *Selected Case Histories in an Approach to an Understanding of Homicidal Psychopa-*

*thology, Together With a Brief Inquiry into Certain Aspects of Aberrant and Divided Personality Among Men of Superior Mentality, by Adam MacComerou, A.B., Ph.D., Litt.D. (causa honoris, Chicago), Sc.D. (Yale) LL.D. (Swarthmore, Columbia, McGill), Lowell Professor of Psychiatry at Harvard,* was the brief title of it.

Old Adam knew his murderers. The dry and ponderous title he had deliberately chosen, I had sometimes suspected, to keep it out of the hands of screwball laymen. Actually it was a fascinating book, brilliantly and lucidly written, witty, though profound, and more absorbing in sheer entertainment value than any fiction I have ever known, in the sparse quiet drama with which its illustrative cases of murderous mentalities were unfolded, and in the penetration of MacComerou's analyses of just what had made them like that. You can have your Sherlock Holmeses, Colonel Primroses, and Ellery Queens. I'll take old MacComerou. As a textbook, of course, it would always be a classic in its field, the final word. It was tops.

It couldn't be the same A. MacComerou, of course. He must be dead, with all that had been in his brain. It mightn't be even any relation, or anyone who had ever heard of him.

Still it wasn't a very usual name.

I felt a momentary clutching of my heart. A catching of my breath. I had been fascinated by MacComerou's *Homicidal Psychopathology.* I had memorized whole pages of it. He was the great mind. Yet I didn't know whether I should care to meet him now, if it was the same.

I must get that item analyzed in my mind—my feeling in that moment. In part, it may have been due to a general feeling of mine that authors and their books are things apart; and that if a man has written a great book, the best of him is in it.

But it was something more than that. MacComerou had found a particular quiet amusement in poking fun at medical doctors in his *Psychopathology,* in a good-natured but mildly ironic way. The medical profession, as a whole, hadn't been very advanced in its understanding of the importance of psychiatry, I think, at the time he had first written it; and some of the more ignorant doctors had even branded all psychiatry as a quack science. He was too great a man to enter into any exchange of name-calling or argument. But he had found his amusement in pricking doctors, one of the most fascinating chapters in his book was titled "Jekyll-Hyde. M.D.", and was devoted exclusively to case-histories of physicians who had been murderers, with analyses of how their aberrations had been related to their profession. I'll admit that he had plenty there.

But it didn't mean that just because I was a doctor he would find a murderer in me, of course. . .

There was a grey bird with a white breast, a phoebe, which fussed and flew low before my eyes in that moment as I paused at the entrance to the drive. She had built her nest, I saw, in the mail-box, almost at my eye-level. There were five nestlings in it. They were probably a second or third brood, at this time of summer. Phoebes have more than one brood, and are devoted parents. Generally they are friendly birds, nesting around houses as they always do, and being accustomed to humans. But this mother phoebe might have never seen a man before, from the way she acted to me. Flying back and forth across my face on grey wings in the twilight, as if I were some kind of bloody panther that she would beat back with her white breast, with her soft twittering cries.

I heard a tinkling sound beyond the hedge as I stared in, and a feline wail. A grey cat with white paws and a white face, wearing a collar jangling with little bells, came slinking out from the roots of the hedge onto the gravel, almost at my feet. It looked up at me, with a hoarse twanging wail coming from its throat, like the wail of a steel guitar.

It wasn't a homeless hunting cat. It was a tame cat, a house cat, with its bell-studded collar. It lived here, since pet cats stay around the places where they belong. And I usually get along with cats. They come to rub against me without much urging. Even those in the experimental laboratory, which I used to take care of when I was a student, poor things. I have always thought I had a way with cats. I stooped and held out my hand to this one now, with a quiet soothing word. But it only looked at me with its yellow eyes, miauling, and veered away. It went loping up the drive, away from me with its head and tail down, leaping into the tall grass a little farther on, with its hoarse and wailing cry.

There was that mangled grey kitten which Yellow Fang had in his arm, and dropped in the ditch beside the highway when Elinor and St. Erme had stopped to see. But there is no way it can be tied up with the wailing of that grey cat of MacComerous at sight of me. No way whatever.

And yet I have a feeling that that incident was not without significance.

## CHAPTER FIVE

### "THAT'S ALL RIGHT," I SAID. "IT'S DEAD."

NO LIGHTS HAD BEEN lit in the old white house yet. I could hear a woman's voice talking somewhere inside, though, through the closed windows, and then another voice replying, as I went up the drive. There was a slow, regular, whacking sound, like someone beating a heavy carpet, out in back. Country houses are usually entered from the kitchen way, and I went on back there, following the sound.

Back of the house there was the garden I had glimpsed, with rosebushes heavy with pale full-blown blossoms—cream or yellow or pink, I could not just be sure in the silver light, but making a heavy fragrance in the air, mingled with the damp smell of grass and good black garden earth. Tall delphinium spikes and hollyhocks, and clusters of little pale summer chrysanthemums, grew in beds around, with narrow stone-paved paths between. A mirror ball, like a clairvoyant's crystal, stood on a white wooden pedestal in the middle of the garden plot, to catch and reflect all the colors of the flowers. Though the bright colors were all subdued now, and the ball was as silver as the darkening twilight sky.

A tall, lean, bent-shouldered, bald-headed old man, clad in striped shorts and a pair of loafer moccasins, was packing down the earth with the flat of a spade in the bed across from me. His milk-white back was turned to me, but I could see that his bald head was rimmed by a thin fringe of clipped whitish hair, and that he had compressed and toothless jaws beneath his big bat ears.

He paused in his whacking as I stepped on the garden path, gripping the spade handle with one brown hand, and waving his other hand around his neck and shoulders, with a long thin white arm like a wavering white snake.

"Get away, you damned bloody little fiend!" he said, in a mushy voice. He wasn't talking to me. He hadn't heard me walking up the broad shallow tire tracks in the driveway gravel, in my pre-war crepe-soled sport shoes. He didn't know that anyone was within three miles of him, perhaps. Just slapping at mosquitoes, and talking to himself, as a man gets to do alone.

"Damn you, you red bloody—"

*Whack!*

"Excuse me," I said, pausing by the mirror ball, with a hand on it.

He had squashed a bloated mosquito on the top of his bald skull. It made a smear on his palm as he lifted it. He stood there with his face to the flower bed he had been working at, holding his hand motionless two inches above his head.

"Yes?" he said, in a mushy whisper.

"I was wondering—" I said, a little hesitantly.

"Yes?" he repeated mushily.

As if his mind had been lost in some far off problem. As if he were concentrating, not quite sure whether he had heard my voice, or had only imagined it. And if he had heard it, and not just imagined it, whether it had come from inside the house, where the subdued voices of those two women were still talking and gabbling, or whether it had come from the general dusk around him, or maybe from the ground.

"Here I am," I said. "Behind you."

"Behind me," he repeated.

He turned around, with his shoulders bent, gripping his spade with both brown hands. There was a grey furze on his pale chest. His face was sun-browned, like his hands, darker than his arms and body, and he had brown, outstanding ears, like a huge bat. He stared at me with compressed and toothless jaws, with large pale protuberant eyes, across the silver dusk.

"Where in hell did *you* come from?" he said mushily, with his toothless jaws, after a moment. "Who are you?"

I took my hand from the mirror ball. I walked towards him.

"My name's Riddle," I said. "Dr. Harry Riddle, of New York. My car seems to have stalled up the road. I wondered if you knew of a garage mechanic around—"

"A garage mechanic?" he repeated, staring.

"I didn't really expect to find one," I said a little lamely. "I think I might be able to take care of the trouble myself, if I had a small wrench. I haven't any tools at all in my car. Any kind of a small adjustable wrench, or a pair of pliers, if you have them."

His face relaxed. His mouth broke into a warm, friendly grin, with a twinkle of humor.

"You gave me a small wrench yourself," he said mushily. "Turn about is fair play. Yes, I should imagine we should be able to find a wrench in the kitchen somewhere. You have a damned light, quiet way of walking, for a red-headed man. What is your name again—Dr. Riddle? My name is Professor MacComerou, Dr. Riddle. I guess you saw it on the mailbox."

He gave his spade a small swing and dropped it on the flower bed, over against the house.

"Are you a gardening nut yourself, doctor?" he said; and I shook my head. "I was just setting in my next spring's early tulips," he told me. "I ought to have been a horticulturist, instead of a psychologist. My flowers are like women to me, only about twice the trouble and expense."

"Are you the Adam MacComerou?" I said.

"The?" he said. "Well, I don't suppose there are so many."

"I had you in Med Psych Twelve my senior year," I said.

"You were at Harvard?" he said, looking at me closely.

"No," I said. "Hopkins. We had your book, I mean. It was almost my Bible."

"Oh," he said. "Well, there's a lot of stuff in it, if I do say it. I suppose a good many have read it. Your car's stalled up the road, you say? I don't know of any garage mechanic around. The only one I go to is in New York, a hundred miles away. But we'll see what we can do. Where is your car located? You must be this side of Unistaire's, or you'd have stopped in at his place. You're heading up towards Stony Falls?"

"No," I said. "I came down from Stony Falls. I'm heading towards Whippleville to get on Route Seven. My car's stalled up that way."

"Oh," he said. "You came from that way?"

"Yes," I said. "From that way."

"I see," he said. "You must have had quite a walk. No one living along the road at all. Did you see that big grey car with the two men in it pass you?"

"No," I said. "Nothing passed me."

"They must have got out to Stony Falls and taken the highway there before you started down," he said. "It may have been a half hour ago."

"I've been stalled for the last hour or more," I said. "Since sunset. Nothing passed me."

"It didn't? Not a grey Cadillac sport touring with red cushions, with a high-pitched horn? License XL 46-something? With a black-eyed young fellow in a panama hat and gabardine suit in it, and a little red-eyed man in a blue saw-tooth hat and a checked coat at the wheel?"

"No," I said. "It didn't pass me."

"It must have turned off down the Swamp Road, then, before it reached you," he said, with a troubled frown. "No place else where it could have gone. It worried me a little when I saw it, I can't say precisely why. But that fellow at the wheel was such an ugly looking little devil. Long yellow teeth, a torn ear, and such a God-damned grin. What happened to your own ear, by the way?"

"My crank flew off while I was cranking—"

But he wasn't interested. He was revolving some problem in his mind.

"It looked like that young fellow what's his name, St. Erme, with him," he said, as he led me up onto the back porch and in through the screen door of the kitchen. "It must have been St. Erme. I met him only once, but a likeable young fellow. He looked ill. Ghastly ill. The Swamp Road is a cul-de-sac. Nobody but John Flail lives on it. I wonder why they should have turned off down that way."

"The Swamp Road?" I said. "You mean that old wagon-road about a mile up? That's where my car is stalled. Nothing turned off down it, while I was there."

We had entered the darkling kitchen. The murmuring women's voices which I had been hearing seemed to come from the wall beside the stove, about three feet from the floor. They came from the receiver of the old golden-oak wall-telephone, which had been left hanging. A country party line.

"He killed Bobbie! He killed Bobbie . . ."

"Oh, my poor Mrs. Wiggens . . ."

Old MacComerou had paused in front of me. He put the receiver up, cutting off the gabbling, weeping voices. In the silence he turned towards me.

"You were right at the Swamp Road?" he said mushily.

"I was right at it."

"And nothing turned off down it?"

"Nothing," I said. "No car, anyway. There was a gust of wind that turned off down it. And there was a man walking away down it when I first got there, who must have turned off down it. But that was before I got there."

"A man?" he said. "What kind of looking man?"

"He had black hair. He was tall, with heavy shoulders. He was dressed in khaki pants and a blue sweat-soaked shirt, and was carrying his coat slung over his shoulder. He was walking with a long Indian shuffle, without lifting his feet."

"John Flail," said MacComerou. "You saw him walking?"

"Yes," I said. "He was just going into the trees when I saw him. He was about a hundred yards away from me. I didn't know his name."

"John was working around my place to-day," he said, with a calm mushy effort. "I didn't notice at just what hour he quit. It was some time before that grey car went howling by, that's all I know for sure. I would have said that John Flail left here only about ten minutes before. But perhaps it was John you saw. I wouldn't know."

Still, for the moment, he stood looking at me with a pale bulging stare, as if he were trying to look right through me. He must have felt convinced in his own mind that John Flail had been walking down the road much later, at least a half hour later, than the sunset hour at which I had said I had seen that figure walking. Perhaps he was wondering if it was an apparition I had seen. Or if I myself was an apparition out of hell.

He picked up something from a shelf beside the stove—a small nickel-plated monkey wrench. He handed it to me.

"Wait a minute till I put on some clothes. I'll go along with you and see if I can help you get straightened out," he said, almost absently.

He was still thinking over a problem that seemed no problem to me at all, as yet. Or one I was particularly interested in, at least. But I hadn't seen St. Erme going by with his whispering, praying lips and ghastly face. And I hadn't seen Yellow Fang.

I haven't yet.

It worried MacComerou. It was then that he took down his black book from the shelf, and called up long distance.

That scene keeps coming back to me. There had been no word of murder yet. There was only something vaguely ominous in the air. A phantasm I had seen. A car I had not seen. To MacComerou, the picture wasn't right.

I don't know which worried him more. But he could inquire about the car, at least.

He laid a big watch down on the phone pledge, while he thumbed through his book. There were people on the line when he picked it up, and he had to ask them if they minded getting off.

"This is Professor MacComerou," he said. "Ring five-five. I'd like to put in just a brief call to New York. Would you mind? Then you can have it again."

"Oh, Professor MacComerou! This is Mrs. Hinterzee, down the road from you! Did you see a grey car—"

"Yes, it passed my place."

"I was going to call you up and ask you if you had seen it, but I was afraid you might be working, and would take my head off, as you always do when anybody interrupts you! It scared Adolph—that's Mr. Hinterzee—right out of his rocking chair! There was a man in a ragged blue hat driving it, a terrible-looking tramp! He ran down the poor Wiggens' dog deliberately, their big kind St. Bernard that the children love to ride on! There was some other man in the car with him who looked as if he had been struck on the head! A nicely dressed man! He looked dead! Mr. Hinterzee had seen the tramp—"

"Yes," MacComerou said with mushy quietness. "Yes, I saw him, too. If you will just let me have the phone for five minutes, thank you. Then you can talk all night."

And he got the long distance operator then, and asked her for Mordaunt 2-8364, looking at his black book, and spoke to Dexter, the garage man he knew down in New York. . . It had been Dexter's car, all right. St. Erme had borrowed it to go some place with his girl, and must have been the fellow in it. But that was all that Dexter knew about it. He was working on some experiment or invention, and couldn't be bothered. He'd be obliged if the professor would call up some other time. And, click, he hung up drily.

A thin, concentrated, irritated-sounding man, Dexter, the grey murder car's owner. With a dry, metallic voice.

MacComerou had still been looking through his black book as he put his inquiries—looking for other numbers to call up, perhaps, if the car had not been Dexter's. But it had been, and the man in it had been the man he had thought. He seemed satisfied for the moment about something.

"A great invention," I said. "The telephone," I explained, as he looked uncomprehendingly at me. "I wish you'd asked your man how much he would charge to come up here, if I can't get my car started."

"Dexter?" he said. "That's a crazy idea. You couldn't get him up here for twenty-five hundred dollars."

"Well," I said, "I haven't got twenty-five hundred dollars, so I won't try."

Nobody would have twenty-five hundred dollars. But St. Erme had. He drew that much out of the bank yesterday morning, just for expenses. Elinor overheard the teller counting it out—but this was at twilight last evening, and there was no way to know that it was murder yet.

But that's how I knew St. Erme's name, anyway, when I met her stumbling up the road down near Dead Bridegroom's Pond. Rosenblatt asked me about that, of course.

I went to the sink and got myself a drink of water while MacComerou slipped on some clothes in the adjacent bedroom. There were some rotted vegetables on the drain-board and window-ledge—an old quarter of a cabbage head that had half turned to slime, a handful of moldy carrots, and a strawberry box that didn't have anything in it except stems and a mess of black mush that had once been good red berries, that nobody would eat now.

The water was good and cold, anyway. It was spring water piped from the water tank behind the barn, I guess.

He came out then, and he had put on a clean blue shirt and a pair of old flannel pants, and shoes on his feet. He must have seen what I had been thinking.

"I should have apologized for the appearance of things, doctor," he said. "I'm undoubtedly the world's worst housekeeper. It's John Flail's job to clean up, but he forgets. You found yourself a clean glass to drink out of, anyway, I see. Would you like something stronger? There's a small amount of medicinal rye in the bathroom cabinet, I think, which might be enough for a potion. I don't touch the stuff myself, and never have."

I told him no, I didn't myself. And I knew it was true about him, too. His flesh was firm, his muscles sinewy and strong, his pale eyes were clear and penetrating, and he moved limberly and strongly, like a man in his prime still. Except for his teeth, or lack of them, he didn't look more than forty-five in the crepuscular light, and might look no more than that in broad day, though he must have been at least twenty years older, when one considered that his book had been a classic for thirty years. There was some kind of a dictaphone on a wheeled stand in the kitchen, with a phonograph attachment and some batteries and wires. He was dictating a sequel to *Homicidal Psychopathology,* he said, and having a stenographer down in New York do it.

We went out through the kitchen door. His station-wagon was out of commission, he said, or otherwise he would drive me to my car. But it wasn't far to walk.

No, I told him. Not above a mile. I took a banana from a box of groceries on the back porch, and peeled and ate it as we set out. I hadn't eaten anything since breakfast at old John R. Buchanan's, and that, perhaps, was a part of my splitting headache.

He still couldn't believe that I hadn't seen anything. He just couldn't believe it. He had brought a flashlight with him, and as we went along the road he kept playing it down on the stony surface.

"What's the name of that tire-tread with a series of C's in it, do you remember?" he said mushily. "Continental, isn't it? Continental Special Service Fleetroad tires, or something like that."

"That's the name, I think," I said. "They used to advertise them a lot. But you can't get them any more."

"But some cars are still equipped with them," he said. "Dexter's car must have them. You can see the tracks along the road here. Still fresh."

We stopped and squatted and I looked.

"Where?" I said.

He pointed a little impatiently, touching the road with a big brown finger. "The characteristic C," he said. "Here, and here. It went along here. Can't you see it? What's the matter with your eyes?"

"I've got ten-D accommodations," I said.

"And you don't wear glasses?"

"People with ten-D accommodation generally wear glasses, don't they?" I said.

Perhaps he didn't believe me. He must have known what ten-D accommodation meant. He knew more ophthalmology than an oculist. More anatomy than an anatomist. I really have the eyes of a fly. Scheduled for flight surgeon in the Navy air arm, stripe and a half next month, after battling for three years to get my release from S. and D.—they need surgeons, too.

I thought he must have hypnotized himself into seeing those tracks. I couldn't see them. The road was so hard and dry. There was no dust to take an imprint. Brown hard clay earth, and flint and granite. Dry.

But the grey murder car had gone along here. He was right. We came to the eyeless house, or just before it, where I had heard the croaking in the ditch after I had picked up that damned hat and thrown it away, and started to walk on. And there was blood upon the road. Drops and little pools. It glistened in the moving of MacComerou's flashlight, as he went along beside me with his bald head bent, his sinewy shoulders bent, though I had not seen it in the dusk.

He was right.

We went down off the road into the high weeds of the ditch, and found John Flail, with his Indian dark hair, with his dark Indian face, in his sweat-stained blue shirt and khaki pants, with his coat still clutched in his right hand beside him, wrapped around it and his arm.

He had been hit and smashed, as hard as a heavy car can smash a man. Half the bones of his body must have been broken, and I could see the tire marks on his shirt—when they had gone over his chest—which I had been unable to see on the road.

It was a wonder he had lived a minute crushed like that. But he had lived, to drag himself down into the weeds of the ditch with his coat still clutched in his hand. I felt his pulse and looked at his eyes. He had died about half an hour ago, when I had passed this way. It had been, perhaps, his last groan or death rattle I had heard, that inhuman croaking in the ditch. A sound I had thought was almost human. And had been, in part.

Hit and run. It looked bad, the way the tires had gone over him. Still it was manslaughter, and not murder, without proof of premeditation, without any knowing how it had happened. It wasn't murder stalking in the night. Black, premeditated.

It wasn't terror. Yet. As I could see it.

"The police will have to be notified now," said MacComerou, drawing and twitching his mushy lips. "You'll have to state that we found him here, doctor."

"Of course."

"If you saw him walking down the Swamp Road at sunset, how did he get here?"

"I may have been mistaken about that," I said.

"Perhaps you were," he said, a little mushily. "Mistaken."

In the weeds then, a dozen steps farther on, going up and down the ditch with the flash to see if there was anything more, we found the blue mutilated hat.

"I'd like to know how it got here," said MacComerou, as we crouched beside it. "I'd like damned well to know."

"I threw it here," I said.

"You threw it here?" he said.

"I found it on the road," I said, "and picked it up. It used to be a hat of mine."

"It used to be a hat of yours?"

"Yes," I said. "Haxler's on Fifth Avenue. There aren't many such hats. My landlady must have given it to the Salvation Army, or perhaps put it out with the trash. I suppose it's going to be pretty hard to trace."

The flashlight lay upon his knees. For a moment he looked at me. He got up.

"Let's go," he said.

If I had shrunk in that moment to five feet three, and grown a beard and long matted hair, small red eyes and long yellow fangs, I don't think it would have surprised him.

A couple of hundred yards farther on we came to a bend of the road, and around it, a hundred feet ahead, there was my coupe, standing where I had left it, right at the entrance to the Swamp Road, blocking it.

We walked towards it. MacComerou had still been examining the road for those tracks I couldn't see. But when he saw the car he lost interest in them. Perhaps he had lost them altogether.

"Perhaps you were mistaken about the time you were here," he said.

"From sunset," I said, "till I came and spoke to you in your garden. You remember?"

"Yes," he said. "I remember."

"I may be mistaken about some things." I said. "Every man can be mistaken—I thought I saw a man looking like that man up the ditch walking off down that road there, as I got here at sunset. But it may have been a mirage or an optical illusion. I'm not standing on what I saw that didn't exist. I'm standing on what I didn't see—that didn't. I was here. No car went by. No one went by in it."

"You're pretty sure of it, aren't you?"

"How else could I be?"

I opened my coupe door, turned on my headlights, and got out my flashlight. I loosened the feedline nut with the little monkey-wrench that MacComerou had lent me, and unscrewed it with my fingers. It just needed a start. I put my mouth to the end of the copper tube, and sucked on it. Some dirt or lint came out, and then a mouthful of raw gasoline that filled my mouth clear down to the tonsils. That was all there was to it. I spat the gasoline out, with the taste still in my teeth. I took the little filter screen and blew through it, put it back in and connected the line again, tightened up the nut, while insects sang, and MacComerou stood watching me.

"You aren't a very imaginative man, are you, Dr. Riddle?" he said.

"What is there to imagine?"

"Most men have some imagination," he said.

"Maybe it's my hard luck," I said. "A screw lacking. But maybe there's enough in the world already without what I might contribute. All I ever see is the facts in making diagnoses. That ought to do the trick, Professor. Here's your wrench, before I forget it."

"Maybe I had better give it to you," he said.

He stood looking at me there with his bulging pale eyes. His toothless gums were working a little. His bat ears seemed to quiver on his head. He held the wrench I had passed to him in his big brown hand.

"No, thanks," I said. "Don't try to give it to me. I wouldn't want to take it."

Insects hummed in the darkness, and there was an owl howling in the woods. He put the wrench away in his pocket after a moment. I suppose I might have taken it. It was only a little fifty-cent wrench. It wasn't very big.

I had thrown my crank away up the Swamp Road at that yellow rattler. I went with my flash and found it, lying across the ruts where it had bounced. I picked it up. In one of the ruts my light showed the snake, lying like a ribbon, with its head smashed down on stone, with its hard eves cold, and its long hooked fangs extruding from its pulped jaws.

My throw had nailed it, though I hadn't known it. It hadn't slipped away, too quick to see. That is hard to do, even for a snake. It had slid just a little down beneath the grass, trying to cover up, but that was all that it could do. The mortal blow had hit it, and it was finished. It had lain there, wounded, hard-eyed, and dying, with what thoughts in its reptile brain, hell knows. It would certainly have liked to bite me, but it hadn't had the chance.

I turned, with the crank in my hand. MacComerou was there behind me. He had a twelve-pound rock in his hand.

"That's all right," I said. "It's dead."

He tossed the rock off into the weeds, and took a breath.

I got in behind the wheel, and snapped on the switch. I had worked up a little juice in the battery with all the cranking I had done earlier, and when I stepped on the starter the engine turned over, caught, and held. I laid the crank across my knees so MacComerou could sit beside me. But it was only a short distance back, and he didn't bother to get in. He stood on the runningboard, holding to the windshield post while we drove back to his place, breathing in the freshening night air.

He would have to notify the state police at their nearest barracks, at Readsfield twenty miles over beyond Stony Falls, in regard to finding Flail killed by that hit-and-run. That was the procedure, he thought. But it might be a couple of hours or more before they got down, and there was no use of my waiting, if I wanted to get back to New York tonight.

I agreed with him. I gave him my address in New York, in case they wanted a deposition from me. But they might not need any statement from me at all, since it would be merely corroborative of his that we had found Flail there. I hadn't been a witness to the event itself, any more than he had, and I had not even seen the car go by.

I dropped him at the mail-box beside his drive where the grey phoebe had made her nest. He went striding up the driveway along which that gaunt hoarse-twanging cat had fled before me in the twilight, almost before I had started on. As if he still didn't believe that I was quite real, somehow, and wanted to dismiss me from his mind.

## CHAPTER SIX

## THE RIGHT NAME

THREE OR FOUR miles down the road there was a California-style bungalow, standing in among fields at my left, on the loop of a wide circular driveway that went off the road. It had wide plate glass windows that were all lit up inside, and red shades half pulled down. There was a juke-box or a loud victrola playing some senseless tune inside. It looked as though it might be a teahouse. I swung in, with a squeal of tires, between two low, cobblestone gateposts placed wide apart, to see if I could get a cup of coffee, for my head was still splitting.

There was some splintered kindling underwheel as I came around the drive. The figure of something, animal or human, swung into my headlights in front of the porch steps, on all fours among the debris. It was clad in a leopard skin and a pale purple gown, and had a feather duster fastened to its stern like a rooster's tail. It leaped up and away from in front of my lights with a rabbit scream as I came around at it, and went rushing up the steps like something in a surrealist's dream.

I went around the drive and out again. Fast. It was still a nightmare road that I was on. I was out on it again when that figure appeared in the doorway with a shotgun in its hands. It banged away with two red flashes and roars, as I went on.

A mile and a half or two farther, there was a shingled vine-grown old house in at my right, with a small light in it, standing among low broad apple trees. A bevy of small figures, four or more, loomed in the middle of the road in my headlights as I approached. They fled like gnomes before me, and from beside the road I heard a man shout. I slowed as I came abreast of the entrance of the place. The figure of a man stood in off the road, with children clustered around him, while his arms tried to press about the shoulders of all of them, drawing them in close. Just the picture of a poor father, frightened, trying to protect his children from something intangible in the night.

"Route Seven?" I called to him.

"Keep on, mister!" he cried quaveringly.

But it wasn't so much a direction as an injunction and supplication to go on, out of his life and his quiet orchard peace.

Two miles farther, down that dark, winding nightmare way, a lamp shone from the windows of a rickety shack-house at my left, close beside the road. The front door opened as I approached, and a thickset, bowlegged man in overalls, with a broken nose and a shock of hair, stood behind the screen door in the rectangle of light, holding a big yellowish airedale-collie mongrel by the collar. He opened the screen door and loosed the dog with a gruff grunt as I came by, and it shot out with a deep-throated growl, in a slavering rush, at my wheels.

For a quarter mile it kept beside me down the stony, winding road, snarling and foaming and snapping at my tires, hoarse and murderous, and hating me with its life. It's said, of course, that dogs, children and lunatics have an infallible instinct for character. If that big savage brute had anything to say about it, I was a demon out of hell and Jack the Ripper. But dogs bark—I had been through blood, of course. There had been Flail's blood upon the road, and the blood of that St. Bernard in front of Widens' place before, and perhaps the blood of St. Erme all along the road. He may have smelt it on my tires!

A nightmare road. I might have dreamed if from the first moment I had turned off onto it at sunset, with a splitting head. Phantasms and a crazy hat of mine; and MacComerou's eyes staring at me through the garden dusk as I appeared, as if I couldn't be alive and real; and a dead man in the ditch. And skittering, surrealistic lunatics and slavering dogs and fright. All down the nightmare road. But the road was real. And I knew that I was real. I'll stick to that. . .

The big snarling, rushing mongrel left off finally. The road was empty again. I only wanted to come to the end of it. I wanted to meet nothing more till I got to level, wide Route Seven, and was headed down fast for home.

Those places I had passed had been all that there were along the road. Nothing was known of murder yet. There had been just a weird horn, and a grey car rushing, and an ugly little demon at the wheel driving it and laughing, and a stricken man beside him who had looked like death. Just a big tail-wagging dog that had been deliberately run down, and some splintered easel frames on a surrealist's drive. Just the information which MacComerou had phoned to the state police by this time—and to which they all must have listened on the party line—of John Flail killed by a hit-and-run car a little after he had left MacComerou's place this evening, perhaps by a grey car that had gone rushing past.

All ugly and a little frightening. Sinister was a word for it. The women in their kitchens were discussing it over their phones. But not yet deliberate murder. Not the terror yet. The first man killed with the sawtooth knife had not vet been found.

He had to be found to make it real—not just a nightmare dreamed of. St. Erme needed to be found. . .

A half mile down the road from that house of the slavering dog, I saw the girl's white-coated form pressed against the rock wall beside the road in my headlights, torn and burr-covered from her hiding and her running, signaling me imploringly to stop. She turned and fled from me when I told her to get in. But I jumped out and stopped her, and got her into my car with me. She had been on her way home with her fiancé, Inis St. Erme, to be married in Vermont. They had picked up a tramp along the road. The tramp had attacked St. Erme, and stalked her through the woods while she hid, and had then gone on. Had I seen him?

No.

I drove on down the road with her to the parking place overlooking Dead Bridegroom's Pond, and got out and felt the grass there. And it was murder I had put my hand in.

None of the nearer houses looked hospitable. I brought her back here to MacComerou's to phone the police.

There was a police car on the road in front already. I drove halfway up the drive to the kitchen door, and pocketed my keys this time when I got out. MacComerou's station-wagon, out in front of the big white barn at the end of the drive, was out of commission, he had said, so I wasn't blocking it for him. I don't like to block people.

Gasoline lamps had been lit in the kitchen and living room beyond. A state trooper was inside, a pleasant sandy-haired man with a broad smiling face. He was phoning in the kitchen when we entered, and nodded to us as he put up the phone, with his meaningless professional smile.

"Trooper Stone," he introduced himself. "What can I do for you?"

She told him her story. His smile did not change.

"Your car's been found," he said. "Your fiancé wasn't in it. That's really a good sign. It looks as if it might be a crazy kidnaping attempt at the point of a knife. The fellow can't have got far. Lieutenant Rosenblatt and Professor MacComerou are down there now, with Mr. Unistaire from the next house below. The lieutenant has sent for more troopers."

Lieutenant Rosenblatt and he had already been on their way, it seemed, when MacComerou had called up Readsfield reporting the hit-and-run, and describing the grey car that had passed. They had arrived about twenty minutes ago, half an hour or less after I had left.

They had come down to question John Flail about his brother, Pete, who had been released ten days ago from Wethersfield after serving three years of a term for manslaughter, and who hadn't reported on probation.

MacComerou had coffee ready for them. They had had a cup of coffee, and then had gone down with MacComerou to where Flail had been hit. They had taken Flail's body on down the Swamp Road to his house. Just a little beyond, the road was mucky. There were Fleetroad tire tracks in the mire. They had noticed them before when they had been to Flail's to inquire about his brother. Now they went down the road and, a little farther on, had found the car.

With blood on its running board and cushions—Stone told me privately, making coffee, when we had got the girl settled in the living room to await developments. It didn't look so good for St. Erme. Not so good as he had tried to make her think. Also John Flail hadn't been killed just by a hit-and-run driver. He had been smashed in the occiput with a stone—a thing I hadn't noticed when I had looked at him—as if he had been knocked unconscious by someone who had stepped up softly behind him on the road, before he had been run over and his chest crushed and the bones of his body broken. The stone he had been hit with had been found in the ditch near him, fitting that terrible blow on his occiput, and with traces of blood upon it. No question but that it had been murder.

I knew already that it was murder. I had put my hand in it eight miles down beside the road. If I had examined John Flail's body more closely, when MacComerou and I had found him in the ditch, I suppose I should have known it then.

"You live around here, Dr. Ridder?" Stone asked me.

"Riddle," I said. "No, I'm from New York. I'm on my way down from Vermont. I wonder when that car passed me?"

"You saw it passing you?"

"No," I said. "I didn't see it."

"I thought you said it passed you," he said. "We're interested in people who saw it and the man who was driving it. He didn't give his name to Mrs. St. Erme. Did she tell you?"

"Miss Darrie," I said. "She and St. Erme were on their way to get married. They couldn't get married in New York, and they couldn't get married in Connecticut, so they just kept coming on up. And picked up this tramp. No, they didn't know his name or anything about him."

"It looks like the same old story," Stone said. "The girl is lucky to be alive. I wouldn't give anything for St. Erme. The guy probably intended to pitch his body down some deep ravine along the road farther up, and keep on going. Only he turned off down this side road by mistake. It's a dead end. He can't get very far on foot."

"Not with that face," I said.

"Did you see him?"

"No," I said. "I didn't see him."

Stone was going back down to the Swamp Road, and I asked permission to accompany him.

Unistaire, the artist down the road—a dapper, bright-eyed little man, with black hair neatly combed, in his ordinary shirt and slacks when I met him down on the road with MacComerou and Rosenblatt—said, as we stood talking when Stone and I had arrived:

"This is definitely a surrealistic murder. It is the murder of a genius. It has symbolism. You, Lieutenant, are too much the unimaginative policeman, thinking in terms of moronic killers for gain, to see it. You, Dr. Riddle, are too scientific and merely realistic. You, Professor MacComerou, have discontinued drinking milk from my beautiful Jersey cow, and it is milk which fertilizes the soul. You, Trooper Stone—oh, pouf!"

And he had laughed heartily at all of us.

"It is a surrealistic murder," he said. "And it takes a surrealist to interpret it and explain it. I have the key. I understand the symbolism. I will interpret it and explain it. Give me two heads of cabbage, an old umbrella, a dressmaker's form, a cube of ice, and a calendar, and I will put the picture together that will explain it."

He had nothing in his mind. Nothing whatever. He was only mildly cracked. There are always those men who gather around a murder, drinking in the excitement, posturing and posing in their vanity. He was only a little more cracked than the ordinary. But maybe Yellow Fang was a little cracked, too, and thought that a surrealistic picture would explain it.

We found Unistaire, anyway, ten minutes later, shortly after we had separated, with his throat cut, down there near the grey car in the swamp.

That is, I found him.

"You were with Professor MacComerou when Flail's body was found, too, weren't you, doctor?" Lieutenant Rosenblatt said to me.

"Yes," I said. "We found it together. Blood upon the road. I had passed by a little while before and heard a groaning, but hadn't realized it was a man. I was thinking about that damned hat. Then MacComerou and I, coming back, found Flail."

"Your hat, you mean?" said Rosenblatt, looking at me with his wrinkled, pug-dog face.

"Yes," I said. "My hat."

"I wish you hadn't told me it was your hat," said Rosenblatt with a sigh.

"I don't doubt you do."

"You seem to be good at finding bodies, Dr. Riddle. Perhaps you can find St. Erme's."

It hadn't been found yet, when he said it. But pretty soon, when the other troopers had arrived, they began finding it. It had to be found, I thought.

When they were about halfway through, I came back here to examine the matter. They have found everything but his right hand, and a certain portion of his face.

MacComerou had got close; he had realized a significance in the fact that I had not seen the murder car go by. He was close. He must have been close. From down towards John Flail's, across the rocky fields behind the barn and through the woods in back, an hour ago his scream came. And Rosenblatt, with his hand on his gun latch, went charging there.

There is no gun or weapon in the house. There isn't even a bread knife, such as he has himself. I went out a while ago to get my crank from my car, but it had been taken. My surgical instruments—not that any of them would do any good for defense—were taken at some moment earlier in the evening from my unlocked rumble. They were what was used to cut St. Erme up with.

I haven't dared go further in search of any weapon.

He didn't do a very good job of it with St. Erme—not a job that any medical man, or that old MacComerou himself, with his knowledge of anatomy, would have been proud of. He didn't do as good a job in my particular field as I did in a garageman's field with my car. As a doctor, I may be only a fair garage man. But as a garageman, he is a—

Why did I put down that word?

Why did I start to assume that he might be a garageman?

The phone out in the kitchen gave its ghostly jangle again. Dexter, the garageman who owns the murder car, A.M. Dexter of Dexter's Day & Nite Garage on West 14th Street, is a hundred miles away down in New York.

Yet his shadow remains sinister.

Suppose I went to that phone in the kitchen, and rang the crank, and asked for long instance, and asked her for Mordaunt 2-8634; and suppose it answered, saying. "Dexter speaking." And suppose I said, "This is Professor MacComerou, you remember me, calling from my place up in the Berkshires." And suppose it said, "What do you want to know, professor?"

In its dry metallic voice. While I looked through a black book, with a big, old-fashioned watch before me.

Or suppose I just said nothing, or said "Tra-la-la-la-la!", or said "How are the oats growing on Times Square?" and it said, "Dexter speaking. What do you want to know, professor?"

But I can't call up. The phone line has been cut.

*Yes,* sinister!

*Sini St. Erme was—*

I misspelled his name there. Sini, instead of Inis. Transposing the S. Or spelling it backwards. A slight slip. I am getting a little tired. Nerves strained. Watching for that shadow, that red right hand so sinister.

*Sinister.*

*Sini St. Erme*

*Sini St. Erme*

*Sinister Me!*

Oh, God!

Before my eyes, all the time, and I couldn't see it. The old man has been trying to help me. How that devil must have been laughing at us all!

It's here before me. All of it.

That case-history study of a murderer which the old man had made a note of:

> Case-history of A, of good family, well educated, colossally conceited of his own mental powers, 45 years old, greedy for money and unsuccessful in any undertaking, who plots his uncle's death so as to inherit—

What A had the old man had in mind? He never wrote a case-history that he did not know intimately. A is not old Adam, old Adam MacComerou.

The notes upon the pad here on the desk:

Call lawyers this afternoon after lunch—
Have John Flail clip syringa and trim privet—
Potatoes, strawberries. . . .

Call the lawyers on what afternoon? And about what? To change a will? Have John Flail trim privet—but the privet was never trimmed. Strawberries in August!

And that mush out in the kitchen sink!

Those books on the shelves before my eyes. The old man's own huge, brown, buckram-bound *Psychopathology*—or that bright green *Garden Flowers.* Suppose I looked up in the index under "Tulips, Planting," to see when their bulbs are set in the ground, and just how they are packed down!

Or that red *Who's Who in America.* He may have torn out the page, but he may have never bothered. I'll look at it, anyway.

MacComerou, Adam Dwight; born Olion, Missouri, June 7, 1862 . . . Married Genevieve Dexter, 1895—

1862! He'd be eighty-two years old. Married a Miss Dexter. Suppose she had a brother, who had a son he named after the famous relative? Adam MacComerou Dexter, A.M. Dexter!

And I thought how few people know their Latin! Me! *Dexter*—right. *Sinister*—left. Partners. The right hand and the left hand. That insurance. It stank.

Before my eyes, the newspaper alone, which I propped up to shield her eyes from light. Who brought that paper here? Quelch said, as patiently set down by Rosenblatt, that the Danbury papers didn't come by mail truck till tomorrow morning. She didn't bring it; her hands were empty. Who stopped on the way out of the little ice-cream and stationery store in Danbury, and tossed down three cents and picked that paper up. Who bought—who has now—the knife?

Ah!

I'll write his name here. I'll slip it here. Beneath the pad. There is some paper underneath already. The old man wrote it, too. He must have been sitting here when that shadow came behind him. With all that he knew of murder, he couldn't help himself. No one with him but the killer. He knew! He knew! With his old brain that knew so much of murder. He wrote the name. He slipped it under here, with the shadow behind him.

My nephew-in-law, A. M. Dexter, is coming now to kill—

He couldn't help himself. But he tried to help me. He tried to help the world, and all the people unknown to him that that killer might still kill.

But no one found it. Now—

I must not let him hurt her—he's behind me—the shadow on the page—

His name is A.M. Dexter.

## CHAPTER SEVEN

## SINISTER ME

HE CAME IN through the dark bedroom, I think. Or it may have been the window out of reach of the lamp across the room behind me. I did not know. I could not know. There were so many ways. He came in quietly. Oh, so quietly. He did not wake her in her breathing. There was just his shadow on the page.

"Here I am," he said quietly, mushily. "Behind you."

I had said it to him in the garden, when he had paused, paralyzed by my voice, not knowing if it came from the ground.

I turned around in my chair and looked at him, with his knife. It made it easier for him. It gave him my heart or throat. But it is better to get it in the front than in the back. About the throat, I don't know.

I looked at him. With black contact lenses on his bulging pale blue china eyes he would be a little blind, of course, and stumble over things. He would look better, though. With his bat ears glued back, and partly hidden by a black silky wig he would look better yet. With white flashing teeth in his mushy mouth, and with a little black-dyed mustache, and dressed in silk shirts and a big floppy panama hat and gold rings and gabardines of a glistening sheen, he might look almost passable. To a girl with myopic vision who needed 500 glasses to see across a room, but was too idiotic to wear them. To a girl brought up by an Amish grandmother, a girl who had never had a sweetheart, not even a high school boy friend before, and was a little afraid of men.

A little afraid. Always a little afraid of him. But she hadn't wanted to be.

Almost passable. Yes, quite passable. He had passed. The insurance company doctors hadn't been interested in his eyes. He was strong enough inside.

That business between him as Sinister Me and him as Dexter had been pretty crude. It stank. But smarter men have tried more stupid plays, and got away with them. Insurance companies can be robbed. In case of death, they pay.

I wanted to get a view of him before he killed me.

That insurance business was clear. About the old man, too, it was fairly clear. Maybe the old man had changed his will; or maybe it gave him only a part of the old man's sayings and investments, instead of all. So he will be the old man, and get his hands on all. Living here. On this road of solitary souls. The old man is a summer recluse. Books and garden. When the phone answers, he barks into it. He will not tolerate visitors. It's not hard to rig up an answering phone bark to a certain ring, with some kind of battery device and dictaphone. I'd seen it in the kitchen.

The same sort of thing down in New York, of course. It was he himself who called, placing Dexter in New York, away from all danger, all suspicion. Reading off his own part of the conversation from his little book, watching the seconds on the clock. Yes, that metal voice. I hadn't gotten it at the time. I hadn't been interested. But I hadn't liked it.

He could live up here as MacComerou, too, for intervals. He has visited the old man, he knows the country, he knows who the neighbors are, though they don't know him. Here he can collect and practice copying samples of the old man's handwriting, and write to brokers, bankers, lawyers. Little by little, not in sudden jumps, so as to frighten them, but little by little, he'll get the old man's property into his own hands. Maybe a hundred and fifty thousand. Not a million. But a nice little sum. Nice.

Only John Flail, who worked for the old man, knew the old man. Knew him, too, perhaps. So Flail must be killed. But that's only an incident.

All right, that's being MacComerou, and that's the insurance. But about Elinor, about the girl here. With her sweet youthful heart, with her lovely face, with her straightforward, blind young eyes? Why, it helped with the insurance, at first. It was Miss Darrie's friend who was getting the insurance—surely you know who Mr. St. Erme is, he's a friend of our shy little Miss Darrie, he must be all right. . . Through her, he built up a character, a substance, a background as Inis St. Erme, an actual, an insurable person. It is other people who make any man a person. Alone, he is nothing.

But more than that, she has a little money of her own, he finds. She has twenty-five hundred dollars in the bank, which she got from her grandmother. So he will get it. He goes into the bank with her, having put into her mind the thought of writing out a check for twenty dollars, and he tells her he will cash it for her while she watches a car out front, pretending that he has one of his own to cash. And he adds "five hundred" to the check she has written, and goes to the window of a teller who knows her. But the teller is a little dubious of a check of that size. So he turns to her and smiles, and she comes towards him, and the teller counts the money out to him, seeing that she is present, and vouches for him.

Perhaps he mentions to the teller that she is going to buy a car or house, and the teller makes some comment about her new venture. To do all that, of course, he must keep talking of marriage to her. To get her set for that last act, he must hurry her along. Let's get married now, today. So we rush down to City Hall, but are disappointed. All right, the next place along. But we are disappointed here. All right, let's go on—

If he had said to her at the beginning, "Let's drive up to northern Connecticut, where I know some deep black lakes I can kill you by and bury you in so deep that no one will ever find you," she would not have gone with him. It would have seemed too far. He had to drag her on by stages, in a spirit of whipped up excitement. To the place where he wanted her. A girl without a family, for whom no search would ever be made.

How could he do it? With her beautiful face. Not human, at all. Look at those damned cold marble eyes, those big brown bat ears, that mushy mouth. Holding the knife.

Maybe he had done it to other girls before her. Who knows? Or will ever?

Poor damned Yellow Fang. Poor Doc. I wonder if he really was a doctor? It's not education that keeps a man from going down. But something hard inside him. Something that says, I'll face the issue. It's my hat. That car did not pass by. I'll not be licked.

But you've got the knife against my throat, haven't you, mushy Dexter. You had the rock in your hand when I turned around, up there by the Swamp Road, after looking at that snake. Why didn't you do it then, Dexter? Because you had got it in the head, and you knew it. just like that damned snake.

The knife across my throat. A serrated blade, sharp and sticky. A big brown hand gripping it. A shoulder behind that hand. A murderous heart and eye.

*Don't move, Riddle. Face it.*

"You meant to nail me," he said mushily. "You meant to nail me! From the moment that you came. You knew when you saw the phoebe in the twilight that she would not nest in the mailbox where anyone was living and got mail! You knew she would not have been frightened if she had been used to seeing men. It was the bird that told you."

"I'm not an ornithologist," I said.

"You meant to nail me," he said. "You knew. You knew when you saw that damned wailing cat of Uncle Adam's, that hasn't been fed, and hasn't been able to stalk its own game with the bells around its throat. You knew when the damned cat wailed and ran from you. It was the cat that told you."

"I'm not a zoologist," I said.

"You knew," he said. "You came to nail me. I read it in your eyes. You knew I'd not be planting tulip bulbs in August. Pounding them down. Pounding them down with a spade."

"I'm not a botanist," I said.

"You with your damned soft voice," he said mushily. "like that red-eyed little drunk spouting his Latin. You knew when you frightened me in the garden. You knew that only I and she had ever heard his voice, or could recognize it, and that I must be me. Saying to me, 'I am behind you!' When I thought you were in the ground. You knew. You knew from the beginning. It was I myself who told you. Don't lie to me."

"Perhaps I knew," I said. "Perhaps from the beginning. Yes, you told me. Everything about you told me. I knew that I had nailed you. I knew."

"But you won't ever tell anybody!" he said. "I have been too smart for you."

I didn't want him to do it there. Not with the sleeping girl. If she were awakened by a sound, he might kill her there before me with a slash. But if me first, I did not want her to see or know.

I didn't want him to do it there. I wanted him to do it outside, in the darkness of the garden. With the smell of the yellow roses that came in the window, and the deep black earth around. In the darkness, where he belonged.

He wanted to do it there, too. Someone might come back and see him through the open windows. He thought of everything. He had a brain.

I arose, at his gesture, and backed before him with my hands stretched back straight from my shoulders, as he wanted them—in his sight, but not overhead, where I might have whipped them down and caught that knife. Step by step, backward. Out the screen door, and onto the porch, and down off it onto the earth.

The earth from which we all come, and to which we will all go some day.

But not for me tonight. I like to think it was the banana peel under my foot that saved my life.

Oh, perhaps it wasn't. Perhaps I would have got him otherwise. I had nailed him at the Swamp Road. He had not dared to give it to me three times before, tonight. He knew that I had nailed him. He knew that he was through. So doubtless I would have got him otherwise, some way. But, if it hadn't been for the banana peel beneath my right shoe sole, I might have been cut a little by that knife.

I felt it beneath me as I backed a step from off the porch, as he drove me towards poor Doc's, poor Yellow Fang's grave. It was the peel that I had tossed there. From the banana in the box that he had bought in Danbury. Backing, I slipped my foot forward on it, with my arms behind me. I caught him in the groin with my right foot as I threw myself back.

I felt the ground beneath my hands and rolled and half got my feet beneath me. He thrust his knife, quick, into the waistband of his flannel pants. He picked up a spade.

That was his mistake.

He sliced the edge of the spade down at me. It caught me across the right foot as I leaped back, and so I had to stand. I shall be lame for life. The thing was very painful. I could not run from him, and so I had to stand. If he hadn't used the spade, I might have got away from him. But he had broken the bones of my foot, he had half cut them through, and so I had to stand.

He had strong hands, but I have strong hands, too. He had strong shoulders; he had terribly strong shoulders, but I am wiry. He outweighed me, he towered over me, but I had twenty-seven years to his forty-five, and I had more to live.

He wrestled for that spade.

He pulled the sawtooth knife out of his waistband then, when I had wrenched the spade from him. He brought the knife up to drive it at my breast, with a mushy scream. But I had the spade lifted at him, and it was coming.

I did it with the spade.

Yes, I did it, and I finished it. Right there. My foot was hurting. And I shall be lame for life.

Rosenblatt has given me a cigar, which is something to get from a policeman. I know something else I'd rather get, from this kid Darrie, but that can wait. Rosenblatt was knocked out by a piece of timber as he passed by a tree, with gun in hand, hunting down that scream. He hadn't believed it. He had thought it was a phony, too. Everything about that marble-eyed man was a little phony. But one thinks of those things afterwards. He had lain for Rosenblatt with the timber, wanting to have me alone. The timber, he thought, was more certain than the knife.

Actually, he used the knife only once to kill—on Unistaire. He had used the car to run down Two-Finger Pete Flail, and the rock to crush John. And he had strangled the little red-eyed tramp, Doc, with his hands, before he knifed him. He wanted some blood along the road. But the fear of that knife was plenty.

Poor little Unistaire. He had got that surrealistic knife across his throat, as near as Rosenblatt and I can see it, because of his remark about MacComerou's having stopped drinking milk, down there on the road when we had first gathered to start the hunt. MacComerou-Dexter decided that the fact the old man wasn't sending John Flail to buy milk any more had told Unistaire the old man was dead. If the mention of the milk hadn't quickened Dexter to the murder pitch, maybe he would have seen something significant in Unistaire's mention of two cabbage heads, a calendar, or a cube of ice. Surrealistic talk may cause more murders than are known. And Unistaire had such an easy throat for cutting.

About Yellow Fang—

"This fellow Yellow Fang didn't trust him." said Rosenblatt, talking it over in the kitchen with some of the tired hunters who had stayed on while the dawn came, and we let the girl sleep. "That's the way I see it. Dexter was going to kill her, down by the lake, and then come back and kill Fang. But the tramp followed down, and when Dexter saw he was being spied on, he had to make sure of the tramp. He chased him. Fang fled for the road, and Dexter caught up to him near the car, and strangled his scream and wrung his neck. Changed coats with the tramp then and slapped his big floppy Panama down on Fang's head.

"The girl heard the scream, as she followed up from the lake shore, and naturally thought it was Dexter. Maybe she screamed herself. Dexter went back to finish her. If he had been nice, calling to her, he would have got her. But she hadn't stayed where he had told her. She had followed him up, and he believed as sure as hell she had seen him kill the tramp, and so there was no use any longer for sentiment. He went after her on the prowl to kill her. Quiet and hard and businesslike. But the twilight was there, and she was able to keep slipping away from him.

"He had to give it up for the time being. Perhaps she would wander deeper into the woods, and feed the crows. Perhaps she'll tumble in the lake, or meet a rattler. He'll come back tomorrow and try to find her. She doesn't know very much. And though he would like to finish her now, the other business is the more important.

"He's got to do the business of murdering St. Erme now. The light is just about right. He has already established through Quelch that the tramp was with them, that they were going to picnic. Now comes the rush up the road, the man in the blue sawtooth hat and checked coat crouching low behind the wheel, the other man in his gabardine coat, with hat down over his face and head on the car door. Attracting attention all along the way. He has passed Hinterzee's, Wiggens', Unistaire's, he'll say that he passed his uncle's place, too. The presumption will be that he just kept going, or that tramp kept going, till he hit the moon. Just to show that he has passed MacComerou's place, he goes on a little farther down the road to drop something, the hat. And sees Two-Finger Pete Flail slugging along the road. Thinks it's John, whom he has to get rid of, anyway, and smashes him like a nut.

"Must have given him a bad moment when you came, doctor, and didn't mention anything about having seen John Flail whom he had left for dead on the road. A worse one when you had seen John Flail walking home down the Swamp Road at sunset and stuck to that.

"Then he goes with you to find the body. Maybe it's when he sees it that he realizes his mistake. He's still got to kill John, so he gets out his grey car, which he had parked in the barn, picks up Pete's body, and drives down to Flail's place fast. He kills that bird with a stone, leaves Pete hidden somewhere where he can cut him up a little at a time later, and takes John back to the ditch beside the road. He has a body for St. Erme now, at least, so he's that much better off in the deal. It's always better when you're dead to have a body."

"It's better when you're alive, too," I said. "There were some moments when I wasn't sure. But I just had to stand on it that I had been there, and hadn't seen him."

Rosenblatt grinned at me. "I believed you," he said. "I felt right along you had something."

I nodded towards the closed living room door, as the tired men got up to stretch, to take their cars back home.

"What do you have to tell her," I said, "when she wakes up?"

"What is there to tell her?"

"Nothing but that it was a nightmare," I said. "A bad dream without reality."

"That's all it was."

And that's all it ever will be with her and me. A shovel dropped on my foot and hurt it. Though I shall be lame for life.

# MY FRIEND DEATH

## CHAPTER ONE

### Dead Earnest

BEASLEY ZILLIP saw the man who had had the package quite distinctly. The package wrapped in newspaper, that was, with its irregular, roughly globular shape, about twelve or fifteen inches in diameter and with its manila binding-twine encircling it this way and that, like a clumsily wound ball of wool, tied with many knots. He was a big man, with big, red-haired hands. He wore a bright emerald green topcoat, a green snap brim hat, a Norfolk jacket of heavy rust brown tweed with green and blue nubs in it, and a pair of old grey flannel slacks with dark, wettish-looking splotches on the right leg, as if he might have sloshed some of his morning cup of coffee carelessly on his thigh, while he sat sipping it and reading his newspaper at the breakfast table, before leaving home to catch the subway downtown. His shoes—for the rest of his attire—were light tan bluchers with big brass eyelets and thick crepe rubber soles, and had been newly polished. He wore a white, soft-collared shirt and a wide, maroon, knit necktie, loosely knotted.

He had a scraggly red mustache, to match the color of the hair on his hands, and a rather big and empty, moon-shaped, foolishly grinning face, which gave a glimpse of a gold inlay in his right upper canine tooth. His nose was big and crooked, giving him a somewhat tangential appearance, like that of a boat with a bowsprit which has been knocked askew, as if he ought to be heading north-northeastward when he was heading north. He had bushy red eyebrows; and beneath them his eyes were a pale and almost colorless blue, like the cloudless October morning sky which lay over Manhattan and the Bronx.

He looked to be about forty-five years old, Beasley Zillip's own age. He was about six feet tall, four inches taller than Beasley's own average height of five feet eight. His weight, Beasley judged, was about a hundred and ninety-seven pounds, forty-eight pounds more than his own somewhat less than average hundred and forty-nine.

He carried the package, wrapped in its newspaper and knotted with its twine, casually and negligently in the bend of his right arm, against the breast of his unbuttoned topcoat, as he strolled down the long wooden platform, away from the little knot of people in front of the house which contained the entrance turnstiles. He approached the bench where Beasley was sitting down at one end, and with an absent-minded air laid the package down on the platform floorboards behind the bench, within two feet of Beasley.

There was no reason why Beasley Zillip shouldn't have seen him. Visible as he was, however, it was quite likely that none of the other passengers on the platform saw him; it just happened that Beasley Zillip was an observant man. Himself one of the most colorless of individuals, he had developed the faculty of observation as compensation, perhaps, for his own excessive insignificance of appearance. Anyway, he got a quiet pleasure, unusual for a city man, out of observing other men and analyzing them.

He felt, with all due modesty, that he had a singularly acute ability for sizing men up at a glance—for determining their characters and backgrounds, what their professions were, whether they were honest or crooked, and a dozen other things about them, from their little mannerisms and expressions. It was an ability which, for twenty-three years, he had put constantly to the test at his station at teller's window three of the 40th Street Branch of the Metropolitan National, often cashing checks without identification just on a man's face, while at other times requiring the endorsement of Mr. Clemgott, the assistant cashier even though all identifications seemed to be iron-clad and gold-plated. He could say that, in all the years, he had never one made a mistake and he sometimes wondered whether, if he had chosen such career, he might not have made one of the world's great manhunters and detectives.

Forty feet below Beasley Zillip where he sat on his bench down the end of the platform—precise and thin, in his seedy grey hat and old grey covert cloth topcoat, with his worn black briefcase resting meticulously on his pressed-together knees—upper Broadway rumbled and hooted. Trucks backfired. A traffic policeman's whistle blew. A news vendor's voice came up through the interstices of the track ties, shouting hoarsely and mournfully: "Legs found! Get your first afternoon edition of the *Globe-Messenger!* Read all about it!" Horns blared, and blared again.

The traffic rumbled on over the vehicular floor of the Harlem River Bridge a hundred feet to the south, above the railroad tracks and the river, below the elevated. The river, roiling with blue and brown flood waters at full tide, flowed sluggishly underneath the bridge; it bent and stretched away southeastward, reaching toward the East River from the Hudson at its back, performing its equal function of separating Manhattan from the Bronx. An eight-oared college shell was out on it, skimming off down towards the bend, with water jeweled blades dipping in the sunlight. There was a tug approaching the bridge, drawing a coal barge against the tide, like a sturdy beetle dragging the carcass of a fat black caterpillar.

Along this side of the river the bright silver tracks of the New York Central stretched out four-fold, following the river's curve, going to—and coming from—Grand Central station down in mid-Manhattan. Coming from, and going to, likewise, Yonkers, Tarrytown, the lovely little suburban town of Ossining-on-Hudson, Harmon, Buffalo, to Niagara Fails and points beyond. The wooden platforms of the little Marble Hill station of the railroad lay on each side of the tracks fifty feet east of Broadway, at the bottom of a flight of steps which went down from the street; there were passengers standing on the platforms down there while an express went racing by. In the blue distance to the south and southeast lay the clustered spires of Manhattan; and over Beasley Zillip, where he sat upon his bench, stretched the whole blue morning sky.

He sat precisely, with his grey-gloved hands folded on the briefcase on his lap. With his meager shoulderblades erect and back. With his mild eyes in his thin wistful face fixed in contemplation in front of him, waiting for the next downtown train. He took cognizance of the different parts of his body, and of their general health, as he sat there, in the quietly analytical way he had. His teeth felt scrubbed and good. His face felt smoothly shaven. His hands, inside their gloves, felt cleanly scrubbed, and his nails felt clean and trimmed. He had breakfasted at a bakery on the way to the subway, enjoying two buns and a glass of milk, and his stomach felt replete and good. His heart felt quiet and good. His mind felt rested and relaxed from worry and pressure—he had slept soundly last night, and was about to start his vacation.

He went over the contents of his pockets in his mind, in an orderly fashion, to make sure that he had everything he should. His purse, with twenty-seven dollars in it, was in his inside breast pocket. The envelope, with the pair of steamship tickets for himself and Minnie, was in that pocket, too. His comb and nail file were in his upper left vest pocket. His watch, which he had just consulted, was in the pocket below. The little brooch which Minnie had admired in the window last week was in its flat white box in his right coat pocket—he would surprise her with it at dinner at Havana on her birthday next Thursday, after pretending beforehand, with a stupidly guileless air, that he had forgotten the day and had no present for her. Little surprises like that always pleased a woman.

His left coat pocket contained his memorandum book, with his careful and precise accounts set down in it, and his small meticulous jottings of Things-to-be-done. His right pants pocket contained his change purse, with forty-three cents in it—no, thirty-eight, he had used a nickel to get through the turnstile.

His right hip pocket contained only a clean white handkerchief. His worn leather keycase, which he ordinarily carried in that pocket as well, he had thrown into a trash-can at the foot of the el steps as he started up them, in a gesture of casual freedom. For one reason, it was dilapidated; for another, he had got his money's worth out of it, he felt, having bought it for a quarter back in 1926 when he had still been a bachelor; while, for a third reason, he had for the time being no use for it, having turned in the keys to their furnished rooms —number 2C, at 4457 Montvale Avenue, five blocks away, they had lived for the past seven years—to Mrs. Flebuddy this morning before leaving, and having given Minnie yesterday the key to the trunk which the expressmen were taking down to the *Saturnalia* to go along.

Keys! There was a sense of freedom in having none to think about, for the first time since he had got married and had begun acquiring trunks, with other impedimenta. He had never owned a car, and so had no car keys. He had never had a key to the 40th Street Branch, of course, nor would he have had if he had been Julius C. Peffersmith, the Metropolitan National vice-president in charge of the bank himself, since the doors were always opened and closed by the bank guards. So good-bye to the keycase.

He went over, in his mind, his notebook memoranda. There were the Things-to-be-done yesterday at the bank before leaving. There were the Things-to-be-done this morning at the apartment before leaving it for good. There were the Things-to-be-done from now until the *Saturnalia* sailed from Pier 13, North River, at two o'clock.

He had—he went over the items in orderly fashion—done everything yesterday that should be done. He had turned over his ledgers and accounts to young Brearley, who was substituting for him during the next two weeks, and had got the proper receipts from Brearley. He had emptied out his locker, stuffing everything into his briefcase except his gray alpaca office coat and an assortment of railroad timetables and resort folders which he had left on the locker floor—not being headed for any of the various play-havens which they advertised with transcendent words and illustrations, though it was nice to think about them all. He had stopped at the desk of Mr. Clemgott, the assistant cashier and his immediate superior, to say good-bye to him and had said good-bye to old Ruggleston, the guard, on his way out.

"Getting your vacation late this year again, eh, George?" said Mr. Clemgott jovially. "Well, it may seem tough to have to spend all summer with your nose to the grindstone, while all of us somewhat bigger birds are taking our turns off soaking in the sun and brine. But virtue is its own reward. Now we August sluggards have to sweat while you get yours. The parable of the grasshoppers and the ant, eh? No finer season of the year. I envy you. Where are you going to spend it, George?"

Everybody at the 40th Street Branch who knew Beasley Zillip well enough not to mister him always called him George. He had given George as his first name when he had come into the bank's employ, twenty-three years ago, having had a boyhood friend named George Allerton back in Vermont whom he had much admired. Nobody likes to be known as Beasley.

"Why, we're thinking of going to Niagara Falls for a few days, a kind of second honeymoon, and then perhaps for a few days on into Canada," he told Mr. Clemgott diffidently.

"Niagara Falls, eh?" said Mr. Clemgott jovially. "A second honeymoon. I'd forgotten whether or not you were married. How long have you been—nineteen years? Well, it's always fun at Niagara Falls. It's fun anywhere, as the old man wired his bridegroom son who wanted to stay on for another week, and so come on back home and help pitch hay. More power to you, George, and don't try going in a barrel down the Falls, you old daredevil, you. Seriously, the coloring in Canada at this season should be gorgeous, and the accommodations should be quite cheap."

"That's what I'd understood, sir," he told Mr. Clemgott drably. "I hope to do it all on fifty dollars, traveling by bus."

He didn't dare—he absolutely didn't dare—to tell about the wonderful cruise which lay ahead for Minnie and him on the *Saturnalia.* Great blue and purple tropic seas, golden sands and palm trees, star-spangled southern nights and all. Havana, Port au Prince, Trinidad and Barraquil and all the other glamorous, romantic ports beyond. Mr. Clemgott, or any of the rest of them, wouldn't believe, they simply wouldn't believe, that he had such an adventure in him at all, though it was something which he had been dreaming of and planning for, for twenty-three years. A bus-trip to Niagara Falls was about his limit. And let them think so.

Julius C. Peffersmith himself had come striding towards Mr. Clemgott's desk, out of his private mahogany-paneled office, while Beasley Zillip had been limply shaking Mr. Clemgott's hand in good-bye. Julius C. Peffersmith—third vice-president of the six-billion dollar Metropolitan National, head of all the civic committees and charity drives, articles published about him every month and week in magazines and newspapers, one of the big men of New York and America; old J. C. himself, as he was known, with his yachts and racing stables and country estates and millions of dollars behind him, and with his long corona cigar in front of him, gripped between his granite teeth in his granite face. Out of his door he had come striding to Mr. Clemgott's desk while Beasley was still shaking his good-bye. Beasley had felt a limp impulse to shake Julius C. Peffersmith's hand, too, and tell him, too, good-bye. For, after all, although Julius C. Peffersmith didn't know him from a picture on the wall, they have been in the bank together five days a week and fifty weeks a year for the last ten years of Beasley's own twenty-three; and it might seem that he was entitled to a farewell, too, without offense.

"No, thanks! No shine!" Julius C. Peffersmith had roared at him, waving away his limp half-lifted hand. "About this Thurakew account, Clemgott—"

Slapping some papers down on Mr. Clemgott's desk, with his burly back turned, and his cigar in his face, dismissing Beasley. He had mistaken him for Tony, the Greek shoe-shine man, this time, Beasley realized. The last time Julius C. Peffersmith had noticed him, bumping headlong into him at the revolving door back in 1939, he had mistaken him for a solicitor from the Salvation Army. But life was like that, Beasley thought without bitterness, and so was he, just a colorless man that other men forgot. With his hat in his hand and his briefcase under his arm, he had gone quietly on his way.

"Starting your vacation, Mr. Allerton?" old Ruggleston, the white-haired guard at the door, had asked him with a kindly beam as he let him out. "It's a shame you always have to have it so late. I went to the seashore myself this summer—had a wonderful time there. But it's a little cold now."

"I dislike the sea, anyway, Bill," he had told old Ruggleston drably. "There's something a little frightening in the vastness and violence of it to a man like me. I prefer things calmer and more contained. I had rather thought of taking a bus trip to Canada to see the autumn foliage. On the other hand. I may go out to visit an aunt of mine in South Bend, Indiana."

"I suppose you're taking Mrs. Allerton with you?"

"Oh, yes, indeed," said Beasley, with the hangdog smile of one old married man to another. "I wouldn't be able to leave her behind, even if I wanted to."

The old watchman had chuckled sympathetically.

"They're hard to get rid of, aren't they?" he said. "Not that we ever really want to, God bless them. But a man does get to thinking at times that it might be fun to jump the fence for a little while and nibble a few stray oats. Not that they have any oats in South Bend, I suppose, even if you weren't taking her with you. Not visiting your aunt. Well, a pleasant time to both of you, Mr. Allerton."

"And the same to you, Bill." he had replied gratefully. "I'll try to find opportunity to send you a postcard. If not, you'll be seeing me again before you know it."

Old Ruggleston, like everyone else at the bank who didn't know him well enough to call him George, always called him Mr. Allerton. That was because when he had started with the Metropolitan National at the age of twenty-two, half his life ago, he had given his last name as Allerton. He had done that in part for the same reason that he had given his first name as George—because of the George Allerton, who had been such a nice guy and whom he had known back in Vermont Also it was easy to spell and remember, had a pleasant sound, and was up towards the front in any alphabetical list of names, unlike Zillip, which has practically nothing after it except Zzyzuzski. Who wants to be always at the bottom of the board?

For those reasons, therefore, and perhaps for others, he had started in at the Metropolitan National as George Allerton; and he had remained there as George Allerton, though his real name, of course, was still Beasley Zillip, and his wife's name was Mrs. Zillip, not Mrs. Allerton, as old Ruggleston had kindly asked about—it might be confusing to others, but it wasn't to him, with his orderly and meticulous mind. After all, there's nothing against the law in a man taking any name he chooses for business purposes—actors and writers do it all the time; and it couldn't make any difference to the bank whether they had him listed as Allerton, George, or Zillip, Beasley.

So the Things-to-be-done in his notebook for yesterday had all been done, before he had left at five o'clock.

He thought over the Things-to-be-done this morning before he had left the apartment. The two trunks had been locked and strapped since yesterday morning, ready for removal; and it had remained merely to give them to the warehousemen and expressmen when they called—the one trunk, which he had marked with a big white "S" for Storage, to be taken to the mothproof cold storage vaults of the Paradisio Warehouse Corp., whose huge dark-red brick building was just a half block down the street from 4457 Montvale Avenue, to be stored there till called for and the other trunk, which he had marked with a big white "W" for Wharf, to be taken down to the *Saturnalia's* wharf and placed in Stateroom A. He had given the keys to that latter trunk to Minnie yesterday, so that she—who would probably arrive at the boat before him, from her sister's over in Brooklyn where she had spent the night—could open it and begin to unpack its contents and lay some of them away.

The trunks had both been removed from the apartment at a sufficiently early hour.

A couple of men had reported from the storage company as early as half past seven o'clock, removing the one trunk; and he had accompanied them down the block to the warehouse, vast and windowless as an Egyptian tomb, and up on the freight elevator to the zero-temperature fur vaults making sure that it was put away inside before stopping at the warehouse office and paying his storage fee in advance and getting a receipt. . . The expressmen for the trunk for the boat had appeared at half past eight, and had taken it away, after giving him every assurance that it would be at the *Saturnalia's* wharf not later than ten o'clock, and certainly before eleven o'clock or noon at the outside, and in any case positively not later than one-fifteen, in ample time before the boat sailed. So he had done everything that could be done about that trunk, too, short of accompanying the expressmen in person; and it would probably arrive in time. If not, there was no use worrying about it.

He had straightened up the apartment after the trunks had gone, though it wasn't necessary—he just liked to have things tidy, and not leave a littered place. He had gone through the bureau drawers and closets, the bathroom cabinet and the shelves of the little kitchenette. He had gathered and stacked up all the old magazines on the golden-oak living room table; had neatly folded the items of wearing apparel for which there hadn't been room in the trunks, and placed them in a pile on the bed: had thrown away the various odds and ends of broken and useless gear into the waste-baskets, such as old combs, a squeezed end of toothpaste tube, the alarm clock that didn't work, hairpins, a half-used jar of cold cream, and a framed picture with a broken glass of a young dark-haired girl seated beside a deep blue pool, which he had bought for a quarter when he had been a bachelor, and had kept through various other movings from other furnished apartments, for no particular reason except that it had been his only adventure into art. . . . The thought had occurred to him, as he dropped the chromo into the wastebasket, that something in the dark-haired contemplative girl, not in her coloring but in the dreaming posture of her resembled Minnie some way. But perhaps that was merely because they were both women.

There was little that a childless married couple who lives in furnished rooms accumulated, even after seven years in one place. The two trunks which had gone had held the most of it.

He had seen that everything was in order, and had stopped to say good-bye to Mrs. Flebuddy at the door of her ground-floor apartment, and to give her the keys.

"Our time's not up for five days more, till the fifteenth, I believe, Mrs. Flebuddy," he told her with his drab smile. "But there's no need for us to keep somebody else from using the apartment, if you can get some other tenants right away. I left our radio. There's something the matter with it, but maybe it can be fixed up. I left some clothes on the bed, too—Mrs. Zillip's old winter coat and some of her house dresses, and some shoes in the closet. If there is anybody you want to give them to, or sell them. There's half a quart of milk in the icebox; some oranges, potatoes, crackers, and other things. Mrs. Zillip and I have enjoyed our stay here. If the firm weren't opening up this new office, we'd like nothing better than to stay on. She meant to tell you good-bye yesterday, but she went over to visit her sister in Brooklyn, and decided to spend the night there. We're taking a little ocean voyage, and she's going to meet me at the boat."

"It's been wonderful having you, Mr. Zillip," said Mrs. Flebuddy, her mud-colored eyes in her fat face moistening with sentimental tears. "Always the rent paid on time. No cats, no dogs, no whoop-de-doop parties. If all tenants were like you, this would be a better world. I wish you all the success in the world in your new position. There are a lot of cemeteries in Westchester. It should be a wonderful place. Mrs. Zillip has a sister in Brooklyn? I didn't know. I always understood her to say that she didn't have any family. But I guess I was mistaken."

"Just the one sister," said Beasley sadly. "They quarreled many years ago. I am glad to say that through my intercessions, however, they have got together again and made it up. Mrs. Zillip is quite happy about it. I believe her sister had a party for her last night in Brooklyn. That was why she stayed."

"Well, tell her good-bye for me, with all I my love," said Mrs. Flebuddy emotionally. "And all the wonderful things in the world to you in your business, Mr. Zillip—you deserve them. Thank you for the groceries and the clothes; and I hope that you and Mrs. Zillip will find time some time to drop back and see me, after you've got settled in your new place."

"Oh, you'll see Mrs. Zillip and me again, be sure of it," Beasley promised gratefully. "It's just *au revoir* and not good-bye, from both of us."

And with his drab little smile, replacing his hat upon his thin drab hair, he had turned from her, and gone out the front door of 4457 Montvale Avenue for the last time.

Mrs. Flebuddy's mention of his new position was in reference to what he had told her when he had given her notice. He didn't like to hurt people's feelings, particularly landladies', and so he always told them whenever he moved that it was because of a change of business location. Otherwise they might think that they had bedbugs, and feel bad about it. In Mrs. Flebuddy's case, he had told her that his firm was opening a new branch in Yonkers, and he had been put in charge.

Her reference to the cemeteries of Westchester was because she somewhat misunderstood the kind of business he was connected with. He had made it a rule quite early in his life never to mix business and personal affairs, because if people know your business they are apt to try to make use of you—if they know you are in the refrigerator or electric toaster game, for instance, they always want you to get it for them wholesale; and if with a bank, to arrange a loan for them. He had told Mrs. Flebuddy that he was in the mortician game, employed by a big chain funeral house. Nobody ever tried to get wholesale rates from you in that business.

So much for the Things-to-be-done this morning before leaving 4457 Montvale Avenue forever. The Things-to-be-done from now till two o'clock, when the *Saturnalia* sailed, were few, and almost non-existent. Item, to catch the downtown subway and stay on it to Chambers Street, down towards the lower end of Manhattan. Item, to get off there and ascend to the street, and pick up a taxicab to Pier 13, North River. Or if there were no cabs at hand, to walk the comparatively brief distance, with no luggage to carry but his briefcase. Item, when he got there, to go on board the *Saturnalia,* to Stateroom A, reserved for Mr. and Mrs. Beasley Zillip, if you please, and wait till Minnie arrived, and the trunk, if they were both not there before him.

Actually, the Things-to-be-done had practically all been done. He had allowed himself much more time than needed. The business of taking care of the trunks and giving a last look to the apartment had consumed hardly any at all. Down to Chambers Street was only about forty minutes. Allowing ten minutes for the cab ride to the pier, or twenty if he walked, a total of no more than an hour. He would be on the boat by a little after eleven—in time to call up the express people if the trunk had not arrived. In time to stock up with magazines, fruit, and candy. In time to smooge a little in the stateroom with Minnie, while they watched through the windows the preparations for departure. . . Actually, maybe it was silly at his age (an old married man like old Bill Ruggleston at the bank would think it was silly), but as he was as crazy over her as he had been the first time he had ever laid eyes on her.

All the time in the world, anyway. Only seven minutes after ten. No, nine and a half, he saw, pulling out his watch again, with one hand on the briefcase on his knees. In four more hours they would be casting off, and down the river. Then heigho for the Caribbees!

## CHAPTER TWO

## FOR WHOM THE BULLS TOIL

ENGLISH SPARROWS pecked on the track in front of him at bits of peanuts spilled from a nearby platform vending-machine. The bending river sparkled. The sky was clear and blue. *Burra-wurra!* the noises of the street came up from below. "Legs found in Brooklyn!" the raucous news vendor's voice rose inanely above the many rumbles, backfires, whistles, and other noises below.

"Legs found in Brooklyn! Get your first afternoon edition of the *Globe-Messenger,* just off the presses! Read all about it!"

Beasley Zillip frowned faintly. He pulled the fingers of his gloves. He never read much crime news; but there had been some gangster named Legs Glass or Legs Ruby, he thought, who had always been getting himself shot full of holes by rival gangsters or the police, until he must have resembled a piece of limburger cheese. A violent, low, and stupid animal. He had had an idea that the fellow had been machine-gunned to death or electrocuted in Sing Sing years ago, back in the Hoover administration, or almost as long ago as that. But apparently he was still alive, and the police had been searching for him again, and again had found him—"Legs found in Brooklyn!"

He closed his ears to that hoarse, senseless bleat.

There was a little knot of half a dozen other passengers waiting up the platform, in front of the el house which contained the entrance turnstiles. A small number, compared to the crowd which was usually on the platform for the earlier trains in the business rush hour. Two or three housewives on their way to a day of senseless shopping in the big department stores around Herald Square. A boy with a violin case under his arm, obviously a music student. An old unshaven collarless bum, and a little man with a black beard. A couple of bobby soxers, probably playing hookey from junior high to go down and see some swoon crooner at a movie house on Times Square.

Beasley had never seen any of them before, but for a boy from a Vermont village, where everybody had known everybody else for twenty miles around, the vast inchoate anonymity of the city was still, after twenty-three years, fascinating and enjoyable. He had never got rid of his own native-born habit of observing and analyzing people. The man in a bright green topcoat emerged from the el house, where the turnstiles were, out onto the platform. He strolled casually, with the package under his arm, down the platform towards the bench where Beasley was sitting at one end.

He wasn't, thought Beasley Zillip, a businessman, or he would have taken an earlier train. He was also not one because of his jacket and unmatching slacks, which didn't belong in a business office. He wasn't an author, because he didn't have a briefcase filled with manuscript to sell. He wasn't an artist, because his shoes were shined. He wasn't a rich man, because he had shined them himself—there was a spot upon one toe that he had missed. He wasn't poor, because his shoes and clothes were of good quality, though a little old. He was careless and absent-minded, because of the way he had spilled his coffee—those dark splotches on his pants leg.

He was undoubtedly, thought Beasley, a college professor. Probably in the department of philosophy, or some other absent-minded subject like that. Probably a professor of Christian ethics, to be specific about it, because of his mild vacant smile. He was probably on his way down to an eleven o'clock lecture at Columbia, New York University, City College, or possibly the College of Brooklyn, depending on where he would get off the subway, after he got on.

His maroon necktie meant that he had gone to Cornell. He was about forty-five years old, which meant about the class of 23. He was married, because his shirt, though spotless, had the soft unstarched look and the amateurish ironing creases about the collar points of home laundry work. He had probably been an athlete in college, and still kept himself in trim by taking hikes or playing golf, because of the loose and casual, yet quietly powerful, way he walked. Football, specifically, had probably been his game in college days, because of the easy way he carried his package in his arm.

Beasley speculated idly on what the package contained. It might contain a large cabbagehead or a very large coconut which he had bought at a fruit and vegetable stand on his way to the subway station. It might contain a bundle of laundry to drop at the Chinaman's. It might contain a jar of tobacco, or a stack of books, or half a dozen ancient Etruscan clay-tablets which he had borrowed from the college museum to pore over at home, and which he was now returning.

No, it couldn't be a cabbage or a coconut, because anything bought at a store would be in a brown paper sack or brown paper wrapping. It couldn't be laundry, because his shirts were done at home. And then, too, a man may wrap laundry in a newspaper, but he doesn't bother to tie it round and round with twine, with forty knots. It couldn't be a jar of tobacco, either, or a stack of books or bricks, because it wasn't cylindrical or square in shape. It was round.

Beasley had never seen a package quite like that before. He gave it up.

Oh, yes—a memory flashed back to him—he had! He remembered with a quiet smile the round, newspaper-wrapped, twin-knotted package which the old bent woman in the knitted shawl and the rusty black taffeta dress that dragged about her patched shoes, had brought into the 40th Street Branch back in 1925, and had laid down on a bench beside the writing counter, while she had pulled out a deposit slip at the counter and made it out, and had then written out a counter-check, and had gone shuffling to join the line in front of one of the paying teller's windows, leaving her package forgotten on the bench.

He had been fairly new at the 40th Street Branch then, and only a kind of messenger and office boy still. He had picked up the package, where it lay unnoticed, on his way out with a bundle of checks to deliver to the clearing house. The old woman looked as if she lived in some cold water tenement room over in Hell's Kitchen, and the package looked as if it might contain meat scraps which she had collected from the floor of some butcher shop to feed her mangy cat. Holding it at arm's length by a section of its twine, away from his nose, he had intended dropping it into some trashcan on the sidewalk outside. However, as he started out the door he had seen the blue back of old Bill Ruggleston in the lobby, and had turned back to poke the old guard in the kidney and give it to him to dispose of: "Here, Bill! Something that that old dame in the line at Mr. Clemgott's window left on the bench." And had gone hurrying out.

It hadn't been till he had returned, an hour later, that he had learned the old dame had been old Mary Brown herself, the hundred-million-dollar miser, and that the package had contained a hundred and eighty-seven thousand dollars in rent collections which she had brought in to deposit. Laying it down on the bench that way, and just forgetting it, while she went to cash a check for ten dollars spending money. Anybody might have walked away with it, if they had known what was in it. He could easily have got away with it himself—nobody had seen him pick it up, and he had already been halfway out the door with it, if he hadn't turned back and punched old Bill to call it to his attention.

A hundred and eighty-seven thousand G's, wrapped up in a newspaper and tied with brown twine! Great Godfrey! Of course his noticing it and giving it over to old Bill had been appreciated by the bank. They had promoted him to a teller's cage after that, as a man who could be trusted with money.

Maybe this big red-mustached man with the pale blue eyes and the gold tooth in his foolish vacant smile was another Mary Brown, thought Beasley humorously. Or maybe he was a bandit, loaded with the swag of some big robbery. There had been a mail truck holdup out in Chicago last month which had netted the robbers two hundred thousand dollars in cash, which the police were looking for. There had been some red-headed man in it, Beasley thought. He never read crime news just for the crime angle; but a two hundred thousand dollar robbery wasn't just crime, it was finance. "$200,000 Loot of Chicago Gang!" he remembered the headlines. And maybe this was the gang big shot himself, with his loot beneath his arm.

Oh, nonsense! Things like Mary Brown don't happen twice in ten million years. The big casual man wasn't a holdup man. They had to be alert and hard-eyed and sharp. And his smile and pale blue eyes were just dreamy, vague, and gentle. A little sappy in his mind, a little screwball, even. Just a college professor of Christian Ethics. And the package under his arm was just something.

He had reached the other end of the bench on which Beasley was sitting. He dug into his pants pocket and pulled out a coin. With a casual gesture he laid his package down on the floor back of the bench, and stepped up onto the platform of a penny weight machine which stood back against the iron guard-rail a couple of feet away.

It was one of these guess-your-weight machines, and he set the dial at a hundred and ninety-seven, the weight which Beasley had calculated for him. He put in his coin. The needle spun around to 197, hesitated, then went on to 198. It didn't return the coin. They never do. He stepped down off the scales again.

He dug into his pocket once more and pulled out another penny. He took a couple of steps back up the platform, to a peanut machine affixed to one of the grey-painted I-beams which supported the end of the platform roof. He put his coin in. Cupping one hand beneath the spout, he turned the handle with the other. He sorted the peanuts he collected in his palm. He lifted one between his thumb and forefinger to his mouth, looking up the track in the direction from which the train would be coming. All his gestures were casual.

He had, while laying his package down and stepping up onto the scales, been within two to five feet of Beasley Zillip, sitting with his colorless expression and pressed-together knees on the bench, with briefcase on lap. He was not more than twelve or fifteen feet away now. He gave no appearance of having seen Beasley or of putting on an act for his benefit. He gave the appearance of a man who had come up on a subway platform to take a train down town, and who had decided to weigh himself, and then to eat some peanuts. A man with no other thought in the world.

Suddenly, with no preliminary gesture, he threw his peanuts to the track and darted off. He ran soundlessly back up the platform, with an almost incredible speed. He darted into the el house, through the turnstiles just beyond the entrance, disappearing.

Beasley gave his head a quiet half turn upon the screw of his neck. Through the platform guard rail back of him he got a glimpse of the red-mustached man's emerald green coat and sage green hat, his flying grey pants legs and polished shoes, descending the covered el stairs three steps at a time in soundless leaps toward the street below. Then he was out of sight for good and all.

A little curious, thought Beasley.

Perhaps he had suddenly thought of something he had left behind him at home, and was hurrying back to get it. Still he hadn't looked at his watch, as any man might be expected to do, to see how much time he had to make it in, if there was such need of haste. Perhaps he was a firebug, and had heard an engine in the distance which he must follow. Being a firebug was a kind of insanity. He had looked a little screwball. Beasley could hear no engine in the distance himself, though. Just the regular yammer of the street.

None of the other passengers up the platform gave any indication of having observed the red-mustached man's departure. In the sixty or ninety seconds which had elapsed from the time of his casual appearance with his package, it was quite possible that none of them had seen him at all. The sparrows were just beginning to gather the peanuts which he had cast upon the track.

He had forgotten his package, of course. It lay on the planks back of the bench, just back of Beasley's shoulder. Beasley reached his arm down and picked it up by its string with a quiet gesture, laying it on the seat beside him. If the red-mustached man came leaping back up the steps to get it, he could save him time in looking around for it by having it in plain sight. Calling it to his attention, saying: "I noticed you forgot your package, and put it here where you could see it. Don't mention it!"

Little helpful gestures like that, little smiles exchanged, made men friends for a brief moment, even in the great city. Little drops of kindliness. Little thoughtful acts. It hadn't occurred to him to try to get away with it. He had just picked it up to put it where it could be seen.

Beasley watched, with his thin colorless face half screwed, the segment of stairs down through the guard rail. Other passengers were coming up all the time. But there was no sign of the red-mustached man with his vague light eyes returning.

A train was coming around the curving tracks from 231st Street beneath the morning sun. Beasley Zillip stood up quietly, with his briefcase clasped beneath his arm. The train drew to a stop, with a surge of opening doors. Poised on one foot, he stood watching a moment from the corner of his eyes. No one was looking at him. It might be hours before the man remembered his package. It wouldn't do just to leave it sitting on the bench unguarded, to be picked up by any dishonest person, as old Mary Brown's forgotten package with a hundred and eighty-seven thousand dollars in it might have been.

Might have been—had actually been picked up by him. Unnoticed. Almost out the door with it. But he had gone back and punched old Bill Ruggleston and turned it over to him, in the most unforgettable gesture of his life. There wasn't any Bill Ruggleston to turn it over to now. Unfortunately.

The car doors were starting to close again. Beasley picked up the package from the bench with a swift, quiet gesture, and caught the rubber flange of the door in front of him, squeezing in.

"Legs found in Brooklyn!" came the gloomy, raucous cry from the street below, like a mournful crow. "Legs found on subway platform down in Brooklyn!"

Then the doors closed.

## CHAPTER THREE

## THE HOMELESS HEAD

THE CAR WAS still comparatively empty. Only two stations before this from 242nd, at the beginning of the line. It would fill up as it proceeded down through other stations—there is no subway car which arrives at Times Square not jammed—but there were still plenty of seats. The few other passengers were reading newspapers, or staring in front of them with blank eyes. Beasley took a seat, with his briefcase clasped beneath his arm, resting the package on his knees. He wasn't trying to hide it—it was too large to be hidden anyway. He wasn't trying to get away with it. If the red-mustached man should find it gone from the platform in the next forty minutes, before the train reached Chambers Street, and frantically phone the police or subway officials to look for someone carrying it, why, he, Beasley Zillip had merely picked it up to turn into the lost-and-found.

And it could hardly be anything valuable enough to get the police to looking for it. There aren't Mary Browns twice in a man's lifetime. If it was money, it might be only a few hundred dollars or so, in small bills. If it was stolen money, no complaint would be made.

And it might not be money, anyway. He didn't know.

He felt the package on his knee with inconspicuous pressings of his hands. The thickness of newspapers wrapped around it was eight or twelve fold. The texture, and even the precise outlines, of what it contained could not be ascertained; except that here or there beneath his quiet probing pressure it seemed to be hard and bony, and here or there yielding a little to his thumbs, like a soft cheek.

It couldn't be a vase, then, either a rare old Ming or a cheap modern pottery, for it wasn't hard all over. But it couldn't be old rags or a round plum pudding, either. Gold and thousand dollar bills, he told himself, laughing with quiet face at himself. He would sell what it contained for ten dollars, that was how much he really thought it was anything valuable. Well, for a hundred, anyway; or five thousand at the most. It was probably just some woman's thing, hard and soft that way. Minnie might be able to tell what it was just by the feel of it. Maybe she could use it. Still it was curious.

The subway had plunged into the tunnel at Dyckman Street, from which it would not emerge again, except for the brief interlude of 125th, till far out in Brooklyn. The car was filling up more at each stop. Men with their newspapers, women with their shopping bags. The seats on both sides of him were occupied now. He made little shifting gestures at each station, squeezing his narrow flanks together to make room for more along the seat—the subway wiggle. Thin and colorless he sat, with the package reposing on his pressed-together knees, with his briefcase clasped under his arm, occupying no more than his meager share of space, or less.

A typical subway-rider, faceless and inconspicuous. No one knew that his name was Beasley Zillip. No one knew that within three hours he would be outward bound on the *Saturnalia* with Minnie. No one knew of the blue seas and tropic islands stretching out before them. No one knew what he had in his briefcase.

HEAD NOT FOUND! said a black headline on a newspaper which a black-browed man across from him was holding open, reading the sports or stock market page on the inside.

Who was Head? Beasley wondered idly. There had been a Judge Head, or something like that, who had disappeared some years ago, with a great deal of mystery. If they had found him it might be news; but hardly if they hadn't. And maybe his name had been Foote, anyway.

Maybe the head of some spy ring or secret revolutionary conspiracy was meant, or perhaps of a criminal gang. There had been a character called The Head in the funny-papers once. Legs found—Head not found. Perhaps the leader of the mob that this fellow Legs had belonged to. They were rounding up the whole gang.

DRAGNET OUT—he could make out words in a smaller heading below.

When the police went after a man, they always put a dragnet out. When Beasley had been small he had imagined it as something with meshes and hooks, sweeping slowly in a grey sub-ocean darkness, to catch the little prawn or jellyfish of a criminal cowering in the depths. He would never have a dragnet out after him, he had decided. Even now, the word made him shiver a little.

It was amazing how they could expect to find any one single individual in all the vast faceless millions of the city, where a man never even saw his neighbors who took the same subway trains with him, who might live right across the street from him, twice. But of course if a man made himself conspicuous, like these well-known criminals, he was no longer anonymous, he was no longer faceless. They had his photographs in the rogues' gallery then. They had his real name and all his aliases, and where he lived, and all his little habits. A fellow like this Legs, as shot full of holes as a limburger cheese, must have been quite a sight wherever he went, even in a New York crowd. Perhaps that was why they had found him.

The Head hadn't been found, though. They just had a dragnet out. Beasley focused his mild eyes across the car to read more. But the man opposite folded his paper back again, having glanced at the inside, and turned it over to peruse the front page himself, with a brief frowning glance beneath black brows at Beasley. No Subway rider likes to have anyone else reading his paper. It is an invasion of his privacy.

Sunlight appeared again outside the windows. They had rushed out of the tunnel momentarily at the 125th Street station-half the distance to Chambers Street. The doors opened and closed. They went into the ground again. 116th. The fat woman with the market basket who had been sitting at Beasley's right side had got up and got off, maybe back at 189th Street. The scrofulous little man with the ratlike face and the bad teeth, in the tieless shirt and greasy cap, who had been sitting at his left side, had got up and got off, too—Beasley had been keeping rather an eye on him, he looked like a dip. A chunky man with shiny jaws, in a brown hat and blue overcoat, with square black polished shoes, had taken the seat at his right side now, unfolding a newspaper. An ethereal-looking little girl with waxed golden curls and a pale wistful face, who had been hanging with upstretched arm to a strap in front of Beasley, plumped clown into the seat at his left side, planting the blue morocco case which she had been carrying on her lap. She opened the front of it. A portable radio. She fiddled with the dials, chewing bubble gum.

HEAD NOT FOUND:
DRAGNET OUT FOR FIENDISH KILLER

From the edges of his eyes Beasley caught the headlines on the paper in the hands of the chunky man at his right. There were a couple of half-tone pictures beneath, looking smudged and dismal: "Police at Brooklyn subway platform where first newspaper-wrapped leg was found. . ." "Lexington Avenue subway station where section of dismembered woman's torso, wrapped in newspapers and tied with twine, was found. . ."

Beasley Zillip sat completely motionless. His hands lay motionless on the package on his knees. With staring eyes aslant, he read down the news story beneath the pictures:

> The discovery of the right leg of a woman's body wrapped in newspapers and tied with brown binding twine hidden behind a bench on the platform of the Mevins Street station near the terminal of the Flatbush Avenue subway at two o'clock this morning, followed by the finding of her other limb and segments of her torso in other bundles, similarly wrapped and tied, behind benches on subway platforms at various other stations on the Brooklyn and East Side lines during the night, has not yet been climaxed by the discovery of her head, contrary to reports, according to the latest word from Police Commissioner Walter J. Hollinger at nine o'clock this morning.
>
> The victim, as yet unidentified, is described as dark-haired, about five feet five inches tall, of medium build, between twenty-five and forty years old. She had an appendectomy scar, and had been vaccinated on the left thigh. There were the marks of rings on her ring finger, presumed to have been from an engagement and wedding ring, which had been removed. A strand of grey wool had been caught beneath the torn nail of her right middle finger, which may have come from the clothing of her murderer.
>
> A dragnet has been put out to find the head, which the murderer may not yet have been able to dispose of. . .

The chunky, shiny-jawed man beside Beasley Zillip shifted his square black polished shoes. He glanced over his shoulder in annoyance at Beasley's craned face and poring eyes.

*Oh, God!* thought Beasley.

There was a roaring in his ears. His heart had ceased to beat. The package on his knees was like a stone. His thumb pressing it convulsively, pressed horribly into a bony circle where a soft thing like a grape moved. It was the socket of an eye.

*Oh, God!*

A screwball, insane murderer.

A damned, red-mustached, foolishly smiling, pale-eyed crazy murderer.

All his own affairs so well and intelligently planned and carried out. All the Things-to-be-done, done. His off-on-vacation good-byes at the bank said, with his briefcase beneath his arm. The two trunks taken care of, the one marked "W" for Warehouse given over to the Paradisio storage people, and the one marked "S" for *Saturnalia* sent down to the wharf, with Minnie having the keys of it, so he could begin to unpack and lay his new shirts and his other new, sporty, cruise-going clothes away. Just the right explanations and good-byes said to Mrs. Flebuddy, with promises to the dear old soul that Mrs. Zillip and he would see her soon again. A modest but sufficient breakfast of two buns and a glass of milk in his stomach. Sitting there on the bench at the 225th Street station beneath the bright blue October sky, on top of the world, with his heart beating quietly and happily, with his digestion good, with his mind carefree. Nothing more to do but take the next train down to Chambers Street, and go to the *Saturnalia's* wharf, and smooge a little with Minnie while they waited for the ship to pull out. Then heigho for the great blue tropic seas, and the palm-strewn Carib isles.

His every move and action carefully planned out, in every details, for days and weeks, and even months. The carefree southern voyage itself dreamed of, looked forward to, the groundwork for it laid since long before he had known Minnie Dreamed of since twenty-three years ago, back when he had been a bachelor. With a cool and precise mind. With a quiet, far-seeing mind. And then a crazy screwball murderer, without a brain in his head, going around as happy as a fool hiding portions of a murdered woman's dissected body wrapped up in newspapers and tied with twine behind subway benches, for some reason known only to the gods of lunatics, had to plant this last and most dreadful package of his down back of the bench on which he, Beasley, had been sitting.

All the police in New York looking for some man carrying the terrible package which the red-mustached man had been carrying since two o'clock this morning, it was evident. But he could lay it down quite casually, unseen by anyone except Beasley; could step up on the scales and weigh himself, could step a little farther off, quite casually, and treat himself to peanuts, and could then run like shadowy hell, getting rid of it.

Now he, Beasley, had it.

He must get rid of it! He must bend over, very quietly, and place it on the floor at his feet, before anyone noticed it. No one would observe such a small and casual gesture. No one ever looked at anyone else in New York unless they carried a sign around with them saying they were somebody important, or did something extraordinary and conspicuous.

Just to bend over casually now, and lay it on the floor. It was a small act, but the most sweating and terrible one of Beasley's life. It is nothing at all to stand on a string laid on the ground. But to stand on a string above the middle of Niagara Falls. . . He tightened the thin muscles of his arms bit by bit. He lifted the terrible package an eighth of an inch off his knees. He eased his shoulders forward by the same amount. Now just to bend over quietly and place it casually on the floor. . .

He slanted his eyes to the side. The chunky man with the shiny jaws was looking at the package. He let it sink down on his lap again. He forced the muscles of his thin colorless face into a smile.

"Nice weather, isn't it?" he said.

"What?" the chunky man shouted above the train roar, bending his face over.

It was, Beasley realized, a mistake. No one ever speaks to a stranger in New York except to ask directions. The chunky man was looking straight into his face now from a foot away, not just glancing over his shoulder.

"Does this train go to Chambers Street?" Beasley inquired, with precise, dry lips.

"What? Oh, yes. Sure, I guess so. I think it does."

The chunky man bent his gaze back to his newspaper. A problem had been put to him, and he wanted to avoid any further. His help had been sought, and he wanted to dismiss the beseeker. That was using his head! thought Beasley, still shuddering with an inward cold horror of the chunky man's close stare. But at the left edge of the page the chunky man's eye moved again to the package on his lap.

He might be getting off in a station or two more. He wasn't riding as far as Chambers Street, anyway, or he would have known definitely that the train went there. It could be got rid of when he had left. Or if someone else might be looking at him, thought Beasley, he could carry it out nonchalantly when he got off himself at Chambers, and drop it into a trashcan on the platform or out on the street.

Cool, that was the way to be. Quiet and casual. That was the way that red-mustached fiend himself had been. No one except Beasley himself had noticed him, thought he had been a hundred times more conspicuous in appearance. No one had noticed the package in his arm.

But that had been when the early editions of the afternoon papers had only just come on the stands—the discovery of the first package at two o'clock this morning would have been too late for the morning papers. *Legs Found in Brooklyn! Head Not Found!*

Beasley sat stiffly, focusing his eyes straight ahead. An orange-haired girl in a brown suit hung on a strap in front of him, reading a newspaper, LEGS—said a minor headline on the back of it—FOUND IN BROOKLYN. "Continued from Page 1." He stared at it.

> . . .murdered woman's head. Tracing the pattern of his concealment of the packages on the East Side and Brooklyn subways, it is believed that he will make effort to dispose of it on the West Side subway, of which he may be a patron, and near which he may reside. A particular watch has been ordered to be kept. . .

The orange-haired girl moved her newspaper aside. She had felt his eyes through it. She frowned down at him, looking him up and down.

His hands felt damp within his gloves. There was a dampness creeping down his spine. He tore his eyes away by the roots. He must not look at any newspapers. He looked past her waist, to the opposite seats. The black-browed man across there, whose headlines he had first looked at, stared at him with a challenging frown, as if expecting him to try to steal more of his news. He swept his eyes away, up and down the car. LEGS FOUND IN BROOKLYN! HEAD NOT FOUND! The black headlines, *Globe-Messenger* and *Evening Star,* leaned at him from left and right, and above him in the hands of strap-hangers.

The orange-haired girl was looking down at the package on his lap. He lifted his eyes to her in his thin colorless face. He stretched his lips again in a ghastly grin.

"Awful, isn't it?" he said.

She stared down at him a moment, with her lip curling, then raised her paper again, without reply. But he could feel them burning through it on him.

Be cool! Be calm! Even if they looked at you, they didn't do anything about it in New York. There might be a holdup or a murder going on right before their eyes, and they would look, of course, but then go on their way, wanting no part of it. If there was a cop in sight, they would just call out to him, and point, letting him take care of it. . . Oh, God, there *was* a cop. The blue uniform, the big impassive face. Down at the end of the car, on the rear platform.

The doors had opened once or twice with more passengers crowding in. But only a few more stops to Chambers Street. Be cool. He would get rid of it in a trash-can when he got off. He could leave it in a cab. Any place where he could be alone, He could get rid of it on the *Saturnalia,* if he had to carry it that far. He could drop it out a stateroom window into the roily waters of the dock, or while they were going down the river, or a thousand miles at sea. Minnie would never tell on him. She would know he hadn't done it. He wasn't crazy enough to kill a woman and go carrying around her head.

A dark-haired woman, between twenty-five and forty, with an appendectomy and vaccination scar, married, in Brooklyn—

Oh, God! Suppose it was Minnie!

His hands damp, his thighs feeling damp beneath the package. Oh, God, they *were* damp! The ghastly package was oozing. There was a redness creeping out along a crease, through the thick folds of newspaper, onto his leg.

The train had drawn into another station. Beasley Zillip jerked to his feet as the doors opened. He dropped the package on the seat behind him.

"Excuse! Excuse! Sorry! I beg your pardon!" he babbled, clawing at the arms and shoulders around him in front of him.

Faces stared at him. Even in New York one just shoves, one doesn't claw. And whatever one does, one doesn't beg pardon. A thin shrill scream came from behind him:

"Hey, mister, you forgot your package!"

The little angel-haired girl in blue who had been sitting at his left. She was too young to be a hardened New Yorker, turning away from other people's affairs. Maybe she was a girl scout and wanted to do her one good deed.

*Your package!* said the faces around him. *The little girl says you left your package!*

Once the hue-and-cry had been started up, they were all ready now to join in. Their faces around Beasley were all a blur. He, who had found his quiet pleasure in observing and analyzing people while they gazed beyond him unseeingly, was surrounded by a faceless blindness now himself, while they all looked at him, with eyes focusing on him, taking in his face.

Be cool. Oh, God! He turned blindly back, forcing a smile upon his face, picking up the package from the seat beside the angel child, who beamed at him, fiddling with the dials of the blue morocco radio on her lap, and chewing bubble gum.

"Thanks!" he breathed. "Wouldn't have lost it for the world."

He only wished for one thing more than that he had never seen it. He only wished that it was her own golden-curled head that was in it.

Her radio was humming. It burst forth with a volume of news announcer's voice which seemed to roar through the whole car and out onto the platform that he was fighting for, and up out onto the streets above:

> A man wearing a grey suit or a grey topcoat, with gloves on. All citizens have been asked to watch for a man on the subways or on the streets with a round package wrapped in newspapers, tied with twine, and notify the nearest policeman. . .

Beasley fled. Head lowered, he plunged through the crowd pouring out the door and milling on the platform, with his package beneath his arm. He clawed and butted, turned up a short flight of stairs. There was a trashcan on the platform above. He put out a hand to push open the swinging lid of it as he came to it. A blue-clad figure, immobile, impassive, was standing beside it. He left the lid swinging, swinging, as he hurried on past, with the package still beneath his arm.

He had fought away from the center of the crowd. Still there was a crowd behind him. A sign at the foot of stairs in front of him said, exit 41st street. It was the Times Square station where he had got out, his regular morning debarking place. Still three stations and three miles short of Chambers Street. The most crowded part of the city. He fled forward through a turnstile, up the stairs, with the drum and shuffle of feet behind him.

He burst out upon the street above. He hurried down the sidewalk, looking back over his shoulder. Men were coming towards him, men were coming along the sidewalk back of him. That chunky man with the big polished shoes, hadn't he followed him off at Times Square? Was that he behind? But the faces were all a blur. The cool October sun shone on his dun-colored hair. Somewhere in the crowd he had lost his hat. He was unaware of it, except by the coolness of the sweat upon his scalp. He was aware only of that package beneath his arm.

The eyes were all around him. They were following him. He must get somewhere where he could be alone. He must get rid of it. He raised his hand, trying to find a cab and signal it. But there were no cabs, only trucks, upon the jammed and narrow cross-street.

There was a patrolman coming towards him—he could see the dark blue tunic with its Russian blouse effect, and the silver shield on the big impassive chest, even though the face above it was featureless. He stumbled in through the open doors of a drugstore beside him. Bloodless of face, with a grin like a skull's upon his thin stretched lips, he went weeviling past the soda lunch counter and the stacks of cut-rate books on tables toward the telephone booths at the back.

A man was emerging from one booth. Beasley pushed aside the girl who was moving to step in, and settled on the bench, closing the door behind him. He was shut off now from all those eyes. He must get a grip on himself, be cool and casual. He would lay his package quietly on the floor while he pretended to put in some calls, and leave it when he went out. People were always laying down things in telephone booths. The gesture was an inconspicuous one.

He looked through the glass of the door. There was a chunky man with shiny jaws standing outside, looking in at him. There was some girl with orange or brown hair. There was someone in blue.

He kept the package on his lap. He reached in his pants pocket and pulled out his coin purse. He pulled out his memorandum book, containing his small careful accounts and his lists of Things-to-be-done, and laid it on the phone counter in front of him, as though it contained many numbers which he must call up. He opened his purse and got out a nickel. He stuck it in the slot, and turned the dial haphazardly.

"Two Hundred and Thirty-first Street precinct house," a voice answered. "Desk."

God, how had he got that? The number had been in the back of his mind, of course. He had looked it up, and the address of the precinct house, when he had first moved to Montvale Avenue. It was one of the first things he had always done, wherever he lived.

Not that he had ever expected to use it. One just likes to know where the nearest police are located.

Out of his subconscious the number had popped up, and he had dialed. He would have to say something sensible, or they would think he was a crank or a criminal, and check the number that he was calling from. Maybe they checked all incoming calls automatically.

"My name is Beasley Zillip," he said. "Of 4457 Montvale Avenue. I gave a trunk of mine to the C. and D. Reliable Express and Tracking Company of 227th Street this morning, to be delivered down to Pier 13, North River, the *Saturnalia.* I am downtown now, and haven't been able to reach them by phone. Would you mind telling them that if they aren't able to deliver it on time, just to hold it for me till I return? There's nothing of particular value in it."

"A trunk. You want it held. Okay, I'll notify them."

The precinct man hadn't got it exactly right. Still it didn't make any difference. There was nothing about that trunk, marked "W" for Wharf, which made any particular difference, whether the expressmen delivered it on time, or whether they failed to deliver it, whether they held it till he came back, or appropriated it for themselves, or dumped it into the river. A dozen shirts, many of them old; his last year's tropical summer suit which had already seen two New York seasons; his two new sport coats of gaudy hues, and some pairs of new slacks—two or three hundred dollars worth of clothes altogether, at the most.

Just something to say to the desk man, since he had dialed the number.

He was beginning to use his mind again, in the shelter of the booth, after that momentary complete panic which had gripped him in the subway crowd. He took a breath. His heart was like a hammer. But show a cool face. Keep his head.

His head. . . . He still had it!

The faces were pressed outside the booth. No, it wasn't the orange-haired girl of the train, it was a brown-haired girl in a green suit. The chunky man with the shiny jaws standing outside was wearing a brown overcoat—the one's on the subway had been blue. Just people waiting to use the phone. Still their eyes were on him through the glass, avid for any movement of his which might indicate departure. He could not put that package down, even casually, in the midst of phoning, without calling it to their attention. He couldn't put it down anywhere where there were eyes upon him.

Perhaps if he talked to someone long enough, they would go away. He took another coin out of his purse and put it in. He dialed Mrs. Flebuddy.

"This is Mr. Zillip. Mrs. Flebuddy," he said in his sympathetic undertaker's voice, when her voice answered. "I just wanted to tell you I left some cheese in the icebox, which you're welcome to, too. I thought I might have forgotten to mention it, and you might worry about it. I wanted to thank you again, for both Mrs. Zillip and myself, for the pleasant time we've had with you."

"Oh, Mr. Zillip," she said, pleased. "That is so nice of you. Mrs. Zillip just called me up, too."

"Mrs. Zillip just called you up?" said Beasley, with a turning over of his stomach.

"Why, yes. I didn't recognize her voice at first, but she said she was Mrs. Zillip. She said if I saw you to tell you she had got down to the boat from her sister's in Brooklyn, and that the trunk was there already. She wanted to know if she should open it with the keys you gave her yesterday and begin to lay some of the things away."

It wasn't Minnie's head upon his lap! Though he was almost too sick to care.

"If she calls again, tell her to go ahead," he said.

"I guess she was going to do that, anyway," said Mrs. Flebuddy. "She sounded all excited and happy—that was why I didn't recognize her voice, I guess. She generally sounds sad. She didn't talk to me more than to ask if you were here, and say about the trunk—then she hung up. I was going to ask her—oh, my land, there's the bacon burning! I've got to go. Thank you so much, Mr. Zillip. Be seeing you and her soon, I hope."

He would have liked to have held her in one of her interminable gabbling conversations, which all through the years he had lived at 4457 Montvale he had dexterously avoided, or cut short. But she had hung up. Burning bacon. He made gestures with his face of smiling and nodding for a few moments more, with the receiver at his ear. But the operator would be ringing presently if he didn't hang up.

He hung up. He opened the booth door slightly. But the crowd was still pressed around outside. He couldn't leave the package, before their concentrated eyes. He didn't have quiet the strength yet to emerge and face them. He must be perfectly quiet and calm. He put another coin into the slot. With the booth door an inch ajar, he dialed the number of the 40th Street Branch around the corner, with an air of great assurance.

"Metropolitan National Bank?" he inquired distinctly of the switchboard girl who answered him, though she had already assured him, in her greeting that it was. "I want to speak to Mr. Julius C. Peffersmith, vice-president of the Metropolitan National, the honorary deputy police commissioner and chairman of the Associated Charities Appeal."

"Who's calling?"

"Mr. Allerton. George Allerton."

He heard the call going through Julius C. Peffersmith's secretary. "Mr. George Allerton on the phone to speak to Mr. Peffersmith. . . . George Allerton, Mr. Peffersmith. Do you want to take it?" No, of course not. Julius C Peffersmith didn't know him from a Greek bootblack. But he was getting the credit of calling Julius C. Peffersmith up, of being a friend of that great name.

"How are you, Georgie!" the granite voice of Julius C. Peffersmith roared at him, with all the joviality and volume he could have desired, with far more than he could have even dreamed. "How are you, you old horse-thief? Boy, did you see the stunts I pulled at the class dinner last night! Was I high! You ought to have seen the blonde I picked up afterwards. Too bad you left so soon. Wait a minute. What time is it now,

Georgie? Eleven-thirty. How about coming around in another hour and having lunch with me?"

"I'm afraid I can't today, Mr. Peffersmith."

"Say, who are you?" said Julius C. Peffersmith, in a diminished voice. "I thought you were George Allison, Cornell 'twenty-three."

Beasley pushed the booth door shut. "No, sir," he said meekly. "George Allerton, of teller's window three. I just wanted to call you up and tell you I'm starting on my vacation today."

"You work in the bank here, do you?" said Julius C. Peffersmith. "I don't remember you. Where did you come from? What were your references?"

"Why, I've been with the bank twenty-three years, sir. Everybody in Trilby, Vermont, recommended me. I'm the man who found Mary Brown's hundred and eighty-seven thousand dollars back in nineteen twenty-five, and restored it to her—"

"You're starting on your vacation now, you say?"

"Yes, sir. Mr. Clemgott knows all about it—"

"Then why tell me?" growled Julius C. Peffersmith, not unreasonably. "I'll look it up."

"And give my love to Mrs. Peffersmith and all the children." said Beasley calmly and distinctly, opening the booth door again. "I'll have dinner with you at the Union Club tonight if I can make it, J.C. If not, extend my apologies to the mayor."

He hung up with a steady hand. To hell with Julius C. Peffersmith. He would never see him again. He had got what he'd needed, a personal conversation with the great man. He must be calm and casual. Use his head. He stood up. With the package beneath his arm, he walked calmly and blindly forth, pushing through the little crowd around the booth.

## CHAPTER FOUR

## NEED A BODY FRY?

THE DRUGSTORE was filled with faceless faces. He felt the burning of their eyes. At the book tables, at the soda fountain, coming in from the street. The street outside was filled with more. Some of them—some of them, certainly—must see the package he was carrying, with all the newspapers and the radio, even with their New York eyes. For the moment, he was a friend of J.C. Peffersmith, that great and well-known name. But if some one of them hadn't heard he was, should start the hue and cry. . .

He must get away alone, away from eyes, to get rid of it! Suddenly he knew this store. Suddenly he remembered that it was one into which he sometimes stepped after lunch to pick up a package of cough drops or soda mints, through a side door from the Dinewell restaurant next door.

He turned aside into the narrow alcove passage at the nearer end of the soda-counter, went through the ground-glass door. None of the faceless drugstore throng followed him in, with their blank staring eyes. That would be too much trouble, even if they suspected the package he was carrying. Let someone else start the hue and cry. Let someone else follow him. It was a matter for the police. They'd get him soon enough.

White tables standing in a semi-gloom, with empty chairs drawn up about them, in the long narrow restaurant. Dull yellow velvet quarter-curtains across the bottom of the front window, on a brass rod, curtaining off the window display of dull green lobsters waving their slow claws on a bed of cracked ice. The same white-clothed tables in the same quiet dusty gloom, the same curtains, perhaps the same window lobsters, as when he had used to eat his dinner regularly at the Dinewell, fifty cents for a table d'hôte with dessert and choice of tea or coffee, and ten cents for the waitress, back in bachelor days so long ago. About as small a price as could be found. And with the dark-eyed, slender, shy Miss Davis at the cashier's desk in front, for him to give his money to, and to give him his change, while their fingertips touched and entangled a moment on the counter. . .

Long ago. Long ago the shy and slender little Miss Davis of the Dinewell had become the plump and contented Mrs. Zillip of furnished rooms and kitchenette-cooked meals and down to the bank and back again and the neighborhood movies and the tired and well-known bed. She had ceased to exist. She was no more—he had never intended to marry. Quite possibly never should have married, with the life of glamorous adventure which he had planned. Yet she had made these intervening years pleasanter. Her meals had been as well-cooked as the Dinewell's, and had cost no more—two *could* live as cheaply as one. And then a man needs a woman. So he did not regret it—he would never regret it, though marriage at the time he first started tangling fingers with her had been a thing he had not planned.

He hadn't dined at the Dinewell for many years. But two or three months ago, having dropped in to have lunch one day as a change from the plate-banging cafeterias of the neighborhood, he had gotten into the habit of coming back again.

The cashier's desk in front was not occupied now. The cashier—a freckled girl with fat hands, whose name he didn't know—probably didn't begin her day till just before noon. There was no patrons yet in the long, dark, narrow restaurant behind the lobster claws; it was never a gay and cheery looking place which attracted a lot of patrons, and it was early yet for lunch. The tall angular waitress, Miss Mowgli or whatever her name was, wasn't in sight. She was probably in the kitchen, beyond the green swinging doors in back.

Beasley put the package down quietly on a chair at one of the white-clothed tables, his regular one, towards the rear. He took off his gloves, with that damp sticky feeling on their fingertips, and put them into his topcoat pockets. He removed the coat, folding it and laying it meticulously on top of the package. He shoved the chair deep beneath the long white cloth, and sat down in another. When he got up, he would just pick up his coat. Why hadn't he thought of it before? There must be a hundred restaurants in New York which still used long white tablecloths, with chairs where people left things.

"Goodness, you surprised me!" said the tall angular waitress who emerged through the green swinging doors, with a little gasp. "I didn't hear the front door open. When did you come in? I thought I heard a rustle, but I thought it was a mouse."

She stood at his shoulder, scratching her scalp with the point of her pencil. "You're awfully early today," she said. "I don't know what's ready. Miss Traxton isn't here today. She's off on her vacation. I'll have to serve you myself, it looks like."

"Who?" said Beasley casually and remotely, consulting the menu which she laid before him.

"Miss Traxton, the blonde girl, the other one. The one that waits on you regular. I thought you knew what her name was. I thought maybe you were sweet on her." She giggled. "The broiled salmon's nice today," she added primly, scratching her scalp again, as Beasley still consulted the card. "I know it's ready anyway. Then there's fishcakes and beans that you generally like, only they aren't done yet. It's awful, isn't it?"

"Yes," Beasley said quietly and casually, consulting the card. "You can't imagine a crazy fool like that cutting her up and trying to get rid of her by scattering her all around, just bringing her to everyone's attention. Why couldn't he have just hidden her in one place? Put her in a trunk and taken it—well, taken it and dumped it in the river, or something."

"Oh!" she said with a little gasp. "I meant the shortage and trying to get things to give people on the menu. We aren't supposed to talk about things like that. It might turn the customers' stomachs. Some people are so refined. Yes, it was awful, though. More exciting than the drowned brides. Did you follow all that one? Honestly—" she scratched her head again—"I've been half scared out of my wits that it might be Miss Traxton. Twenty-five to forty, and she's twenty-five if she's a day, though she says she's only twenty-three. She has an appendectomy scar, too—she's often showed it to me when we've been up on the roof to sun ourselves in summer, telling me how they put her under ether—and a vaccination scar on her left limb. She used to be married, too, and has her engagement and wedding rings she wears, except she takes off her wedding ring when she's on duty—a wedding ring scares away the fellas, you know. She lives in Brooklyn, too, with her sister there, where the first limb was found. It said dark-haired, and she's a blonde, but it's only peroxide-deep—"

She paused, a little confused and embarrassed, scratching her scalp again, at thought of the segments of that headless and dismembered body.

"Well, anyway," she added, "I wondered if it might be her."

"Oh, I'm sure it couldn't be—ah, Miss Traxton," said Beasley calmly. "No doubt everyone thinks of someone they know who might fit the description, until she's been identified. I'll take the salmon and the french fries."

*Not Minnie, anyway!* he thought again. Minnie had phoned Mrs. Flebuddy from the *Saturnalia* pier, inquiring when he'd be there, and if she should open the trunk. She was down there now on board, in Stateroom A, putting things away, and singing to herself, waiting for him to come. Her head was still on her shoulders.

Not Minnie. But, oh, God, what difference did it make whose head it was? He almost didn't care if it had been Minnie. It was somebody. It *was.* He had it.

Just be calm. Be casual. Eat his lunch, as much of it as he could stomach, taking his time, taking maybe half an hour, until the place would be fairly filled; then call for his bill, leave a tip, pick up his folded topcoat quietly from the chair seat beneath the tablecloth, pay his bill on the way out, and go out onto Seventh Avenue or Broadway, free of it—as free as that red mustached fiend had been when he went leaping down the stairs at 225th after leaving it behind the bench. Only much more casually and calmly.

Catch a cab then down to the *Saturnalia,* as planned. Plenty of time to make it.

"The cops expect her head to turn up any minute, almost any place, they say," said the tall and bony maiden, writing his order down. "They think he may be carrying it around with him, kind of crazy, looking for a place to get rid of it, now that the rest of the things have been discovered and he knows they're looking for him. Honestly, a place like this—kind of dark, I mean, and no customers hardly ever before noon, and right off the street—why, it would be just a natural for him. I've kept looking on all the chairs and under the tables since eleven when we opened up, to see if he had slipped in the front door or maybe in from the drugstore while I was out in the kitchen a minute with Oscar making up the menus, and had left it. But you don't need to worry! He hasn't left it yet. There's nothing on any of the chairs. I looked just before you came in."

She giggled brightly and scratched her scalp. Beasley laid down his menu card with a bored and casual air. Casual! Maybe that red-mustached fiend had thought that he was casual. But he had put it down in a place where no one knew him, before the newspapers were all about the town. He, Beasley Zillip, was twice the man that that crazy fiend himself was, when it came to casualness, if anybody wanted to know.

"And the lemon jello for dessert," he said. "A cup of coffee."

He would get rid of it. He had to.

But he saw things more clearly now. The very thing which made the Dinewell temporarily a haven and gave him a feeling of security in it—his familiarity to it—made it an impossible place to leave that ghastly package. They might not know his name or where he lived, but they did know his face. He wasn't just one of a million here. He had an individuality. Little mannerisms he had, which he might not be conscious of himself, they had absorbed unconsciously during the sixty or eighty times he had been in. If the package were found on a chair at his table after he was gone, they would know he had left it. They would know that he worked somewhere in the neighborhood. When the police started their slow grinding search, the Dinewell's description of him would be accurate enough to identify him with George Allerton of the 40th Street Branch, just around the corner.

His fingerprints, on file at the bank—it had been a thing which he hadn't been able to avoid when he had first gone with them, since it was required of all employees—his fingerprints would be broadcast. Wanted for murder.

It was one thing to be wanted for absconding. Then they looked for you at Niagara Falls and up in Canada. And in South Bend, Indiana, where you might be visiting your aunt. They looked for you in all the resort places whose beautifully printed and illustrated folders, on glossy paper, in four colors, you had carelessly forgotten on your locker floor when you cleaned out; and they looked for you in all the towns on all the railroad timetables which you had left for them, too, from Squeedunk to Boohoo. They even looked for you in places to which you had given them no lead at all, although with less attention to the seacoast cities, naturally, since they knew that you didn't like the sea.

But it would be three or four weeks, at least, before they started looking for an absconder. Not till after the sixteen days of his vacation during which he was supposed to be away. Not till after a week more, when they received the telegram he had mailed to Western Union in Chicago to be sent at the end of his vacation time, requesting another week because Mrs. Allerton was down with the flu and he had broken his hip in a roller-skating rink. And perhaps still another week, and maybe months, before they had worked their way into all the maze and jigsaw of triple entries and dummy accounts, which he had built up patiently during the last twenty-three years with his eyes upon this day, sufficiently far to be sure he was actually an absconder.

Oh, they looked for you, yes, when they knew you were an absconder. But they wouldn't begin to look for you right away, today. And all you had done was just walk off with ninety thousand dollars, which wasn't all the money in the world to a six-billion-dollar bank. The bank would be pretty mad, and they would like to get you, but they wouldn't keep hunting for you forever, and through all the world away. Just a quiet, colorless, fifty-dollar-a-week teller who's absconded, the dirty crook. Send out the alarm for George Allerton, and charge it up to profit and loss.

Ninety thousand bucks was all. Yes, all that he had been able to get away with, after twenty-three long years. And yet in one moment, on one day, when he had been not much more than half his present age, he had picked up a hundred and eighty-seven thousand bucks, unseen, and could have walked away . . . Just for a few minutes, an hour or two ago, he had thought that he might have picked up an Old Mary Brown again; though of course he had really known he hadn't, that those things don't ever happen in a man's life again.

It hadn't happened. Oh, God! That package!

"Here's your salmon. It was the boiled potatoes you ordered, wasn't it, Mr. Zillip?"

The tall bony girl stood over him again, scratching her head with her pencil. They even knew his name. Minnie must have told it to them. He hadn't been sure. Maybe even his address, and Mrs. Flebuddy's telephone number.

Beasley Zillip, 4457 Montvale Avenue, weight one-fifty, height five eight, aged forty-five, thin features, poker face, wanted for murder.

No, thanks.

He would take the package up with his briefcase quietly and casually when he departed. He would find some other place to get rid of it.

His briefcase. . .

## CHAPTER FIVE

## A LIFETIME TO DIE

SUDDENLY, and quite calmly, Beasley Zillip realized that he didn't have his briefcase. It was as if it were something that he had known for more than twenty years. He was an absconder, with nothing to abscond with. He had left it in the phone booth. He had dropped it on the subway stairs as he clawed his way upward in his panic. Or perhaps it had been gently and expertly slid from beneath his arm by the fat woman with the market basket who had been sitting on his right side, while he watched from the edges of his eyes the pickpocketish-looking little man on his left and thought about the package on his lap, as far back as 189th.

He didn't have it any more, anyway. The fruit of twenty-odd years of quiet and meek and patient work and planning. That was that.

He ate his salmon and boiled potatoes slowly and carefully. The Dinewell had filled up with the noon hour. There were lunchers at every table. A man came to his table and put his hands on the back of the chair beside Beasley and asked if he and two friends might share the table. And with a calm, bored air Beasley removed his coat and the package from the chair seat, underneath the table. He kept the package on his lap, beneath the folds of the cloth, and stowed his folded coat underneath his chair. He went on eating, with it on his lap; and when he had finished ordered more coffee, and then another cup.

He had let panic overtake him once.

He had lost his brief case. In three or four weeks he would be wanted. A man without a dollar, without a job, drifting as a day laborer and a tramp. And that was that. But he did not care to be wanted for murder. No, thanks, not for him. He must not lose his head again.

He had lingered over lunch and over his coffees. Eight or nine men—the Dinewell's cold dull green lobsters with their waving claws in the window had more appeal to men, it seemed, or terrified them less—eight or nine had at one time or another sat down at his table with him, chewed with their faces to their plates, and got up and gone. Now he was alone at his table again. The restaurant was thinning out. It was half past two. The farewell whistles of the *Saturnalia* had long blown.

Had long blown, and down the river. And farewell for him to the blue Caribbees and the coasts of Hi-Brasil and Minnie. She didn't have a ticket, poor thing. He had hers and his both in his purse. But he had given her the key to the trunk yesterday, anyway. Maybe she could cut down one of his new sport coats into a skirt.

"Another cup of coffee, Mr. Zillip? Goodness, but you look sad! Maybe it's because Miss Traxton isn't here to wait on you. Aren't you due back at your undertaking parlors, or wherever it is you work? I hope business hasn't been too bad with you, to make you look so awful."

"It's nothing. Minnie—ah. Miss Gogley. Nothing," Beasley said. "May I have my check, please?"

He examined the green slip which she laid down before him. Pointed out that she had overcharged him ten cents. Got out the quarter that was in his change purse, while she made the correction, and laid it beneath his coffee cup for her. Reached down and pulled his grey topcoat from underneath his chair, unfolded it, and laid it over the package on his knees beneath the tablecloth. Wrapped the coat around it with a casual gesture, and got up.

He paid his slip at the cashier's desk, to the fat-handed freckled girl who sat there, where once had sat the dark and lovely girl with her shy, shining eyes who for almost twenty years had been Mrs. Beasley Zillip. There had been many others since her time. He did not mention that his wife had once worked here. There was no need. He went out onto the street again, quietly and casually, with that dreadful thing concealed in the bundle of his coat beneath his arm.

A hatless man—but many other men went around without hats. A man who liked the bracing October weather, and carried his coat in a loose bundle, instead of putting it on. A thin and colorless, inconspicuous, almost featureless man. A man of around forty or forty-five, his face a little lined, his hair receding. A man in a dark brown thirty-five dollar suit, like a million other men in New York.

No one would know him—no one—for a murderer. Just a mild married middle-aged white-collar man upon the street.

He would get rid of it. He must.

He turned up 42nd, the street of huge dingy movie houses. He went in one of them, up to the balcony. It was fairly crowded, not too crowded. It was dark, and they were watching the screen, and it was all just right. He took a seat in the darkness at the back, between two empty seats, in the middle of the row. He readied down to lay it quietly on the floor, beneath his coat.

A pencil stream of flashlight from the aisle swept towards his down-reaching hand abruptly. He straightened up, laying the package on his knees beneath his coat.

"Lady lost her purse," said the usher at the aisle end.

He came side-stepping in. He turned up the empty chair seat beside Beasley, and played his flashlight on the carpet. He stretched over

Beasley, sitting quiet and motionless with his coat balled on his lap, and played his light on the floor beneath the empty seat on the other stale.

"Excuse me," he said.

He went sidewise back out of the row again, past the other people sitting along it, and played his flashlight from the aisle along the row in front, and went in to look more closely.

Maybe it was a lost purse, and maybe it wasn't. He had appeared very quickly with his flash, at Beasley's bending gesture to put something on the floor. But whether it was a lost purse or not, it was quite useless to try it, Beasley Zillip knew. Darkened movie houses along the West Side subway would be the first place, after the subway platforms themselves and the trashcans, on them, that they would be keeping watch on.

The usher went on down the rows of the balcony with his light, and came climbing back up the aisle steps again, snapping his light out. Beasley sat with his arms folded above the bundle of his coat. The movie on the screen was about some man who killed his wife. After a while he picked up the bundle of his coat, and went down the stairs again.

He went down into the basement to the washroom. But there were other patrons in it, of course, as well as the attendant, and the white tiled walls were brightly lit, One of the patrons at the washbasins was a uniformed patrolman. Beasley didn't even start to go into a booth.

He went out into the cool, late afternoon again. He walked along 42nd Street quietly, as inconspicuous as he had even been in his life, towards Grand Central station.

Cops. Newspaper headlines. Subways, Trashcans. He must get out of town, out somewhere where there was space, and no eyes. He couldn't hope to get rid of it in New York.

He went in the entrance of the vast terminal, with the early returning commuting throng. He went down the ramp, and turned left down the stairs to the lower level. There was a train gate open, the gateman standing beside it with hand uplifted, looking at his watch. A black, white-lettered sign beside the gate said, 125th STREET, MARBLE HILL, YONKERS, TARRYTOWN, OSSINING-ON-HUDSON. Reading down.

Somewhere where there weren't cops and newspapers. Ossining-on-Hudson, a lovely-sounding town. That was where they had the big grey prison and the death-house for murderers. No thanks, not for him, not Ossining-on-Hudson. Tarrytown, perhaps, might be a place. He had taken a trip up the river once. There was a dump heap at the river's edge right by the Tarrytown station, as he remembered it. Or at some other town. If he couldn't drop it on the dump heap or into the wide quiet river waters, in the night that soon would come, he could catch another train to someplace further on. Up to Buffalo and Niagara Falls, if need be. Leaning casually over the rail beside the falls, with his coat in a bundle in his arm, quite accidentally he could lose his hold on it, and—white in the white spuming waters, swirling just for an instant—the damned thing would go down.

A dozen ways to quietly get rid of it, a thousand places to do it, outside New York.

Even if they caught him there at the Falls as an absconder—it would be the first place they would look for him, as soon as they knew—even then it would be no more than five years, with a third off for being good. And he had lost his briefcase—he didn't care too much if they did catch him as an absconder, any more.

But not that. Not murder.

He had descended to the lower level, where the local trains pulled out because on them you didn't have to have a ticket for anywhere to get through the gates. The guard just assumed you were a commuter somewhere up the line and had a ticket. The guard waved Beasley Zillip in, along with a hurrying twenty or fifty more.

Beasley sat quietly in the smoking car up at the front end of the train, with his bundled coat on his lap. A colorless man, not a murderer. Not in anything about him would anyone know. He looked out of the windows idly at the 125th Street platform, ten minutes from Grand Central, where a small bevy of passengers got on, and one or two got off. He looked out at the Marble Hill station in ten minutes more.

There were more passengers who got off there. A good half of those in the car that he was in arose and moved in a slow line down the aisle past him, to debark; while from the other cars in back of him an equal proportion poured out onto the platform. They were residents of the vicinity whose business lay down near Grand Central, and who found the short twenty minutes of the train-ride, as against the subway's and shuttle's forty-odd minutes, more than counterbalancing the railroad's less frequent trains and somewhat higher fare. They had all been Beasley's neighbors, like the riders on the subway, for a part, at least, of the last seven years. All living within half a mile of him, at most. Perhaps some of them residents of the Bronx Gardens right across the street. But no more than the subway-riders had he ever seen any of them before, nor would he expect to see any of them again.

A big man in an emerald green topcoat, and wearing a sage green hat, a knit maroon necktie and a white shirt, too, and a reddish-brown Norfolk-jacket beneath his coat—a man with a red mustache, with a foolishly smiling face, with a gold inlay in his right upper canine tooth, with a big nose pushed aslant like the bowsprit of a boat that has been knocked askew—passed below the window out of which Beasley Zillip was quietly and casually gazing, and moved quietly with the surging crowd up the steps towards the street.

Quietly and casually amidst the throng. Quietly and casually. Up the steps in the dusk.

"Stop!" yelled Beasley Zillip, beating on the glass. "Stop him! Murderer! The fiend killer! Stop him—out of my way!"

He had risen madly. His grey coat dropped from his lap in a heap between the seats. He didn't stop to pick it up. He held the bloody package beneath his arm like a football. He clawed the outgoing passengers in front of him still moving down the aisle.

"Murderer!" he yelled. "The head! The fiendish killer that you've read about! Out of my way!"

It was unquestionable that he had succeeded in attracted attention. Twenty motorcycle policemen, the governor and mayor and the police band, could have done no more. They scrambled backward in between the seats out of his clawing way. Some of them ducked down their heads. A woman screamed, with a long unearthly wail.

"Out of my way!" yelled Beasley. "The fiend killer! I've got her damned head!"

He had reached the car vestibule in a rush. He sprang down to the platform in a single leap, with his eyes distended in his head, with his wild yell. They melted and dissolved before him on the platform. With his damp red-stained package beneath his arm, he leaped to the steps towards rumbling upper Broadway. He plunged across the street against the lights, between the trucks coming over the Harlem River bridge, past the traffic officer standing in the center of the street beneath the el.

"The fiend killer!" he yelled with bursting lungs.

He ran, a thin man in a brown suit, coatless and hatless, with his thinning hair rumpled wildly on his sweating scalp, with glaring eyes in his strained and sweating face, up the cross street off Broadway. There he was! Just turning left at the end of the block, with his bright green coat's skirts flaunting about his grey flannel trouser legs, with his sage green hat set jauntily on his head, striding at a quiet powerful ground-covering pace quite casually and with an air of great unconsciousness around the corner.

"Stop!" yelled Beasley. "I've got her head!"

He half turned around upon the sidewalk, pausing in his headlong race, with haggard eyes, to see if he would have to face that red-mustached fiend alone. A long file of people, men and women, were streaming up the sidewalk after him like harriers, from clear across Broadway and the railroad platform steps, and around the corners of the street from both sides. The traffic policeman from the intersection was in the van of them. As Beasley paused to look wildly back at them, the foremost of them paused. But the traffic policeman kept straight on. He'd not be alone, Beasley thought with a sobbing breath, when he caught up with that fiend.

"Stop!"

He rounded the corner. There he was! With his long easy powerful strides, upon his rubber soled shoes, there he was walking away along the sidewalk three quarters of a block ahead—no more! He must have heard Beasley's yells behind him if he wasn't deaf as stone. Still he kept on, casually and without a turning of his head, without a slowing of his pace or an increasing of it, and turned left around the corner of the next block, onto Montvale Avenue, disappearing.

A shot roared out behind Beasley as he ran towards the corner. The traffic policeman behind him had fired into the air.

"Stop!" the bellow came behind Beasley. And the screams.

He had no more breath left to yell himself. He went sprinting and gasping around the corner.

There he still was! Walking along past the front of the Paradisio Warehouse down the block, walking with his unchanging stride, quite unconcernedly! Heading down towards Mrs. Flebuddy's at 4457, it seemed. Beasley's breath sobbed from his lungs. He pulled the bloody package from beneath his arm. and held it in both hands against his breast as he went running.

"Stop!" the bellow came from back of him. "Stop, or I'll shoot!"

A bullet zinged, ricocheting from the curbstone beside Beasley. The shot roared behind him up the street. The damned red-mustached fiend, not forty yards ahead of Beasley now, kept quietly on.

Beasley ran with sobbing lungs past the great windowless red brick structure of the warehouse that was like an Egyptian tomb, where only this morning—it seemed a thousand years ago—he had accompanied the "S", for Storage, trunk up to the zero vaults. No, the "W", for Warehouse, trunk, he meant. The "S" trunk had been for the *Saturnalia*—the "W" trunk for Wharf. He couldn't think. A thing-to-be-done that had been done. He had it down in his book. He had his book in his pocket. No, he had left it on the ledge of the phone booth.

He couldn't think of it. He must get rid of the head, that was all. He must give it to that fiend. 4457 was ahead, down the sidewalk. A little knot of half a dozen people, some blonde girl in blue, Mrs. Flebuddy's own dumpling figure, and some men, were on the stoop and the sidewalk in front. Some man with a big granite jaw, who looked like Julius C. Peffersmith himself. Some plump little man with a strand of hair across his hatless dome, who looked like Mr. Clemgott, the assistant cashier of the 40th Street Branch, though what Julius C. Peffersmith or Mr. Clemgott, either, would be doing up here it would take heaven to answer. Two burly men in dungarees and caps, along with them, who looked like the expressmen who had taken the trunk down to the wharf this morning.

There were burning red spots before Beasley's eyes. His heart and lungs were bursting in his throat. His brain was drained. He had almost forgotten what he had in his hands. He had almost forgotten why he had to get rid of it. The blonde girl in blue at the top of Mrs. Flebuddy's stoop looked like Minnie, though the *Saturnalia* had pulled out three hours ago, and was now out on the deep Atlantic past the Hook.

The red-mustached man was heading for that knot of dreamed-of visionary, unbelievable figures in front of 4457. No, he wasn't! He was stepping casually and quietly out into the street before he reached them. He was cutting across the street towards the entrance archway of the Bronx Gardens Apartments, with their forty-five hundred units housing twelve thousand souls.

*The fiend!* Beasley tried to move his lips. But they were paralyzed. He held the package against his breast. He cut out from the sidewalk, across the street.

"There he is! There he is!" shrilled the gibbering voice of Mrs. Flebuddy from the stoop. "There he is! Mr. Zillip! He said that he'd come back!"

The red-mustached man was no more than ten yards in front of Beasley Zillip now. He was turning into the archway of Bronx Gardens. Casually, quietly, as if he lived there. Maybe he did. No doubt he lived some place. No doubt he would try to lie that package away. No doubt he had some alibi.

"Take it!" yelled Beasley, sobbing, with his last breath. "I've carried it long enough for you! Take her damned head, you fiend!"

Staggering, he lifted, the package in both hands above his head. He hurled it at the back of that green coated figure entering the archway.

The package hit the top of the arch, just above the entrance. It burst, it spilled and slathered, raining down upon the sidewalk. A horrid dead and yellow eye, blood, soft yellow membranes, flesh and bones.

It had missed the red-mustached man as he went in the archway. It rained down on Beasley.

The red-mustached man went on, quite unconcerned.

But Beasley Zillip had no time to think of him any more. He had no more thought to spare on the package which at last he had got rid of, after these nightmare hours. His mind was turned all inward with a greater horror. He was trying to remember whether he hadn't meant that trunk labeled "S" for the *Saturnalia,* not for storage. And whether the "W" on the other trunk hadn't been for Warehouse, not for Wharf.

"Zilly!" he heard Minnie's hysterical scream. "Why did you do it, Zilly?"

He turned to flee madly down the street. But they had caught up with him. They were all around him then. Some of the men who had been running after him, and the men from across the street. Big men and hard men. They were all around Beasley Zillip by the dozen, and they had him.

The harrier chase he had drawn after him by his wild bug-eyed yelling, which trailed out all the way behind him from the Marble Hill railroad station, with swarming additions from the el platforms, from Broadway, from stores and newsstands and barber shops and apartment buildings on all the streets between, would catch up with him—most of them—in time to see him with the bracelets on him being hauled away. But there would still be thousands who had missed the sight and sound of him, who would come together on the street in front of the house at 4457 Montvale Avenue where the Monster Murderer had lived, to stand and stare at it, all evening, and all the next day. . .

Professor George M. Allison, Cornell A. B. '23, Harvard Ph. D. '26, of the Chair of Christian Ethics, Department of Philosophy, Manhattan University, hunted around in his pockets for his door key.

The key to 19-C, Section A, Entry 3, of the Bronx Gardens Apartment at 4444-46-48-50-52 Montvale Avenue, which was the little nest that he called home.

It should be in his upper right vest pocket, or else in his lower left vest pocket. Perhaps, though, he had put it away in his purse for added security, or in the band of his hat. He had always meant to buy himself a key-case—it was really the only way. He hoped he hadn't lost it. He wasn't sure just how he had got in last night. Perhaps he had lost it in the lobby of the Pennsylvania at the Class of '23 Dinner while he and Pooch Peffersmith had been demonstrating, somewhat late in the evening, the famous quarterback-to-full-to-guard play—requisitioning one of the elevator boys to be the quarterback—which had beat Yale.

He couldn't remember how the subject had come up, or what had impelled him to the demonstration. Pooch had a deleterious effect on him, he was afraid.

He might, of course, have left it at his office today. He had taken some small object out of his pockets and tied it to the end of the piece of twine which he had diddled beside him while he sat reading themes in his arm chair, to keep Tabitha amused—the Philosophy cat, which otherwise would have insisted on perching on his shoulder and licking his ear with loud hoarse purrs, in the way of female Siameses. He had dropped the string absentmindedly into the wastebasket afterwards, he was afraid. He had thought it was his gold penknife, but it might have been his key—

He remembered now. Of course! There had been a keycase lying behind the trash-can on the sidewalk at the foot of the subway el stairs when he had been starting up them this morning on his way down town. A worn leather case, quite dilapidated, and of no value. It had only one old trunk key in it, the sort of key which people may have in their keycases long after the trunk it belonged to has been disposed of. Probably someone had thrown the case away, along with the old key in it. He had picked it up. It would serve him to contain his key until he remembered to buy himself a case of his own. He had hooked his key in it.

And there the keycase was, right in his right hip pocket, where he had always meant to carry his keycase when he had one. His key was in it. He unlocked his door.

He removed his hat and bright green topcoat and stowed them away in the hall closet—Martha was always so particular and didn't like them draped around on lamps or chairs. He attached his little hearing device, which he never wore between the university and home, avoiding thereby the city roars which might disturb his meditations.

When a man is somewhat absent-minded, and more than a little deaf, there is a great deal about him which he misses. Not unhappily.

"Is that you, Bunny?" Martha called to him from the kitchen.

"Home again, my dear."

He washed his hands in the bathroom. He settled himself in the living room, in his favorite leather chair. Martha had come out of the kitchen with a salad bowl in her hands, to sit on the couch beside him while she made some last dinner preparations, as she always did. It was a nice thing, he thought, a nice thing, to have a wife. How any woman was willing to be a man's wife, he didn't understand. She had a white block of margarine in her mixing bowl, and was mixing coloring into it with a fork.

"A tiresome trip home, Bunny?" she said. "Was the subway very crowded?"

"No, I don't believe so," he said. "I didn't notice it particularly. I had a seat, I think. As a matter of fact, I came home by train," he said, remembering. "I went down by Grand Central this morning, too, it seems to me. Yes, I'm sure of it. I went up on the subway platform, but then I happened to notice there was a little crowd of passengers waiting on the downtown platform of the Marble Hill station below. A train must be just about due, it occurred to me. And since it would be more expeditious, I hurried down and caught it, just in the nick of time."

"That's nice," she said, working the margarine with her fork into a shapeless mass. "You've always said you were going to get a time table someday, and take the train regularly. It was dreadful about the murder, wasn't it?"

"What murder?" he said resignedly.

Martha had a curious, mild interest in murders. She read the murder serials in the women's magazine she took, after she had finished with the food and household hints. He couldn't understand what interest she found in them. Abhorrent characters doing nasty things. Of course they were just fiction.

"Some gangsters who killed the woman that belonged to them," she said. "The police had found her head right away and knew who she was, and who must have killed her, though they pretended that they didn't, to lure them out of hiding. They didn't catch them till nearly noon today. I thought maybe you heard people talking about it downtown."

"No," he said. "I didn't hear anything about it."

"It's a quarter of six," she said. "Time for Elwell Cordy on WQM. You always like him. At least you say he's the least terrible of the lot. Supper won't be ready for another fifteen minutes."

"Yes, I suppose so," he said resignedly. "One should keep up with the world. After all, it's the world we live in."

She stuck her fork in the margarine, and turned on the radio beside her at the couch end. She sat working in the yellow coloring placidly, while Professor Allison stretched his legs out, settling lower on his spine. The radio hummed. It began to speak.

> This is Elwell Cordy, with your five-forty-five edition of the front page, brought to you this evening for the first time by Purr, the wholesome Food for Cats. A terrifying experience awaited Miss Minnie Traxton, blonde twenty-three year old waitress of the Dinewell Restaurant in the Times Square District, at noon today when she opened the trunk which her fiancé Beasley Zillip, of 4457 Montvale Avenue, The Bronx, had sent down to the *Saturnalia* at Pier 13, North River, to accompany them on a southern cruise which she believed was to be their wedding trip and honeymoon, and found the trunk to contain the remains of a dark-haired middle-aged woman, dead thirty-six hours, whose body had been dissected to fit neatly into the space. The ship's

officers, summoned by her screams, immediately notified the police, and an alarm was put out for Zillip.

The remains were identified as those of his wife, Genevieve, whom he is recorded as having married at City Hall on January 7. 1927. Relatives of the former Miss Davis, who gave her home address as Portland, Oregon, are being sought by the police of that city.

It was found that earlier this morning Zillip had stored another trunk, of the same size and color, in the cold-storage vaults of the Paradisio Warehouse Corporation at 4437 Montvale Avenue, just down the block from his residence, paying a year's storage in advance. This trunk was opened by the police under court order, in absence of a key. It was found to contain merely an assortment of male summer attire, some old and conservative, and some new and leaning to the bright side. It is the theory of the police that this was the trunk he had intended to send down to the boat, and that he had intended to send the other one to cold storage, to leave it in the vaults indefinitely, paying a small annual fee, thus obviating discovery of his crime, until in some distant future year he might have opportunity to dispose of it. But that, in the terror of his crime, he had confused the trunks.

A connection between him and George Allerton, teller employed by the 40th Street Branch of the Metropolitan National Bank for the past twenty-three years, who started on his vacation yesterday, is being sought. Allerton called up Mr. Julius C. Peffersmith, vice-president of the Metropolitan National, honorary deputy police commissioner and Chairman of the Charity Drive, before noon today, informing Mr. Peffersmith with inexplicable braggadocio of his absence from the bank. Audit was immediately started of his books, and the references which he had given from his home town of Trilby, Vermont, when he had first come with the bank, were questioned by telegraph. It was learned that George Allerton, a well-esteemed youth in his native town, had left there in 1923, following the death of his grandfather and only relative, to go to New York to seek employment, at about the same time that one Beasley Zillip, the son of a local police character and known himself as a petty thief, had also left town. George Allerton had references with him from all the leading citizens of Trilby, and the police are working on the theory that Zillip took these from him, and disposed of him in some way. The rooms which Zillip occupied on Montvale Avenue are being examined by the police, to ascertain if fingerprints of his left there may match with those of the George Allerton employed by the Metropolitan National. If so, he will be required to explain, when caught, the whereabouts of the real George Allerton, on the supposition that Allerton may have been murdered, and that his body, more easily disposed of in the country than in the city, may have lain for almost a quarter of a century buried in some lonely district between Vermont and New York.

Zillip's former landlady at 4457 Montvale Avenue, Mrs. Evangeline Flebuddy, has informed the police that he promised to return to see her, and that she is convinced he will keep his promise, since he is a man of the utmost reliability who always paid his rent on time, besides having no dogs or children. The police, however, remain sceptical of that, unless he is even more stupid than he has given evidence of being in his other heedless acts which thrust him on their attention.

"Flash! He was! He did! Boy, let me see that! According to flash just coming in, Beasley Zillip, alias George Allerton, has been caught just across the street from his home at 4457 Montvale Avenue where he murdered his wife the night before last and cut her body up and stored it in a locker trunk, after leaping off a New York Central train for Ossining in the vicinity yelling that he was a murderer, and drawing after him a great crowd—"

Mrs. Allison stuck her fork in the by now smoothly yellowed mass of margarine. She snapped the radio off. Poor Bunny's aid had slipped from his ear; it lay at the end of its black cord upon his breast. His big red-haired hands were folded on his stomach. His eyes had closed on both sides of his big crooked nose. He was asleep, tired out from his day. A Professor of Christian Ethics has much to make him tired, when one considers the young hellions that college boys are, and that he can't swear about it.

There was a little frown upon her face. She had meant to listen to Elwell Cordy herself. He had such a pleasant soothing voice, it went nicely with coloring the nut-butter. But his first words, mentioning his new sponsor, the Purr Company, had turned her thoughts away. Bunny hadn't said a word about Tabitha, the Philosophy cat. She wondered if he had lost the package.

A striking detail in the case is the similarity in the backgrounds of the two women in Zillip's life. The dead woman, prior to her marriage, had been employed in the Dinewell restaurant—where Miss Traxton, Zillip's current intended, worked as a waitress. Zillip had met both as a patron of the restaurant.

Professor Allison opened his mild blue eyes, as blue as the bluest October morning that ever lay above Manhattan and the Bronx. He rubbed his red mustache.

"What are we having for supper, Martha?" he said. "It smells good."

"That perfectly enormous salmon that Julius C. Peffersmith sent you yesterday, don't you remember?" she said. "Goodness, I don't know what he expected us to do with it. I gave half of it to Mrs. Lund over in 412 of Section M of Quadrangle 3 with her perfectly enormous family of seven children, and a quarter to the janitor's wife. I'm broiling the rest in butter, even though we have to eat margarine for a week. There'll be enough for over Sunday. Oh, Bunny, what did you do with the beautiful huge head and tail and all the insides that I gave you to give to Tabitha, the Philosophy cat, and her husband and her children? After your telling me how much Siameses love raw fishheads. And after I had wrapped it up and tied it up so carefully. I hope that you didn't just forget it somewhere. It was such a lovely head."

He was a Professor of Christian Ethics, and he disapproved of lying—it weakens the moral fiber. However, he had been married twenty years, and he had learned the utility of mild evasions at times.

"Tabitha was quite happy, playing with a string I dangled for her," he said. "Who can say precisely the pleasure which anyone gets out of anything? Still I think there is no reason for you to be afraid that your package, so thoughtfully prepared, didn't serve a good use today."

# THE CRIMSON VAMPIRE

"FIVE HUNDRED ACRES of woodlot and meadow old man Hamilcar owns," said William Hicks—"but I'd not trade places with him for all the money in the world."

He turned his round, freckled face to look curiously at Captain Sparrow, resting his forearms on the shuddering wheel of the little car as he swung it around a stone in the road. A stony, hard-rutted road it was, rising steadily between dim, graying upland meadows and somber groves of pine. The storm had long since passed, and the light of morning was in the eastern sky.

William Hicks was a confiding youth, yet there was something in the air of Captain Sparrow which was not altogether friendly.

The captain's face, as well as it could be seen by the pale dashboard light and the sky still gray with darkness, was pleasant enough. His thin, smallish nose was straight-edged as a knife. His cheekbones were sharp, his jawbone grim. His skin was tanned the color of leather.

Now Captain Sparrow turned his glance directly on William Hicks. It was those pale eyes, gleaming from beneath eyebrows straight and black, which gave the freckled youth a strange feeling of uneasiness.

"Are you a detective, mister?" asked Hicks with a sudden surmise.

After a thoughtful pause Captain Sparrow shook his head.

"No," he said. "But why wouldn't you like to trade places with Mr. Hamilcar? What do you mean?"

"I mean," said William Hicks—and his voice sank low, so it was hard to make him out above the rumbling and squeaking of the rusty little car. "—I mean that to the best of my knowledge and belief, something terrible was done to poor Dick Hingham—old man Hamilcar's grandson-in-law—last Sunday night, up there in Hamilcar's fine home on Bald Knob mountain. There's plenty of us suspect foul play of some kind or other. Maybe murder."

Captain Sparrow sat silent a little while.

"Murder is a black word," he said at last. "What makes you speak of it?"

The pale-faced driver coughed and hesitated, his worried eyes fastened on the road ahead.

Captain Sparrow waited patiently.

"Old Hamilcar never got used to the idea of Miss Irene's being married to a poor man," said William Hicks quietly. "He had another multiplied millionaire as rich as hisself picked out for her. He always hated Dick. And many a devilish thing he's done to him, Dick has told me in confidence. And if Hamilcar wanted to get rid of Dick Hingham, I'd not put it beyond him to do it."

"What do Hamilcar and Mrs. Hingham say has happened to Dick Hingham?" asked Captain Sparrow.

"They tell a cock-and-bull story that nobody would believe," said Hicks with a snort. "They say that last Sunday night Dick Hingham was out walking on the lawn. And all of a sudden a great big giant bat came screeching and yelling down out of the sky—"

"A what?" said Captain Sparrow.

"A flying bat, a vampire." said William Hicks, his voice growing hoarse. "A flying bat as big as all get-out, with great red eyes and claws as long as your arm, hollering and flapping its wings. And before Dick Hingham could do anything, or turn and run, it had grabbed him up and torn the life out of him. Away it flew, dangling him in its claws like a dead rat. They found his blood all over the lawn."

Captain Sparrow sat tight-lipped, nodding silently.

"That's the story they tell," said William Hicks. "I ask you, mister, does it sound reasonable?"

"No," said Captain Sparrow, "it doesn't sound reasonable."

"I could think of a million stories to tell, myself, better than that, if I wanted to hide some foul and dirty work," said William Hicks.

"That's what makes *this* story reasonable," said Captain Sparrow, "however far-fetched it may sound."

The gray pre-dawn was clammy chill, though the stars were fading in the east behind them and the dawn would come soon.

Across the road ahead stretched a high, white picket double gate set in a low, thick wall of fieldstone, and with a mail box on a post beside it. This was the boundary of old man Hamilcar's domain, on the summit of Bald Knob mountain.

"Here we are at the top of things," said William Hicks, "and we couldn't get no higher unless we flew."

Captain Sparrow stepped out to open the gates and stood beside them waiting for Hicks to drive through. But the country youth had begun to back and circle, and was plainly of no mind to go farther.

"Well, mister, much obliged to you," said William Hicks, pocketing the bills which the captain had offered him.

He put his little car in gear and, with a farewell nod, went down the rutty road much more speedily than he had come up. In a moment he was out of sight beyond the somber pine woods; in two he was out of sound.

Captain Sparrow closed the gate behind him and walked sturdily along the well-laid, graveled road between the poplar rows, over the rolling lawns to Hamilcar's house—a slight and silent little man, with an unafraid look in those shrewd eyes which were as pale as the dawn sky above him.

Down in the valley a cock crowed. A dog began to yap furiously. But up here about this silent house, no giddy cock or foolish, cheerful dog welcomed up the sun. Captain Sparrow lifted his fist and knocked, well aware that from the dark interior someone was watching him.

## II

An old negress with a weazened countenance admitted him, shuffling to the door in carpet slippers. Her little eyes were red with sleeplessness. She peered at him like a watchful rat.

"Mrs. Hingham telephoned," said Captain Sparrow.

But the withered black woman only made strange sounds in her throat, shaking her head—a deaf mute. . . .

Captain Sparrow scrawled a message on a card. She led him upstairs to a book room on the second floor, and knelt at the hearth to apply a match to the wood piled there in readiness. Softly she went out, her big checked gingham gown billowing about her.

Left to himself, Captain Sparrow pondered the object of this strange visit. What had it been—that inhuman and unbelievable giant beast which, if the story was to be believed—had come flying over these hills on the night before the last, to seize poor Richard Hingham in its claws, as an owl seizes a running rat? Had it been a reality—or the imagined image of a crazed mind? Or was it all some malignant, lying game, with death as the stakes and prize of it? Now beneath the sun no thing flew. The wind itself was motionless.

Irene Hingham was a woman who moved with quiet footsteps. She had come into the room before Captain Sparrow was aware of her. Turning from the window suddenly, he saw her—a large woman, clad in black, with great dark eyes staring from her pale face.

"I expected someone yesterday," she said. "It was two days ago—what day is today?"

"Tuesday."

"Then it was only yesterday I telephoned," she said quietly. "It seems longer."

"Today is Tuesday," said Captain Sparrow again.

"I haven't slept," she said. "We are here alone, you know. The village people, I suppose, think we are lunatics. They've given us no help. Yet we need help."

Captain Sparrow bowed. Standing with his back to the fire, he could examine Richard Hingham's wife (or widow, he had better say) at leisure. She had sunk down in a divan facing the hearth, with the firelight and the clear sunlight on her face.

"We are in trouble, Mr. Sparrow—have I the name right?" she said. "How shall I begin? What do you want me to tell you?"

"The truth," said Captain Sparrow.

"I'll try," she said.

"It's the hardest thing in the world to tell," said Captain Sparrow. "Not that I'm impugning your veracity, ma'am."

"You will have to believe what I tell you," said the woman quietly, "though it sounds like an impossible nightmare."

"I will believe whatever is possible, ma'am," said Captain Sparrow. "It is only the impossible I will not believe."

"Before another night is done, if you stay in this house," she said with a deepening of her quiet voice, "you will see with your own eyes what is not possible, Mr. Sparrow."

Captain Sparrow narrowed his pale glance a moment. His teeth shone as though he might be laughing.

"I have seen many strange things," he said, "but I have never seen the impossible."

He was studying her. Pretty, he thought, but like a languid chrysanthemum, without perfume or fire. About thirty years old, Captain Sparrow guessed. Her brown eyes were wide and frank.

Yet appearances may lie, knew Sparrow.

What dismal images gathered behind that smooth mask of face? If mad, what was her madness? But she had begun her story now, and the Captain listened.

"We first saw it—this Thing that we have learned to call the Crimson Bat—on the night of—the night of Thursday last," said Irene Hingham. "Or rather my grandfather saw it. I was down in the city that night with Richard. I remember I called up home about midnight—I had gone to the show with some college friends, and Richard, who had been in conference with our lawyers, joined us afterward for supper. At midnight I called up grandfather, as I always do when I'm in the city, to see how he was getting along. Is all this boring you?"

"On the contrary," said Sparrow.

"It was that night the Crimson Bat first came," said Irene Hingham, lowering her voice. "Grandfather had been dozing on the sun porch after dinner. He was awakened by a scream and it came flashing down over the house. He said. . ."

"What *you* saw, please," suggested Captain Sparrow politely. "What *you* did."

"I telephoned grandfather," she said weakly. "He told me about it. He had been startled, naturally. The connection was weak, or else he wasn't speaking clearly, so I had a hard time understanding him. Richard talked with him then. Richard thought it had been only a nightmare. I remember he laughed. He got me and the other girls laughing, too."

"I wonder if he'd be laughing now," thought Captain Sparrow. But he said nothing.

"That was Thursday night. Friday evenings Richard drives up for the week-ends. I came home Friday morning. That night about nine o'clock *I* saw it. Brian Boru, our Airedale, began to groan and whine. He came and crept under my chair. His hair was up, and he shivered steadily. Then I heard it—a sudden wild scream, growing into a horrid yell as it came swooping down with wings outstretched and eyes blazing. It passed over the house as though looking for some prey, and turned and came back again, so close this time that I think it must have clung a moment to the roof ridge."

"Describe it, please," said Captain Sparrow.

"Why, it had crimson eyes—dull red like coals—the kind of eyes an animal has in the dark. Its wings must have been as wide as this room from tip to tip when they were outstretched, and they were indented along the edges like a bat's wings. There wasn't time to see. . ."

"Its head?"

"It had pointed ears, claws outstretched. . ."

"What kind of claws?"

"As a matter of fact, I didn't see them, that time," said Irene Hingham. "That was later. It must have curved up its claws ready to strike as it came swooping down."

Captain Sparrow paced back and forth in front of the fire. His hands were clasped behind his back, his head bent. He frowned.

"Did the others see what you saw?" he asked. "What did they think of it?"

"What others?"

"Your grandfather and your husband, and this person you call Minna, whoever she is," explained Captain Sparrow impatiently. "I take it there was no one else in the house?"

"No one else," said Mrs. Hingham. "Richard had a blow-out on the way up from the city, and didn't get home till later. It frightened grandfather. Yet I suppose he felt a sense of victory in proving it was more than a hallucination—he is sometimes afraid that his mind may be failing him. Minna, I think, was sleeping."

"That was Friday night," said Captain Sparrow.

He watched her dark eyes. The red firelight played on them. Her pale countenance was smooth and expressionless, but her fine hands bad begun to tremble. She picked at a pillow beside her, and turned the ring on her finger.

"The next night it came again," she said, in deepening tones. "Richard hadn't yet seen it, and I think that he didn't half believe in it. That night after dinner he went out. He was going to walk down the mountainside to the village, to play cards with some of his friends. He went out shortly after dark."

"Alone?" asked Captain Sparrow.

"Alone," said the woman. "No, the Airedale was with him. Brian Boru was frightened, that was plain. Animals have a sixth sense, people say. I don't know. But the dog must have had some premonition, for he hung back and yelped, and once he broke away from the leash in Richard's hand to come whining and crawling over the ground to me. His eyes were bloodshot, his hair was bristling up. But there was nothing to be seen except clouds in all the sky. Grandfather and I watched Richard going down the road, head up and whistling, dragging the dog behind him."

"Men don't seem to have the premonitions of animals," remarked Captain Sparrow.

Irene Hingham twisted a handkerchief with tense fingers. She made a ball of it and touched her dry lips. Captain Sparrow watched her intently, his head cocked on one side.

"Richard was down beyond the pine woods when it dove on him." she said. "He had just stopped to light his pipe. Perhaps it caught the flash of fire in the mist. The first Richard was aware of it was when he heard its wild scream above him, and looked up to see it crashing through the trees. Its wings were folded overhead, its head was stretched out and swaying, and its long hooked claws reached down to seize him where he stood—"

Captain Sparrow nodded soberly.

"He dropped—Richard dropped—no time for anything else. He rolled into a narrow gully beside the road. Screaming again, it swept over him, not two feet above his face. It was so close he could see the reddish fur which covered all its body."

Irene Hingham leaned back on the pillows of her couch. She closed her eyes. Her bosom stirred heavily. Again she put the ball of handkerchief to her lips. In a moment she had herself under better control.

"He must have been a brave man," said Captain Sparrow with soft respectfulness. "I'd not like to have been where he was."

"He was afraid of nothing." the woman whispered. "Yet I think even he was afraid of it."

Captain Sparrow examined his fingernails. His eyes were as pallid as the mist which had lain on Bald Knob mountain during that dismal night.

"He fought it off?" he said. "He saw it could be wounded—was flesh and blood like any living thing?"

"He fought it off that night—but, wounded and furious, it remembered him."

With an intensity resembling hypnosis she was staring at the fiery coals. Captain Sparrow did not alter his position to look at her, but watched her movements out of the corner of his eye.

"What more is there to tell you?" she whispered. "It may have been a madness, but it had gripped us all. The next night—Sunday night—the night before last—Richard determined to go out and face the creature once and for all. I pleaded with him. I would have gone out with him gladly, to face any death with him. But he would not have me. He was fierce and savage—he was going to slay the monster. In the twilight he went out alone to meet it."

Again Captain Sparrow examined his blunt fingernails, giving her time to compose herself.

"We went out at twilight," said Irene Hingham wearily. "We were all of us mad, perhaps. He carried a rifle with him—a big-game gun that would have blown the heart out of an elephant. We watched him going down between the poplars, hurrying to find a safe hiding place before darkness fell. We never saw Richard again."

Now Captain Sparrow turned on his neat heel, and gazed at the woman searchingly. She shook her head, shuddering, and lifted her eyes from the fire. Slowly she swung about, and like a blind person felt her way to a seat on the divan again.

"We waited hours," she said. "The night had come, without a moon. There was nothing to be seen, no sound. Richard had found concealment and was waiting, too. The thing was late in coming that night. It was sly and wise. It must have flitted through the darkness silently, knowing in its monstrous cunning brain that some danger beset it. Where it was flying, or hiding, or stalking its prey with eternal patience, we had no means of knowing. But we waited.

"What happened? We do not know for sure. Richard may have made a movement in his concealment, tired of watching and not knowing it was near. But suddenly we heard the bang! bang! of his rifle—heard him screaming: 'It's got me! It's got me!' Between the poplars we saw it rise up like a swift shadow, as though it had snatched up something from the ground, and it gave a prolonged yell of jubilation—"

"The first sound you had heard?"

"Except the rifle shots, and Richard's cry."

"Now, what sort of a sound did it make, ma'am, that you call a yell?" asked Captain Sparrow.

"It was a loud, piercing, crazy shriek of laughter," said the woman, "like no other sound I've ever heard."

Captain Sparrow nodded briefly. But it was plain he was puzzled.

"It poised a moment there between the poplars, with its wings outspread, then came swooping toward the house and shot down the slope beyond skimming low over the grass as it went by. And Richard screamed again from the air as it passed—oh, a terrible and frantic cry that froze our blood! It had him then in its claws, and was tearing him apart with beak and talons."

"But you could see, as he was carried off, that he was still alive?" said Sparrow.

"He was screaming, and was still alive."

"What next?" asked Captain Sparrow.

"I don't remember—the night passed somehow. I have not closed my eyes since then."

The moon was not yet risen at nine o'clock that night. And the sky was black—a night for hobgoblins and flitter-mice and flying things that like to remain not too clearly seen. Nimbus clouds in long billows drifted a mile above the earth, so thick that a man standing on the summit of Bald Knob mountain would have had difficulty in seeing the brighter stars.

In a fire-lit room of the Hamilcar home Captain Sparrow was speaking guardedly into the mouthpiece of a telephone:

"All right, Hicks—Yes—In about an hour—See that the plane's tanks are filled and that she's ready to take off." A brief silence filled with the distorted mumbling of the voice of William Hicks at the other end of the wire, then Captain Sparrow spoke again and his calm, quiet voice was warm with appreciation:

"You've done well. Hicks. Send Peter's men on up to the house; we may need them."

Captain Sparrow hung up and moved quietly across the shadowed room—out upon the night-shadowed porch where old man Hamilcar was waiting. He sank down into a chair beside the haggard-cheeked grandfather of Irene Hingham. A tall old man was Hamilcar, with staring black eyes and body as lean as a spider. A white point of beard quivered now like the chin whiskers of a goat as he stared curiously at the little captain.

"You've heard our story. Captain Sparrow," he said, "what do you think of us—are we both crazy?"

His voice sounded singularly loud and harsh for so old a man. He bent forward now to stare once more at the younger man, and there was the look of plain terror in the old fellow's eyes.

"I don't know that I've formed a final opinion yet," replied Captain Sparrow calmly.

"But—but you've come up to see if we're nuts?" demanded old man Hamilcar tremulously.

"No," said Sparrow. "I'm not a detective, nor a psychiatrist, either. I'm only an aviator—a man supposed to know something about the various kinds of birds and beasts—and devils that inhabit the upper air. I heard about your case from the Peters Agency—the detective firm Mrs. Hingham called up. Frankly, sir, they thought her story sounded hysterical. Since they weren't ready to send a man out on a wild-goose chase, I volunteered to come on up—partly curiosity, I'll admit."

"What do you think of it now?" asked Hamilcar.

"I haven't seen it yet," replied Captain Sparrow cautiously.

"You will tonight," old Hamilcar said with conviction. "When you do, I'll not trust your sanity any more than my own!"

"I'm always quite sane," said the captain. "We'll find an explanation somewhere."

"Eh? What do you mean?" snapped old Hamilcar.

"I mean," said Captain Sparrow, "that I don't believe you've dreamed this thing—that your mind has failed you, as you seem to fear. The thing—whatever it is—is real and dangerous. Already it has harmed you. It has given you the name of being a lunatic. If you or your granddaughter were killed tonight, whether by some diabolic thing from out the night sky or by a creeping human assassin, there is no man would bother to hound your killer down."

"Give a dog a bad name before you hang him, eh?" said old Hamilcar grimly. "You have a keen idea, young man. what this devilish thing may be—Tell me."

He eyed Sparrow keenly.

"If I told you," said Sparrow, "you'd think me crazy, myself." He threw back his head and laughed silently. "I've telephoned for a guard of men from the Peters agency who don't believe in devils," he said. "They will be here before another hour."

"And you, sir—what do you propose doing?" asked Hamilcar.

Captain Sparrow clasped his hands behind him and stood very erect. "I intend, sir," he said, "to meet the. . ."

But old man Hamilcar never heard the finish of that brave speech, for the captain cut short his words on a suddenly gasped breath. Rising shrill and terrible on the silent winds of night, there came a long-drawn, awesome shriek as of a soul in agony.

Captain Sparrow, though he was a brave man, felt the cold fingers of fear crawling against the skin of his back before that terribly weird and hopeless cry died suddenly away in the midst of its own grim echoes.

Then, disregarding the trembling old man, he had leaped the low rail of the veranda and was racing out across the smooth-rolled lawn—reckless of the horrible death that might there await him. High above him, as he reached the gates and passed through them, he caught the dim shadow of outspread wings, saw for a brief instant two searching eyes of burning crimson. Then he was in the hard-rutted road, speeding downward through the darkness, on his way to William Hicks and the plane that was held in readiness against his coming. In a very few minutes now he'd learn which was the greater flying devil—himself or the Crimson Bat!

## III

High in the empty night above Bald Knob mountain. Captain Sparrow glided silently. Far below him, the clustered lights of the valley village twinkled faintly, but up there in the quiet darkness of the overcast sky his sharp eyes could catch no slightest shadow of stealthy movement. Above Bald Knob he hung, poised like some swift, unseen midge, waiting patiently to hop upon whatever flying fiend might drop from the rolling blanket of smoky cloud above him.

A mile above the earth the night was sharp, and a stiff west wind rushed swiftly through the night. Down at the three thousand-foot level Sparrow knew that only a small breeze was stirring, but up at his own level the wind was so strong and steady that his stub-winged little Vought, heading into it at half throttle, hung directly above Bald Knob without visible motion, caught on a sky hook. There he remained, watchful and unseen in the dark night, and the turning world was motionless below him.

Gone from the sky was the creature with shadow wings and crimson eyes. To Sparrow it seemed that he held the night alone, yet less than an hour before his own eyes had visioned the grotesque shape of the Crimson Bat; his own ears had rung with the shrill wail of the diving monster. Alone now in all the sky, the little captain clung grimly to his vigil.

But a strange feeling of uneasiness was coming over him. The night was *too* quiet, too calm and peaceful. Out of its very silence his straining ears conjured the stealthy beat of feathered wings. He could understand now, alone in the night sky, the panic that had been Irene Hingham's. He could sympathize with old man Hamilcar's fear.

Ten minutes passed, and Captain Sparrow felt a touch of ice on the back of his neck, as a vaporous shadow cut across the faint stars to the east. He swallowed hard, banked uneasily to gain further altitude. The shadow was gone—a heavier cloud that had drifted by into the night. That was all. The little man sighed his relief and once more cut the motor to half speed. But the wind, sweeping through his uncovered hair, tingled his scalp with needles of cold.

Dimly he felt the near presence of another creature of the air. Somewhere above him, he was now sure, some other living thing was poised behind the cloud murk, watching the mountain top with eager eyes.

Once more, impatient of his vigil, the little captain zoomed upward, cutting the lower layer of cloud. Would the creature ever return? Would his night flight, after all, prove in vain? But he could not hold such doubts for long. He had seen it with his own eyes. He knew, so he believed, the explanation of its being. He knew its purpose, knew the scheming of its cunning and malignant brain. It had set out to harry the old man and the woman to insanity. That failing, it would kill them fiendishly.

The lowering cloud wrapped about him. He snapped his engine switch, feeling his way down toward the clear air below. Now he could see nothing. So suddenly dark was it, that he could not see the lights of the tiny towns below him, nor the faint flare of stars above him—nor even the engine head before him. But in that brief moment when the ship still lingered within the cloud, Captain Sparrow heard a sound that bristled the hair on his head.

A scream it was, a shriek like a wild and rumbling laugh—and it echoed from the darkness close above him. A vast shadow plunged downward through the clearing air, diving from out the empty wastes above the world, its horrid cry shattering the night.

Then silence, as the creature passed not twenty feet before his ship, a shadowy, bat-winged monster, streaking vertically down the caverns of the night. Its bottom side, or belly, was turned toward him, and Captain Sparrow breathed a sigh of relief that it could not see him. Swift as a falling rocket, it passed by, with the form of its stiff wings like a shadow on the mist.

Sparrow's fist was frozen to the control stick. His legs were pressed like rods against the rudder bar. The unexpectedness of the creature's coming, the unearthly fierceness in that wild shriek, had left him for the moment utterly incapable of movement. As stiff as an ice statue he sat. while his ship dropped off in a slow glide through the foggy billows of the lower clouds. Presently he shuddered, filling his lungs with a great draft of the cool night air.

"Like a bat," he whispered. It had passed him by, but for long moments his flesh would still feel cold, his scalp would still crawl.

Then, quite suddenly, the little captain was laughing. A hard sound it was—and angry. Pale eyes slitted, he shoved the stick far forward, dived headlong down through the whistling night. His heart was roaring.

The taut guy wires sang in the racing wind. His body was flattened against the back of the seat. Once more the air was sucked from his lungs. Blood swept to his head, and blind spots danced before his eyes. Yet he still rushed down through the darkness.

Then, when it seemed that a sudden check must tear the wings from the racing body of the little ship, Captain Sparrow hauled up its nose like the tail of a figure J. Wings groaning, the little Vought twisted up out of that breathless dive, and the captain kicked right rudder and sent her tumbling over into a spin. It was rough treatment for the ship he loved, but down there below him the Crimson Bat was diving upon Bald Knob mountain. He must follow him down, must close with him, must drive him for all time from the air.

At a thousand feet he leveled off, and at the same instant caught sight of the howling thing just below him. It was soaring on long and rigid wings but a little way above the lighted house. For the moment it made no sound.

Instinctively Captain Sparrow cut his engine and glided with the wind. Now he was but eight hundred feet above the mountain top. Now he was down to five—now three. He leveled his ship. Powerless, it fell off on one wing. He righted it, but it slipped away on the other. Right and left, swaying like a pendulum, it drifted like a falling leaf, dropping down toward the shadowed fields.

He was near enough now to see the glowing, crimson eyes of the thing that flitted about the house. Handling his ship with sensitive hand, he watched its every sweep and dive. He started, as once more that weird shriek swept through the night. Stiff-winged, the howler swooped low across the house roof. It seemed almost to touch. Above the poplar trees it turned, wafted upward, lifted by the warm currents of air which flowed up the mountain slope. Recovering now from his first terror at the thing's horrible voice, Captain Sparrow watched it through narrowed, speculative eyes. He banked above it, staring down from his swaying cockpit. And presently his brow cleared, and a hard little smile twisted his thin lips. The mystery of the Crimson Bat was satisfactorily explained—for the dim shade that glided beneath him, motor dead as his own, was a monoplane! Jaw set at a fighting angle, Captain Sparrow nosed his ship down out of the night.

## IV

Drifting down on that unsuspecting monoplane, Captain Sparrow laughed silently—bitterly and without mercy. He was above it, had the upper hand of it. And he wasn't afraid of it now. It was, after all, only a thing of wood and metal, captained by a pilot as human as he. He could even understand that howling voice—a mechanical whistle probably, so rigged that the wind, shrieking through it, would produce that wild tone and huge volume, and so adjusted that it could be turned on and off at will. A simple mechanical trick it was, nothing more.

The other devices of horror, the glowing eyes, the bat-shaped wings, the pointed ears, he had already reasoned out. These shining eyes would be two crimson searchlights on either side of the propeller hub, the bat wings a rim of scalloped material on the edges of the monoplane's true wings.

But Captain Sparrow realized, as he swept downward, that were he on the earth below, he would not look so contemptuously at the "Crimson Bat." For it was, in truth, a devilish thing, of evil devising. Once more it howled its empty cry and fled over the rooftree of the house.

Its pilot had not yet seen the biplane dropping so quietly down from above. Now was the time to strike! Without further hesitation, Captain Sparrow pushed the nose of his ship over and dove like a bullet on the tail of the Crimson Bat.

Wings whistling, he shot above the monoplane, missing its wings by a scant ten feet. Head craned far out from his cockpit, he glimpsed for a moment the white, upturned face of the other pilot.

Lips tight-pressed, the little captain motioned the monoplane toward the ground. The surprised terror in that upturned face below him was plain to the angry Sparrow.

Abruptly he switched on his engine and gave the ship full throttle. With a roar that splintered the silence, the engine caught. He zoomed upward, saw the earth drop away below him. The biplane's nose was pointed toward the clouded stars. With a jerk he snapped the ship over on its back.

At the crest of the loop he cut his engine. He heard the silence, the ringing, screaming silence. He slipped on one wing, knifing downward through the air. Once more he was behind the helpless monoplane—and above it. Down he hurtled, like a thunderbolt from the blue.

"Make a landing, or I'll rip your tail off!" he roared above the whistling wind.

But the terrified pilot of the Crimson Bat had opened up his engine, was trying desperately to climb away from the Vought. Straight up he rose, almost stalling in the steepness of his flight. But the monoplane had no such speed, no such maneuverability as that swift, two-winged ship that rolled and streaked above it. The frightened pilot was climbing it too steeply. It wavered in mid flight, and again Captain Sparrow caught a brief glimpse of that white, terror-stricken face.

The night prowler was flying recklessly, taking desperate chances to elude his pursuer. He Immelmanned, but the captain spun about with him, once more swept upward like a rocket, to come sweeping back across the tail of the Crimson Bat. Engine silenced, he nosed up slightly, flattened across the other's tail—dragged his ship to a stall. His speed slackened. He pancaked down on the monoplane that drifted below. He was mercilessly determined to knock it down from the air.

His wheel had struck the monoplane a glancing, downward blow on the left wing. There had been no force to it, for that would have sent his own ship crashing down with the other. But it had been enough to knock the Crimson Bat out of the air. It would fly no more with its howling voice, its horrid eyes, its wide, hobgoblin wings.

It fell into a flat spin. Twice its wings went around. Then upon the somber earth it crashed with a thundering roar—in the meadows down by the apple orchards, at the far end of the mountain crest. From the first impact it bounced, and crashed down again. Its wings crumpled like paper in a man's hand. Its tail snapped off. The scalloped sheets which had given its wings their bat appearance fell off like rain-gutters from a toppling house.

Like a falcon to the strike Captain Sparrow came down. The meadows swept up to meet him, indiscernible and black. He opened the engine throttle part way, stalling down to a landing by feel, with bow high and tail dragging. Then he knew he had met the ground. The tail skid was bumping over grassy hummocks and the wheels had begun to roll. Swiftly he taxied over close-clipped meadows toward the wreck.

Out of the great lighted mansion a quarter mile behind him he heard the shouting of men. Peters' men were on the job. Their circling flashlights came like fireflies across the meadows.

Out of the crumpled wreckage a dark form arose.

The fugitive had taken stand on the open meadow. His legs were straddled wide, he shook his head warningly and shouted some indistinguishable word. Then his right arm swept upward, and he emptied a revolver point blank at Captain Sparrow.

Echoes yelled. Sparrow saw that pointed arm not twenty paces in front of him, jerking with the recoil and leveling again. Lead pinged on the propeller cap, and caromed off. A hot streak seared Sparrow's face, and there was a blow against his thigh. He felt no pain of it, but when he pressed his hand on it, it grew sticky and wet.

Shouting again, the man on the ground hurled his empty weapon from him, and turned to run.

Springing to his feet, Captain Sparrow tried to leap to the ground in pursuit. But his wounded leg crumpled beneath him and he slumped back in the cockpit, suddenly dizzy with pain. Teeth clamped, he opened up his engine. The heavy propeller swept like a sickle at her nose. Swaying at the controls, he drove across the ground after that running figure, which sprawled and stumbled in desperate haste, making toward the stone wall and the deep woods beyond.

"Stop!" shouted Captain Sparrow, striving to lift his voice above the engine's clamor. "Stand where you are!" he gasped, feeling sick and faint. "Stop—or I'll run you down and carve you to mincemeat."

The runner stumbled. Flinging his arms overhead, he sprawled forward on his face. Frantically he scrambled to his knees, but Captain Sparrow was behind him. On his knees the fugitive stayed, as though in prayer to Captain Sparrow or whatever were his patron fiends. The bright half moon was coming up. It flooded the crest of the mountain with wan light. The pallid face, the writhing lips, the popping black eyes of the man who had driven the Crimson Bat were lustrous beneath the moon.

"What do you want?" he croaked. "What do you want of me, you flying fool?"

Captain Sparrow poked his sagging head overside. The blindness was coming over him, and his loins were drenched with his own warm blood. But still he kept his hand on the throttle of the ship he knew and loved so well.

"I want you," he gasped, "for clubbing a poor Airedale dog to death last Saturday night. I want you for spreading lies about old Hamilcar and Irene Hingham, till the whole world believed they were crazy. I want you," he said, "for trying to terrify them into the madhouse or their graves, so you could get your claws on Hamilcar's money. I want you for the black determination in your heart to kill them in their beds if they did not succumb to your madness. But most of all I want you," he said with a deep, triumphant breath, "for thinking you were a greater flying devil than Captain Sparrow!"

He labored heavily. The blindness was creeping over him. The darkness rose and roared about him like the darkness of a great salt sea.

"Stay on your knees!" he said. "I've done my work. But here come the men to get you, Richard Hingham!"

That night Captain Sparrow lay in bed in the best guest suite on Bald Knob. The doctor in attendance on Irene Hingham had bound up the wound in his thigh. The shot had missed the great artery and the thigh bone, yet it would be many days before he would again streak through the air in his swift craft.

Old man Hamilcar sat grimly beside the man who had brought an end to the weird flights of the Crimson Bat. His fierce old face was knotted up with wrinkles. His glittering black eyes stared, unblinkingly, at Sparrow. The fear was no longer in them, for he had proved to himself that he was sane—and, with that knowledge, a man need be afraid of nothing.

"How did you know?" he asked.

"Richard Hingham was the only person who might have derived benefit from your insanity or death." said Sparrow quietly. "At the very first I suspected him—last night, even, when I talked with William Hicks. Hicks is a talkative youth, and Hingham had filled him with fantastic lies. My suspicions became almost a certainty in my own mind when I learned that he had been patiently and cunningly isolating you from all human contacts. Then, too, he was a chauffeur; it's not a far jump from piloting an automobile to piloting an airplane.

"These facts aroused my suspicions. Then when I learned that neither you nor Mrs. Hingham had seen the Bat and Richard at the same time—though neither of you seemed to realize this—then I had no more suspicions. I *knew!*

"On that first Thursday night Mrs. Hingham was at the theater several hours. She *thought* her husband was at his lawyer's. She'd probably have sworn to it as a fact. But during those hours it would have been easy enough for him to fly up to Bald Knob, pay you a little visit of horror, and return for supper with Mrs. Hingham. On the next night—Friday—when she saw the Bat for the first time, Richard Hingham was not in view; he'd broken down on the road, he said. And on Saturday night it was Hingham, alone, who claimed to have seen the Bat. He had a broken walking stick and a dead dog to show for his encounter—and a description of the creature's appearance much more detailed, and impossible, than any you had given as your own observation.

"When Richard Hingham stepped out the door on Sunday night with a gun, you never doubted the reality of the terror he was going out to meet. Hours passed—hours to increase your frenzy and your fear. And they gave Hingham time to get his quick little monoplane and come flying back over the trees."

Captain Sparrow smiled at the intent old man, lighted a cigarette.

"What did you hear?" he asked. "You heard a gun go off. But he could have shot it from the air. You heard him shrieking. But he could have shrieked from the air. What did you see? You saw the plane come sweeping over the poplars, rising on the warm air currents from the valley, and drifting toward you. You may have thought you saw Hingham—for you were listening to his yells from the air.

"The next day you found a broken gun; he'd thrown it from the ship. You found his torn shirt where he'd dropped it in the poplar branches, soaked with the blood of the dog he'd clubbed to death the night before."

Sparrow paused and laughed. Old Hamilcar stared at him with glittering eyes. Slowly the old man nodded. Like a man just awakening, he nodded his scraggly head.

"His plan," said Captain Sparrow quietly, "was to continue his night visits until you'd both become screaming maniacs. . . If that plan failed, there's no question but that he'd have murdered you in your beds. He would have been safe enough; you had told an impossible story of his disappearance; you were thought to be lunatics."

Sparrow closed his eyes, still grinning. Old Hamilcar muttered deep in his throat. He pulled at his sliver of beard.

"How did you know the Bat was not a creature of the air—no matter what suspicions you might have had of Richard?" the old man asked.

Sparrow smiled patiently. "I've flown up and down the air, sir —east and west and crossways," he said. "I've flown through mountains and over the big blue pond. I've flown half a million miles, I guess, and I've seen everything that flies—But I've never yet seen a flying thing—bigger than a buzzard—*that wasn't a man-made ship!"*

# MURDER OF THE DEAD MAN

## CHAPTER I

## THE DEAD MAN WALTZ

SLOWLY AND WAVERINGLY in the night silence, the tropic heat, the dead man came creeping along the dimly lit rear corridor of the Royal Tarpon's top floor, towards the room where Hilton Bannerwell was sleeping. *Creak creak creak* he came along the green matting runner, the brightly varnished floorboards complaining faintly beneath his slow, fumbling feet in the hushed midnight stillness. His face was white with a clammy sweat. The pupils of his eyes were dilated and rolled upwards. His lungs were strangling. Yet he made no sound, except for the creaking of his feet, as he moved down the deserted corridor towards Hilt Bannerwell's door, with his hand upon the wall.

He carried his coat, a white sport jacket, dragging from one dead hand. His silk shirt collar was torn wide open on his heaving chest. In life he had been a strong man, big and blond, with shining eyes full of laughter, of health and vitality, with a ruddy face. But now he was a dead man.

He had rounded two turns of the corridor or the great four-square winter pleasure hotel, from the front wing into the empty south wing, and now into the west wing at the back. Last turn to make. Endless steps. Past rows of locked and empty doors.

One hour after midnight. Far off a clock struck with an unending note, with a *bong-g-g* that trembled and trembled, like the timeless strike of eternity.

Perhaps it was. No clock, but that, the Fatal Hour. For him sounding. Everlastingly.

He was a dead man, and he knew it. This strangled, poisoned death had got him, him who had been a live man, strong and buoyant, five minutes ago. Five minutes ago. Within a time so short as that the terrible snake venom had rushed from the two tiny blue pinpricks on his wrist into every nerve and limb with its dark hellish fire. The swift abominable poison was flooding his heart with every surge and beat.

Here, in this quiet place. This rich and quiet pleasure hotel, on Florida's silken coast. Here he was dead as men die in the jungle, while far off music blared; and people laughed and danced, played at cards, counted money.

Nothing could save him, bring him back to life. He was dead, he was dead. Oh, God! The sweat budded out on his cold face. His muscles were already stiffening in the rigidity of death. He was dead, he was dead! A dead man five years in the ground was not more dead than he.

There was that one last glimmering spot of consciousness still amidst the breakdown and dissolution of his mind. Still in him struggled, in the despair of hell, this everlasting will.

He must reach Hilt Bannerwell's room . . . an anti-venine . . . Hilt was a doctor . . . should be able to do something . . . He had started out to reach Hilt quickly and at once . . . Too late, too late . . .

He paused. He swayed, suffocating, reeling, clinging to the wall. He rubbed a slow blind hand over his sweating forehead.

"Hilt! Hilt!" his strangling throat struggled horribly to shout. But no sound he made. He was on his hands and knees.

No one would realize the fiendish thing that had happened. A tragic accident, Hilt would say with horror, making the autopsy of him when they had found him. Somehow he had had an encounter with one of the cold deadly creepers of the swamps, Hilt and everyone would say. A great Florida diamondback, the most vicious of its breed, or else an even more venomous coral snake, the deadliest of them all, had done for him. An accident terrible and rare, but not unique. So it would seem to Hilt and everyone. But he wanted to tell Hilt Bannerwell that it had been no accident . . . that he had been murdered . . .

Only eight steps more . . . knees buckling . . . could not move . . . he was falling here . . . now . . . this was . . . silence . . . death . . . forever after . . . but he wanted to tell Hilt he had . . . been murdered . . .

Oh, cards and dice! Lorraine Somers' unforgotten lovely face! Rita's scarlet lips that were a stab, a flame. The bright sweet Dutch Indies orange brandy of Digger Jeffries. Music, and flowers in darkness. All the loveliness and glory of this earth. No more . . . He must tell Hilt . . .murdered . . .

Suddenly, in the hot stuffy darkness of his remote and lonely resident physician's bedroom, on the top floor of the Royal Tarpon's rear wing, Dr. Hilton Bannerwell sat up in bed with an affrighted jerk.

"Yes?" his dry lips moved soundlessly.

For an instant the slender, dark young hotel medico sat staring into the quietness, a little confused and bewildered. Silence, except for the whirring of the fan on his bureau and the blaring of that radio from the front wing of the great hotel across the quad, which had been playing dance tunes for an hour.

He hadn't realized that he had been asleep at all. The sultry late April night had seemed too hot and oppressive for any rest. There was the shadow of some ghastly nightmare in his brain now, and he had awakened with nerves twitching and on edge. There had been no sound he could remember which had so suddenly startled him, but the sweat was over him, and something impelled him to get up now.

With dripping lean-ribbed torso, clad in pajama trousers only, Hilt swung his legs over the edge of his bed and slipped his feet into straw beach sandals. Stumbling, he arose and crossed to his bureau. In the darkness he found his ice carafe and a bottle of Bacardi still half full. He mixed himself a stiff drink, squeezing in half a lime.

"Damn that radio!" he muttered with quiet fury.

He had first lain down on his bed at eleven. It was a few minutes after one o'clock now, the luminous hands of his wrist watch showed. He could not sleep again.

He did not bother to turn on his room lights. He had left his shutter door wide open onto the dimly lit and deserted corridor before lying down, in the vain hope of a little more ventilation, but the shadows which came in only served to make the stillness and heat more tangible. Sluggishly the fan on his bureau whirred, and revolved to the right. Whirred, and revolved to the left. With a monotonous and irritating drone.

Glass in hand, he moved to his window. He stood there a moment while he swallowed the strong rum steadily and rolled the coldness around his tongue. There was an itching on his left side just beneath his heart which felt like a mosquito bite, and he scratched it. With relief, if not with any particular elation, he felt the alcohol weighting his limbs and blurring the sharp edge of his nerves. If he took enough he might get some sleep, when that radio ever stopped.

Moonlight flooded the farther half of the tropical gardens which filled the hotel quad in front of him, in the silver shadows four stories below. A hundred feet away across the quad the Royal Tarpon's front wing, its yellow clapboards, iron-railed Spanish balconies, and long door-windows, stood washed in the moon whiteness. Millionaires' Row, the front wing was called.

The season was late, the great hotel no more than a quarter filled. Most of the windows in Millionaires' Row were closed and dark now, untenanted. Only two or three of the suites on the top floor opposite were still occupied—that one directly across from Hilt where the party was going on, with windows wide open and lights blazing and half a dozen figures weaving around to the music of the radio, and another suite to the left of that with lighted windows closed and shades pulled down and quietness in it, and a third suite to the right which was dark except for the intruding moonlight through its open balcony windows, but a white-clad dimly glimpsed woman's figure to be seen at intervals moving about inside with the restlessness of insomnia . . .

Voices, shouts of laughter, once the clash of a bottle or a broken pane of glass, had been echoing across the quad from the middle suite since midnight or earlier, mingled with the crooning and wa-waing of that infernal radio. Hilt glimpsed figures passing as he stood and downed his drink. A tall bald-headed man in white mess jacket dancing with a tall, limber, red-haired woman in green. A paunchy man in linen knickerbockers and yellow polo shirt, staggering around with a bottle. A short, pompous man in formal evening clothes, with round horn-rimmed glasses and a stiff pompadour of black shoe-brush hair, strutting by with hands clasped behind him beneath the tails of his coat, like a penguin. A woman in coolie coat and pajamas, with a white flower in her midnight hair. The big bald-headed man in the mess jacket again, in a moment more, dancing this time with a dumpy brown-haired woman in yellow, about whose throat something striped red and yellow lay circled, like a glittering, poisonous snake.

A necklace, of course. Rubies and yellow diamonds, perhaps. Or garnets and topazes. Only a necklace of bright stones. But a repulsively beautiful thing. Like the bright harlequin, the rare and deadly Florida coral snake, which its glittering coils had seemed for an instant to be.

He rubbed the mosquito bite on his left ribs. He tried to recall what had impelled him to get up. Not the heat altogether. There had been something else. Not that damned radio, either. Something had happened which had caused him suddenly to get up.

Idiotically and maddeningly the banal radio tune blared on, with a discordance of saxophone, a calf-voiced crooner bleating.

"Yah!" he gargled with a jeer, quoting from memory Smiler Dunbar's alluring word-picture which had drawn him down to take this winter berth. "A hundred and fifty smackers a month, the life of Riley in one of Florida's swankiest joints, plenty of chances for valuable professional experience . . ."

Smiler Dunbar, the big hound, was probably over there right now. Wherever the drinks and the music and the girls were, there Smiler was generally to be found. Big, blond, easygoing, and handsome as a movie hero.

Smiler was the only friend, almost the only person the lonely young physician so much as knew by name, in all the great hotel. The big blond fellow was social director of the Royal Tarpon. Smiler had always been a smoothie, from the time Hilt had first known him back in Yale eight or nine years ago. His sole ambition was to get the maximum fun he could out of life with the minimum amount of toil. Since flunking out of college in sophomore year Smiler had been pursuing the butterfly life as best he could manage in settings of wealth and luxury, now at this soft berth on Florida's gilded coast. Smiler belonged to all this sort of thing as a fish belongs to deep wet water. But it was all just a gob of mud in Hilt's own eye.

Yale A.B. '27, Harvard Med '31, both *magna cum laude.* Two years of interne work in Post Graduate, specializing in neurology. Walking the streets of New York last fall with a dime in his pockets, looking for a berth. Bumping into Smiler, tanned and beaming, on Broadway. Come on down, Smiler had urged him. Florida. The tropics . . .

It was a laugh. Official pill-pusher in a tinsel winter fairyland. But the patrons of the Royal Tarpon, he had speedily learned, regarded a resident physician as a kind of servant one degree above a bellhop. To hell with them.

Sweltering in the airless heat of his rear wing room. Bored and lonely. Swigging rum to deaden his nerves and put him back to sleep.

Why had he waked up, anyway? Nothing had happened. Nothing was about to happen. Nothing ever would happen at the Royal Tarpon.

Profanely he stirred himself another stiff hooker of rum and ice at his bureau, finishing the bottle. That first one had helped. It had made him feel numb and fuzzy, though not gay. A couple more good heavy slugs ought to put him under. In the last month or so he had been going at it rather heavily, he suspected. Smiler Dunbar had suggested as much to him only this morning. Though Smiler was a fine one to talk.

"Getting yourself a rep, Hilt," Smiler had told him only this morning. "Somebody saw you carting up a couple of bottles in the front elevator the other day, it seems, and they've started a rumor that you're a secret dipsomaniac. Holding regular sessions of the d.t.'s with yourself. Counting pink elephants."

So that was the kind of a reputation he had got by keeping to himself.

Old Smiler. He was damned fond of Smiler. They were so antithetical they had always got along. He would go through hell for Smiler, the big useless hound. And Smiler would do the same for him, he hoped.

Suddenly, as he stood there in the darkness in front of his bureau with the cold drink to his lips, the young physician had a queer, giddy feeling that Smiler had come softly into the room with him. Smiler's hand, as light as silk, lying for an instant on his shoulder. Smiler's big tanned friendly face. Beside him. In the breathless darkness. But no one.

No one. Only the whirring of his fan in movement. Only the vague masses of his room furnishings to be seen. This stuff was hitting him. The sweat on his body felt cold.

Why had he waked up in the stifling night? Why so breathless and strangled now? There had been a voice within his ears, a cry. Like the voice of a far-off bell. A feeling of crawling silk. A horror in his flesh.

Vainly he wrestled to recapture the memory of that tossing nightmare from which he had awakened on his bed, and a voice crying out in his ears of his own death as he lay there, and the sweat over him . . .

Moved by some unconscious impulse, he felt his way to his door, shuffling over the grass rug in his straw sandals, avoiding the dim shapes of remembered chairs obstructing his path. He emptied his glass, and stood at his door peering forth into the corridor. White walls, green grass floor runner, closed doors, six wall lights at intervals of twenty feet. That was all.

Whom or what he had expected to see he didn't know. He had no word for it. But the corridor was empty. No one there.

## CHAPTER II

## HILT SEES A MURDERER

OUT ON THE iron-grilled Spanish balcony of the party suite opposite the tall, bald man in the white mess jacket and black trousers whom Hilt had glimpsed dancing inside when he first arose was standing now, smoking a cigarette. In the white lustrous moonlight Mess Jacket's concave bony face was pale as a skull's, his egg head shaved and naked. His face twitched as he smoked. He half turned, glancing around him at the glass doors through which he had come. His right hand came out of his trousers pocket and he lifted his left hand, seeming to slide back the cuff as if tightening the strap of a wrist watch. He dropped something in his fist over the balcony rail. Bracing his broad shoulders, he turned and went back in.

Presently another of the party guests strolled out. The short shoe-brush-haired man in evening clothes, this time. Black and white like a strutting penguin. His horn-rimmed glasses reflected the moonlight, shining like the eyes of an owl. Penguin surveyed the fair night sky with hands clasped behind him, rocking on his toes. His hands came up presently, and he took something out of his inner breast pocket with deliberation. A flash of silver. He squeezed something between his thumb and forefinger firmly and carefully, with a rolling motion, and dropped it over the balcony rail. Then he was putting a cigar into his mouth, and lifting up a foot to strike a match on his heel. Clasping his hands together again beneath the tails of his coat, blowing Havana smoke contentedly, Penguin in turn reentered through the glass doors.

It was only a moment afterwards, it seemed to Hilt, when yet a third man was out on the balcony across there. This last man slipped out rather briefly from the dancing floor, and was outside only an instant. Long enough, however, for the picture of him to be clear. It was the same gray-haired, purple-faced man who had been reeling around inside with a bottle, his paunchy figure garbed in crumpled white knickerbockers and a short-sleeved sport shirt, with a wide belt that looked like mottled silk around his squashy middle. He was glancing over his shoulder as he came quickly and deftly out. His hand went over the balcony rail as if dropping a cigarette ash. He turned at once, and went back in.

That was all.

Hilt Bannerwell rubbed the palm of his hand over his dripping chest. Sweat crawling down his spine. Meaningless pantomime of three men on a balcony. Against the black mass of the rear wing, on the moonless side of the quad, his little window and himself standing at it were as invisible as ink, he believed. None of those three men had supposed himself observed by anyone.

It was a little comic. The way each one of these three in turn, quickly or methodically or casually, had made the same gesture of dropping something over the rail.

The twitching face of Mess Jacket as he looked at his wrist watch, if that was what he had done. The glaring spectacled eyes of Penguin as he had surveyed the gardens below him. The broad glistening belt which had been shinier than mottled silk around Purple Face's middle, a belt not silk, but more like mica, or like sequins of colored steel.

No, it hadn't been silk, of course. It had been a snakeskin belt, a great Florida diamondback. The Seminoles of the swamp country made those belts. They were on sale, Hilt remembered now, in the curio shop on Beach Avenue. Queer tastes some people had. To wear a slimy crawling thing like that around one's body!

Again there had risen the shadowy horror of his forgotten nightmare to bring the sweat out on him. An eerie sense of terror.

He almost had that forgotten dream a moment! Wait!. . . No, he had lost it. The horror of that dream! A man who wore a snakeskin belt around his middle.

That gaudy necklace of rubies and yellow diamonds, if that was what it had been, which the dumpy woman in yellow had been wearing around her throat in glittering coils, over there dancing! Harlequin, the coral snake, the rare bright Florida cobra. The woman in yellow was no longer wearing that string of barbaric gems now, he was glad to see, as her plump and middle-aged figure came into view again through the French windows, strolling and chatting gaily with Penguin, the man in the dress suit.

That infernal radio! He couldn't stand it any longer. He'd go over there with an empty bottle in a minute and crack a few of their brainless heads.

Smiler wasn't over there. He had seen everyone in the party suite, he felt sure. There were only five. The woman in the coolie coat with the flower in her hair had gone. The three men and the two women were all. The dumpy woman in yellow and the tall red-haired woman in green. He snatched up his phone furiously, calling Smiler.

"Smiler, this is Hilt!' he raved, to the voice which answered him in a few moments. "For God's sake, can't you pipe down on those half-witted whoopee-lovers in the suite across from me?"

"This is Clarence Durkee, the night desk clerk, sir. Is this Dr. Bannerwell? Mr. Dunbar isn't here, Doctor. The party in the Ambassador suite, you mean?"

"That's the joint, Durkee! There's a limit to everything! It's after one o'clock—"

Durkee laughed soothingly.

"That's Mr. and Mrs. Wellington Jeffries' suite. Mr. Digger Jeffries, as he likes to have you call him, the multi-millionaire Australian copper king. Mrs. Jeffries was Adelaide Deacon of the Philadelphia Deacons, who owns a big chunk of this hotel. The Jeffries belong to that big white baby liner, the *Stella Australis*, that's lying out beyond the breakwater. They're just having a farewell party for their friends. It probably sounds much louder on your side than it really is. Anyway, you can't very well crack down on people like that."

"Is Digger Jeffries," demanded Hilt irritably, "that gray-haired tub of lard with the rum-blossom nose and the purple face, prancing around in a yellow shirt? I don't care how many yachts he has."

"Your description sounds a little like Mr. Chance, I'm afraid," said Durkee with a discreet laugh. "Alfred Merton Chance, the well known mystery writer, Doctor. Mr. Chance has just come back from an auto-camping trip through the Everglades, where he's been gathering material for a new mystery he's going to stage down here. Mr. Jeffries is a big bald-headed man."

"Mess Jacket is the Anzac millionaire, is he? And Purple Face is an author. Who's Penguin, the governor of the Federal Reserve Bank?"

"Penguin, Doctor?"

"I was wondering who the other one of the three sisters was. The pompous twirp in soup-to-fish, with the big owl glasses."

"That's probably Professor Stumpfwasser you mean, Doctor. He and Mrs. Stumpfwasser have the suite on the third floor just below the Jeffries'. He comes from Berlin. They say he's a very distinguished scientist in his own line."

"Stumpfwasser, the German herpetologist?"

"I don't know about that. He's a reptile authority, Doctor. Been making a study of the snakes of Florida."

"That's what I meant by herpetologist. I've got a book of his."

"Yes, that's what the prof is. He's got a wife who's the best looking redheaded woman you ever saw, Doctor. Rita. Kind of Spanish. Mr. Dunbar has been giving her plenty of rush, and he knows how to pick 'em."

"Smiler isn't there now," said Hilt.

"Then he must be still playing poker with Mr. Camponello, Doctor."

"Who's Camponello?"

"Mr. John P. Camponello. Why, he's from St. Louis. He's"—Durkee's smooth well-trained voice hesitated slightly—"well, some people say that he's a regular gunman, Doctor. A kind of self-made, not very polished type, I will say that about him. But about his being a gunman, I don't know. I never asked him. Maybe he's just a politician. He's got the suite next to the Jeffries', and he plays poker for pretty big money. He took Digger Jeffries for an awful loop, they tell me. And some more of the boys with big wads. Mr. Dunbar got started there in a game about eight o'clock, and he must be still at it."

"The suite to the left, to the north, of Jeffries'?"

"That's it."

As he held his phone at his window, talking with Durkee, the young physician had seen the shade-covered windows pushed open in the quiet lighted suite to the left of the party suite. For a moment a coatless man with hairy forearms, wearing a green eyeshade, had been standing there in the window opening. Behind him, in a living-room hazy with tobacco smoke, a brass-haired woman in black was sitting idly shuffling cards at a table on which bottles and glasses glinted. The man at the window had turned now, and gone back to the woman. He was bent over the card table, conversing with her, while she shook her bent head and shuffled cards. The hairy man seemed to have some object in his hand like a short piece of pipe or a heavy monkey-wrench and he was tapping it slowly on the table for emphasis, while he talked. The woman, sitting stiff-faced, a woman of wood, doggedly shook her bent head again while she continued shuffling cards.

Like two figures dimly seen through glass they appeared in the smoky room. Mr. John Camponello talking to Mrs. Camponello, presumably. The poker game had broken up. Only the two of them.

"Smiler isn't in Camponello's suite now," stated the young physician.

"Well, that's funny," said Durkee in a witless voice. "He hasn't come downstairs. He must be somewhere."

"There's another suite occupied over in Millionaires' Row," suggested Hilt. "Maybe Smiler's there."

"No, that's Miss Lorraine Somers' suite. She just arrived from California at nine o'clock this evening by plane. She's tired out and gone to bed."

"Lorraine Somers?"

"The movie actress, Doctor. She's the niece of Mrs. Jeffries. She's going to join them on their yacht when they sail for the Antipodes. Mr. Dunbar has told me he used to know her in Hollywood. He was counting on seeing her at the Jeffries' party tonight, too."

That damned wa-waing radio! A burst of laughter, shrill and giddy, a woman's.

"How long does this party of Jeffries keep up, Durkee?"

"Their yacht is scheduled to head out at five o'clock this morning for Panama, Doctor. I don't know, but I suppose they'll be more or less celebrating and telling their friends goodbye till sailing time."

"There'll be somebody dead if they don't stop before then, Durkee," Hilt promised savagely. "You can put it down in your book I told you so."

With a jerking hand Hilt slammed the receiver up, cutting off Durkee's squeak of protest and alarm. Probably Durkee thought he was bottle-screwy, too. Maybe he was. He leaned over his bureau, staring at his dark hollow-eyed reflection in the obscure silver of the mirror.

He did look drunk. Clammy and sick. With ghastly paleness, sweating and drawn, his own face stared back at him from the dim refulgence like the face of a dead man. Like a ghost.

To the right of the party suite, through the open windows of that quiet darkened room, the white-clad figure of a girl was stepping out onto her balcony. It was she whom Hilt had obscurely glimpsed at intervals stirring back and forth sleeplessly inside her room. Lorraine Somers.

Durkee had been wrong. The blond movie star in that third suite of Millionaires' Row had not been asleep.

## CHAPTER III

## THE THING IN THE DARKNESS

Half past one. That ceaseless radio had drooled through its last hellish jazz note and calf croon at last. Silence now and suddenly, except for the murmur of voices and laughter from the Australian millionaire's suite. The very silence was loud and full of portent.

Lorraine Somers had come out onto her balcony adjacent to the Jeffries'. Hilt didn't go to the movies much. He had remembered the name of the blond movie star only vaguely.

She had thrown a deep-fringed Spanish shawl of some light color, blue or foam-green, over her gleaming shoulders as she stepped out. Her hair was like spun gold and platinum in the moon shadows. She seemed to be staring straight across at Hilt as she paused by her balcony rail, across at the blackness of the rear wing where he was. Her eyes, dark as the dead volcanoes of the moon, seemed to meet his sweating drunken glance directly, with a mute appeal. For a panic instant he wondered if she could see him. But that was impossible, he knew. In a moment her eyes drifted away. She turned her head and glanced up at the moon.

Her lovely face seemed a little drawn in the pale silver light shining on her. Her mouth down-curled, and a little haggard. Like him, she had not been able to sleep. Or if so, like him a nightmare had awakened her.

Mess Jacket, Digger Jeffries, the big shaven-headed millionaire Australian had strolled forth onto his own balcony once more, adjacent to the slender blond girl's. Jeffries turned his bony face and saw her.

"Hello, Lorrie."

In the silence, so loud and clear now, his big voice boomed. Her small voice answered something. He strolled down to the end of his balcony near her, separated by a five or six-foot space from hers.

"Better change your mind and come on over," he boomed. "Too late now for any sleep tonight. We're all aboard in three more hours."

Lorraine Somers replied something, leaning on her rail, smiling strainedly at him.

"Dunbar?" he boomed. "The big blond young chap. No, I think he's gone. There were swarms of people in, but most of them seem to have gone. Oh, maybe half an hour ago. We're going to stay up, anyway, till the last dog's killed. You'll come over, will you, Lorrie?"

She answered something in her faint voice, with a laugh and a nod.

"Good girl!" Jeffries boomed. "Make it now!"

Suddenly he had stepped out over his balcony rail on the side next to her. With one foot on the outer edge beyond the rail, he reached with his other foot to the edge of her balcony. Easily and with firm strong nerves he spanned the intervening space, with long legs stretched to their utmost, like a split dancer, four stories above the ground.

"Digger, you fool!"

Her small, golden voice had lifted sharply, half laughing, half frightened. Swiftly Digger Jeffries reached over and caught her in his arms before she could have known what he was doing. He lifted her clear.

"Digger!" her frightened scream rang.

Hilt Bannerwell would never forget the horror of her half completed cry. With a strangling throat and sweating eyes he stood helpless at his little window a hundred feet away. Sheer nausea gripped him. Yet before the girl's cry had been completed, it was all over. Laughing, the big bald man had swung her clear of her rail and over the emptiness, cradled in his arms. Her legs slid over the rail onto his own balcony. He set her down, and his pale bony face was laughing still as he pulled himself back to join her.

For a moment she leaned back against the wall, limp. Then her dark eyes opened wide at him, and she laughed with him. He caught her hand, and they went gaily in through the door-windows together.

"My God," Hilt breathed with rage. "You damned bony-faced fool!"

Death, yes, death in the instant it might have been, for both of them. Except for Digger Jeffries' iron nerves and not less than superhuman strength, in the moonlit gardens down below both he and she would now be lying where the match sticks and cigarette butts tossed over by the purple-faced murder author and the brush-headed snake professor and Jeffries himself had fallen, amidst the flowers.

Lorraine Somers. She had nerve and courage, too, though she had been surprised for an instant into that half completed frightened scream.

A scream—had it been a scream which had caused him to wake up? A few minutes after half past one now. It had been half an hour ago, a few minutes after one o'clock, when he had waked up and got from bed, so suddenly and startled.

*Creak-k-k!*

Over his shoulder, standing at his window, Hilt turned his face.

Why, that was what it had been, of course, which he had heard in his sleep! A creak. He remembered being unconsciously aware of that quiet sound amidst his distorted dreams. A slow and endless creaking that had been coming towards his door down the long corridor outside, hot with the night heat, dimly lit, in which no wind blew.

There was no one else but himself who lived on the top floor rear. In season the small back rooms up here were reserved for minor hotel functionaries, for the secretaries and valets of the rich. Now that the season was largely over the other hotel employees had been given a choice of more comfortable and desirable quarters. Hilt himself could have moved, had he desired to. But the lonelier the better. All other rooms in the rear wing were closed off and locked. So, for that matter, were the rooms in both side wings. The top floor was unoccupied except for Millionaires' Row in the front. No one ever came down the rear corridor except the chambermaid of mornings. If the office wanted to reach him, it did so by telephone. That was the reason why, no doubt, the slow and endless creak of an approaching step had registered in his tossing sleep.

He didn't know why he was listening so intently for that faint creak to resume again now. There was a silent roaring in his ears. He breathed slowly and with effort.

"Hello?" he said quietly, but aloud. "Anybody out there looking for me?"

He felt the sweat trickling down his naked torso. Silence. Voices across the quad. Only the whirring of the fan on his bureau.

Again, after a moment, he moved reeling and lurching to his door. His head swayed. He looked up and down the corridor with a blurred stare. But there was nothing. That creak had been only the give and snap of raw unseasoned woodwork in the night stillness.

He turned back heavily inside. But still, now that he had recaptured a part of it, he could not evade the horror of that dream.

Cold crawling silk . . . There had been something of that in his dream.

Almost he could feel it now again. Almost as if he smelled the fusty odor of the cold, venomous snake. Every nerve in his body was recoiling.

Sick.

Something was in this room!

In shaky fright he fumbled for the light switch by his door. With a click the ceiling dome blazed on. All the darkness of the stuffy room went fleeing on black darting shadow wings like a caveful of bats. He stood in the middle of his room. Slowly he cast a glance around. The tumbled bed from which he had arisen. The big deep upholstered armchair beside the writing desk, strewn with his cast-off clothing. The bureau with ice carafe, Bacardi bottles, a handful of limes, the slowly whirring fan. His closet door—

"Get up, Smiler, you big drunk!" he said. He laughed crazily with relief.

## CHAPTER IV

## THE CORAL DEATH

SMILER DUNBAR! Lying there in a drunken huddle at the foot of the bed, in the corner by the closet door, half hidden both by the door and bed's foot.

Smiler must have wandered around drunkenly from his poker games and girls and parties to pay an aimless visit. It had been his heavy creaking step which Hilt had heard, asleep. It must have been half an hour ago. And Smiler was still sleeping.

Laughing a little breathlessly, the young physician reeled to his window. Jerked down the shade. Mustn't let Smiler's girl friends and millionaire pals over there look across and see the big hound sprawling. Great social error. Great disgrace.

"Get up, Smiler! You're—drunk!"

Smiler's tousled yellow hair was damp and dark with sweat. He lay in a sprawling heap. Too paralyzed to move. His face was flung sideways under one arm, half hidden. His linen sport jacket lay across his thighs. He had taken it off and had been carrying it, still gripping it by the collar with a tight hand. He had torn his lavender silk shirt wide open, too, down the front of his smooth brown chest.

Hilt Bannerwell crouched dizzily on his haunches beside that recumbent figure. Took hold of Smiler's shoulder and tried to shake him awake. Smiler's head was rigid on his neck. His teeth shone, locked and grinning.

"Smiler, get up!"

He was heavy. Inert.

Swaying on his knees, Hilt grasped hold of Smiler's jacket and wrenched it away from Smiler's stiff, unconscious grasp. There was a crackle in one of the pockets. He thrust his hand into it, groping numbly, his brain reeling with his own drunkenness, trying to find something in Smiler's coat, a flask, a bottle, which would give an explanation of this terrible inertness and drunkenness which had come on Smiler Dunbar.

Money. Left coat pocket stuffed with bills, fifties, tens, hundreds. A couple of thousand dollars in a crumpled careless wad. It had been Smiler's lucky night. A woman's handkerchief in that pocket with the money, too, yellow silk, lace-trimmed, initialed "L," with a rich and gorgeous scent.

Right coat pocket, nothing in it. Just a feeling of something a little warm, a little tingling. Hilt drew his hand out quickly from that pocket almost the instant he had inserted it. There was a tiny spot of blood on his knuckle, no bigger than the head of a pin. With a convulsive gesture he hurled the jacket away from him across the room. He rubbed his knuckle quickly and thoroughly on the rug at his feet. A gesture spasmodic and involuntarily. He was hardly aware that he had made it. Blood. It was his business. He had seen dead men and living cut wide open. Just a tiny spot of cold thick blood on his knuckle, and something like a flake of mica on his nail, which he flicked off.

Smiler hadn't moved, hadn't aroused. With a queer feeling of desperation Hilt was trying to lift the big blond man with both arms around his waist.

"Smiler, for God's sake!"

With terrific taxing of his thigh muscles Hilt staggered to his feet, hoisting the bigger, heavier man around the waist, trying to hold him upright, to plant him on his feet. But Smiler's head rocked stiffly. His legs were sluggish.

Hilt was staggering with his shoulder beneath Smiler's armpit, his arms locked around Smiler's middle. Suddenly and fearfully the big, inert man seemed to get his sluggish feet beneath him. A spot of diabolic consciousness seemed to leap to life, within his brain. He seemed to rise on his toes. He towered over Hilt's shoulder with arms dangling. He seemed to push the smaller and lighter man backward off balance by sheer weight, contemptuously and malignantly.

And suddenly in that terrible moment, as he stumbled backwards helplessly and horribly, off balance beneath that weight which was pushing him, the drunkenness fled from Bannerwell's brain. He saw this thing that he would not believe, he would not face. The body of this man he was wrestling with was dead. It had been dead many minutes. Its face across his shoulder was all blue and horrible like a hanged man's. Its teeth were locked tight upon its swollen tongue between purple lips!

"No!" he choked with a strangled throat. "For God's sake, no, Smiler!"

In blind horror he tried to recoil backwards, to get out from under, to thrust this cold dead man from him with both frantic arms. The dead man seemed to surge forward in that instant ponderously, fiercely, terribly, with the staggering push of his heavy cold body, with one suffocating arm thrown about Hilt's shoulder, with his locked purple grin. The edge of the bed caught the young physician behind his stumbling knees. He felt himself going backward, and the dead man falling on him.

Smiler's left wrist! Even in that moment of horror, of helpless sprawling, Hilt saw it, adding to the madness of the instant. Those two blue punctures on the dead man's wrist, little more than an inch apart!

This dead, poisoned mass of flesh crushing him down. His shoulder-blades were flattened on the bed, amidst the tangled sheets. In paralyzed horror he struggled to arise. He was in a madness close to screaming. Beneath his pinned-down shoulders, beneath his naked, sweating flesh, amidst the tangled sheets he felt a sudden cold writhing, and a twist!

The silken death! The silken death, oh, God! That was what had been crawling in his bed to waken him and touch his flesh with horror! And it was there yet, writhing in the sheets beneath his naked back, and it had been no dream.

His weight, the weight of the dead man crashing down on top of him, had bruised that sluggish thing. He felt that cold silken thing beneath him whip angrily in hurt, twist like a spring, and slash! Two times it slashed beneath his leaping, twisting shoulders, left and right.

Oh, God, the thing had fastened in his arm beneath his shoulder! It was hanging on!

"Ah-h-h!' he breathed.

Maniac laughter, silent and terrible, strangled his throat. His lips were dry. His throat muscles were stretched like cords, panting with his breath. That thing was still fastened in his arm.

He managed to twist his stiffened neck. His eyes must stare upon it. He must see this death. There, oh, God, at the back of his arm, beneath the curve of his right shoulder, hooked into his flesh it was hanging, the harlequin!

As he had thought. He had heard no rattle klirr. The striped and sluggish harlequin.

A thing like a worm, not more than eighteen inches long. A headless thing, or rather with a head that was merged into its body like a worm's. None of the broad triangular savage snout of the copperhead or rattlesnake. Looking no evil. Wide stripes of scarlet and saffron yellow, separated by narrow bands of black. Scarlet snout and gaping, wide-stretched jaws from which those fangs extruded, those curved needle fangs that were hooked into his flesh. One fang, he was cool and detached enough to see, had actually been broken off in his shoulder by his desperate horrified writhing. The thing was hanging by one fang only. A lovely thing. But its name was death.

Small, black, beady eyes, glaring just below his own twisted straining glance, there upon his shoulder. He looked at it coolly. His moment of maniac despair had passed. He was dead, but this thing was going to die, too.

Very coolly in that terrible moment the young physician looked upon that snake there. Coral snake, lovely and bright. American cobra. The sluggish worm. His medicine-kit contained anti-venines for rattler and cotton-mouth and copperhead, for all the poisonous vipers. But for this thing, which was not a viper, which was more venomous than any viper, he had no anti-venine.

He got his left arm free of the dead man on him. Breathless and sweating, he reached around. He seized the bright cold thing just beneath its head with thumb and forefinger. He jerked it free. He hurled it sickeningly and blindly, with a slap against the opposite wall.

Oh, God, if he hadn't killed it! If he had left it alive, as Smiler had left it, to crawl and slash and strike again within this night!

## CHAPTER V

## THE THREAD OF THE KILLER

SLIDING SLUGGISHLY, the body of Smiler rolled and sprawled inertly to the floor. Hilt stood up on weak collapsing knees, breathing quietly. He stepped carefully, a little giddily, across to his bureau. His medicine case. Potassium permanganate. He must incise his flesh around the focal point of the poison. Try to drain as much as possible. There was nothing he could do, really. He could only make the gesture of doing something, so long as his mind and strength were still in him.

After that, morphine.

Alone. Alone with a dead man and a mortally stricken man, Doctor. You are going to lose this patient, Doctor. He is beyond all aid of your science. He is going to die very soon.

A crazed sense of unreality filled his brain as he opened his medicine case with calm professional fingers. As if his personality had split into two parts. The physician's mind of him which was immortal, and this poor snake-bitten fellow, this doomed and dying man who was his patient. He must make the pretense of doing something to keep the poor devil's spirits up. That was all.

"Just take it quietly. We're going to do everything we can, old man," his lips moved.

There were those people across the quad.

But there was nothing that any of them could do to help, either. No, not even if they came running with an anti-venine in hand, which it was not one chance in fifty million any of them would possess against a snake so rare. Too late for that. Too late for everything. The poison had been caught up into his blood stream, already. Was surging through his heart. Already it must have begun its work.

It was better to fight it out alone. Not scream like a terrified woman for help which could not be given. Not call anyone in to watch him die in the way he must.

He knew approximately how this thing would work. That dead man told him how it would be. There was a book he had, whose learned dissertation on the coral snake and the way its poison worked he remembered in fragments. A heavy book, translated from the German, "The Cobra, and Allied Venomous Snakes of the World" by title. Written by some profound and learned Teutonic professor. He would think of the learned author's name. And of why he was trying to think of his name. Presently.

How had that cold, abominable thing got in here? Had Smiler met it in here, in the silent darkness as he entered? No; Smiler had been creaking down the corridor. He had been walking so slowly. And at the last he had been crawling, as his knees showed. He had got that ghastly bite somewhere else, somewhere else on this same floor, since he could have climbed no stairs with the swift poison in him.

Smiler Dunbar had known what was coming, too. The instant he had felt that savage double puncture he had set out to reach Hilt, to get help, at once. He had thought that he could make it. He had done the quickest thing, the best way he could. At the first he must have hurried, running madly. Then in a moment more he had been walking and staggering, more slowly, more slowly. At the last he had fallen, crawling and dragging himself in here. But he had been a dead man already.

Somewhere else Smiler had got the bite that killed him. How? How had that damned thing got into this hotel? From its dark and slimy swamps miles back in the hinterland. Had the one that struck the death at him been the same that struck death at Smiler, too, or were there more than one of them? An army of cold creeping harlequins! They were weeviling all through the Royal Tarpon!

No, that was fantastic. Impossible! It had been the same snake for him and Smiler, too, and only one. The ghastly thing had crawled into Smiler's pocket somewhere else, when he had pulled his jacket off at Camponello's poker game or in his drunken exhilaration at Jeffries' party. Then, perhaps, long minutes afterwards, he had thrust his hand into that pocket, and the lurking death had struck him. And it had crawled its sluggish evil way out after Smiler had collapsed, and had got on Hilt's bed, awakening him.

He remembered the quick abhorrent feeling which had come to him when he thrust his hand into the right side of Smiler's coat. The spot of cold, thick blood on his knuckle. The flake of pale, pink coral scale which had been like mica, and which he had so quickly and instinctively flicked off. There was something else Hilt remembered, too, from the German scientist's book, which was that the coral snake in spite of its deadliness was one of the most sluggish of reptiles. Children had been known to find them and handle them without harm. Sluggish, needing to have its fury roused within it. Coiling in Smiler's pocket, it had torn its skin. It had brought blood. And so there had been aroused its dark, venomous hate, which had caused it to strike the stroke to Smiler when all unawares he had thrust his hand into that pocket. So it seemed.

He stood with his slender, muscular brown back half turned to his bureau mirror, surgical knife in hand. He could see just a little red swelling on his right shoulder, marking the place where the venom had gone in and the snake's fang was still snaggled. He wasn't trained to work in a mirror backwards, but he would have to do the best he could. Strike straight and clean and deep, with his left hand. He should have been a dentist, trained to work backwards in a mirror. Dentist. That was a good one. Cutting a snake's tooth out.

The knife. No anesthetic. He didn't want to feel the numbness. He wanted to feel the sharp sweet pain one last time in his life again. The pain and the pleasure, they were all the same. They were life.

Bending his shoulder in towards his breastbone, he could just reach it with the knife in his left hand. Deep! Sweat sprouted out beneath his eyes. His lips went pale. His teeth chittered softly together. Deep, and a long straight cut. Now another one, across. That had cut to the shoulder bone, and under.

He clamped his suction-pump to the deep red-flooding cross-incision. That red flood had washed the snaggled reptile's tooth out. Perhaps had washed out a little of the venom. He was drained white. Now a solution of potassium permanganate crystals. It wasn't an anti-venine. It was the old remedy before anti-venines were developed. But it was supposed to do some good.

He had done all he could. All that anyone else could have done for him, or that he could have done for another. There was the white strong searing pain at his shoulder. His eyeballs were moist and hot, and a great knife was in his brain because of that deep throbbing. But it was good to feel the pain, for pain was life still. Clumsily with one hand he wrapped gauze bandages around the shoulder, pulling them tight with his teeth.

No more he could do. Moving softly, so as not to start his heart to too quick beating, he located that bright and lovely coral death again, creeping sluggishly along the baseboard under his bureau.

Streaked death of red and yellow, banded black. Crawling warily and silently with its bruised flesh. Crouching on his knees and reeling, Hilt reached in to it with an empty bottle. He hit it on the head, and it lashed in a coil. Lashing, threshing, it whipped out from beneath the bureau into light. Its jaws, with one fang broken, were open wide at his naked feet. It was not dead. It was trying to strike him yet. He hit its scarlet head again. Again. The base of the bottle cracked in his fist. He struck, he struck, he struck. Till the green grass rug was frayed and broken. Till the bottle was cracked and broken in his hand. Till of the head of that cold writhing silken thing there was only pulp left.

"That got you! That got you!" he choked. "Oh, you black son of hell, try it again!"

A little crazy in that moment.

He was cool enough to pick the damned thing up by its tail after a moment. He could see where the scales had been torn a little back towards its tail, and a spot of dried blood there. A linen thread was caught beneath the scales, cutting into the serpent's flesh. The thing had been in Smiler's pocket. His surmise had been right as to that.

He held the striped thing up before his eyes, turning it with care, following with his eyes the white thread around its silken body. His surmise had been right, but not right enough. It had not been any accidental movement of the snake in Smiler's pocket which had cut it with that thread and whipped its sluggish anger up to fury. The thread went clear around the dead snake's body, beneath its scales and its pale colorless ventral plates, cutting into the flesh in a bloody circlet, and it had been tied with a tight knot.

This snake had been handled by a man. It was not a horrible accidental intruder from the swamps. The thread had been tied tight around it by someone to torture and madden it, before it had ever found its way into Smiler's pocket.

## CHAPTER VI

## A DRINK BEFORE DEATH

MR. DIGGER JEFFRIES, big, bald, bony-faced, but fashionable and elegant looking in mess jacket and black cummerbund, turned easily from his niece Lorraine Somers and from the bristle-headed German professor who had buttonholed him at the improvised bar in the living room of his suite.

"Excuse me," he said. "Excuse me, Lorrie. The doorbell, I think. Another guest."

"Oh, Digger, could it be—?" the blond girl breathed.

There was weariness and fright in her dark volcano eyes, the Australian millionaire thought. Could it be that she was afraid of meeting this big, brainless blighter they called Smiler Dunbar? Maybe that was the reason she hadn't come over earlier in the evening.

"I don't know who it is, Lorrie, I'm sure," he said. "But I'll see. And we'll have the rest of our dance later."

"Digger!" his plump, brown-haired wife called to him in her tiresome voice, from across the room with Chance, the author. "The doorbell rang."

"Thank you, my dear," he said.

He had learned manners from Adelaide, who had been one of the Philadelphia Deacons, just as he had learned a cultivated intonation of voice, and how to dress distinctively but in good taste. He owed his brains to himself. He owed his money and his success as well, hard fought for and hard won in youth. But he owed to his fifteen years with Adelaide the fact that he was a civilized and an attractive gentleman.

He opened the door. He stared with a fixed and inquiring smile at the small, mouse-faced man in the dinner coat who stood there straightening his tie apologetically. He had seen the man's face vaguely before, was Digger Jeffries' impression. One of the hotel staff.

"Yes?" he said in his booming voice. "Just what seems to be the trouble?"

"I'm C-Clarence Durkee, Mr. Jeffries. The d-desk clerk downstairs, and a friend of Mr. Dunbar's. I was up at your party around midnight before, and Mrs. Jeffries said I might drop back again, if everything w-w-wasn't over."

"Of course, Mr. Durkee," said the Australian millionaire. "I remember you threatened to come back. Come in."

"Mr. Dunbar is still h-here, isn't he?" Clarence Durkee said diffidently, loosening his collar.

"No, he went some time ago." Digger Jeffries threw an arm around the little toothbrush-mustached clerk's shoulders hospitably, dragging Durkee along with a twisted head and a squeezed neck into the center of the big chintz and wicker living room. The radio was murmuring with the faint and barely audible music of a Los Angeles dance orchestra, and Lorraine Somers, with her sea-green embroidered Spanish shawl thrown loosely over her white arms, was waiting there to resume the dance with him.

"The party isn't over yet by any means, Durkee," the big Australian millionaire said amiably. "The drinks are still holding out, and there are a few die-hards still left around. Professor and Mrs. Stumpfwasser are still on deck. And Al Chance. That's him crawling on the floor over there beside Mrs. Jeffries with his head under the end of the couch."

"I took the l-liberty, Mr. Jeffries, of asking Dr. Bannerwell, he's the house physician, to drop around," Clarence Durkee said, loosening his collar. "He's a kind of f-friend of Mr. Dunbar's, too. A kind of l-lonely buzzard. I hope you don't mind? He hasn't shown up, has he?"

Digger Jeffries frowned faintly.

"The house medico? Dark fellow? Glad to have him, Durkee. But he hasn't showed up yet. Do you know my niece, Miss Lorraine Somers?"

Clarence Durkee grinned at the little golden girl from California. He fingered his collar, rolling his eyes with what he intended to be a devastating and heart-crushing look. Like all small and insignificant men, Clarence had a tremendous ego in regard to women. Look at me! his quivering toothbrush mustache commanded, his ghastly grin, his rolling eyes. Am I not handsome, clever, charming?

"I've been h-hoping this would h-happen to me," he fingered his collar at the blond girl, grinning with red gums. "I saw you coming in this evening, Miss S-S-Somers. I've been wanting to meet you ever since I first heard Mr. Dunbar mention your n-n-name. Believe me, if you don't mind my saying so, everything he told me about you isn't half true. And I'm ready to tell him so right now."

Lorraine Somers had glanced at the mouse-faced, vain little man at first with remote dark eyes in her tired and lovely face. But at the name of Smiler Dunbar she stiffened. And at the thought of what Smiler might have said, not knowing what it could have been, the blood receded from her face.

"Yes, Mr. Durkee?" she said in her small voice. "What did Mr. Dunbar tell you about me that you're so sure isn't true now?"

"What did Mr. Dunbar tell me? Why, he told me that you were the niftiest looking little bunch of blond sweetness—I mean the best looking blonde in fourteen states. But I s-s-say you're the best looking in twenty-eight states. Mr. Dunbar didn't half tell the truth."

"Oh, I see. Thank you."

"Gosh!" said Digger Jeffries with a burst of laughter, as he put his arm around her again and they began dancing to the faint radio tune. "You looked positively white, Lorrie. What was the matter?"

"It's just been a surprise finding that Smiler's here, that's all."

"Lord, if I'd only known that Dunbar affected you that way! I thought you were still in love with him, head over heels. If that's the way it is between you, how are you going to stand him for three months? Your Aunt Adelaide has told you, hasn't she, that he's to be one of our party on the *Stella* for Australia?"

"He isn't!"

"He isn't? But I thought he'd accepted, and it was all set."

"I mean I don't want him to go, Digger!" she breathed. "If he does, I simply won't. I didn't have any idea that he'd be here. That he'd be sailing with you. It would be quite impossible for me."

"I'm sorry. Of course he shan't go, in that case," Digger Jeffries assured her. "We can make some excuses. To tell the truth, he rather forced an invitation out of your Aunt Adelaide, and there's no reason for being delicate with him. It won't be the first time he's been snubbed, I fancy."

Clarence Durkee stood on one foot and then the other. He wiped his forehead and fingered his collar-button again. The big bald Australian millionaire and the lovely young cinema star had forgotten his existence. The party wasn't nearly so lively and hilarious as it had been at midnight, even with Lorraine Somers' presence. He wondered where Mr. Dunbar had gone, Smiler Dunbar always made a party lively.

Thrusting his hands into his pockets with an air of nonchalance, Clarence strolled over to the improvised bar at one end of the room. Herr Professor Stumpfwasser was standing there as if glued to the spot.

"Going to stay till the last dog's killed, I hear, Professor?" Clarence remarked gaily.

"*Was?*"

"They'll be heading out in a couple more hours now, I expect, won't they? We've got a lot of stuff here to finish first, I see. It looks like it's up to you and me."

"Pardon?"

"*Ik soggen, vee gate es eenen, Herr Professor?*"

"Speag more zlowly, blease! Der English, him I do not so vell yet oonerstondt."

Clarence had been introduced to the professor socially by Mrs. Jeffries during his previous brief visit, while for several weeks he had enjoyed a speaking and smile-exchanging acquaintance with the professor's dashingly beautiful red-haired wife, Rita. In fact, he nourished the belief that Rita Stumpfwasser was secretly but overwhelmingly infatuated with him. But the professor's glare on him now was the same as on a species of curious and abnormal reptile which the professor had never seen before.

"I — say — it — is — a — hot — night, Professor," Clarence tried again.

"Iss dot so?"

Clarence swallowed his glass of orange brandy mixed with soda.

With a little swagger, an air of being very much at ease and in it all, he turned away, while the professor's beady eyes glared after him. Straightening his collar-button, he sauntered over towards a bedroom door from which Rita Stumpfwasser's willowy, green-clad figure was emerging.

"Dance?" he said gaily.

The tall red-haired woman looked down at him with an unseeing glance. She sank into a chair without replying, lighting a cigarette. Her hands were a little unsteady.

"It's a hot night," he ventured, standing by her.

Hands jammed in pockets, he teetered on his toes beside her with an air of nonchalance. Her orange-colored eyes were stony and motionless, fixed straight ahead of her at the slender figure of Lorraine Somers stepping back and forth in the arms of Digger Jeffries. She had just made up her face afresh in the bedroom, Clarence thought. Her lips were a bright poppy red. There was bright red on her cheekbones.

He fingered his collar-button. "I hope you don't mind my calling you R-Rita. It's the n-n-name I always think of you by."

"I beg your pardon?" she said wearily, turning her strange, large eyes up at him. "I'm afraid I didn't just hear what you were saying."

"Do you mind if I call you R-R-R-Rita? Do you think your husband would m-m-mind? You know, I think the old boy's just a teeny-weeny bit upset and jealous of you and me, R-R-R-R—"

"Oh, for God's sake, get me a drink," she said.

She had arisen. Beneath the carefully applied powder on her right arm, as she retreated from him, Clarence Durkee saw the marks of finger bruises, purple and round, and for a moment he almost thought he saw the shadow of the same around her throat. But it could not have been her husband, the good and learned Professor Otto Stumpfwasser, who had made those bruises, for she drew her arm in his as she reached his side, with a sleek and sinuous writhing of her naked spine.

A little hurt, Clarence Durkee strolled across the wide room towards his hostess, Adelaide Jeffries. During all the five or ten minutes since he had been here the dumpy pleasant-faced lady in yellow had been moving around in circles over there with her eyes bent to the floor, while on hands and knees in the same vicinity the paunchy figure of Alfred Morton Chance, the mystery author, had continued exploring beneath chairs and chintz-covered couches.

"Oh, please don't bother any more, Mr. Chance."

"I've been wondering if that was a game you two've been playing," Clarence said archly.

With Mrs. Jeffries he always felt at ease, almost a little condescending and superior. Adelaide Jeffries' broad pleasant homely face had no beauty to excite and disturb him.

"Well, it's our nice young Mr. Durkee back again," she smiled at him good-naturedly. "Mr. Dunbar's friend."

"I wondered if you'd lost something."

On the floor Alfred Merton Chance turned his gray head, his purple heavily jowled face around, peering at Clarence beyond the broad bottom of his dirty white linen knickers. He got to his feet heavily. He stood swaying a little drunkenly, right and left.

"Losh shumping?" he said. "Losh shumping? Hell, no."

He grinned sardonically.

"Just a little necklace of mine, Mr. Durkee," explained Adelaide Jeffries pleasantly. "It seems to have slipped from my neck and dropped somewhere."

"What kind of a necklace, Mrs. Jeffries? Perhaps I could help you hunt?"

"Why, it was an odd thing, Mr. Durkee. Rubies and yellow Brazil diamonds, separated by small beads of black jade. It looked like—why, it looked like some kind of a rather horrible snake, I suppose," she laughed a little helplessly. "You couldn't miss it. I rather liked it because it was so odd. But please don't bother about it now. I've been telling Mr. Chance not to, but he insists. Those things always turn up eventually. The chambermaid will probably find it."

"Valuable, Mrs. Jeffries?"

"Well, the rubies were rather nice. I think my father paid something like forty thousand for it."

"Holy Moses!"

"Oh, please don't bother. Mr. Chance has looked all around here, anyway. He's been a lamb."

Alfred Merton Chance stood swaying on his feet.

"Want my 'pinion," he said thickly. "Want my 'pinion, 'Delaide, some cock-eyed shun of gun went off wizh' ish. Forty thousand buckarinos no small sum of money. Suggesh we all lesh ourshelves be searched. Turn pockesh inshide out. Inshide out—"

Hiccoughing, he pulled out the pockets of his dirty crumpled knickers, dropping keys, a wad of small bills, and loose silver to the floor. He laughed a little foolishly. He thrust one hand, after several futile stabs, into the open neck of his yellow polo shirt.

"Searsh me," he hiccoughed. "Bet you twenty—twenchy—trenchy dollarsh 'at shun of gun Dunbar went off wizh ish. Never liked his fashe."

Swirling around the room with Lorraine Somers in a grand finish, Digger Jeffries had brought the slender blond girl to a stop beside his wife and the two men as the faint radio music ended for the moment. The big Australian released the girl. He looked at the drunken purple-faced murder author with pale stony eyes in which anger burned.

"I'm quite sure you're mistaken, Al," he said coolly.

"I was jush shaying—"

"It's my impression that Adelaide was still wearing the necklace after Dunbar left, whenever that was," Digger Jeffries stated flatly. "I'd rather lose ten necklaces than have any guest of mine named as a thief. The damned thing will turn up somewhere, Al. And if it never does, to hell with it."

The drunken author took a deep breath. His broad diamondback belt creaked. He stood staring at the big Australian with swaying head.

"Hell wizh ish ish what I say," he declared. "Want dansh, 'Delaide?"

"I think I rate one myself, Adelaide," said Digger Jeffries good-humoredly, holding out his arms to his wife. "After all, I've been doing my duty by the younger generation long enough. If I don't watch out, I'll lose you."

"You could never lose me, Digger," she replied gaily, settling into his embrace with a look of ineffable happiness on her broad homely face. "I'd never let you."

They moved off. The purple-faced murder author looked at Lorraine Somers with a query in his bloodshot eyes, but she did not seem to see him. He shrugged. He thrust his pockets back in again. He stooped and picked up rather carefully the money and keys he had dropped, fishing for each last dime, and went swaying, staggering away.

The slender blond young girl sank back against the arm of a chair. There was a kind of fright in her dark eyes. She closed them for a moment. Her lips moved.

"God keep me from a man like that!" she whispered.

Clarence Durkee fingered his collar-button. Why she should hate Mr. Chance so much he didn't see. Mr. Chance did look like an awful old sot, a regular satyr. And there was a kind of greasy look in his yellow, bloodshot eyes.

"Do you dance, Miss Somers?" he murmured.

She opened her eyes, looking at him. She had forgotten he was there, her look said plainly.

"No," she said. "No, never." Clarence picked an invisible thread off his sleeve. With a swagger of his hips he turned and walked away. Professor Otto Stumpfwasser and the tall, lovely red-haired woman who was his wife were still at the bar when he sauntered back there again to revive his feeling of departed joy. Yes, the mouse-faced little clerk saw as he approached, unmistakably Rita Stumpfwasser's throat as well as her arm had been bruised with strong brutal fingermarks, though thickly powdered over.

They were talking together, however, confidentially and intimately, as he reached the bar beside her on his rubber-soled shoes, too rapt in their discussion for the moment to observe him. He heard Rita's low-pitched murmuring voice.

He did not pour a drink. Shrewdly, with his mousy look, he drew a little back behind her shoulder where he could listen.

"Couldn't have got away?" he caught her murmur.

"Nimmer! Umpossible! He could not haf grawled a hundret feet, Rita. I hat gifen him dot hypo dwice."

Otto Stumpfwasser's guttural voice deepened till the words were indistinguishable.

"Are you sure you used all the care necessary, Otto?" she murmured in reply.

Clarence heard no more. She and Professor Stumpfwasser had been talking about some of the professor's experiments with his reptile specimens, Clarence Durkee supposed. The professor was always making expeditions back into the Everglades after strange and curious reptiles. And sometimes he came back greatly elated and excited. That he kept some of his living specimens in his suite below, Durkee was aware. In wire cages in his closet. The chambermaids, snooping, had discovered them, and reported to the management. Strange, bright, curious serpents and lizards and salamanders of all kinds. And while to have such things in one's room was against all the laws of the Royal Tarpon, still a tacit exception was made in the case of a scientist so world renowned as Otto Stumpfwasser. The order had therefore gone out from the management to ignore the professor's little playmates.

The professor's little beady eyes were suddenly watching him unwinkingly behind those huge glasses, Clarence felt. It nattered him to realize that his instinct had been right, and that Otto Stumpfwasser was jealous of him.

"Mr. Dunbar and I shall think of you often with great pleasure, indeed," said Clarence with his gummy smile.

"*Was?*" said Otto Stumpfwasser. "Pardon?"

His beady eyes blinked. He had the deaf and heavy look of a man who is very drunk.

"I said that Mr. Dunbar and I shall think of you—and of Mrs. Stumpfwasser—often, Professor," articulated Clarence carefully. "It has been a pleasure while you have been absent on your scientific trips—I mean it has been a pleasure to know you have been on your scientific trips. It has been an honor to the Royal Tarpon. And to Mr. Dunbar. And to me. Having you. And Mrs. Stumpfwasser."

"*Nein,*" said the bristle-headed man. "You are mistaken."

He shook his head.

"You are mistaken," he said again.

He poured himself four fingers of bourbon, with a grave and deliberate gesture.

"You are mistaken, *herr,*" he said. "Herr Dunbar vill nefer think of mine vife again yet."

He sipped his glass in little careful swallows. His face was brick-red.

"Nor you, eider, do not fool yourself," he said.

With a grunt he walked away.

The red-haired woman leaned back against the table, highball glass in hand. She laughed. Clarence watched her over the rim of his glass as he sipped his orange brandy.

The dumpy yellow-clad figure of Adelaide Jeffries had come waddling up to them.

"Now you must promise not to break up the party, Rita," Mrs. Jeffries said pleasantly, with her vague smile. "And you, too, Mr. Durkee. I want everyone to stay and see us on board. But I'm not so young as you two, and I'm really frightfully tired. Digger has persuaded me to lie down for a little while. Where he gets his own inexhaustible energy from I don't know, but he always seems to have a new reserve to draw on. I want you both to stay and keep him company, of course."

"I heard Al Chance saying you'd lost your necklace, Mrs. Jeffries," Rita said. "Have you found it yet?"

"No, but doubtless the hotel people will, if it doesn't turn up before we sail. I'll leave it in the hands of Mr. Dunbar. He's always been so kind."

"But he's going with you!"

"No. It seems that the cabin accommodations wouldn't be sufficient," explained Adelaide Jeffries carefully. "Digger had already asked some people to join us at Panama that I hadn't known about. It is too bad we are going to have to disappoint Mr. Dunbar at the last moment, but that's the way things are."

Rita stood staring, clutching her bosom. "Then he wouldn't have gone with you anyway?"

"Anyway? Oh, you mean if Lorrie weren't joining us. Why, yes, I suppose he might have then, Rita. She's taken the cabin he was to have had."

Rita Stumpfwasser stood swaying a little. Her scarlet lips trembled faintly over words unspoken. There was a wild light in her eyes. Suddenly she threw back her head and laughed hysterically.

"There is a God!" she said. And walked away. Clarence Durkee finished his drink alone. He poured himself another, and with it in hand strolled out onto the balcony. Digger Jeffries and Alfred Merton Chance were out there with highball glasses, beneath the placid silver moonlight, with arms on the rail looking down at the mottled moonlit mass of the tropical foliage beneath the balcony.

"I thought I saw it glittering for just an instant," stated Digger Jeffries quietly.

"Digger shinks he shaw shnake," explained the purple-faced author with drunken belligerence to Clarence. "Noshing down 'ere, I claim."

"Just a glitter for an instant," said the Australian millionaire quietly, "when the moon came out from behind that chimney pot of the wing across the way. But I don't see anything more now, I'll admit."

Clarence looked across the way. "Well!" he said. "The doc's still up. I wonder why he doesn't come around."

There was light behind the shaded window of Dr. Hilton Bannerwell's hot little room up beneath the eaves in the rear wing opposite, he saw. The window was up but the shade was pulled to the bottom, unstirring in the windless night heat, and he could see nothing beyond it.

"I wonder if the ol' doc's found Mr. Dunbar yet," said Clarence with a vacant laugh. "He was telephoning for him. They're probably sitting there now with a couple of bottles between them, both dead cold."

## CHAPTER VII

## THE TRACK OF MURDER

But Hilton Bannerwell wasn't cold, not yet. Not in the way that Clarence had meant. Nor in the way that Smiler Dunbar was, either.

His shoulder was white-hot with pain. He breathed in gasps. With all the horror of this thing he couldn't think quite clearly. But he had been able to see that fact about the thread which encircled the body of the dead bright snake. There had been something devilish in the tying of it.

Yet he couldn't connect the tortured snake with a deliberate and fiendish plot to murder Smiler. There were more certain ways to accomplish murder, if a man had a heart so black.

The young physician had collapsed into his armchair now, weak and sweating. The fan whirred on his cheek, and whirred away. He took deep, quiet breaths. It was slower in hitting him than he had expected.

What hours, what years and eternities in hell Smiler must have lived through, during the brief minutes he had been making his agonizing way around the corridor!

He felt an itching on his left ribs, just beneath his heart. He had noticed it when he had first awakened and sprung from bed, he remembered. Bitten now by the cobra death, and still conscious of such a small irritation as a mosquito bite! Perhaps even dead men noticed things like that.

Involuntarily he rubbed his finger tips over that itching on his left ribs, glancing downward. The skin was red and angry. It was not a mosquito bite. There were two tiny red punctures approximately a half inch apart, or three-eighths of an inch, in the center of the red angry spot. It was a snake bite. The hellish thing had struck him twice.

To left and right, the lashing snake. He remembered now having felt the double lash of that ghastly thing beneath his twisting, horrified shoulders, though he had not felt its strike either time, too numb with horror. But here, as well as his right shoulder.

"Almighty hell!" he breathed.

He sat holding his breath, looking down at the angry spot and the two tiny punctures beneath his heart. The joke had been on him, making that cool and desperate effort with his shoulder. Like operating on a man for appendicitis when there was a bullet in his heart.

He laughed breathlessly and silently, sweating.

His fan whirred in the silence. He heard the creak again of green unseasoned wood in the night silence from the long empty corridor outside. He heard the ticking of the watch on his wrist. Through the unstirring shade which covered his window he heard voices and laughter at intervals still from Millionaires' Row. The radio over there was operating again, though faintly.

Time. "You have just listened to . . . Wur-rp! wur-rp! wur-rp! . . . Hollywood, California. The time is now one minute of eleven . . ."

Hilt Bannerwell sat there, sweating.

One o'clock. It had been one o'clock, or only a little after, when he had felt that silken thing in his nightmare sleep, and had sprung out of bed. It had been half past one, or only a little after, when he had found Smiler Dunbar crumpled on the floor, a half hour dead and cold.

His wrist watch said two o'clock here. And that bright-striped death had struck him at least twenty minutes ago. Possibly all of twenty-five. Had struck him twice.

Wait a minute! About that strike on his left side, beneath his heart! The swelling there was redder, was older, was more inflamed appreciably than the redness on his shoulder had been where it had struck the second time. There had been a difference of time between the two strikes. Lying pinned on his bed beneath the dead weight of Smiler, he had felt the snake beneath him twist and slash its wormlike body twice, that was true. But it would not have had time to strike twice in that moment, to have imbedded its fangs, and extracted them, and then have struck again.

It had lashed twice in that horrible jerking movement, but had actually struck only once. This first, this older strike upon his ribs beneath his heart, had been dealt to him while he lay sleeping, and it had been the needle stab of it as well as the writhing of the silken thing which had awakened him. He had got up, and had stood at his window rubbing it while he drank, thinking it was a mosquito bite.

At one o'clock, or only a few minutes after! A good long hour ago.

His mind was clearing. He breathed quietly, summoning his thoughts. A statement in Stumpfwasser's book on the cobra arose in his memory. He could see that paragraph almost word for word, in letters of fire before his eyes.

"The bite of the American coral snake or harlequin, *Elaps Fulvius,"* the eminent German herpetologist had written, "must be said to be always fatal. It has been known to cause death to a man within so brief a time as three minutes, while there is no known case of anyone who has survived the toxin of this small and most deadly cobra, without the prompt use of an anti-venine, for so long as half an hour."

Half an hour, the maximum. But he had been bitten twice, and a full hour had elapsed since the first strike. And he was still alive.

He was going to stay alive! The pain in his right shoulder had settled down into a deep slow throb and ache, blessedly full of feeling. The bite on his left side was no more than a mosquito itch. Why it was he didn't know, but he had won out on that striped, hellish thing somehow.

Why hadn't Smiler, who had been a stronger man, and who had been bitten only once, in a less fatal place, there upon the left wrist? Hilt startled, stiffened.

There was something here incredible.

Somebody put that damned snake into Smiler's right pocket, he told himself.

But Smiler had been bitten on the left wrist!

Why, these fang marks on his own ribs, which that damned snake had made, were no more than a half inch apart. Three-eighths of an inch, more like it. But the two jabs on Smiler's wrist were more than a full inch.

That damned thing had not bitten Smiler at all! Smiler had more than likely never even known that it was coiled in his jacket pocket.

No coral snake ever grew large enough to have a bite that wide, Hilt realized in growing bewilderment. No doubt a great diamondback would leave fang marks like those on Smiler. But it had not been a diamondback's poison which had killed Smiler, by all the symptoms. It had been a coral snake's.

"Almighty God!" he breathed.

It was impossible that it could have been this snake that had been in Smiler's pocket, it was impossible likewise that it could have been any other coral snake, it was equally impossible that it could have been any other kind of a snake, which had injected the venom into Smiler Dunbar.

Coral death, but not struck by a coral snake! Not struck by a snake at all. What did that mean?

The young physician arose on shaky knees.

"Murder!" his dry lips moved.

And Smiler had known it. Smiler had come to tell him. That was why Smiler had fought so desperately to reach him, a dead man crawling.

One of the two thrusts in Smiler's wrist appeared to have gone in deep and straight, while the other had penetrated slanting, at a tangent, shallowly beneath the skin. They had not paralleled each other, as a snake's fangs would. Those thrusts had been two quick and vicious jabs of a hypodermic, filled with venom extracted from a snake's poison glands.

Murder of a kind so foul it revolted the imagination. A killer more horrible than the striped snake itself had done this thing to Smiler.

Who was he, and where! What kind of a madman had done this diabolic thing! It was someone on this same floor of the great hotel, for Smiler had climbed no stairs. It was someone in the Australian millionaire's or else the gambler's suite in the front wing opposite, for there were no other places where Smiler could have come from.

Creak-k-k!

With horrified ears Hilt heard that faint hushed creak in the silent corridor outside! On knees like water, yet with a fierce and desperate bound, he sprang up. He whirled to his bureau drawer. Snatched out the flat blue .32 lying in there at the back, behind his socks, silently jerked back the oiled carriage, throwing a cartridge into the chamber. With glaring eyes he watched the open door. His right hand was numb and weak with pain and loss of blood, almost useless. And he was not left gun-handed.

On naked feet he tiptoed to the threshold, grasping the doorpost with a light tense hand, and listening. No sound. In a moment he looked forth. Empty. Only the snap of woodwork in the night heat again.

Gropingly, the understanding of how it had been done was shaping itself in Hilt's mind. The tortured snake had been slipped into Smiler's pocket when he had removed his jacket somewhere, or else possibly while he still had it on him. To strike and poison him again, if it would, and add a moment of last foul horror to him, dying. But in case the sluggish coral thing's venom might be exhausted when it struck, or in case Smiler might not happen to thrust his hand into that pocket where it lay coiled, the murderer had made certain of his victim's death by stabbing the venom into Smiler's wrist while he was drunk and helpless somewhere, off his guard. Had stabbed it in two times, viciously and quickly, simulating the snake bite.

Only a little too quickly and hurriedly. The vicious double thrust had been spaced too wide. And had been injected into Smiler's left wrist instead of his right wrist, not coinciding with the snake already in his pocket.

That was the way it had been done. And yet, Hilt realized with growing hate and horror, it could never be proved. There was only his own instinctive assurance that the snake had been in the right pocket, not the left. He himself had destroyed the snake's head which would have shown that the wide punctures on Smiler's wrists could not have been inflicted by its fangs. Impossible to prove that it was murder. Even more impossible to prove, and perhaps even to guess very definitely, the identity of the living devil who had done it.

Smiler was dead, who had never encountered the hidden, angry snake. But he himself had encountered it, and he was still alive. The answer to that was beyond him yet. But he thought that his book on the cobra might be able to tell him something as to that. He went to his closet and pulled the heavy tome down from the shelf.

Stumpfwasser! As he opened the book to the index, suddenly the name of the German scientist who was the author struck Hilt with full force. The thing he had tried to remember, in his half-crazed horror couldn't at the time. Why, Dr. Otto Stumpfwasser was here in person, in residence at the Royal Tarpon, Clarence Durkee had said! The distinguished German herpetologist had been Penguin, that owl-eyed man in evening clothes on the balcony. One of the guests in the Australian millionaire's suite tonight.

Smiler had been in Digger Jeffries' suite and Camponello's both, tonight. He had come straight from one or the other. In one or the other he had got it. Little more than an hour ago.

Stumpfwasser might be able to tell something about this terrible death which had come to Smiler. And the purple-faced drunken murder author newly returned from the Everglades, Chance might be able to tell something, too. As for the big millionaire Australian himself, the gambler and his brass-haired woman in the suite adjoining, the rest of them, that golden girl in the moonlight on the balcony, yes, even she . . .

One of them! As God lived, he had seen the murderer tonight.

Hilt stood swaying on his feet a little, thinking, thinking. For God's sake, let him only remember now what item had seemed queer!

Mess Jacket had appeared first, Jeffries. Then Penguin, who was Stumpfwasser. Then Purple Face, Chance. The tall red-haired woman in green he had glimpsed inside, through the windows. The dumpy woman in yellow, likewise, with the glittering snaky necklace around her throat which had later disappeared. Then the windows of Camponello's suite had opened while he had been talking to Durkee, and he had seen the hairy gambler and his brass-haired woman. After that, the golden girl on her balcony.

It had been a gun which Camponello had been tapping on the card table as he talked to his brass-haired woman, Hilt was certain now.

What had Lorraine Somers been doing as she strolled out to the rail of her balcony beneath the pallorous and deceptive moonlight? Her competent hands had been twisting slightly. Why, she had been tearing up a letter, of course. Scattering the scraps into the foliage below.

Hilt was going back, going back.

He must make his way unseen, if possible, down the back staircase to the courtyard gardens. Must search there thoroughly and patiently for the scraps of the letter which Lorraine Somers had torn up and dropped into the thick dark foliage; and for what the big, bony-faced Australian millionaire had dropped, and Stumpfwasser, and Chance, each in turn. There might be nothing he could find down there which would give a clue or point a trail to the perpetrator of Smiler's ghastly death. But it was a bare chance there might be. Under Jeffries' balcony, or under Camponello's. A hypodermic, half filled yet with snake venom, and with fingerprints upon it.

That was too much to hope for. The killer had that hypo yet, and filled with venom. A man like that wasn't stopping at one murder.

The killer was over there, and awake. He would be awake all night. Wherever he was, he was waiting for the scream of horror, the raising of the alarm.

And yet the damned killer didn't know for an absolute certainty that Smiler was dead. He didn't know it as Hilt knew it. Only Hilt and he knew that Smiler had been poisoned. But only Hilt knew that Smiler was dead. A poor card to play. But on it the young physician knew that he was going to gamble his life.

"We mustn't let him know now, Smiler!" his dry lips moved silently. "We've got to make him think you're still alive to hang it on him! Then watch out for his strike!"

He dressed in haste. Crumpled gray flannels, a pair of crepe-sole black and white shoes, no socks nor tie. His quick-growing beard, eighteen hours old now, was bristly beneath his palm as he rubbed it, and in his bureau mirror it was raffish and dirty looking. His hollow face was drawn and dark-shadowed, pale with drink and loss of blood. His eyes were bloodshot, his black hair unkempt. He still stank of rum, no doubt. He looked like the devil.

The drunken doctor. He was glad now for the word that had got out about him. Let the killer think him drunk when they should meet, though keen-brained and wary and awake. Let the killer think Smiler alive, though dead. His life would depend on how well he played the part.

It was the only way. If it failed. . .

He thought a moment. He took his wrist watch off, and stuck a pin twice into the leather strap. He put the watch on again upside down.

He pushed his big deep armchair nearer the window. He had a time getting Smiler's stiff heavy body hoisted up into it, and it was all pretty horrible to go through with, but at last he had it done. He must come back, after he had explored the garden below, and pull the shade up before he went to confront the killer.

He thrust his gun into his hip pocket. He was going to have to risk a dose of that venom himself before he was through. The damned murderer would try to give it to him, in the same way that it had been given to Smiler. One quick vicious thrust, or two. It could be given to him while shaking hands or passing him a drink. It could be given to him by a woman throwing her arms around him.

## CHAPTER VIII

## THE DEAD MAN LAUGHS

Millionaires' Row . . .

Suite B was Camponello's, and C was Jeffries', and D was Lorraine

Somers'. These were the doors of the places where Smiler had been. One of them was the door out of which Smiler had come surging, with his death in him, little more than an hour ago.

Running, running, running around the corridor.

The door of Camponello's suite was closed tight, and the door of Lorraine Somers'. But that of the millionaire Australian's was an inch ajar, he saw. From here he must trace Smiler on.

Suddenly, as he stood there in front of the gilt elevator cages, hesitating, the door of Camponello's suite burst open. The hairy-armed gambler came rushing out. Camponello did not see him, or if so, only with a cursory glance. With a thrust of his stocky shoulders, not pausing to ring the bell, the gambler pushed through Jeffries' door, leaving it open behind him.

Hilt followed. He paused there just inside Jeffries' living room for a moment, leaning back against the wall, with his hand thrust in the pocket of his wrinkled gray flannel jacket and touching the cold stones there which he had found in the garden below. Touching the colder flesh of that dead striped snake which he had killed, and which had not killed him. Dark, hollow-eyed and sweating.

Cobra death. In here. They were all here now. The snake killer was before him. In view of his bloodshot eyes as they swept the room.

There were two women in the room he had entered, the blond young movie actress and the red-haired woman with the snaky walk, Rita, Stumpfwasser's wife, as Durkee had described her. There were five men, the three whom he had seen out on the balcony in the moments following Smiler's death, and mouse-faced little Clarence Durkee from downstairs, and Camponello whom he had followed in. The dumpy woman in yellow, Mrs. Jeffries as she had been, was no longer in evidence, she who had been wearing that bright and terrible necklace around her throat, as if for a symbol.

A murderer before his eyes. One of seven. For even if the murder of Smiler had not been done here, the murderer was here. Was waiting.

Digger Jeffries was standing at the bar with the sinuous red-haired woman, Rita, whose red lips were a stab, a flame. Hand thrust in trouser pocket, nonchalant and at ease, the big bald Australian millionaire was laughing with his head thrown back at something she had said to him. Carefree and buoyant, on top of the world. He touched the rim of his highball glass with hers, laughing, and hoisted it and drank. Didn't he know that across the room, slumped on a couch between the balcony door windows, Otto Stumpfwasser was watching him with motionless drunkenness?

Near the bar, upon the bare floor, to the imagined music of the radio which had been a quarter of an hour turned off, Alfred Merton Chance, the murder author, was dancing solemnly and alone a drunken dance of his own devising. Purple-faced and yellow-eyed, scaly belt stirring like a snake alive about his quivering paunch, solemnly and ludicrously the author danced, while in a big chintz chair not far away Lorraine Somers watched him, leaning forward with hands clasped between her knees, a steady and hypnotized and somewhat horrified look on her tense face. Was there a meaning in that drunken dance? Some barbaric ancient tribal rite he had learned from ancient Seminole medicine men in the Everglades out of which he had returned? Some Dance of the Snake. His swaying head was drunken, his wavering arms seemed drunken, but he wove through the intricate step without a falter, and there was a keenness, there was a terrible wakefulness and sobriety in his eyes.

On the opposite end of the couch from Otto Stumpfwasser little Clarence sat fingering his collar.

Murder! Can it wear a face like that?

Whether he had been seen prowling down in the garden below the balconies of Millionaires' Row, Hilt didn't know. He had not dared look up and show the whiteness of his face while he had been down there. If the murderer had happened to be at the balcony rail and had seen his creeping figure in the shadows, his life was not worth a shoebutton in this moment. Not because of what he had found, for he had more than likely not found anything of any consequence. But because the murderer would know that he was not drunk, that he was following a trail now, that he was keen and sane and awake.

It had been less difficult than he had anticipated to locate even scraps of paper in the dense foliage down there. The very thickness and size of the great elephant-ear leaves had formed a kind of table on which objects dropped from above had fallen, without dropping through to the tangled ground. Beneath Digger Jeffries' balcony, a cigar band, Flor de Fino brand, rolled in a tight cylinder, for one object. For another, a crumpled cellophane wrapper, with a meaningless design printed on it in red and green. For a third object, a string of red and yellow stones, interspersed with beads of black jade, the rare and glittering necklace which Adelaide Jeffries had been wearing —the items which Stumpfwasser, Jeffries, and Chance had thrown over in their moments in the moonlight. Though it was only a guess which had thrown each, and in what order.

Beneath Lorraine Somers' balcony, three scraps of a note, written on Royal Tarpon stationery.

Lorrie :

Will try. . .if you give me any po . . . one o'clock tonight.

Smiler.

Yet nothing by which murder could be hung on anyone. Nor anything that pointed exclusively and alone to the damned snake killer. But the killer was in this room. One of these five men or these two women.

None of them, he thought, in that brief instant of survey as he followed Camponello in and paused against the wall, had looked across yet to the lighted window of his room in the rear wing, with the shade up over there now. None of them had seen Smiler yet, sitting in the deep armchair beside the open window. He was in time to get the first reaction which he had counted on. Would that picture of the dead man fool the killer? Make him think that Smiler was still alive to name him? It was a desperate, but the only, chance.

Then watch out for the venom!

"Thanks, Mr. Chance," the murmur of Lorraine Somers' small voice reached Hilt. "I've got the idea now, I think. I have to use something like it in this next picture, as I've said. But I ought to get away with it."

"Hands like zhish. Throw your head back," said Chance with a grin. "Just faksh ish. Thash ish always the trick. Faksh anything."

It might mean anything. But Chance, it was certain, was not drunk . . .

"Excuse me, gents," said Camponello.

Truculently the hairy gambler had surveyed the room beyond him, crossing towards the bar.

"I'm looking for Dunbar! Where the hell did he go?"

"What do you want to know for, may I ask, Mr. Camponello?" said Digger Jeffries.

"The lousy son got away with twenty-two hundred bucks off me tonight," said Camponello with quiet fury.

"Really?" said Jeffries with a crinkling grin. "Well, as I believe you yourself have remarked, somebody's got to lose when you gamble. I remember it from the night when I had the pleasure of playing with you."

"Yeah? Don't get too funny. Dunbar was playing in cahoots with that double-crossing frail of mine to ream me! Believe me, Lucille opened her yawp finally when I got to working on her! And I'm going to catch the big pink geranium and beat the everlasting hell out of him! I'm going to get my dough back! Where the hell did he go?"

"I had the impression," said Jeffries coolly, "that he was going back to his place to continue his game with you, Mr. Camponello."

"He didn't come back to my place."

"Then I couldn't say."

Otto Stumpfwasser had arisen heavily from his couch across the room. With his hands clasped together beneath the tails of his coat he had approached with a swaying motion.

"Oxcuse," he said. "Did I oonerstand Herr Dunbar you vos it looking for, mine friendt? I oferheardt Herr Dunbar saying dot he vos going to Miss Somers' vroom ven he vos telling you goot-pie, Herr Chefrries."

Crouched in her big chintz chair, with hands clasped together, Lorraine Somers stared at the scientist with her dark volcanic eyes.

"You are mistaken!" she said with difficulty.

"You must be mistaken, Professor," said Digger Jeffries evenly. "I heard nothing like that."

"I heardt him," affirmed Stumpfwasser obstinately. "I am a man off science, dot is aggustomed to being brecise. Howefer," he said, with a stiff and heavy bow towards the blond movie actress, "if you do not vish it so, madame, it mocks no tifference to me.

None of them had seen Hilt yet, the drunken doctor, standing with his swaying head and gaunt, ghastly look near the door through which he had come in. But he was near enough to overhear the interchange of words, to see the expressions on their faces. Beneath heavy lids with bloodshot eyes he watched the slender blond young girl.

"No," she said, shaking her head. "I haven't seen him at all, I'm sorry. He sent me a note that he would try to see me, if I gave him any possible opportunity to do so, sometime this evening before one o'clock. He used to be—I used to know him in Hollywood. I've told you and Adelaide about that, Digger. But I didn't see him."

"You are quite obviously mistaken, Professor," said Digger Jeffries pleasantly.

"Where is he then?" asked Rita, sharply and eagerly.

"Why all zhis curiosity about Dunbar?" inquired Chance, with a creased drunken grin. "Lishen, I shaw big old shun of gun when I got out of elevator, minute or two before one. He was running down hall. He got 'way with 'Delaide's necklace, was why he was running, bet you. Coursh he didn't shtop see Lorrie."

So that was it! Hilt stiffened. Not Camponello's room, not the blond girl's! Here! He had followed the trail back. But perhaps he had never really been in doubt of it. There had been a voice which had told him all along. Here, here, Smiler had got it!

"Running down the corridor, Al?" said Digger Jeffries curiously.

"Running sosh-eyed, down around the turn, Digger."

"Maybe he was just going around to see the doc, and have a drink with him," suggested Clarence Durkee.

"The doc?" said Jeffries.

"Doc Bannerwell, the house medico. I told you about him," said Clarence Durkee apologetically. "I asked him around here, you remember. He's a kind of souse, lives in the rear wing."

"Just another shouse," giggled Chance. "Jush a big shouse like me."

The murder author's rotund frame shook with his laughter. His yellow bloodshot eyes rolled towards the door. They rested on Hilt with surprise, with abrupt fixity. The laughter left his face so suddenly that it was almost comic.

"For goshall's sake!" he said.

Then simultaneously and all at once the rest of them seemed to catch sight of him.

Oh, he must look ghastly! With what he had been through. With what he knew. And that thing that was in his pocket. He must look like a ghost or demon, and like hell itself to that foul murderer with his keen snake brain, with the venom ready.

Only that damned killer and he knew that Smiler had been poisoned! And could he keep that knowledge from his eyes, while he read the same knowledge in the killer's?

With an apologetic word Clarence Durkee had started towards him. And at the same moment the rest of them seemed to start towards him, moved by a mass impulse. Chance. Jeffries. The hairy gambler. The slinky red-haired woman. Even the blond young movie star who had been watching Chance's snake dance with such hypnotic interest. All except Otto Stumpfwasser, who sat in heavy drunkenness.

They were all coming towards him.

Had they all been in on Smiler's death together? Now, he thought! The fear of that swift unseen needle jab shot like white fire down his spine. Cobra death.

Now! No, not yet.

He was just the bottle-screwy doctor.

"How are you feeling now, Doc, old socks?" said Durkee familiarly.

"I'm Digger Jeffries, Doctor. Kind of you to join us."

"Tell your friend Dunbar that he'd better cough back tomorrow, or he'll cough up in a coffin," said Camponello harshly. "And with that I'll bid you gents good night."

Hilt swayed, with a maudlin grin, a drunken look. His face was white. That ghastly poison near him! The killer's terrible and watchful eyes probing into him behind a mask! He must act. Act for his life. Only the killer and he knew that Smiler had been poisoned. But only he knew that Smiler was dead.

"Smiler—" he said thickly, in a voice which he let trail off drunkenly.

Digger Jeffries' cold stony eyes bored him.

"Old Smiler—" he repeated thickly.

With a drunken grin he waved an arm towards the door-windows.

They were turning their heads at his gesture. Even Professor Stumpfwasser, on the couch across the room, was slowly and heavily turning his glassy glance around the corner of a window beside him to look across the quad. All except Chance. With his intoxicated witless air, the murder author thrust his face close up to Hilt in that instant, breaching in his ear.

"You're not drunk!" Chance breathed terribly, in a voice that was barely audible. "Don't try to pull that stuff on me! What's your damned game?"

Now!

The murder author's thumbs were hooked beneath his armpits. Hilt watched those hands. Chance glared at him, terrified and awake and keen. But not now. If Chance was the man . . . With a stifled oath Chance had stepped away from him. He, too, turned his head.

"Why, there Mr. Dunbar is now!" exclaimed Clarence Durkee with a drunken giggle. "Across in the doctor's room."

They were looking out across the open balcony windows. It was all black across there except for the window of Hilt's room opposite. But there the shade had been pulled up to the top, and all the lights were lit. Against the window over there Smiler Dunbar was sitting in Hilt's big armchair, with his purple shirt torn open wide on his brown bosom, and a bottle lying loosely on his lap, and a glass tumbler clutched tight in his right fist on the chair arm.

In that instant of silence, while Clarence Durkee laughed foolishly, Smiler Dunbar slowly heaved his shoulders. His yellow hair, tousled and sweat-dampened, rolled a little and swayed on the back of his chair with his restless heavy movement. Slowly he heaved his shoulders again, in a deep slow gasp. There in the lighted window across the quad the big blond man sat like a man alive, with a glass in his stiffened hand, stirring and twisting slowly.

"Oh, God!"

There was that one muted voiceless scream. Lorraine Somers. With stiff and terrified hands, desperately and blindly, the movie actress pushed past Jeffries, past Camponello, and fled from the room.

## CHAPTER IX

## STAB OF THE FANGS!

It had worked! For this instant, anyway. Only the killer and he knew that Smiler had been poisoned. But the killer, unlike him, believed now that Smiler was still alive. What hell in that man's brain!

He had played his act. He had done his work. He had better go now.

"Wait a minute!" Digger Jeffries' nervous twitching grip, with tight and stony fingers, had dug into Hilt's arm! "Just what the hell did you come around here for, Bannerwell? What's in your mind?"

Hilt swayed against the wall beside the door, dark hollow-eyed, with a wavering grin.

"Smiler," he hiccoughed. "Pie-eyed. Took belonging Mrs. Jeffries by 'stake. Apologies."

He had thrust his hand into his jacket pocket. He had it, that cold, silken slimy thing. He jerked it out and held it up drunkenly. The striped red and yellow snake with its crushed bloody head!

"Jumping codfish!" croaked Camponello. "I never seen a thing like that before."

"Harlequin!" screamed Rita Stumpfwasser. "Oh, my God, the harlequin! Otto!"

The red-haired woman had staggered back. Her hands were before her eyes.

"Take it away!" gagged Clarence Durkee.

"That happens to be a harlequin, my friend," stated Digger Jeffries with white and twitching jaws. "A cousin to the Indian cobra and the krait, and the African black mamba. One of the deadliest things that crawls on this green earth. Where did you get it?"

" 'Sense," said Hilt drunkenly.

He dived his other hand into his other pocket. He brought out the glittering necklace of rubies and yellow diamonds. He saw the bloodshot eyes of Alfred Merton Chance bulge in his face like a strangled man's. The murder author's complexion had turned gray-white. Gagging an unintelligible oath, with a glare of sickness and hate at the young physician, Chance stumbled forward out the door, and fled.

"Where did you get that thing?" repeated Jeffries.

It wasn't the necklace the big bony-faced Australian meant. He meant that dead and headless thing that Hilt was still holding drunkenly in his right hand, that striped thing of red and saffron which would slash its fangs no more. The necklace slipped from Hilt's grasp to the floor, and no one noticed. Hilt swayed. Out of the edges of his eyes he was aware of Rita's blanched face and stifled breathing. Across the room, in answer to her cry, Otto Stumpfwasser had slowly, heavily arisen from the couch, with hand fumbling in the pocket of his coat.

"Found in Smiler's pocket," Hilt said thickly. "Pulled out by tail. Stepped on it."

He laughed foolishly, facing their staring eyes.

"It might have bitten you!" said Clarence Durkee.

"It's a wonder it didn't bite Dunbar in his pocket!" whistled Camponello.

"Say!" Hilt exclaimed, with a drunken grin. "*That* must've been what made holes in old Smiler's wrist-watch strap! Never thought of it!"

"Dunbar had a wrist watch on?"

That hoarse and almost voiceless exclamation of surprise came from Digger Jeffries, Hilt thought. Hilt held his left wrist up, with his watch on it upside down. Slowly and ponderously Otto Stumpfwasser was advancing towards him across the room, he was aware. Every muscle in his body was tensed.

It would have to happen in a moment more! A moment more, when Stumpfwasser saw that snake. But let him get it planted first why Smiler was still alive, seemingly.

"Sure, old Smiler's," he grinned. "Old Smiler cock-eyed. Drunk. Old Smiler tried to tell me. Something. Something hit him. Bit him. On old wrist. But damned snake didn't know old Smiler had old wrist watch on, did he? See 'ose holes?"

"Good God A'mighty," breathed Camponello. "Punched right in the strap! Two fang marks! If that guy Dunbar isn't shot with luck!"

"He'd better watch out!" gasped Clarence Durkee wildly. "Its mate might come back!"

"I've heard they do that," said Jeffries quietly.

Otto Stumpfwasser had crossed the floor at his slow and ponderous pace. His hand came out of his inner breast pocket, clasping a silver cigar-case. He extracted a panatela from it, a Flor de Fino, and rolled the band into a cylinder with a methodical and unconscious movement of his fingers, dropping it on the floor. He paused three feet away, and made an effort to strike a match on his heel indifferently. He thrust the cigar into his face cold.

"He iss not mine!" he croaked in deep anguish and agitation, before he had even had time to focus his eyes on the dead snake in Hilt's right hand. "I deny dot he iss mine! Veref er yoi foundt him, he does not pelong to me. I vi'l consult mine lawyer if dere has been an accident!"

He had come close, breathing hoarsely. Through glaring glasses he stared at the dead striped thing that Hilt was holding up. His moist lips trembled.

"Vy, dot iss not—" he croaked.

But Hilt Bannerwell had made up his mind—from the time when he had first seen that killer on the moonlit balcony, perhaps, before he had even known his name. Certainly from the time he had read Stumpfwasser's book. Not Chance, the murder author. A puerile fool like Chance would steal a necklace when faced with sudden opportunity and temptation, and would try to blame it on Smiler. But not a killer. And that left only one.

Hilt never gave Stumpfwasser a chance to complete his croak. Before the words were out of the learned professor's mouth, he had slapped the foul dead thing hard across Stumpfwasser's sweating face.

With the swing of the blow, dropping the snake in the same instant, his doubled knuckles had crashed Stumpfwasser's jaw. He crashed his right fist again, with a twelve-inch jolt, while Rita Stumpfwasser screamed, and Stumpfwasser's eyes went glazed behind his glasses, with his startled mouth still open. The heavy drunken man was out cold on his feet. He swayed, and crashed like a log to the floor.

An instant of silence.

"Dr. Bannerwell, what have you done!" Clarence Durkee squealed like a rabbit.

"Why, you dirty thug!" yelled Camponello.

He heard Rita Stumpfwasser's deep indrawn breath. Then her hysterical laughter ringing. Camponello was gazing at him with disgust, and Durkee with trembling alarm. For an instant Digger Jeffries stood glaring stony-eyed, with one hand thrust in his trouser pocket.

"I think," the big stony-eyed Australian said, "that he had better go!"

Camponello and Durkee had hold of him by both arms as Jeffries swayed towards him with a murderous eye. They rushed him staggering out the door at a run, and down the corridor. Shaking and weak-kneed, he let them half push, half-drag him along. Playing the act of the bottle-screwy doctor to the end. His only chance of life.

"Crazy!" Clarence Durkee gasped.

"He never had no bringing up!" grunted Camponello. "A gent is always a gent, even drunk, is my motto."

But at the turn into the rear wing Hilt could stand it no longer. With a wrench he tore away from their combined grasp. He went sprinting down the corridor away from them with lunging, staggering strides, while they halted, astonished.

"You're drunk!" yelled Camponello after him. "Say thank you next time!" He had left his room door open. He dashed into it, with a breathless gasp, closing the shutter door behind him with a slam. In the darkness, with the dead man.

Out in the corridor he heard them muttering. In a moment they turned, and retreated.

He crept a step across his room, in the darkness. He could just make out the vague shape of Smiler's dead body in the big chair by the open window. The lights had gone out in Jeffries' suite across the quad, and there was a light on in Stumpfwasser's now, on the floor below. They had got Stumpfwasser down to his room, probably still unconscious from drink and that terrific double blow.

Darkness in his own room here, and silence.

But he had left the lights on when he had gone hurrying around to Jeffries'. And he had left his fan whirring. Now the lights had been turned off in here, and the fan was still. In the utter, the unstirring silence, he was aware after an instant of mute, stifled sobbing. He saw a white form crumpled on the floor beside the chair in which dead Smiler sat.

"Yes?" he said quietly.

He felt her shoulders with a fumbling hand. Lorraine Somers. Huddled here on the floor beside the dead man, holding one of his cold lax hands against her cheek.

"He's dead," she whispered.

"Yes, he's dead. You knew, didn't you?"

"You sat him up," she whispered in terrible agony. "You put the fan back of him so that its movement would make him seem still alive. So that I would think he was still alive. Oh, how cruel of you!"

"This was more cruel, Lorraine."

"You're not drunk," she said in her small weary voice. "I knew it when I first saw you. I knew something awful had happened. A snake bit him?"

"Yes," he said. "A damned snake."

Her hand reached his in the darkness. He pulled her to her feet. She stood swaying, and he threw an arm around her. Her face was white as her gown.

"You had better go," he said.

"Oh, God," she said, "I loved him once! We were married five years ago. The father of my little girl. It wasn't me he ever loved, of course. I was just somebody to take care of him. I supported him two years. He was no good, I know. Even lately he has been trying to get money from me. Threatening to take little Lorrie away. The shock of finding him here, and expecting to sail with us! I was afraid to see him. But now I'll never see him again. Oh, I loved him once! Do you blame me?"

"You had better go," he said. "For this death is not yet over."

"Oh, he was no good, they all said. I suppose you would call him a blackmailer and a gigolo. No good. He was going to try to get money out of me tonight, I think, because he thought I was in love with Digger."

"Are you?" he said quietly.

"I hate him," she said, shuddering faintly. "The cold touch of his hands!"

"Hush!" breathed Hilt. "There is death in the night still, girl! The snake is still creeping! The snake is coming back!"

"Oh, God!"

"Hush!" he breathed. "Into the closet! For God's sake, lie still there! It's death!"

Breathless he listened to the terrible silence in the empty corridor beyond the shutter door, with his gun drawn in his fist. *Creak-k-k! Creak-k-k!*

No snap of green unseasoned woodwork in the night heat this time, but a man! Coming with a slow inaudible creak, as Smiler had come in his nightmare dreams! He heard it a yard away, as silent as the creeping of a snake over forest leaves. He saw the shadow beyond the shutter door.

He fell softly back into his bed, with heavy breathing. Across the room from the dead man in the chair. He breathed stertorously, like a man in deep sleep. But the gun was like a rock in his hand.

The venom was near him! It was coming! Softly and silently the door opened with a key. Oh, yes, he would have stolen Durkee's pass-keys from him. A man so keen as that. Breathless. The door had opened, and it had closed. The venom was in this room, Hilt knew. The young physician felt, more than saw, that silent shape. Felt that hushed soft breath. Saw those pale, glaring eyes.

Bent over Smiler.

Hilt's hand was on the light switch of the lamp beside his bed. He snapped it on. He leaped to his feet with a wild inarticulate shout.

"Drop it, you damned snake!"

Whirling, Digger Jeffries turned his ghastly glare. He had one of Smiler's wrists in his left hand. His right hand jabbed at the pocket of his trousers in a frantic gesture, but he did not get the hypodermic thrust away quick enough. He did not get it thrust away at all. His whole body jerked, and he held the silver cylinder up, then hurled it at Hilt with a choked and strangled cry. His face was white as death as he beheld the open closet door and the horrified face of the blond young girl who had emerged from there.

"You thought you'd kill him again?" said Hilt bitterly. "You couldn't stand his being between you and Lorraine? And this time you would not miss. You would blame it on the snake's mate coming back. But you didn't miss the first time, Jeffries. How many times is enough?"

The white face of Digger Jeffries stared at him like a skull.

"Brilliant," said Hilt with tight lips. "You're a junkie, aren't you, Jeffries? I kind of had an idea afterwards that I had seen you giving yourself a shot in the arm out there alone on the balcony, pulling up your sleeve. And when I found a cellophane wrapper below without any lettering on it I figured there was nothing else it could have held that didn't want to be advertised except a deck of morphine. That turned me to the idea of a hypodermic. A special one filled with snake venom for Smiler.

"That was an interesting discussion of yours on the coral snake and its cousins, Jeffries," the young physician went on, with bitter mockery, with dark and steady eyes, holding his gun steady against that tall wavering shape. "Smiler's not the first man you've pushed out of the way with a fake snake bite, is he? There was that one thing you didn't know. The snake you planted in Smiler's pocket happened to be a false coral snake, the scarlet king, *Ophibolus Doliatus Cocchineus,* if I've got Stumpfwasser's name for it right. The false coral's snout is red, where the true coral's is black. And its stripes are wide scarlet and yellow, with narrow black, instead of the true coral's narrow yellow and wide black. So you see that even if it had gone off as scheduled, Smiler's death could not have been blamed on that damned snake in his pocket. But you had to be caught like this red-handed, Jeffries. That was why I lied about the wrist watch, to make you think you had not got poor Dunbar. So you would come back and try to kill the man you still thought living. That was why I hit Stumpfwasser—to shut him up. Because he would have told you the snake was the false coral and that would have spoiled it all. You would see your plot was no good. You wouldn't have tried to get Dunbar again in *that* way. And I wanted you to try—so I could catch you red-handed, Jeffries, trying to kill the dead man twice!"

But Digger Jeffries was not interested. It was doubtful if the tall Australian had heard more than a word. Digger Jeffries was holding his thigh just below his trouser pocket with both white-pressed hands. The look of his eyes was stony as death, and sweat was over his shaven skull like dew.

"I jabbed myself!" he breathed.

Hilt's face was white, too. He understood now. The startled killer, wheeling as the light flashed on as his voice sounded, had tried to thrust that hypodermic out of sight too quickly. He had thrust it, with his thumb still on the plunger, through the cloth into his side.

"There is no anti-venine," Hilt said. "You must understand that."

"I was afraid not."

Digger Jeffries was breathing hoarsely and heavily. A peculiar flush had come upon his twitching face.

"You had better go, Lorrie," he breathed.

"Nothing," the white-faced girl whispered, "nothing at all to do?"

"You had better go!" said Hilt desperately.

The tall man swayed. He crumpled forward. Hilt caught him in his arms, and swung him to the bed. His breath was coming hoarsely.

"This is hell," he gasped.

"Yes, hell."

"Thought," he gasped—"have Lorrie alone. On yacht. There was one snake—I found myself—for Dunbar. Another I stole from Stumpfwasser's room—for Adelaide. He had it doped—I think—must be worrying where it got away to!"

He strangled laughter.

"That was—real thing, I know. Should have given it to Dunbar. Then never you—"

"Where is the snake you stole from Stumpfwasser?" demanded Hilt desperately. "For God's sake, it makes no difference to you now. Do you want the girl to get it?"

"Adelaide," he gasped. "Adelaide's bed. Sent her to bed. Lorrie to go back with me—with Adelaide's body. Me alone with her—but wish no harm. To Adelaide. Too late! Too late!"

"Run!" Hilt swung to Lorraine Somers desperately. "There may be time! The thing is sluggish. It may not have struck!"

But the girl had fled already.

"Lorrie!" Digger Jeffries gasped. "I always loved you, Lorrie. From little thing—so beautiful and sweet. You don't know. How a heart like mine can love. Too old, too old? Why, look at me, I've got the strength of ten—when I'm feeling right. Can leap mountains—Lorrie!—Lorrie! Laugh at me!—Air! Give me air!"

In a moment his stiffened, writhing body subsided again. A sweat was on his stony eyes, but he lay looking up at Hilt belligerently.

"Morphine," his lips moved.

"I'm afraid you've used too much," said Hilt heavily. "You would never even feel it."

"No, this is—"

"Yes, it is hell," said Hilt.

And it was hell for him, too, for he was a physician, and he had to stay. But it was over for Digger Jeffries quicker than it had been for Smiler.

On this side of death, at least.

He went down the corridor to the Jeffries' suite.

Lorrie, thank God, had been in time to save Adelaide Jeffries.

# THE HIDING HORROR

## CHAPTER I

## CREEPING MURDER!

SHE WAS ALONE in the house when the killer came. The fire burned on the hearth, and the night rain was beating at the windows. The dog dozed on the rug at her feet; the parrot balanced upon its perch with its head beneath its wing. Upon the lounge beside her the black-faced cat purred lazily.

She sat with her slender, silk-clad legs tucked under her, her yellow dressing-gown open at her throat. One yellow satin mule had slipped off her foot, and unconsciously she cupped one hand around her instep as she sat reading. She hummed a little unconscious tune as she read, as contented as the purring cat.

Somebody went past the house outside, along the brick sidewalk, the only passerby in a long time. There were not many people out in such a pouring rain. The step was too quick to be that of Officer Rounds, the policeman on that beat. Then the steps died away down the street.

But the huge yellow dog on the hearth beside her had growled. It opened its eyes, it lifted its head, hackles bristling. ears pricked up. Grumbling deep in its throat, it listened.

"Greta, be quiet!" she commanded.

Slowly the dog settled down again.

The rain beat on the window pane. The branches of the old elm out in front creaked in the wind and rain, and brushed the pane with its leaves.

She laid down her book, and picked up the mending basket filled with her stockings. The fire crackled cheerily. On the black marble mantelpiece was a bowl of yellow jonquils. Beside it were three carved jade Buddhas, one cream, one green, one pale blue.

The telephone downstairs rang. With a little impatient frown she swung her feet to the floor, undecided whether to go down and answer it, or not.

But it would only be another newspaper reporter, calling up to ask for Miss Lane—Miss Lila Lane. He would say: "Hello, Miss Lane, this is the *Morning Sun.* Oh, Miss Lane has gone out, has she? Now, just wait a minute, Miss Lane, you can't pull that old Hollywood gag on me! I—"

Lila Lane, Lila Lane, Lila Lane! Always the newspapers must have news about her, even when there was none. Or perhaps it was only a wrong number this time, at the phone.

The dog growled again.

She sat still; she did not go down. The telephone rang, and then after a while it stopped ringing.

The yellow dog arose. It arose growling. Its hair was bristling.

"Greta, be quiet!"

*Creak!*

*What was that sound?*

Oh, God, there was someone at the window! Or was it only the elm branches stirring?

No, no, there *was* someone in the house! Someone had come in out of the night and the rain, silently. She heard the soft, stealthy footfalls creeping up the stairs!

She clutched the dressing gown above her beating bosom in terror. The dog howled, the cat arched its back and leaped away, the parrot on its perch awoke, lifted its head.

Who, who, *who?* Coming up the stairs so silently!

Breathless, choked with horror, she crept out to the stairhead. She peered down the winding banister. There he was! There he was, creeping up from below!

She saw him in a dash, before he saw her. With a gasp she sprang back into the bedroom. She tried first to hide behind the curtain, but that would be too easy to see. Wringing her hands, terrified, she hid in the closet, bolting the door behind her. Perhaps he would not know that she was there.

The killer had come in!

She lay there breathlessly in the narrow darkness, while the dog barked and the cat wailed and the parrot squawked upon its perch. Screams of gibbering and maniacal laughter filled all the room beyond the door! *He* was hunting her! She heard in her mute terror the sounds of his hunting. In the bathroom! Beneath the bed! His loud, fierce breathing, and his soft, devilish cursing. Just beyond the closet door!

"Damn you!" he was saying. "Damn you—!"

She heard him cursing, stumbling, hunting. And she lay, not daring to breathe, in the narrow, dark closet. But even then she knew that in the end he would surely find her, for he knew she must be here somewhere.

Now he was just outside! He knew! *He knew!*

"Where are you? Oh, *there* you are! Hide from me, will you? Damn you, you must have known what was coming! Then take it! *Take it, you—!"*

It was just after midnight when Hapgood Bye paused in front of the three-story old Van Nieman house which Lila Lane, the famous moving picture actress, had rented for the season. There was a broad yellow rectangle of light shining through the upstairs windows. Standing there in the rain, his shoulders hunched, the young newspaper reporter looked up at that yellow light. The famous screen star must still be awake.

"Well, all the other reporters have already made their pilgrimages to the goddess," he remarked whimsically. "I suppose it's time I made mine."

The old residential street was deserted beneath the midnight deluge, and dark, except for this house and the All-Nite drugstore down at the far corner. An odd neighborhood to be living in for Lila Lane, that gay, brilliant, famous daughter of Hollywood. Or perhaps he only thought it was odd, reflected Hapwood Bye, because he didn't know her.

Anyway, someone was awake in the house. Lights gleamed behind second and third story windows, even though the black sweeping rain blurred and obscured them at times. Somewhere upstairs he heard a dog's muffled barking—and then a burst of high, shrill laughter.

*"You've a—"* someone shouted hoarsely and abruptly, as Hapwood stood hesitating.

That was all. But somehow faint, icy fingers began to crawl up his spine.

He took a drag at his cigarette. Then, wet to the bone and shivering from the pelting rain, he turned up the stoop towards the iron-grilled front door.

Again that weird, grating voice shrilled inside the house. *"More tea!"*

No, that was not it. It sounded more like *"Murty."* He didn't quite get it. But there was something strange, inhuman, frightful, about that weird cry. He didn't like it. He had come here for news, and there was an instinct now which told him he had found it.

Midnight—and this damned cry! He was afraid, suddenly, for Lila Lane.

Lila Lane, the famous blonde star of KGS Films, had arrived in town from Hollywood two weeks ago. She had brought all the traveling equipage of a Hollywood star, including her pet parrot and her prize dog, her Siamese cat and her Brazilian ringtail monkey. She had even brought her pompous and unimportant little husband, along with her furs, her jewels, and her costly collection of carved jade Buddhas. She had rented the old

Van Nieman house—the very house which not so long ago she had only entered through the back door, when she had been the Van Nieman's chauffeur's daughter, and her name had been plain Nellie Lang.

But she had risen in the world faster than the Van Niemans had gone down. Now she was the highest paid star in pictures; her life was insured for a million dollars—and a crown prince from Europe had presented her with the ringtail howler monkey known to the world as "Wails." A far cry, this, from her earlier days of misery and abuse, as a servant's daughter. But no farther than the weird noises inside the house were from what might have been expected in a wealthy actress's home.

As he mounted the last steps to the door, Hapwood Bye again heard that shrieking laughter from above. It seemed too high-pitched to be quite human. It was more like a screech. Then, glancing upward, the reporter suddenly caught glimpses of a shadow darting across the middle window of the top story straight above him.

It was gone almost before he saw it. But in that fleeting instant, it had looked to Hapwood Bye like the shadow of a little bent man—or like the shadow of some leaping, monstrous spider.

Suddenly the weird inhuman voice cackled again. "Who's knocking at my door?" it shrieked. Then, "Cut the dirty beggar's throat!"

Hapwood Bye shivered.

That diabolical cry had come from one of the windows above him, from the very same top story whence the shrieks of laughter had come. Yet he could see no one. The wide living-room windows of the second story directly above him were closed and the shades drawn. And now the lights in the third story windows, where he had seen that spidery shadow leaping, were suddenly turned out.

The rain beat on the reporter's puzzled face. Suddenly, apart from the steady downpour, a solid half-bucketful of water came splattering down. It had come from the rain-soaked leaves of the huge old elm which rose from the sidewalk and spread out its long limbs until they brushed the house.

There was something odd about the shape of the tree, though. On one of its limbs, above his head, the shivering reporter made out a dark silhouette of something like a great catamount clinging belly-flat, at about the height of the third story. A great cat, or else a monstrous and distorted man. Clinging and crouching there beneath the cold rain, and swaying with the wind.

Hapwood Bye stared. No, there was no one in the tree. The half-bucket of water which had fallen from the tree had merely been shaken off by a sudden gust of wind. And that horrible dark shape up there was only a limb which had grown thick along part of its length from some unusual tree disease. No, it did not move or breathe. But God, how it had scared him!

Now there was that devilish voice again. "Who's knocking at my door?" it screeched. "Youva! Youva! Murty! Murty! It's only me, said Barnacle Bill! *Quarr-a-rawk!"*

Suddenly Hapwood grinned despite chattering teeth. He felt like a fool. It was Lila Lane's parrot, the famous Barnacle Bill, of course! He had heard the big dog barking, too, and that shrill inhuman shriek of laughter from upstairs, gibbering and insane. He had that latter sound placed now, too. It was Leaping Leander, the Brazilian ringtail howler. And the dog was Greta, the prize Boxer. And there would be Piou-Piou, the cat, too—the whole nationally known menagerie. Why Lila Lane's dogs and cats were better known to most people than the names of the President's cabinet even!

"Hee, hee! Whi-yee!" The ringtail monkey howled again.

"You win," Bye murmured with shivering lips. "You win the laugh, Leander."

He realized the moment he had said it, though, that Leander wasn't the name of the ringtail monkey. The monkey's name was Wails, of course. It was Lila Lane's insignificant little husband whose name was Leander.

"Well, what a sweet fool I turned out to be!" said Hapwood to himself in disgust. "There's nothing here—there may not be anyone home, even. I've just let myself be scared out of my shirt by nothing at all!"

The dog had stopped barking now. Hapwood extended his hand toward the bell-push, to give it a ring as a gesture, and then go. But suddenly, before he touched it even, there was the crash of breaking glass above.

Jumping back from the door, Hapwood looked upward just in time to see a naked arm jutting out over the window ledge in the third story where the lights had just recently been turned out. It was a hand—and the hand was clutching something!

"Hey, up there!" he shouted. "What's going on in this damned house?"

The arm suddenly vanished at his shout, leaving only the shattered window pane, and the window sash shoved up four inches from the bottom.

Yet something had dropped from the grasp of that suddenly withdrawn hand, at Hapwood's shout. It had come hurtling down. It had almost hit the brim of the reporter's hat, and then struck the walk with a leaden sound. He saw the fragments of it on the wet stone at his feet. Broken fragments of white jade—evidently at one time a carved statuette of a seated Buddha. But its smile was gone now, broken into six pieces, and its dead eyes looked up from a bodyless head. Broken pieces of a carved jade god!

Hapwood Bye gave a long, steady push to the bell beside the grilled glass door. The black rain poured. It sluiced off his hat, it ran off his ankle into his low shoes. He was as wet as a drowned man hauled from the sea, and he was shivering, shaking.

He got out his matchbox and jammed a match into the electric bell button, holding it down. *Kling-g-ggg!* he heard it ringing far away inside of the house. Ringing and ringing.

But no one answered.

The grilled outer door was not quite latched. The last person in or out had failed to close it securely. Bye put his shoulder to it, and shoved into a small marble-tiled foyer out of the rain. He tried the inner door, but it was locked. Through the yellow silk that covered the glass upper panel he could see the dim glow of a hall light inside.

He found an iron knocker on the door. He banged it. The noise echoed and reverberated through the house. The jammed electric bell was clanging steadily inside the hall. The howling monkey screamed its laughter from somewhere in the upper stories. But there was no other answer.

No answer at the door. Yet quietly and keenly the young reporter was aware, in every sense that he possessed, that there was someone crouching close-pressed against the door, inside! Someone who had heard him ringing and had come down —someone who was crouching and listening to him now, just on the other side of that inch and a half of wood! Crouching and listening in utter, appalling silence!

Hapwood Bye shook. He was afraid!

Yes, though he had tried to grin and whistle it away, he had been shaken with terror ever since he had first paused in front of this lighted, strangely noisy, yet strangely silent house! A terror of sinister and ghastly deeds. Of crime. Of murder!

What was it that damned bird had been crying?

"Youva! Murty!"

He hadn't quite got the words before. Now he realized. It was Spanish—*lluvia* and *muerte.* "Lluvia, lluvia! Muerte, muerte!" the parrot had been crying. "Rain, rain!" And, "Death, death!"

Death behind this door!

Hapwood Bye fumbled for a cigarette with stiff, tense fingers and thrust it between his lips. He turned away. He emerged from the little entrance foyer, closing the grilled glass outer door behind him, but leaving it a little off the catch as he had found it. Nonchalantly and not too rapidly he forced himself to loiter down the stoop. He even paused half-way down to light his cigarette with a cupped hand beneath the rain, though the hair was rising on his neck and the goose-flesh on his spine, and he felt the threat of that voiceless, nameless, hiding horror there at the door behind him every instant. He reached the sidewalk with a steady step. But once upon it he clutched the folds of his raincoat about his lean gasping ribs, and ran!

## CHAPTER II

## PROWLERS IN THE NIGHT

HE SPRINTED FAST and breathlessly, looking back over his shoulder at the screen star's home. If anyone had come rushing forth to follow him or to escape he would have seen him. But no one emerged. No one!

His feet pounded down the rain-flooded walk beneath the elms, past the line of darkened and sleeping residences, towards the gleaming lights of the All-Nite drugstore at the corner.

He must reach a telephone! He must find out if Lila Lane would answer—if she was all right. He didn't want to make a fool of himself with Sergeant Hennessy. Perhaps, he tried to argue as he put distance between him and that house of horror, he had been mistaken. But his keen crime instinct knew better. A broken window. A screaming, frightened little monkey. A bird that had been crying "Rain" and "Death". . .

He cut across the street at the corner and slowed his pace at the drugstore's entrance. The telephone booth was in the front beside the wide plate windows, where he could still keep an eye on the screen star's gleaming house.

But the telephone booth was occupied at the moment, and in front of it bulked the raincoated figure of the patrolman on the beat. The drugstore clerk sat sprawled at a marble table in the rear, half asleep, his face resting on his palms.

No one had yet come out of the front door of the house down the street. Hapwood was sure of it. And there was a memory in the back of his mind that all those old houses in the block were built back to back, without rear entrances or an intervening alley. Whoever had been in there was *still* there—could not get away unseen.

He snatched the telephone book from its hook beside the booth, under the vague inquiring eyes of the patrolman. He would have to tip off the police, of course. But he wanted to make sure first. A little of his excitement and fright had evaporated now. Lila Lane might answer the phone.

There might be some logical explanation for all those fantastic details which had so scared him. He didn't want to get a laugh from Hennessy at headquarters with a false alarm.

Quickly, he riffled through the book. She had rented the house only recently. The number would be under Van Nieman. *Van Nieman, Adelbert Q., res* 1175 *Mass Ave., Elm* 3014—that was it. He reached for a nickel. Then he remembered, and cursed. The phone was in use.

The man in the booth apparently was settled down to an all-night conversation. The door was open. His hard heavy voice was audible. It was Hennessy, the red-faced, white mustached, bat-eared Sergeant Richard P. Hennessy himself, of the headquarters squad.

"So I think." Hennessy was saving from the corner of his mouth, "that we'll be able to lay hands on him pretty soon for you, Mr. Van Nieman . . . Sure, we'll keep it out of the newspapers . . . Don't mention it. G'bye."

At last! Hennessy heaved his heavy shoulders and stepped out. His hard blue eyes lighted on Hapwood Bye with anger and alarm.

"Wait a minute, you!" he said. "Don't you go telephoning in that I'm looking for young Van Nieman!"

He seized Hapwood's arm as the pale reporter pushed into the booth. Sergeant Hennessy credited Hapwood Bye with a sinister kind of mind-reading magic.

"Now listen here!" he said angrily. "There's no story in it, you snooping squirt. The old man simply asked me to help him locate his boy Howe, confidentially. There's no charge against him."

The gray sergeant evidently was looking for Howe Van Nieman, and was trying to cover it up. That much clicked in Hapwood's mind. Howe Van Nieman was the youngest of old Adelbert Q's sons, the one who was an architect. Hapwood remembered him distantly from college—a tall thin handsome fellow with a terrific pride in the Van Nieman honor and importance, mingled with an earnest intellectual Bolshevism. Hapwood had always considered him worthless and a nut.

"Take your hands off me!" he snapped. "I don't want any of your dirty washing, Hennessy."

"Listen, Hap," Hennessy wheedled. "There's one thing I always did like about you. When a man gives you something confidential, you can be trusted not to spill it. Before you telephone your story in, let me give you the facts."

"Oh, for Christmas sake!"

Hapwood wrenched free from the burly sergeant, who was trying to hold him pinned against the wall. He dropped his nickel in. It was a pay phone.

"Elm 3014!"

The "busy" signal sounded. The coin came rattling back down. He inserted it again with quick excited fingers, rattling the hook.

"Listen, sister, don't kid me with the busy signal! Wake up, and ring them for me!"

He heard her ringing.

"Now, wait a minute!" said Hennessy, still beside him. "Listen, wise guy. All there is about young Van Nieman is that he left his family a couple of months ago—after his old man had lost all his dough and moved out to the country. The kid had no job or money and the family is worried. But Patrolman Rounds here, and two or three other people, have recognized him prowling around the neighborhood, wearing a cap pulled down over his face and a crazy long black coat."

"Oh, great Greece!"

At that instant the telephone operator cut in. "They do not answer. Shall I ring them again?"

"Ring them again!" said Hapwood. "Keep on ringing!"

There was still no movement from the house down the street.

"Listen, if you think you've got a story, you're mistaken," said Hennessy angrily. "The young fellow always was a little queer anyway, his family tell me. A kind of an artist and parlor anarchist. Now some people might jump to the conclusion that he's been prowling around this neighborhood because he's got some socialistic bug in his head that it isn't right for Lila Lane, who used to be only his father's chauffeur's daughter, to be living in that fine old house with all her servants to wait on her. And some damn fools might even jump to the conclusion that he's planning to slip in with the keys he still has and rob her of her famous jewels one of these fine nights. But—"

The telephone was whirring its long, rhythmic ring. Still no answer. Hapwood closed his other ear as well as he could against Hennessy's muttering voice. He was listening, listening.

"Wait!" he breathed. "Wait!"

"They do not answer. Shall I r-r-ring—"

"Wait!" he shouted.

At the other end of the humming wire he had heard the faint, almost inaudible click of the receiver being lifted from its hook at last! Lifted without a word. Someone was listening to him back there in the screen star's home, in an utter appalling silence! He had anticipated that move—the intolerable curiosity, the watchfulness of the criminal unable to endure the ringing of that bell. The man, the beast or fiend who had crept down to the front door when he had demanded admittance a little while ago—the man who had waited there in utter silence beyond the door—that man was listening to him now!

"This is the police!" Hapwood shouted. "Do not attempt to escape! We have the house surrounded."

There was no answer. Only silence.

Hapwood Bye stood shivering. Still from that house with the gleaming lights down the street no one had emerged.

Now he must persuade Hennessy to enter. That was not easy. He had no complaint, except for a barking dog and a screaming monkey. No proof of crime except a parrot croaking "Death"—and Hapwood's own dark intuition.

"So it wasn't young Van Nieman at all you're after, damn your hide!" said Hennessy, chagrined. "What are you pulling now?"

"Lila Lane's house. Dick!" said Hapwood, trying to speak steadily. "All the animals are screeching and raising hell! I went up there to interview the dame. Somebody busts a window on the top floor. Yet no answer when I ring the bell for about five minutes. But there's someone behind the door, and listening! It's damned strange!"

"Some servant at home alone, and afraid to answer the door," said Hennessy incredulously.

"I thought of that. But why don't you phone, too?"

Sergeant Hennessy brushed his white mustaches with his forefinger, thoughtfully.

"Is Miss Lane at home tonight, Rounds?" he said.

"I haven't seen her." The big patrolman frowned with thought. "Mr. Eggleston, her husband, went out about half past eight, and walked down to the corner here with me. He was going to the Armory fights, and I happen to know one of the boys in the prelims, so we stood talking about them for a few minutes. He didn't say anything about Miss Lane going out, but she may have been going out later. Her house was lit up when I went by last, about ten or half past."

"What about the servants?"

"I'm acquainted with Miss LeClerc, the madame's personal maid," said the patrolman slowly. "That's all I know. The rest of them are all old Van Nieman servants, I think. Miss Lane took the staff over with the house. I had a date to take Suzanne—Miss LeClerc—to the movies tonight, only I got called for extra duty."

"Dating up the French high-stepper, Rounds?" growled Hennessy. "They come high for a harness bull."

"Miss LeClerc's not that kind, sergeant," exclaimed Rounds with reddened cheeks. "I met her in church last Sunday, and I had to work to get this date out of her. But Miss Lane must be home now," he said with sudden thought. "It's their whole night off. The staff's, I mean. Miss Lane lets them all off at the same time, Suzanne told me. But somebody's got to stay home with the animals. That monkey's like a baby."

Hapwood Bye stood shivering. Oh, he had known it! The girl alone, in that house of screaming beasts. He looked at Hennessy with tragic eyes.

"For God's sake, come on!"

A car went rushing down the street past the All-Nite as they emerged. A yellow or orange taxicab, going down the rain-washed pavement with swishing tires. Down the street the lights still gleamed in Lila Lane's house.

"Ten o'clock was the last time you passed by, Rounds?" said Hennessy, buttoning up his coat.

"Yes, sir, about. That was the time I saw young Mr. Van Nieman like I was telling you before Mr. Bye came in to telephone. He was standing across the street under a tree with his collar turned up and his cap pulled down over his eyes, watching Miss Lane's door. I started to cross to speak to him, but he walked away fast. He must have thought I took him for a tramp or something, and was kind of ashamed."

"You ought to've stopped him. His family is looking for him."

"I didn't know it then, sergeant. Didn't think much about it, anyway. The rain was beginning to come down heavy, and I was beating it back to the station to get my raincoat. The night had started out fine and clear, but all of a sudden it got to pouring."

They had crossed the street with hurrying heels. The rain leaped and splattered on the asphalt. It had worked its way down Hapwood's collar, down his spine. His bones were shivery to the marrow. *"Lluvia, lluvia! Muerte, muerte!"* the downpour seemed to beat a hushed refrain.

"Hey, that taxi's stopping there!" said Hennessy.

"It must be Mr. Eggleston getting back," said Rounds. "The fights ought to be about over."

The taxicab which had gone swishing past the corner came to a stop in front of the screen star's home. A man had got out and started unconcernedly and unsuspiciously up the stoop. At that instant all the lights went out upstairs.

"Holy night, they're laying for him!" roared Hennessy.

All three of them broke into a wild pounding run down the splashing walk. There rose a faint but piercing yell of terror from the dark house door. The taxicab hadn't yet had time to leave the curb. Suddenly the figure of a man came leaping out of the house and down the steps. He plunged headlong into the waiting cab.

"Devil damn him! It's what he was waiting for!" yelled Hapwood. "A perfect break!"

"Stop!" roared Hennessy.

He tugged at his gun. Rounds had his whistle between his lips, sounding a piercing blast. But the cab had got under way at once. It was streaking off down the street, picking up speed as it rolled.

It was possible the driver didn't realize that the whistle blast was meant for him. It was possible he had a gun at the back of his neck and could not stop. He went swishing away at forty miles an hour. It was too far for Hennessy to throw a furious blind shot at the cab's tires. The cab turned the corner, disappeared. Hapwood Bye was not even sure of its color in the night and blurring rain.

"Did you spot him?" gasped Hennessy.

"Kind of tall and thin!" breathed Rounds. "Wearing a cap and a long dark coat."

"Check!" said Hennessy grimly.

Checkmate was more the word for it, thought Hapwood. A tall man in a coat—what sort of identification was that? Leaping wildly down the steps that way, even a dwarf might have looked tall. Hapwood cursed. A big story had been within his grasp, a grim and terrible story with all details. A murderer caught red-handed. Now it was too late.

## CHAPTER III

## THE HOUSE OF HORROR

"WHO'S THAT knocking?" came down the parrot's hideous scream, from the broken upstairs window. "It's Barnacle Bill, and I want to come in! Toads and fishes!"

The front door, the grilled glass outer door of the screen star's home, was open a foot or so as the two police officers and Hapwood went charging up the steps. Inside the little tiled entrance foyer cowered a smallish man with goggle eyes, dressed in a light tweed topcoat and a light gray hat, holding a rolled umbrella clasped under his arm. He was unhurt apparently, but scared out of his wits.

"Did you get a good look at him, sir?" Hennessy asked tersely. "You're Miss Lane's husband, aren't you? Was it anyone you knew?"

Leander Eggleston was a man of about forty-five years of age, with a dudish look and a round puffy face. He wore a tiny wisp of green feather in the band of his pearl-gray hat, a pair of evenly folded chamois gloves extended an inch from his topcoat's breast pocket, and his black calfskin shoes were small and pointed and polished to a mirror gleam. His jaw worked inarticulately, and his eyes popped with terror.

"Who—who—"

They had all crowded into the foyer. Eggleston stood squeezed against the door. The keys did a St. Vitus dance in his shaking fingers, and he had dropped his silver-handled umbrella. He looked with a dumb horror at the hard red face of Hennessy and the pale, rather sinister face of the young reporter, not seeing at the moment the big patrolman behind them.

Hennessy flashed his shield.

"From headquarters!" he said. "Don't be alarmed. Is your wife at home?"

"Why—why, I don't know. What's happened?"

"Steady, Mr. Eggleston, just be calm. Did you get a good look at the man who came busting out of the house just now and beat it away in the cab you come home in?"

"Who—" gasped the little man, "who was he?"

"Probably just a sneak-thief," said Hennessy easily. "But could you give us a description of him? Anyone you knew?"

"Great heavens, no!" Eggleston managed to articulate. "Never saw him before. I'd like to lay my hands on him, the way he ran, confound him! He—he pushed me! Knocked the breath right out of me. He was all dark. Looked like a Hindu. You're from police headquarters, officer?"

"There's been a little epidemic of sneak-thievery around," lied Hennessy soothingly. "I just wanted to get this bird straight, Mr. Eggleston, that's all. Was he, now, did you happen to notice, a tall thin man about twenty-six, five feet eleven and a half tall, wearing a cap and a long black overcoat?"

"I—I didn't notice," the screen star's husband said blankly.

"Do you know Mr. Howe Van Nieman by any chance?"

"Van Nieman? Certainly. He's the owner of this house."

"No, I mean his son."

"Never even heard of him," said Eggleston blankly.

"Who was the taxi man who brought you home, Mr. Eggleston?" said Hennessy. "One of the regulars from the armory hackstand?"

"No, no! Just one of the hundreds you find cruising on the streets. I had walked several blocks before he picked me up." Ineffectually, he was still fumbling at the lock of the inner door. With a smooth unobtrusive gesture of authority, Hapwood Bye relieved him of the keys. He found the lock.

"You said he looked like a Hindu, Mr. Eggleston?" he suggested.

"Did I say that?"

"I quoted you."

"Yes," said Leander Eggleston, with a sudden burst of shrill intensity. "That's what startled me so, officer. Everybody knows that Miss Lane used to be acquainted with the Maharajah of Rangore. Nothing in it, I assure you. Just a friendship on her part. But the damned heathen devil, he tried to shoot her once when she wouldn't leave me for him. He made threats."

The puffy little man broke off, with trembling lips, with a voiceless whimper. The Maharajah of Rangore, repeated Hapwood Bye to himself! He recalled the sensational story three years ago about the fabulously rich and powerful Hindu prince who had tried to kidnap Lila Lane. Yet so much manufactured publicity comes out of Hollywood that it is difficult to remember all of it, or to distinguish what may be true from what is sheer publicity. A Hindu!

But the arm which Hapwood had seen against the upstairs window a while ago had not been a brown Hindu arm. No, it had been a white man's arm, with the shirt-sleeve rolled back. Or possibly a woman's.

The dog was still barking. There was a ceaseless whispering, a rustling and a pattering upstairs in Lila Lane's silent house as the four men entered the dim-lit hall. The house was not dead, alive, though death might be in it. Though death *was* in it, as Hapwood Bye knew with all his soul and intuition.

"Lila!" Leander Eggleston called.

*"Lila!"*

The dog barked.

It wasn't right. Hapwood jerked his head. He was cold to the bone, and shivering, shivering yet his brain was on fire. If only they had reached the house before Eggleston's damned cab had rolled up! That other creeping devil, whoever he was, had thought himself cornered, surrounded by the police. He had not dared to break and run. A half a minute sooner, and they would have caught him. Though that would not have saved the woman who had been alone in this house of terror with him. Who had not answered the telephone, nor the door.

Leander Eggleston paused to lay his umbrella down on a priceless antique table. He slipped his raincoat off and folded it, laying it down mechanically with his pearl-gray hat beside the umbrella, neat and careful as a cat in some subconscious compartment of his brain. His bald head shone. He straightened his polka-dot tie with a nervous finger. He advanced to the stairs.

"Lila, darling, are you awake?" he called shrilly.

The dog barked.

"You're sure she's home?" said Hennessy.

"She *must* be home! But—but she doesn't seem to answer."

Hennessy moved towards the stairs. "The servants are all out?"

"Yes, it was their night off. Till one o'clock."

"They had all gone before you left?"

"All. All, that is, except Navewoh, the butler. And Navewoh had changed to his street clothes. He was going out, too."

"Navewoh! What a queer name. Is he Russian or something?" said Hennessy frowning.

"I don't know. I hardly know him. You see we got him with the house."

Leander Eggleston pressed a button in the newel-post of the stairs. After a moment he called towards the back of the house, in a shrill breathless voice. Yes, they were all out. She had been alone. She was still alone, amidst the gibbering animals in this silent house. And if she did not answer now, would she ever?

Then Hapwood's whole body stiffened.

On the carpeted stair in front of him there were wet blotchy footprints, going up!

Going up, going UP. *But none coming down!*

"I don't want to alarm you needlessly, Mr. Eggleston," Hennessy said. "But I think we had better go up."

"I wish you would!" Leander Eggleston exclaimed fervently. "Her bedroom's at the top of the house! She's probably just asleep! She probably—Is it necessary for me to go up with you?"

"I'd rather you didn't."

With shaking fingers the screen star's husband straightened his tie again, staring at the wet footprints on the stairs. He rubbed a hand mechanically over his forehead and the top of his bald head. Hapwood Bye, alert and shivery, pushed past him to follow Hennessy. Suddenly a look of fearful horror came into the little man's bulging eyes. His puffy face turned the color of clabbered milk. He beat the air with his hands like a man strangling.

"Oh, damn me!" he choked. "I've *got* to see!"

He clawed the staring reporter out of his way and leaped up the stairs after Hennessy. "Wait!" he gasped. "Oh, please wait!"

Some dreadful intuition must have suddenly struck him, a foreboding of the horror they would find upstairs. He seized Hennessy by the tail of his coat, halfway up the stairs.

"I—I forgot!" he said with chattering teeth, while they stared at him. "You had better wait a minute, gentlemen! She—she might be undressed!"

"For God's sake!" said Hapwood Bye.

Undressed! She whose white limbs had posed and languored seductively on the screen for millions. The man was crazed with terror.

"Listen!" Leander whimpered, clinging to Hennessy, pursuing the stocky, gray sergeant up the stairs. "If—if anything happened to Lila, it was that devil Rangore—the Maharajah! He was mad about her! Oh, there's something happened to her now, I can see it by your faces! In God's name, gentlemen, we must be careful! We must be careful! There's someone upstairs now!"

It was horrible to see his corpselike face, to hear his chattering voice. This puffy cowardly fool whom Lila Lane had married, God knew why.

Hennessy mounted steadily, following the wet footprints. But he had his gun out now.

On the second floor they passed the doorway of the living-room, vaguely shadowed by a dying hearthfire. With a whisper in his throat Leander Eggleston paused to find the light switch inside the door. Hapwood Bye hesitated a moment, too.

The wet footprints had paused at the threshold of this room, but they had not gone in far. With a glance of his hot tired eyes, shivering against the doorpost, the reporter took in the scene. A huge red divan was drawn up before the fireplace down at the far end. Lamps and easy chairs, white book-shelves, flowers, pictures. On the grand piano near the door was a gold-framed photograph of Lila Lane. In the curbed bay window looking out at the street, a French telephone stood on a little red desk, the receiver hanging by the cord.

That telephone! There at that red desk in the window alcove, the criminal had softly picked up the telephone. He had heard Hapwood's wild threat, then let the instrument fall.

But how long ago? How long since he had fled from this room? There was the feel of him—almost the smell of him!—still lingering in this room. Why, he had been in here until he had heard or seen Leander Eggleston's cab stopping at the curb below! He had turned out the lights, as he fled downstairs and away.

But why had he turned out the lights, in that quick instant of darting through the door? To avoid being recognized by Leander, entering below? Yet Leander had said it was no one he knew! Why, then, had the killer turned out the lights?

The wet footprints had only hesitated a few steps inside the living room doorway, hunting her. Then they went on up the stairs, missing every other stair-tread now, leaping swiftly on the last of the murderous hunt. Near the top of the stairs Hennessy paused in his quickened ascent. He picked up a black fountain pen with three gold bands and a gold clip.

"I suppose the stairs are swept every day, Mr. Eggleston?" he said casually. "Last thing in the afternoon, usually? Then the man who owns this, lost it going up or down these stairs *tonight!*"

There was a name stamped in the rubber. But Hapwood, though he sprang up to Hennessy's side, didn't have time to read it before the headquarters man thrust the pen away inside his pocket.

"My washing, Hap," he said grimly. "This is one case I'm going to break before you."

## CHAPTER IV

## THE ROOM OF DEATH

THE BARKING DOG launched its strong chunky body against the inside of the door of Lila Lane's bedroom, at the top of the stairs. It growled savagely as they stood outside.

"Greta!" soothed Leander.

"Toads and fishes!" the parrot screamed.

The door was locked. Hennessy stepped back, and drove his iron heel against the panel above the lock. He split an aperture through which he could reach his hand. Through the crack the fire was visible in the bedroom grate, burning darkly red. The growling dog was inching backward towards the hearth, a stocky shadow with bristled ruff and glowing eyes. Upon the mantelpiece a spitting cat arched its back. There was furniture overturned. That much could be seen. And there was a flapping sound which Hapwood identified as the window shade, soaked with rain, flapping at the broken window.

Hennessy's groping fingers had found no key inside. He launched his burly body against the door. The lock gave, and Hennessy catapulted in across the threshold.

"Turn on the lights, Eggleston!" his hard voice cracked in the darkness. "Quick! There's something—"

Hapwood Bye, at the threshold, felt swiftly for the light switch. His groping fingers touched the clammy hand of Leander Eggleston upon the wall, reaching more quickly behind his back. Leander's hand leaped like a cold fish at the touch. He seized the reporter's wrist with a spasmodic clasp of terror. A yell tore from his throat.

"It's Rangore—the Hindu! Watch the window!"

"Watch out, Hennessy," the shivering reporter gasped. "It's—"

"Stop where you are!" snarled Hennessy.

The wet shade at the window jerked aside an instant. A swift shadow leaped across the room, went hurtling headlong out through the shattered glass. With an oath Hapwood tore himself free from Leander Eggleston's desperate clutch. He went sprawling across the room, stumbling blindly against chairs, tripping over debris scattered on the floor. His flying foot lit for an instant on something soft—something soft like hair. Touched it in the darkness on the rug, and leaped from it convulsively. Squashy! God, what had it been?

"Damn his hide!" Hennessy swore fluently. "He's got away!"

He had ripped the wet shade from its roller, thrusting his head and gun hand out through the window frame.

"No. It was just Leaping Leander, Hennessy," said Hapwood Bye with a deep breath. "I mean Wails—the monkey. I tried to yell at you, but I couldn't think of his damned name. I'm glad you didn't shoot the little fellow, anyway."

Out in the tall old elm in front of the house a small swift dark shadow, half spider and half man, with a whipping prehensile tail that was longer than its body, was swinging and flying downward from branch to branch, while the leaves rustled and the rain slathered. It looked back with its wrinkled little old man's face, its beady eyes.

"Whi-yee! Ya-wa-whoo!" it jeered.

"Damn his hide!" swore Hennessy. "Made a monkey out of both of us."

"From the beginning," said Hapwood softly. "From the beginning, I'm commencing to think."

But he couldn't think. He was cold, shivering. The rain was in his bones. There was a ghostly shape rustling and muttering in the corner—the parrot on its perch. And there was the slinking, rumbling dog, and the spitting cat on the mantel.

Policeman Rounds, at the door, black and stolid, had found the switch; he flashed it on. The ceiling light illuminated a scene of savage wreckage and destruction all through this room where the murder hunt for Lila Lane had ended.

The screen star's bedroom had been insanely demolished. Bureau drawers were emptied out on the rug. Chair turned upside down. Bedding and mattress had been pulled off the bed springs. A chiffonier of satinwood and chromium lay over on its side. The glass of the gilt clock on the mantelpiece was smashed. Over in a far corner a painted screen, portraying white peacocks beside a blue Indian lagoon, was sprawled at a crazy angle against a closet door.

As a last touch to the picture of whirlwind chaos there lay scattered over the floor, over the hearth, over the upset chairs and the bedding piled on the floor, dozens and dozens of little carved figures of pale green jade, figures of mottled old white jade, of cream and blue-veined fade—the famous and priceless jade Buddha collection of Lila Lane.

Here was destruction without conceivable meaning. The gorilla of Poe's Rue Morgue could not have wreaked more meaningless upheaval. Yet it could not have been the little ringtail howler that had done this. This was man's handiwork. The hands of the gilt clock which had been smashed on the mantelpiece had been turned back to nine o'clock, to set a misleading hour. Monkeys don't make alibis.

There were other details which Hapwood saw but thought of only afterwards. But the whole effect was the thing—the details did not matter. *Premeditated madness!*

Leander Eggleston was still sitting in the middle of the room where he had sprawled when the monkey fled, his face the color of putty, his mouth opened in a horrible grimace. He was holding one hand plastered to the top of his brown hair as if he had just been dealt a blow there. Rounds still stood at the door, gun in one hand, his other hand pressed over the light switch that he had just turned on. The black-faced Siamese cat arched its back on the bureau top. The parrot ruffled on its perch, rattling its light chain. Crouching and growling by the hearth, the tawny thick-shouldered dog was circling with bristled ruff. With a sudden rush and snarl it charged the door and shot away out of the room between the big patrolman's wide-spread feet.

In front of the hearth the lounge lay spilled over on its side. Beside it lay a soiled yellow satin bedroom mule—a book—a sewing basket, out of which a jumble of black silk stockings, darning silk and needles had been spilled.

"Black stockings!" breathed Hapwood Bye.

Already there had been born a curious idea in the reporter's mind, even before he saw the dead girl or the manner of her death. The overturned lounge, the book and sewing basket, seemed to have a meaning which the rest of the picture of whirlwind destruction lacked. She had probably been sitting there in front of the fire when the killer came. She had seen him—perhaps before he saw her. Frantically she had sought to escape, to hide from that death coming up the stairs! Hiding panic-stricken, terrified. Where *had* she tried to hide? Where was she now? And where was *he?*

In the middle of the room Leander Eggleston sat holding his dazed head where he had fallen. Leander's bulging eyes were fixed in incredulous horror on the mirror of the satinwood vanity across the room from him. He got to his shaky knees, pointing inarticulately.

"Siva!" he croaked. "The sign of Siva!"

He staggered backward towards the door. The hair seemed to leap from his head, and he whirled with a gurgling scream as he came into contact with the large body of Rounds at the threshold. With frantic hands, he pushed past. He fled in whimpering leaps down the stairs.

Upon the middle mirror of the vanity there had been drawn a curious mark in red, about a foot high, consisting of a circle, a dot inside, and two vertical parallels underneath. Hennessy's roving glance found it. He stared.

"What the hell?"

"It's a Hindu religious symbol," said the reporter wearily. "Eggleston had seen it before, somewhere—in India probably. It's the sign of the Hindu God, Siva the Destroyer."

The headquarters man moved to it. He ran a thumb tentatively down the glass beside the thick red lines. He picked up something from the vanity top.

"Lipstick," he said. "Lila's own."

Hapwood was shaking. The rain that had drenched him through had given him the flu. He would be a sick man tomorrow. His thoughts whirled giddily. "You get the picture, Hennessy?" he said.

"Sure, I get the picture! Siva, the Destroyer—it means whoever killed her left that sign. But what did the devil do with her?"

The sergeant's roving glance had completed the circuit then, to the far corner of the room, to the painted screen that leaned crazily against the closet door. The door was closed, but there was a split in the wood from top to bottom. And underneath it, over the threshold, a thin dark stream had trickled forth.

Hennessy strode to it. He jerked the screen aside. The closet door was inconspicuous in the corner—no wonder they had failed to see it at first glance. The murderer himself must have missed it at first, when he had come in. And perhaps for a minute or two he had been baffled, thinking she had gone away, cursing her, hunting around for her, hunting her like a rat. Snarling, kicking over chairs, pulling open the bathroom door, peering under the bed, cursing and wild with murder all the time, while she waited, tense and breathless, frozen in her terror; waited to be murdered while the parrot screamed and the dog barked and the damned monkey laughed.

But the killer had found her, at last. He had found her hiding place. And it was there, behind that narrow door in stifling darkness, that she had met her death.

The lower panel of the closet door was split, splintered half a dozen times with bullet holes that had gone crashing through the wood. And there was that dark stain which had seeped out at the bottom over the sill, darkening the edge of the rug. Hennessy whipped out a handkerchief and laid it over the knob. He pulled, but the door was locked or bolted on the inside. He got down on his heavy knees. Pushing his hat to the back of his head, he pressed an eye to a crack, staring in.

"Dead, of course?" said Hapwood, shivering.

But, hell, he thought, what a stupid question! That dog's weird howling had meant only one thing, Death! And the awful silence he had met at the front door—and the silence over the phone.

And still there was something in Hapwood Bye's confused brain which refused to believe that Lila Lane was dead!

Hennessy got up heavily.

"Open it up, Rounds!" he said.

"Is it Lila?" whispered Hapwood.

"Yeah, she's crumpled up on the floor. There's a little light shines in through these cracks. I could just see the back of her yellow dressing gown, and one arm twisted around behind her. It must have happened an hour or more ago, by the looks of the blood on her gown. She was dead when you first come knocking at the door. Cheer up, smart guy! You've got a story that will knock their eye-teeth out. Lila Lane murdered—the famous movie actress!"

Rounds had got the fireplace poker, and was jimmying at the closet door.

"Did you say she had on a yellow dressing gown?" echoed Hapwood Bye.

"Yeah. She was undressed for bed, you see."

"I don't get it," Hapwood said, closing his eyes, with a tired shake of his head.

"You don't? Why, she was sitting reading or sewing when she heard him, see, and run and hid from him in the closet. There is the book she was reading, and the sewing basket she dropped. She locked herself in the closet. He found her, jammed his gun against the door, and blasted it five times. A .32 would be my guess. He shot through the lower panel, so if she was standing up he'd drop her, and if she was crouching, which was more probable, he'd get her in the body or head. He knew she would be alone. He knew her husband and the servants were all going out. He—"

"I know, I know," whispered Hapwood. "But she couldn't have been color-blind, could she?"

"What do y' mean?"

Hapwood stared at Hennessy with a sigh.

"It's not Lila Lane," he said. "It's not Lila Lane at all in there."

"You're out of your head!" said Hennessy, glaring. "I told you I *saw* her!"

"The yellow dressing gown, the frayed old yellow mule," said Hapwood wearily. "Would a girl as *blonde* as Lila Lane be wearing *yellow?* The book she was reading—it's French, see?—the sewing basket—the pile of *black* stockings waiting to be mended. That was the picture I couldn't get. The million-dollar star of KGS wouldn't be mending her own stockings, you can bet a dime! And I don't think she'd be reading French."

"French! You mean—?"

"Yes."

"Why, damn you!" shouted Hennessy. "You're right!"

With a last ripping heave, Patrolman Rounds had wrenched open the closet door. The yellow-clad form, the dark-plaited hair of the slender girl inside rolled out across the door sill.

## CHAPTER V

## "DON'T DO IT!"

SHE HAD BEEN shot through the head and neck, the little dark French maid, Suzanne LeClerc. Two of the bullets that had gone crashing through the wood from the murderer's gun had missed her. One had grazed her arm. But the other two had indicted mortal wounds. She had died quickly.

"About an hour ago," said Hennessy heavily, on his knees. "Not more than two hours ago. Not earlier than half past ten."

"What time were you to have had your date with her, Rounds?" said Hapwood Bye.

"Eight o'clock." said the patrolman dully. "We were going to meet at the corner by the church."

"Did you tell her you'd been called for duty and couldn't keep the date?"

"I didn't get a chance."

She had waited a while, and then returned home, thought Hap. And Lila Lane had decided to go out then, since there was someone to mind her menagerie. Then the killer had come. The frightened maid had heard him creeping up the stairs, had peered down, and recognized him. He was someone she knew! He was someone whom she feared!

Whom had she had a chance to meet in town since she arrived with Lila Lane? Not many people, certainly. She knew the Van Nieman servants, probably. And, of course, she knew Rounds.

Rounds!

Rounds had admitted that he had come past the house, on his way to get his raincoat, around ten o'clock or a little later. About the time, or within a half hour of it, when the murder had been committed. The man who had been in the house when Hapwood knocked, the man who had leaped out and away in the cab as the reporter had come hurrying back with Hennessy and Rounds—suppose *he* had not been the murderer at all! Just a casual sneak-thief, for instance, who had found himself in a house where murder had already been done.

Suppose that Rounds, as he passed by at a quarter after ten, knowing the girl was alone, had entered softly and quietly with his police key, crept softly up the stairs—

No, that entire theory was preposterous! Rounds' big dull face was his best alibi. He certainly would not have had enough imagination or knowledge to have put that sign of Siva the Destroyer on the mirror.

No, Rounds was out of it. Who else, then, had this dead girl known? The Van Nieman servants. There were five who lived in or had access to the house, Eggleston had said, the butler, the cook, an upstairs girl and a waitress-parlor maid, and the furnace man part time. The name of the missing butler, Navewoh, came curiously up into Hapwood's brain. There was something damned queer about that odd name—

But he was too tired, too cold and wet, to think. Let it *go.*

"God, if I'd known this, I never would have stood her up on that date," the big patrolman was saying dully. "She was such a shy pretty kid. Never had stepped out with any man in all her life before, she said."

"And you fell for that old line, did you, Romeo?" sneered Hennessy.

Rounds' impassive face grew dark. "She was a good girl," he said stubbornly.

"Yeah? Well, I might as well tell you now that she was playing around with young Van Nieman. Last week somebody seen the two of them down the street having some kind of a palaver. She was crying, and saying no, no, she wouldn't do it, and he was telling her not to be scared, he'd take care of her."

"It couldn't have been Suzanne!" said Rounds with a whitened jaw.

"It *was!* Old man Norton, who lives a couple of blocks down the street, saw them when they stopped right in front of his house. He sneaked the window up to listen. He couldn't have been mistaken in either of them. He's known Howe Van Nieman all his life, and he knew the girl."

"Maybe it was Van Nieman. But she—"

"Old man Norton thought it was just the usual thing between 'em," said the old headquarters man stonily. "And so did I when he first told me about it. But you can read back to what they were saying, now. They were working together on some crook job. To get Miss Lane's jewels, most likely. The girl was losing her nerve—and she knew too much. So he killed her!"

Hennessey had arisen from his knees as he spoke. There was something, a scrap of paper it looked like, which he had extracted from the pocket of the dead girl's yellow dressing-gown. He put it carefully away into his wallet, grim satisfaction on his red face. He did not show what he had found to Hapwood, and the reporter knew it was no use asking.

"All right, Hap, go peddle your papers," he said with rough good nature. "It wasn't so big a story as you thought, but still it's a good one!"

"Where's Lila Lane now?" said Hapwood, shivering.

"What difference does that make? Out having a good time, I hope, on her night off from that half-wit clown she married."

Hapwood thrust a cigarette between his cold, shaking lips. "For God's sake, we've got to find her!"

"Why?"

*"Why?* Because she's in deadly danger still, with this damned killer loose and prowling! And I'll have the story I expected before the night's over, unless we use our heads! Don't you get it? This poor girl was killed in *mistake* for Lila! The killer expected to find Lila Lane in the house alone. Suzanne had hidden before he saw her."

"Oh, yeah?"

"Maybe he doesn't know his mistake yet," said the reporter, with shivering teeth, trying to speak calmly. "But suppose he happened to see Lila on the street. He's gone too far. All hell's not going to stop him from finishing what he set out to do!"

"Yeah? So she was killed in mistake for Lila Lane, huh? Tell me another! And maybe it was a Hindu that killed her, too!" sneered Hennessy.

"I didn't say that."

"It wasn't young Van Nieman, eh?" Hennessy said harshly. "We didn't see him making his getaway from the door not fifteen minutes ago, huh? Oh, no!"

"How the hell do I know what we saw?" said Hapwood. "How the hell do I know it was Howe Van Nieman we saw? How do I know we saw *anybody?"*

"Maybe it was all done with mirrors, Hap, and the killer was really hiding under the doormat all the time," jeered Hennessy. "And maybe I'm getting feeble-witted in my old age and ought to be sent to the home for incurables."

"Maybe," said Hapwood.

Hennessy's face swelled redly.

"Is that so? You're too smart for your own good, wise guy. All right, Rounds! Stay on guard, here, and leave everything just as we found it. And watch out that this bright guy here doesn't start biting off chunks of the mantelpiece for clues, just to show he's Sherlock Holmes. Where's the telephone? We'll have Van Nieman in the bag and all sewed up before our feet are dry."

Pushing his derby on the back of his head, the burly gray-haired headquarters veteran hurried forth and down the stairs. Hapwood Bye lingered, feverishly hot and confused, looking around the disordered room in puzzlement, cursing himself for something he had failed to see. Or that he saw and hadn't recognized.

"What was he wearing, Rounds?" the reporter murmured wearily. "The man that got away, I mean. A dark coat and a cap?"

"Sure, a coat and a cap."

"Great Greece! Any man would be wearing a coat in this rain tonight. But the cap! There aren't many men that wear them any more."

He was all hot and burning with his fever chill. He should have his wet clothes off him, and be between blankets. Hot! His whole body was hot.

The black-faced cat arched with fluffed fur upon the bureau still. The parrot squawked on its perch. What a story they could tell, if they could only speak!

"Toads and fishes!" the parrot squawked.

"Yes!" said Hapwood almost hysterically. "Toads and fishes. Toads and fishes were what it was raining. And the monkey went out in it without his rubbers."

There! What thought had just escaped him? Oh, dear God!

There was a photograph in a silver frame on the bureau back of the bristling cat. He reached for it. For a moment he studied the photograph with tired eyes. It was an enlargement of an informal snapshot, showing Lila Lane on horseback with two men accompanying her, riding on a California beach beneath bright sunlight. They had halted, it seemed, after a canter, to pose while the photograph was snapped. The beautiful blonde screen star had her head back, laughing. Her hair was in disorder. Her pretty face, her wide expressive mouth, her large laughing eyes, all seemed terribly youthful and alive.

On her left, Leander Eggleston sat smugly in his saddle, wearing a sporty tweed riding coat and white breeches, his boots polished to a mirror gleam, his brown hair neatly parted in the middle. Wearing a smug look on his low-browed and vacuous face.

But it was the other man, the one on the other side of the beautiful screen star, who interested Hapwood Bye. He was a small man, lean and dark. He wore a cap, a polo shirt, and long riding trousers of the sort known in India as "jodhpurs."

"The Hindu—Rangore!" mused the young reporter.

Rounds had turned his back an instant. Hapwood slipped the photograph out of its frame. On its back there was written, in what was doubtless Lila Lane's heavy careless scrawl, "Riding with Popsy and Buddha. Malibu Beach, May, '32. Doesn't he look like the devil?"

Popsy, of course, was Leander. Buddha, then, must have been her mocking name for the grim, dark, humorless little maharajah. And the photograph had been taken, by its date, about the time of his famous and somewhat ridiculous attempt at shooting her. Who looked like the devil—his Hindu majesty or her husband?

The photograph told Hapwood Bye nothing about the dark crime tonight. He slipped it back into its frame.

"The man in the cap was rather tall, wasn't he, Rounds?" he demanded curiously.

"Six feet or more. Don't touch nothing more in here, Mr. Bye. You heard what the sergeant said."

"About five feet eight or nine, at the least," mused Hapwood. "Yes, that was my impression, too. And this Hindu high muckatamuck is a pint-sized little hellion. Not above five feet three or four. Nothing as tall as Lila Lane herself. He *couldn't* have been the man who ran from the door. Maybe he was what we thought was the monkey."

"That damned monkey!" said Rounds.

"Yes," said Hapwood, sighing. "Yes, 'damned' is correct, Rounds. I still have a feeling, Sergeant Rounds, that he made a monkey out of all of us."

"I'm not a sergeant, Mr. Bye," said Rounds.

"No," said Hapwood, with a grin, "and I'm not Sherlock Holmes, either, I'm beginning to suspect. It's a slight wooziness in the head, Lieutenant, from a dry stomach and wet feet. The peerless Bye brain, I'm afraid, has been disrupted by an intrusion of the flu bug, and is not quite coordinated. My God, there's something dancing before my eyes as clear as the almighty sun, and I can't see it! Oh, well! Which would you recommend as the best remedy for a touch of incipient fever and a marked case of mental incompetence, Inspector—whiskey, or whiskey? And if so, straight or neat?"

"I'm not a lieutenant, and I'm not an inspector, neither, Mr. Bye," said Rounds with a changeless face. "But I've heard that if you take a bullet and put it in the glass of whatever you're drinking, it's the best cure for colds."

"A bullet?" said Hapwood, startled.

"Yes, sir, it's what I've heard. There's a tonic in it that acts straight on your heart."

For an instant the reporter stared at Rounds' impassive countenance. In this quiet room with the dead woman, there had seemed something sinister in the slow quiet words. Rounds took a slow step in his direction. Yet there was nothing behind the big dull patrolman's suggested remedy, he decided. Why was that uneasiness and jittery fright still in him? Fever, no doubt.

But where was Lila Lane? When had she left the house? Where had she been at half past ten tonight?

"You're shaking," said Rounds with sympathy. "You're ill. Better go home and stick your feet in a hot water bucket."

"My head, too," said Hapwood wearily.

There was nothing here. Nothing here in this insane helter-skelter room where death had stalked. Stepping carefully between and over the scattered jade Buddhas, he made for the door. He paused on the threshold to drag a last lungful out of his cigarette. He hurled the butt across the room at the mirror of the satinwood and chromium vanity.

"Lipstick!" he swore.

"Hey, don't do that, guy!" said Rounds angrily.

"Don't do it!" squawked the parrot in the corner.

"Lipstick to both of you!" said Bye wearily. "You're a pair off the same bush."

"Don't do it, Howe! Don't do it, Howe!" the parrot squawked suddenly.

Hapwood Bye stared at it in fascination, shivering and rattling his teeth. If that bird could only say, with an intelligent brain, what its scaly drooping eyes had seen! It would be the star witness of the murder!

"Pretty bird!" the reporter said softly. "Nice bird. Where's Howe? Where's Howe?"

"How are you?" squawked the parrot.

"Howe? Howe?"

"Ha, ha, ha!" the parrot laughed. *"Lluvia! Muerte!"*

"Don't?" Hapwood urged persuasively. "Don't?"

"Don't let my husband know! We'll go through with it this way! Ha, ha, ha!"

"Lila?" said Hapwood, trembling. "Where's Lila?"

The parrot shifted its position on its perch. It craned its head, blinking one eye.

"Lila?" urged Hapwood softly.

"Be quiet!"

"Be quiet? Be quiet?"

"Be quiet! It's Suzanne coming back!"

"Gun? Gun?"

"Son of a gun!" the parrot screamed, flapping its wings in anger. "Son of a gun!"

"Where's Howe?" said Hapwood again, softly and persuasively. "Where's Howe?"

"How are you? Toads and fishes! Ha, ha, ha!"

Ruffling, the parrot subsided. It drew its scaly eyelids down. Digging its claws more deeply into its perch, it went to sleep with its head beneath its wing.

"Holy Jerusalem!" muttered Patrolman Rounds. "What do you make of an inhuman bird like that?"

Hapwood Bye shook his head.

Suddenly, standing in befuddlement at the threshold there, turning to go, he remembered the thing that his foot had touched as he came in, rushing in the darkness towards the window. The soft and squashy thing which had given him a strangely abhorrent feeling to step on, like a small hairy animal underfoot. He had not seen it since. Nor could he identify now what it had been, though he looked a little carefully, among all the many scattered little gods of cream and pale green and mottled blue jade which lay with their wise faces on the floor.

## CHAPTER VI

## DISGUISE

IN THE LIVING ROOM on the floor below, Sergeant Hennessy was seated at the red desk in the front bay window, talking over the telephone.

"Howe Van Nieman, formerly of 1125 Massachusetts Avenue, present address unknown," the headquarters veteran droned. "Wanted for murder. Age twenty-six, height five feet eleven and a half, weight about one sixty-five, dark curly hair, dark blue eyes, sandy freckled forehead, square chin with a little dent in it, long narrow ear lobes. Unemployed architect by profession. He will probably be found dressed in a long dark coat and a cap.

"Last seen fleeing from 1125 Massachusetts Avenue about 12:08, in orange or yellow cab, number unknown. If he has left cab, endeavor to locate driver who picked up passenger four or five blocks from the armory after the fights tonight, driving passenger to 1125—and find out where he dropped Van Nieman, whom he had picked up there. This man is armed."

The veteran detective set the phone down as Hapwood Bye came into the long, quiet living-room.

"Huh!" he snorted to the reporter. "What've you been doing, Sherlock—counting the flowers on the bedroom wallpaper or third-degreeing the parrot?"

"Aren't you a little previous?" Hapwood said.

"Previous! In sending out the alarm for Howe Van Nieman, you mean? What should I do, wait till next December and send him a Christmas card? He can't have got very far away yet, but that doesn't mean I'm going to sit holding my fingers till I hear from him in Mexico. When you're going after a killer on the run, you've got to move fast!"

"Could you," said Hapwood tiredly, "identify the man who fled from the house as young Van Nieman? *Did you* identify him? If you did, why didn't you say so then?"

Hennesy looked confused for a moment.

"Well," he said with a hollow laugh, "well, naturally I didn't recognize him right off the bat."

"How about his ears?" said Hapwood ironically.

"His ears?"

"Height live feet eleven and a half, dark, curly hair, dark blue eyes, sandy, freckled forehead, square, dented chin, *and long ear lobes,"* quoted the reporter ironically. "I don't doubt in the least you made a detailed observation of all the other features in the split second we saw him. But how can you be certain about the ears?"

"Oh, go to hell! You saw him yourself."

"You can't tell me what *I* saw."

"At least you'll admit you saw a man beat it out the door, won't you?"

"A human being," said Hapwood slowly. "Man or woman. Yes."

"Say, that's a good shot, Sherlock. Maybe it wasn't the killer at all. Maybe it was just Lila Lane catching the midnight train."

"Except that there isn't any midnight train," said Hapwood. "That's about as intelligent a thing as you've said tonight."

Hennessy pulled out the fountain pen he had found on the stairs and passed it to the reporter gloatingly. The name stamped in the rubber was "Howe Van Nieman."

"Maybe," said Hennessy with a grin, "you'll say *that* was left in the house when Lila rented it. Only fountain pens aren't left in houses. Or maybe you'll say young Van Nieman lost it, and the killer found it, and then the killer lost it out of his pocket tonight. Only there were some fingerprints on it. And you see, I had already got me the classification of Howe's prints from the National Guard files, *and they check!"*

Hapwood Bye took the pen which Hennessy extended and stared at the name on it with tired eyes.

"And here!" said Hennessy. "Don't say I never gave you nothing. Found it in Suzanne's dressing-gown upstairs while you were gagging with Rounds. I kinda hate to show it to you, but it's too good to keep. You can copy it for your story." From his wallet he extracted the piece of paper that Hapwood had seen him secreting above. It was a fragment of a letter which the girl Suzanne had no doubt torn up and thrust into her pocket after reading, to dispose of later. But this one triangular scrap had stuck to the fabric of her gown. The writing was distinctive, square and bold.

> . . . *after Mr. Eggleston has left to-ni* . . . *kill her. She suspects S* . . . . . . *over bet.* . . .

"Are you sure that's Howe's writing?" asked Hapwood.

"Sure. A sample of his writing was one of the things I got when I started out to look for him. If she didn't burn the rest of the letter, we may find it all."

"But," said Hapwood. "the presumption from this meager scrap, if anything in it is worth a button, would be that Howe Van Nieman and the girl Suzanne were planning to kill Lila Lane. Yet Suzanne was killed in mistake for Lila! That's my story, and I'll stick to it."

"Oh, stick your head in a tar bucket!" said Hennessy in disgust.

Somebody hiccupped mournfully.

"What have you two gen'lemen been muttering and muttering about?" a sad voice said, from the other end of the room.

Over the back of the wide red velvet divan in front of the fireplace at the far end of the living-room a man's head peered at them. It was Leander Eggleston's puffy round face. Leander got unsteadily to his feet, a tall highball glass in his hand. Hiccuping again, he came weaving up the room towards them.

"Pardon my—*hic!*—not doing my duty as hosh," he said with gravity. "But couldn't stand it."

Hapwood Bye had not known that the foolish, pompous little man was in the room, and probably Hennessy hadn't, either. The reporter was glad now that their voices had been subdued. Even Hennessy's over the phone, sending in the call for the coroner and the alarm for Howe Van Nieman, had been pitched to a confidential professional tone that must have only vaguely reached Leander, reclining on the big divan. Some of the rather hardboiled and callous references to the dead girl or Lila Lane which they had made might have been unpleasant to the little man.

He sat down heavily in the bay window on the curved window seat, back of the desk. The glass he was holding was half full of straight whiskey. His bulging eyes were bloodshot, his complexion pasty and pale. Hapwood Bye, soaked and shivering, regarded Leander's glass with envy. About three inches of that would do him a lot of good against the ravages of the flu bug which made his spine creep with shivers and sent queer jolts of a cold, unreasoning terror all through his heart.

If it was the flu only—

Whiskey with a bullet in it, Rounds had recommended. Strange how that remark of the dull, big patrolman recurred to him now! Someone was going to have a bullet tonight before that roaming killer was discovered! A killer with a gun, roaming wild, as cunning as a fiend, as cruel as death. Where was he now?

What time had this butler, Navewoh, gone out? He had still been in the house when Leander Eggleston had left, earlier that evening. Navewoh! What an extraordinary name!

Hapwood was still fingering the fountain pen which Hennessy had given him.

"I may be no detective, gen'lemen," hiccupped Leander, "and I may be no murder expert, as you two gen'lemen are. And I may be only a drunken shun of a gun—but I can see the whole dark and bloody business!"

"Where did you get the licker, Leander?" murmured Hapwood.

"Shorry," said Leander with drunken gravity. "Most fatally shorry. Failed my obligations as gentleman and hosh. All this terrible business mosh upshetting, a man of my poshishion. Would you care for drink, officer?"

"Since you've nominated me as both an officer and a gentleman," said Hapwood with a freezing grin, "I'd be glad to qualify as a judge of good whiskey, too. In other words, I *would.*"

The puffy-faced little man arose a moment unsteadily on his polished feet. He gave a yank to a silk cord at the side of the window which Hapwood thought was only a part of the heavy portière curtains, but which might have been a bell cord at that. Gravely Leander jerked it three times, before sitting down again.

"No, gen'lemen," he said thickly, "I may not be detective, but I could read what happened like a book. Rangore's damn Hindus broke in window, and hunted till they found her! Poor girl, poor girl, poor girl! Mosh unfortunate."

"Pretty good for an amateur. Mr. Eggleston," said Hennessy with an amused grin. "But you're wrong about one little thing. Rangore didn't have a thing to do with it. That Hindu business—all the furniture turned upside down—the little heathen idols scattered about, and all the rest of it, was just a damn fake. The rawest kind of a plant, and laid on too thick."

"Not Rangore?" said Leander Eggleston in bloodshot amazement. "But—but the sign on the mirror! The scattered Buddhas! Who else could have climb' up the tree outside, and broke in window?"

"The man who did it didn't bust through any window," said Hennessy. "He planted it to *look* like he did, sure. He was careful to bust the glass from the outside, which shows he was a smart man. But Bye here saw him reaching out his arm from inside, saw him break the window long after that poor girl had been murdered. The man who killed her had a key, and he came up the stairs!"

"But," Eggleston cried, "tha'sh impossible, officer! Nobody had a key—not even the servants, except the butler. But if you are sure it was inshide job, it leaves everybody open to sh'spicion. I better give you account of my own whereabouts t'night." He hiccuped, but controlled himself. "I left house at eight twenty-five—no, eight twenty-eight. I met patrolman out in front—Officer Rounds—and we walked down to corner together. We stood discushing fights about four or five minutes—until about eight thirty-two. Then, shince it was bright pleashant night—that wash before any rain, and the moon wash out—I decided to walk to th' armory. I arrived there at precishely three minutes after nine. I shtill have a ticket stub somewhere. I wash there, of courshe, from—"

"Never mind the alibi, Mr. Eggleston," said Hennessy with a wave of his hand, half amused, half grim. "We know who the murderer is."

"You know?"

"Yes, Adelbert Q. Van Nieman's youngest son, Howe Van Nieman. He used to live in this house, and he'd have a key."

Leander Eggleston sat silent a long moment.

"I don' know him," he said. "Far as I know, Lila didn' know him either. I never heard her—*hic*—mention him."

"We have indications to the contrary. At least he knew your wife's maid, Suzanne. We have evidence that they were planning to rob your wife's jewels."

Leander reached for his glass again. He treated himself to a stiff one.

"Congrashulations," he said, "on extra-or'inary piece of detective work. And where ish this man?"

"I'd like to know. Sherlock here looks like he's going to locate him from his pen."

Hapwood Bye was still fingering the fountain pen which Hennessy had found on the stairs, turning it around in his hand while he meditated with a confused brain. He heard the sergeant's slurring remark indifferently. He put his thumb over the "Nieman" part of the name engraved on the pen, and turned it upside down. For a moment he stared.

"What now, Sherlock?" grunted Hennessy in sour amusement. "Have you found him in the ink reservoir?"

"I may not be able to tell you where he is now," said Hapwood, in a voice cracking with repressed excitement, "But I can tell you where he's been during these last weeks, and up to a short time ago tonight! Read it and weep! I knew there was something in that pen!"

He thrust the pen beneath Hennessy's eyes upside down, as he had held it. Hennessy stared.

HOWE VAN

"Navewoh—Howe Van, upside down!" said Hennessy. "Navewoh! The missing butler!"

"I don't un'erstand," said Eggleston.

"Navewoh ish one of the Van Nieman shervants. We got him—"

"He's Howe Van Nieman!" Hennessy said grimly. "He's been lying low in this house to play his devil's game! And he was still here when you left tonight. *He* was the man who busted out past you at the door! You didn't have much chance to take a good look at him. You had hardly more than reached the door, as I remember, before he came busting out."

The reporter stood shivering. The silences of this animal-tenanted house were so deep and whispery that a man imagined things. A little while ago he had almost imagined that he had heard the front door-lock softly click, and had heard a quick, quiet footstep pattering towards the back of the house down on the first floor below.

But it must have been only the dog, Greta. Upstairs the dead girl lay, and Rounds' feet moved slowly back and forth across the floor in patient vigil. Upstairs the parrot slept, ruffling its feathers in its sleep. Upstairs the black-faced Siamese cat prowled on soft padded feet. Somewhere the dog was prowling, too. Shivering, Hapwood heard with straining ears the quick, light step that was coming up the carpeted stairs from below. Yes, it must be the restless dog which was coming up so quickly and so softly towards the door.

"Where's that drink you promised, Leander?" he asked, his teeth rattling.

Whiskey, with a bullet in it.

And all at once here came the whiskey. It was coming in on a silver platter, two bottles of it, tall rye and squat, black Irish, along with mineral waters, tumblers, corkscrew, and an ice tub. The butler whom Eggleston had rung for was carrying it. He entered the living room in his plum-colored cutaway and brown-and-yellow striped waistcoat—tall, lean, sedate. He had dark blue eyes, dark curly hair; his lean and rather long face had a sprinkling of sandy freckles, *and there was a little dent in his square chin.* Howe Van Nieman, disguised in butler's uniform!

"I was just getting home, sir," he said quietly, approaching the desk with his tray. "I thought I heard you give your whiskey ring as I came in the door. It took me a moment or two to change into uniform, sir—"

Sergeant Hennessy took a whistling breath. His powerful bulk launched itself from its chair. He snapped the handcuffs on the tall, smooth man in livery before Van Nieman knew what he was doing.

Terrified the butler looked down at his locked wrists.

"You've got me!" he gasped.

Hennessy could not forbear a triumphant glance at Hapwood Bye as he frisked his captive for a gun. But the reporter had dived down on his hands and knees on the floor, rescuing the bottle of rye which had fallen when the fake butler had dropped the tray.

Hapwood pulled out the cork. He still didn't think that Van Nieman had been the killer. It was the chill and fever, no doubt, which made him so stupid that he couldn't see what the police sergeant saw, probably.

Howe Van Nieman's knees were sagging.

"You've got me, officer," he repeated lifelessly. "Though how you found me, I don't understand yet. I thought I'd covered all my tracks. I suppose there's no use asking you to keep this from my father."

"If you make a clean breast of it," Hennessy promised, "I'll try to make it as easy as possible for your family. Will YOU make a voluntary statement before these two witnesses?"

Van Nieman nodded.

"Where do you want me to begin?"

"At the start—the whole story," said Hennessy grimly. "Just to convince Bright-Eyes here, the boy detective who doesn't believe me yet, that he missed a few tonight."

"It started five years ago, I guess," Van Nieman said, "when Nellie—Lila Lane, she is now—was sixteen. I had always thought she was a pretty, bright little thing, but that summer I realized she was beautiful. I fell in love with her."

He swallowed, looking down at the floor, avoiding the glaring, bloodshot eyes of Leander Eggleston.

"I couldn't say anything to her, of course," he continued. "She was too young, and it'd be years before I could marry. I didn't have any right to tie her down with a love affair. We were just friends. Then there came the time when that drunken brute of a father of hers beat her and tried to kill her. She had to run away. Luckily, I had a couple of hundred dollars in my savings account, which I forced her to accept. I drove her down to the station. That was five years ago.

"Let me give you my word," he said desperately, lifting his haggard glance an instant to Eggleston, and then to Hennessy, "that until two weeks ago I never dreamed that the famous Lila Lane was the lovely and pathetic little Nellie Lang I loved. I want you to understand there was no premeditation in it. I had never seen Lila Lane on the screen; I'm not a movie-goer. The last I had heard from her was six months after she ran away. That was more than four years ago, and she was still using her own name then. She sent me a check for the two hundred I had given her, and wrote that she had married a camera man out in Hollywood. She had done it, she said, because he could give her an opening into the movies."

"Why, damn you, you thin, prune-faced, half-witted gigolo!" burst out Leander Eggleston with a wild glare. "Do you mean she took *my* money to give to *you?*"

"Calm down, Mr. Eggleston," said Hennessy.

"I know how you feel about me, Eggleston," said the tall young architect wearily. "But YOU have my word that I had no idea who the famous Lila Lane was, when she rented this house a few weeks ago. It seemed a simple thing for me to take this job as butler. Old Harris, who had been with us forty years, was retiring on his investments, and the place was open. I needed a job. Harris and the rest of the staff, of course, helped me. It was a job that gave me room and board, and a hundred and twenty a month clear, besides. Better than walking the streets trying to get a draftsman's job at ten dollars a week.

"Then I saw her! In this very room two weeks ago, when I presented myself to her for orders. She knew me. of course. She began to cry. How was I to know that she had always loved me as I loved her?"

"You dirty dog!" bubbled Leander Eggleston.

"I swear to you," said Van Nieman, "that I never touched her. Never spoke a word out of my place to her. There was nothing —until tonight."

"And *tonight?"* prompted Hennessy.

"All the servants were going out," Van Nieman recounted wearily. "Even little Suzanne had a date with some big cop. Nellie—Lila—wanted me to stay and talk the whole situation over. I said I wouldn't. I couldn't, you know. Not in *his* house, behind *his* back! Lila—I'll call her Lila—and I had a kind of quarrel about it."

"A quarrel?"

"Yes. Then little Suzanne came back."

"Yes?" purred Hennessy.

"Yes. Her cop had failed to show up. She returned at about a quarter of nine. Lila wanted to go out some place then, and talk with me outside. I wouldn't do that either. After some discussion I went out alone, leaving Lila in the house. She—"

"She was in the house with Suzanne *alone* when you left?" said Hennessy. He frowned. Just for an instant the shadow of a fleeting and confused thought must have crossed the sergeant's brain—the same thought, perhaps, which had occurred to Hapwood Bye at the moment when the dead girl was discovered in the closet. "What time was that?"

"About ten o'clock or a little after," said Van Nieman. "I went out, but I waited across the street. I saw Rounds, who knows me, coming down the street, so I walked away. It was just beginning to rain. Lila was out looking for me when I got back. We walked around the streets in the rain, and talked. I was weak to listen to her, I suppose, but I couldn't fight against it any longer. She had never loved him, she told me. He was more than twice her age. He was brutal and mean and a drunkard like her father. She had only married him to get the money to pay me back. She had tried to he a faithful wife to him, but he was getting worse all the time. He spent her money on other women. He hadn't worked for years. She couldn't stand it any longer. She was through, she said, and had already told him so."

"Huh! Is this your fountain pen?" Hennessy asked curtly.

"Why, yes. I must have dropped it somewhere in the house."

"What does *that* prove?" murmured Hapwood Bye.

Hennessy's face was a dark red. He had lost the thread of his conclusion.

"Is this your handwriting, too?" he said, holding up before Van Nieman the scrap of paper which he had found in the dead girl's dressing-gown.

"Why, that must be a scrap of the note I handed Suzanne just as she was going out this evening," Howe Van Nieman said slowly. "Where did you find it? You see," he explained, "Suzanne had an idea in her silly little head that Eggleston was pursuing her. She was sure he had tried to break into her room a couple of times, and she didn't like the way he was always pawing her. She got quite hysterical one night last week when she was alone in the house with him, I remember, and came rushing out in the street after me. I calmed her, and told her to go back, as I wouldn't let anything happen to her. This morning she told me she was going to complain to her mistress about him. I thought it over all day, and advised her not to. But Eggleston himself was waiting in the hall when she went out. I had just a chance to slip her a note. I said—what did I say?—oh, something about that it wouldn't kill Miss Lane if Suzanne complained. That she already suspected something about him, but there was no sense stirring up trouble. Yes, that's what I said."

He sat there a moment without saying anything more, looking at Hennessy anxiously. "Is that all, officer?"

"All?" roared Hennessy. *"All?* Why, you haven't begun to tell us a damned thing yet! Come on, give us the details of the crime!"

"But I thought I had," said Van Nieman.

"Come on! What did you do with the gun!"

"What gun?"

Hennessy arose in wrath. He jerked the tall, young architect to his feet.

"The old run-around, is it?" he said. "Well, I know a place where some of the answers can be slapped out of you! And I know the boys who can do it!"

Hapwood Bye downed his drink.

"Just what, may I inquire, Mr. Van Nieman," he put in gently, surveying the accused man's confused face, "do you think you have been arrested for?"

"Why," explained Howe Van Nieman stutteringly, "for impersonating a butler."

Hapwood Bye laughed. He threw back his head while the drink surged in him, and opened his mouth and shouted with laughter. And that was the greatest mistake of his life.

"The old run-around!" snarled Hennessy, furious and incoherent. "Come on! We'll lather it out of you, Van Nieman!"

The reporter's laughter had aroused the headquarters man to a blind fury. He did not stop to ponder more, as he might have done otherwise. He had his man, and his man was making a fool of him in front of smart-alec Bye. With a twisting grip on the elbow he propelled Van Nieman, stumbling on long legs, towards the door.

"You'll laugh on the other side of your mouth yet, Bye!" he snapped.

Hapwood Bye still laughed. The rye was strong.

Leander Eggleston had been holding his whiskey tumbler in a shaking hand all during Van Nieman's story. He lifted the tall glass now and downed the last of it with a gulp. With bloodshot eyes, puffing like a porpoise, he sprang up. He crashed his glass down on the floor. He started after his ex-butler with murderous fury.

"Ask the dirty dog why he killed Lila, officer!" he croaked triumphantly. "Ask him why he sneaked back in at half past ten when the rain was falling and there was no one on the street to see! Ask him why he hunted her with a gun in his hand, till he found her hiding in the clothes closet!"

"For God's sake!" gasped Howe Van Nieman, looking back as Hennessy propelled him out the door. "Why, Lila is on a train for Reno! I went down to the station with her, and watched her leave!"

Leander Eggleston's puffy face went white as chalk. A strangled sound was in his throat.

"*What?*" he croaked. "She wasn't here? It was Suzanne then? You didn't tell me!"

His jaw moved more, but the rest of what he said was unintelligible. He followed Hennessy and the sergeant's prisoner out the door. And Hapwood Bye stared at Leander's feet!

Those neatly polished, those dry and shining feet!

"Oh, great holy goose grease!" the reporter gasped in a hushed whisper. "Strike me blind with a horsefeather and let the cuckoo bird eat out my brain! *Gemültlicher Gott!* The umbrella! The hair!"

Wild-eyed, with a shaking hand he seized the telephone on the desk.

"Information!" he yelped into the phone. "I want to trace a call! This is the police! Get this! At five minutes after midnight tonight I tried to get this number, Elm 3014, from the pay station of the All-Nite drugstore. I was given the "line busy" signal at first. Check what number was being called from Elm 3014 at that time! I'll hold the wire! Yes, this is the police! Twelve-five o'clock, that's right! You've got it."

He pushed aside a bronze paperweight which stood on the desk in the way of his elbow. Holding the receiver to his car, he reached shakily in his pocket for a cigarette. In the middle of the gesture his hand stiffened. His whole spine stiffened. His body went cold, as cold as a man a long time in the grave. He knew that he had made the greatest and most fatal mistake of his life.

He had heard a step upon the stair!

## CHAPTER VII

## THE DARK MAN

HE HAD HEARD the click of the inner door and then the slam of the outer as furious Hennessy had gone out with his prisoner. He had heard them on the stoop below the bay window. Hennessy was going down to the drugstore to telephone, having left in such a fury that he had forgotten to summon a wagon from the house. Hennessy had gone out, and Van Nieman. But *Leander* hadn't gone out with them. Oh, no, Leander hadn't gone out!

That step upon the stair, creeping back up! Creeping back up!

Hapwood Bye's spine was frozen. He knew what a gun could do in the hand of a madman.

Whiskey with a bullet in it. The whiskey was in his stomach, and the bullet was on its way!

He sat there, frozen. He wanted to yell to Rounds moving around stolidly in the room above. He wanted to yell his head off to Hennessy walking away down the sidewalk below with his prisoner. He wanted to leap backward out the window himself, or stick his head ostrich-like down beneath the desk.

But he had waited too long in that dreadful frozen moment, and Leander had come back too quickly. The killer was coming back through the doorway quick and catlike on his shiny polished feet, while Hapwood Bye still sat helplessly at the phone fingering the bronze paperweight.

The killer was coming back with his right hand thrust beneath his coat, in the same gesture he had used before in this very room when he had thought that Hennessy suspected him, when he had thought that he was cornered. And his feet moved as a cat's feet move, and his bloodshot eyes were bulging and his plump lips were sucked in purplishly, and his face was very evil.

Leander had heard Hapwood's wild excited yelp for information. And Leander understood what he had wanted to find out. Oh, Leander understood!

With an expressionless face Hapwood held the phone, not looking at Leander coming towards him, but staring down at the bronze paperweight in his left hand. His back was frozen, and he felt very sick inside. He had only a moment—he had only his wits and a moment—between himself and death. Now he forced those wits to work, lightning-like.

"What? You can't check it at all you say, supervisor?" he said breezily into the silent telephone. "Well, never mind! It was of no importance, anyway. Give me the *Evening Comet,* Main 2900. . .Is that the *Comet?* City desk, Bye speaking. . .Hello, Bill!" he said cheerily. "This is Bye. Sorry to interrupt your poker game, Bill, but there's a big story at Lila Lane's house. Her French maid's been murdered. Young Howe Van Nieman, son of old Adelbert Q. Van Nieman—"

Leander was standing almost at his shoulder now. He had his gun softly and quietly half-withdrawn from beneath his hunched shoulder. And Leander's breath made a little sighing sound between his purplish sucked-in lips, and his eyes were bulging with murder.

He can shoot me, thought Hapwood Bye, and get away with it. He can say I found the murder gun in the desk drawer here, and was examining it when it went off. It would be just like me, Hennessy would agree, to be snooping and fooling around where I shouldn't.

Leander's smooth brown hair, that was a little too brown to be real, was somewhat askew on his head. Leander's wig—his brown toupee—had been stepped on tonight. Yes, that soft hairy thing, which Hapwood had felt beneath his foot in the darkness as he ran across the murder room, had been Leander's toupee. For it had been his hair which Leander had forgotten, had lost and forgotten during those wild moments, those still and awful and terrible moments of the death hunt.

Leander had clean forgotten his toupee, and had not realized his loss till he had rubbed his hand over his shining bald head after he took off his hat down in the hallway in front of Hapwood and Hennessy and Rounds. That was why Leander had suddenly been afraid, why he had tried to be the first up the stairs. That was why Leander had put his hand over the light switch on the wall inside the murder room before Hapwood could reach it, and had shouted out to call Hapwood's attention away from the meaning of his gesture, yelling "Rangore!" at the monkey leaping through the window.

And Leander had found that damning toupee on the floor in the dark while Hapwood and Hennessy were making monkeys out of themselves. Leander had been sitting on the floor patting his wig into place when Rounds had finally flashed on the lights. Which was the thing Hapwood should have noticed. For Leander had been baldheaded when they had first seen him!

But his toupee was askew now upon his bald veined head, and his eyes were red with murder.

## CHAPTER VIII

## THINK QUICK, OR DIE!

ALL THESE THINGS passed through Hapwood's mind in an instant. And he did not look up as Leander jerked the curtains across the entrance of the window alcove in front of the desk, shutting the two of them off together within this narrow space. He did not move a muscle of his frozen face. He merely gave a casual abstracted nod, recognizing Leander's presence indifferently. He continued speaking into the silent phone to a mythical Bill at the city desk of the *Comet*—where there was not even a lobster-shift man on duty at this hour—without a break in the flow of his brisk, newsy voice.

And Leander had the gun within six inches of his head. But Hapwood had his wits. He knew that Leander wouldn't fire that gun while he was talking.

"Young Van Nieman did it, Bill," he said cheerily, fingering the bronze paperweight. "Howe C, that's right. Murdered the girl. Suzanne LeClerc, that's right. Nieman was caught red-handed trying to give some poisoned whiskey to Mr. Leander M. Eggleston, the distinguished West Coast Movie magnate and Miss Lane's husband. Leander M. Eggleston, that's right. I think that's right." A moment of silence.

"P." said Leander in his ear. "Not Leander M—Leander P.!"

"Oh, wait a minute, Bill," said Hapwood quickly into the phone. "Mr. Eggleston's here with me right now, Bill. He did a lot to help unmask the murderer by his smart questioning—you want to play that up in your story. You'd like to have a little statement from Mr. Eggleston for publication, you say? Why, no doubt he'd be glad to. Just hold the wire a moment."

The reporter forced himself to look around. He looked at Leander. Guilelessly. Unconcerned. He held the phone for Leander to take.

"Just a brief statement for the press, won't you?"

For a long, long time Leander Eggleston stared at him with a bloodshot suspicious glare. Trying to read into his mind. Trying to read what Hapwood might know. At least it seemed to Hapwood a long, long time. And he did not breathe, but smiled.

Slowly Leander reached over and took the phone in his left hand.

"Hello?" he croaked.

Very neatly, then, and with considerable force and speed, Hapwood Bye crashed the bronze paperweight against the side of Leander's head, just back of one ear. Leander pitched forward across the desk.

"Murder!" yelled Hapwood. "Murder! Help! I've got him! Help!"

He was quite hysterical now that it was all over.

However, he had done a pretty good job of getting Leander tied and knotted up with the portière curtain-rods, and even the silk bell-pull, and everything else he could lay his hands on, before Rounds awoke and lumbered down the stairs. Leander lay trussed on the floor in front of the red desk like a particularly poisonous species of beetle wrapped 'round and 'round in a cocoon of knots and ropes and stays and hitches.

"Call Hennessy at headquarters!" gasped Hapwood in wild excitement. "It's the murderer! *It's the murderer!* Look, Rounds, he was supposed to have *just* come in from the rain—*but his shoes were dry!* Look at him, all dry! He was right there before us all along, and we didn't see him! Get hold of Hennessy, quick!" But there was no need of calling Hennessy, for at that very moment Hennessy was reentering through the front door below and coming back up the stairs with his bewildered prisoner. The fact was, that Hennessy had not progressed as far as the drugstore before heavy doubts had begun to assail his ponderous brain. Just suppose young Van Niemen's story was true. Just suppose he could prove he had been down at the station with Lila Lane at the time the murder had been done. It would never do to get caught in a break like that. Hennessy had turned back a little sheepishly.

"Look here, Bye, I kind of got to thinking," he said, as he came in the door, argumentatively. "More and more I've got to thinking that maybe it was this heathen Hindu Rangore, after all. That—"

He stopped and stared at the bound man on the floor.

"I'm afraid I dented the paperweight, Hennessy," said Hapwood Bye a little shrilly. "But I had to crack down on him. It was that gun he had. I was rather afraid he had reloaded it again. Would you mind awfully seeing if the thing is loaded? Yes, by jingoes, it is! I had an idea that it was!"

The headquarters man was in a daze. It was Rounds who had to find the handcuff key and release Howe Van Nieman. Hennessy could only kneel on the floor, examining the murder gun in befuddlement.

"Christmas day!" he said. "His wig has fallen off! Why, he was bald at first, wasn't he, Bye? I kind of mentioned it to you at the time."

"Yeah, you mentioned it!" said Hapwood, sarcastically.

He poured himself another drink. "He came creeping back at half past ten, Hennessy." he said. "No one would miss him in that big mob at the armory. He expected to find his wife alone. He came creeping up the stairs on his wet feet. He looked for her in the living-room where he had left her, then went stalking her up to her bedroom. Suzanne saw him. She thought he was coming to make a play for her, and so she hid. He shot her thinking it was Lila. He changed his wet shoes and clothes for dry ones, and then staged that scene of the broken window, and the sign of Siva, and all the rest of it. And he came rushing down to the door when the cab drove up, with his umbrella and his raincoat, to make us believe he had just come home, in the taxi. Why, he wouldn't have had an umbrella or a raincoat if he had just returned from the armory in a taxi! The night had been bright and fair when he left home at half past eight. Hell, the rain hadn't begun till ten o'clock. He didn't have a raincoat when you saw him on his way to the lights, did he, Rounds?"

"Now that you mention it," said Rounds heavily, "he didn't. He was dressed in a brown suit and brown shoes, and didn't have a topcoat on at all."

"We'll probably find that wet suit in his closet," the reporter said, "along with his wet gloves."

And find them they did, later on.

"There he was at the door when we came rushing up, all of us soaked to the bone." Hapwood said now, breathing more warmly as the rye took hold of him. "And he was supposed to have walked several blocks from the armory in that downpour. *Yet he was dry as a bone!* Shoes shining and dry! Not a drop on his pearl-gray hat. Nor a drop on his raincoat nor on his rolled umbrella. You don't roll a wet umbrella, anyway. Do you remember how he laid them all down on that priceless antique table in the hall when he came in with us? Would a man as neat and careful as he is lay wet things down on a polished piece of furniture; do anything with them, in fact, except hang them up? No! There Eggleston was, standing right in front of us, dry from hat to shoes, proving he'd *already* been in the house and changed his clothes! We were nuts not to see it all sooner, Hennessy!"

"You remember," said Hennessy, "you remember I told you Suzanne had been killed in mistake for Lila? You remember I kind of questioned him, don't you?"

"I remember a lot," said Hapwood, winking at Rounds. "Yeah."

Hennessy turned his red self-assured face to Howe Van Nieman.

"Thanks, Mr. Van Nieman." he said, slapping the tall dark-haired fake butler jovially on the back. "You played the game beautifully. We had to catch this guy Eggleston off his guard, you see, because we knew he was a killer and a tough one. It worked out just as I had planned. Many thanks for the swell help YOU gave."

"But I thought you meant it, officer!" said Van Nieman with a sickly grin. "Really."

"Hell, don't kid yourself," said Hennessy grandly, snapping the bracelets on Leander Eggleston's plump wrists. "They've got to be smarter fellows than this one before they fool Richard P. Hennessy."

"Lila thought he had tried to kill her once before." said Van Nieman in a low-apologetic voice. "There was a million dollars insurance he had persuaded her to take out, you know, and which would have gone to him. And he knew that she was going to leave him. He had to cash in quick."

Hapgood Bye said, "You'd better run along now, and telegraph Miss Lane to rush through that divorce of hers before the state electrician beats her to it, Van Nieman. It ought to take about two months for Leander to get through the courts to the hot squat, if his lawyer's a good one. And Reno's only six weeks."

"Do you mean," the tall young fellow said, darkly flushing—"do you mean that I can marry N-N-Nellie—Miss Lane—in six weeks?"

"Why ask me? Ask her!"

"She did," Van Nieman stammered redly. "I mean, she asked me already."

"Hell!" said Hapwood.

The chalk-faced killer on the floor was beginning to grumble and stir and blow bubbles from his puffy lips. He opened his bloodshot eyes. He was trying to sit up. With a dazed look he tried to reach his manacled hands up to his head.

"But there's one thing, Bye," said Hennessy. "There's one little thing I can't understand even yet. We saw somebody come to the house in a taxi. We saw somebody else leave. You and I and Rounds here, all three of us. We saw both of them."

"Both of *him.*" said Hapwood.

The telephone which he had forgotten for ten minutes was ringing steadily now. He picked it up.

"About that call which went out from Elm 3014 at twelve o'clock to-night," said Information. "There was only one call from Elm 3014 to-night. It was to the Paramount Day-and-Night Taxi Service on East Third Street."

That was how Hapwood had figured it out, already.

"Give me that number, will you, sister?" he said.

With a jerking grin he motioned Hennessey to share the receiver with him.

"Pa'amount Day-'n'-Night Taxi," said a tired negro voice over the telephone.

"Hello," said Bye. "You got a call a little after midnight to send a taxi in a hurry to 1125 Massachusetts avenue. Did you send a cab?"

"Lawd, I'll say I did! I went mah-self," said the voice complainingly. "I stopped in front of the house and I went up to the do'. The front do' was open, and I went inside the foyah to knock, when all of a sudden a baldheaded white gen'man with great popping eyes comes busting out the do', cramming a hat on his head and waving a rolled umbrella in one hand and a gun in the othah. Lawdy, when I see that gun I sho' let out a hollah, and I run back down them steps so fast you couldn't see me fo' dust. I got in my cab and I stepped on it. I heard the cops whistling. Did you get him?"

"Thanks," said Hapwood. "One thing more. Why does a man turn out the lights when he leaves a room?"

"You mean in his own house, sah? Why, lawdy," the rich negro voice laughed uproariously. "A man turn out the light when he leave a room to save electwicity! He do it without thinking, if it's his own house."

"Thanks," said Hapwood.

"Don't mention it."

"One last thing." said Hapwood. "Are you a Hindu?"

"No, sah!"

"But dark, very dark." murmured Hapwood as he hung up. "I couldn't believe that Leander was lying in every particular. It was a dark man, Hennessey, that Leander said ran out and got in that taxi and beat it. The taxi driver, of course. But an American negro is a whole long way from a Hindu if you want to be real particular about it!"

# AFTERWORD

## IMMINENT MENACE IN THE SHORT MYSTERY FICTION OF JOEL TOWNSLEY ROGERS

By Alfred Jan

*For those who do not want advance information on these stories, in the following article I plan to discuss the plot structure and the endings of the following:* "The Hiding Horror" (from *Two Book Detective,* January 1935, "The Red Right Hand" (from *New Detective,* March 1945), "The Murderer" (from *Saturday Evening Post,* November 23, 1946) and "Killing Time" (from *New Detective,* July 1947). Bibliographic information was taken from the web site on the author, established by the author's son, Tom Rogers.

Joel Townsley Rogers was one of the most prolific, yet critically undervalued writers from the pulp era. Although he was included in Chris Steinbrunner and Otto Penzler's "Encyclopedia of Mystery and Detection", Lee Server omitted him from his recent "Encyclopedia of Pulp Fiction Writers", and Jacques Barzun and Wendell Hertig Taylor, in their "Catalogue of Crime", revised edition, condemned *The Red Right Hand,* the novel, as "overwritten", "often illiterate", and "a case of bore-dumb." Yet it was the best selling title to that date, 1945, at Simon and Schusters' Inner Sanctum Mystery series. It was awarded the French Grand Prix de Litterature Policiere in 1951 and reprinted in paperback at least three times. In this essay, I intend to examine one of Rogers' many literary devices which gives his stories such emotional force: the sudden realization by the main character that his life will be snuffed out in the next few seconds by a killer located a few inches or feet away.

Born in 1896, in Sedalia, Missouri, Joel Townsley Rogers attended Harvard, graduating in 1918. In 1921, he edited Brentano's newsletter called "Book Chat." Back then, Brentano's sold and published books, including Rogers' first novel, *Once in a Red Moon,* in 1923. During the 1920s, Rogers also wrote for the aviation pulps, including such titles as *Air Stories, Flying Stories,* and *Wings,* his flight instructor experiences during the waning years of World War I providing much material for this genre.

In addition, he contributed to fluffy "risque" pulps like *Snappy Stories* and *The Follies,* which presented romantic escapades rife with mistaken identities, awkward situations, and misunderstandings, but not the sex act itself, of course. Even compared to the girly pulps of the 1930s, these were tame indeed. He wrote the majority of his mystery stories during the 1930s and 1940s, venturing into science fiction in the early 1950s. Those published in *Thrilling Wonder Stories* and *Startling Stories* dealt mainly with consequences of time stoppage and possibilities of righting wrongs and changing history. Rogers died in 1984.

Commentator Elliot L. Gilbert suggested that the novel *The Red Right Hand,* expanded from the short story, is "expressionistic," because the woman character's dream constituted the novel's plot. I agree that Rogers' mystery stories are expressionistic, but in a different sense.

Loosely defined, an expressionistic theory of art claims that an artwork, or literary text, induces an emotional response from viewers or readers. Imminent menace to the protagonist causes the reader to feel vicarious panic and fear. This nightmarish situation occurs when you suddenly realize the person standing nearby is a killer who knows you know, and you will be his next victim. The expressionistic quality of Rogers' stories sets him apart from both traditional English mysteries, where detectives logically deduce the murderer's identity, and American hardboiled lone wolf private investigators who expose corrupt institutions. Rogers' protagonists are medical doctors, reporters, even pulp magazine writers, average people caught up in murder, not unlike those of his contemporary, Cornell Woolrich.

"The Hiding Horror" takes place in a creaky old mansion, where in the opening paragraphs, somebody stalks and kills a lone woman in the house. Lila Lane, famous movie star, grew up in that house as the chauffeur's daughter and had recently rented it to get away from Hollywood. She brought a dog, cat, monkey, parrot, jade Buddha collection, and a milquetoast husband, former camera man Leander Eggleston. A reporter, Hapwood Bye, and policeman Sergeant Hennessy investigate the corpse in the closet, which turned out to be Lila's French maid, not her. Howe Van Nieman, son of the mansion owner and socialist-leaning architect, had anonymously hired on as a butler, using the none "Navewoh", an anagram of "Van Howe".

Eventually, Bye realized Eggleston was the killer, who at the very same moment entered the room with a gun, knowing that he knew. With only seconds to devise an escape, Bye tricks him into taking the phone, bashing him over the head with a bookend and avoiding getting shot.

Before this occurred, Van Howe had been taken into custody by Hennessy, who mistakenly thought he had killed the maid after she refused to go along with a plot to steal Lila's jewels. In fact, Van Howe loved Lila, and he had escorted her to the train station earlier for a trip out of town. Eggleston, on the other hand, was abusive and had plotted to kill Lila for the insurance money. He had stalked the maid into the closet and shot her through the door, thinking she was his wife.

In addition to presenting the ineffectual weakling who turns to violence as a frightening character, Rogers showed support towards societal "others." Van Howe, a socialist, was a sympathetic character wrongly charged by the police. Secondly, Eggleston tried to throw suspicion off himself by insinuating, and planting false clues, that dark skinned Hindus had committed the crime, but Bye was not fooled. The anagrammatic name device returns later, belonging to a decidedly unsympathetic figure.

Rogers' menace plots occur in large spooky mansions at one extreme, to the cranked urban apartment, where "Killing Time" takes place. Reginald Meice Little, a struggling pulp writer tries to break into print by studying *Five Fundamental Rules for Writing Murder Stories* by Richard C. Morgelhead. After much deliberation, he plots a story based on water habitually leaking into his apartment from the upstairs bathroom belonging to a woman who uses her bathtub regularly. According to his story, someone kills her, and places her body in the tub with water running to delay rigor mortis, thus freeing the killer to build an alibi. When the tub overflows, water seeps into his apartment.

Little submits his story to *Banner Murder Stories,* edited by Morgelhead himself who personally visits to buy it, and to offer him a trip out of the country on a "special assignment." Before long, Little realizes his editor killed his wife the woman upstairs, exactly the way his story described it, and because Little was aware of his plot, Morgelhead is going to kill him if he does not accept the foreign assignment. Morgelhead pulls out a gun, but Little heaves a typewriter at him, wounding and disarming him. At this key point in the story, because he was World War II vet, Little could "smell murder" up close and imminent.

Rogers makes fun of pulp editors, portraying Morgelhead as a money hungry author who became an editor because his book was not profitable, but it was worshiped by Little, who was disillusioned to discover his hero was not a purist. In addition to the close proximity threat, Rogers employed another common device of his, that of a real murder matching a fictionally plotted one. In this story, the degree of fear and panic is only slightly mitigated by humor and self-referentiality.

A more elemental dual between two men can be found in "The Murderer," which was reprinted several times and adapted for radio and television. . .John Bantreagh, knees wobbly, truck engine crank in hand, sees his wife Mollie's dead body on the ground, her throat and ankles run over by truck wheels. When a uniformed deputy sheriff drives up in his patrol car and investigates, John tells him she was his wife, and that a younger neighbor woman would now have to look after his children on a more regular basis.

The cop surmises that she knew the killer, perhaps someone tired of her nagging who wanted her out of the way so he can marry a sweet young thing? When he asks John if she had a man on the side, he replies yes, because diner patrons had reported to him that they saw her taking food for a companion waiting outside, plus he had discovered dainty underwear hidden in a drawer. The cop asserts that "married ones are hard to ditch," so perhaps this other man had grown tired of her and killed her, all the awhile being careful to avoid being seen with her in public. Finally, the cop says there is not much to go on.

All this time, Rogers describes John as having knees which kept caving in, eyes looking at the ground and sweat dripping down his face, leading the reader to suspect him of killing his wife. But when John tells the cop Mollie had whispered the killer's name before dying, it causes him to reach for his gun, catching the reader by surprise. Cracking the other man's wrist with the crank, John disarms and handcuffs him.

He then explains how he knew the cop, the "other man," had killed his wife. He had never asked John directly whether he had killed her, but more importantly, he spelled Mollie's last name correctly, rather than phonetically, in his notebook. All of John's nervous behavior merely represented his fear of being falsely accused.

In this story, Rogers distills his device to its essence: a suspenseful confrontation between two characters only, one in which the killer will eliminate the other unless the latter can take action within seconds of the first that knowing he knows. There is no humor here to temper the emotional shock the climax delivers.

Rogers' most well known story is "The Red Right Hand", which was expanded to novel length after being published first in a pulp magazine. From the opening paragraphs, Rogers grabs the reader by the throat and does not let go. Based on primal fears resulting from picking up a weird hitchhiker, horrible possibilities present themselves at the outset. One of the moodiest and atmospheric of Rogers' mysteries, it is not meant to be interpreted literally, because some suspension of disbelief is required to feel the maximum emotional effect; hence critics like Barzun who value realistic narratives miss the point.

Dr. Henry Riddle, a surgeon, investigates the death of Inis St. Erme, supposedly killed by "Yellow Fang," a tramp whom the dead man and his fiancée, Elinor Darrie, had picked up on their way to be married. (St. Erme's real identity is A.M. Dexter of Dexter's Day and Nite Garage in Manhattan; Inis St. Erme is an anagram for Sinister Me.) He tricked Elinor into believing the tramp killed him, whereas he had really killed the tramp and then assumed his identity by wearing his clothes, going off on a killing spree.

One of his victims was a pedestrian whose right hand was cut off to simulate "St. Erme's" corpse. He also killed his uncle, a Professor MacComerou, whose psychiatry textbook containing a case history of his nephew as a pathological narcissist Riddle had used in medical school. Dexter had planned to murder his uncle for insurance money and then assume *his* identity to live on his property for free. Dexter also swindled Elinor out of her savings by altering a check she had written and cashing it prior to their trip.

The moment of crisis in the story comes when Riddle realizes MacComerou is really Dexter, with the killer standing right behind him. After a struggle, Riddle kills Dexter with a garden hoe, but not before sustaining a crushed foot.

Coincidence and considerable suspension of disbelief play prominent roles in this story, the most glaring being Elinor Darrie's vision, which Riddle knew to be 20/400. How he knew is never explained, but a person with that visual acuity can only see the big E on the eye chart, yet she was able to drive a car at night. On the other hand, consistent with her high myopia, she could not recognize her fiancée in the guise of his uncle. This is obviously a contradiction, but according to Riddle's theory, Eleanor, being female, refused to wear glasses due to vanity.

Another major coincidence involves similarities between Riddle and Yellow Fang the tramp, who gave his name as "Doc". He also knew Latin, and wore a hat which once belonged to Riddle but which he had previously discarded. When Riddle encountered a frantic Eleanor on the road at night, she initially mistook him for Yellow Fang, which can also be explained by her poor night vision and being nearsighted.

Rogers' cautionary tale urges us not to jump to conclusions based on appearances, because after all, Yellow Fang was murdered by a psychopath who seemed "normal" at first glance. Moralizing aside, this story requires more than one reading to appreciate the many layers of revelations, correlations, and connections which lead up to the horrific climax.

Many of Rogers' short mystery fiction can stand with those of Cornell Woolrich and Robert Bloch, but unfortunately, except for "The Murderer", I am aware of none of his stories that have been adapted for radio, television, or the movies. (In 1955 "The Murderer" was the basis for one episode of a short-lived dramatic series called *Star Tonight.)* I hope that this article will initiate increased recognition of Joel Townsley Rogers' short mystery fiction, and his writings in general, including perhaps a published collection, which also has never been done.

## Biographical Note

A practicing optometrist, Alfred Jan collects and writes about pulp magazines. In 2001, he co-edited with Bill Blackbeard *Footprints on a Brain*: *The Inspector Allhoff Stories* by D. L. Champion (Adventure House). Later, for Black Dog Books, he edited *Death's Detour* (2002) and *Gallows Heritage* (2003), The Surgeon of Souls Collection Volumes 1 and 2, written by Robert Leslie Bellem. He currently writes for *Blood 'N' Thunder*, a magazine for pulp and old movie fans. Alfred has a Masters degree in Philosophy specializing in Aesthetics, and has published freelance art criticism.

# RAMBLE HOUSE's

## HARRY STEPHEN KEELER WEBWORK MYSTERIES

(RH) indicates the title is available ONLY in the RAMBLE HOUSE edition

The Ace of Spades Murder
The Affair of the Bottled Deuce (RH)
The Amazing Web
The Barking Clock
Behind That Mask
The Book with the Orange Leaves
The Bottle with the Green Wax Seal
The Box from Japan
The Case of the Canny Killer
The Case of the Crazy Corpse (RH)
The Case of the Flying Hands (RH)
The Case of the Ivory Arrow
The Case of the Jeweled Ragpicker
The Case of the Lavender Gripsack
The Case of the Mysterious Moll
The Case of the 16 Beans
The Case of the Transparent Nude (RH)
The Case of the Transposed Legs
The Case of the Two-Headed Idiot (RH)
The Case of the Two Strange Ladies
The Circus Stealers (RH)
Cleopatra's Tears
A Copy of Beowulf (RH)
The Crimson Cube (RH)
The Face of the Man From Saturn
Find the Clock
The Five Silver Buddhas
The 4th King
The Gallows Waits, My Lord! (RH)
The Green Jade Hand
Finger! Finger!
Hangman's Nights (RH)
I, Chameleon (RH)
I Killed Lincoln at 10:13! (RH)
The Iron Ring
The Man Who Changed His Skin (RH)
The Man with the Crimson Box
The Man with the Magic Eardrums
The Man with the Wooden Spectacles
The Marceau Case
The Matilda Hunter Murder
The Monocled Monster
The Murder of London Lew
The Murdered Mathematician
The Mysterious Card (RH)
The Mysterious Ivory Ball of Wong Shing Li (RH)
The Mystery of the Fiddling Cracksman
The Peacock Fan
The Photo of Lady X (RH)
The Portrait of Jirjohn Cobb
Report on Vanessa Hewstone (RH)

Riddle of the Travelling Skull
Riddle of the Wooden Parrakeet (RH)
The Scarlet Mummy (RH)
The Search for X-Y-Z
The Sharkskin Book
Sing Sing Nights
The Six From Nowhere (RH)
The Skull of the Waltzing Clown
The Spectacles of Mr. Cagliostro
Stand By—London Calling!
The Steeltown Strangler
The Stolen Gravestone (RH)
Strange Journey (RH)
The Strange Will
The Straw Hat Murders (RH)
The Street of 1000 Eyes (RH)
Thieves' Nights
Three Novellos (RH)
The Tiger Snake
The Trap (RH)
Vagabond Nights (Defrauded Yeggman)
Vagabond Nights 2 (10 Hours)
The Vanishing Gold Truck
The Voice of the Seven Sparrows
The Washington Square Enigma
When Thief Meets Thief
The White Circle (RH)
The Wonderful Scheme of Mr. Christopher Thorne
X. Jones—of Scotland Yard
Y. Cheung, Business Detective

Keeler Related Works

**A To Izzard: A Harry Stephen Keeler Companion** by Fender Tucker — Articles and stories about Harry, by Harry, and in his style. Included is a compleat Keeler bibliography.

**Wild About Harry: Reviews of Keeler Novels** — Edited by Richard Polt & Fender Tucker — 22 reviews of works by Harry Stephen Keeler from *Keeler News.* A perfect introduction to the author.

**The Keeler Keyhole Collection:** Annotated newsletter rants from Harry Stephen Keeler, edited by Francis M. Nevins

**Fakealoo** — Pastiches of the style of Harry Stephen Keeler by selected demented members of the HSK Society.

**RAMBLE HOUSE**
**Fender Tucker, Prop.**
**www.ramblehouse.com fender@ramblehouse.com**
**318-455-6847 443 Gladstone Blvd. Shreveport LA 71104**

## **RAMBLE HOUSE**'S OTHER LOONS

**Slammer Days —** Two full-length prison memoirs: *Men into Beasts* (1952) by George Sylvester Viereck and *Home Away From Home* (1962) by Jack Woodford

**The Organ Reader —** A huge compilation of just about everything published in the 1971-1972 radical bay-area newspaper, THE ORGAN.

**Dr. Odin** — Douglas Newton's 1933 potboiler comes back to life.

**The Chinese Jar Mystery** — Murder in the manor by John Stephen Strange, 1934

**The Julius Caesar Murder Case** — A classic 1935 re-telling of the assassination by Wallace Irwin

**The Contested Earth and Other SF Stories** — A never-before published space opera and seven short stories by Jim Harmon.

**Freaks and Fantasies** — Eerie tales by Tod Robbins, collaborator of Tod Browning on the film FREAKS.

**Vixen Scandal** — Two sleaze masterpieces from the 60s by Jim Harmon: *Vixen Hollow* and *Celluloid Scandal.*

**Maniac Siren** — Two more sleaze marvels by Jim Harmon: *The Man Who Made Maniacs* and *Silent Siren*

**West Texas War and Other Western Stories** — by Gary Lovisi

**Marblehead: A Novel of H.P. Lovecraft** — A long-lost masterpiece from Richard A. Lupoff. Published for the first time!

**The Secret Adventures of Sherlock Holmes** — Three Sherlockian pastiches by the Brooklyn author/publisher, Gary Lovisi.

**The Universal Holmes** — Richard A. Lupoff's 2007 collection of five Holmesian pastiches and a recipe for giant rat stew.

**Tales of the Macabre and Ordinary** — Modern twisted horror by Chris Mikul, author of the *Bizarrism* series.

**The Gold Star Line** — Seaboard adventure from L.T. Reade and Robert Eustace.

**The Werewolf vs the Vampire Woman** — Hard to believe ultraviolence by either Arthur M. Scarm or Arthur M. Scram.

**Black Hogan Strikes Again —** Australia's Peter Renwick pens a tale of the outback.

**Four Joel Townsley Rogers Novels** — By the author of *The Red Right Hand: Once In a Red Moon, Lady With the Dice, The Stopped Clock, Never Leave My Bed*

**Killing Time —** New collection of short novels by Joel Townsley Rogers

**Night of Horror** — A short story collection of Joel Townsley Rogers

**Twenty Norman Berrow Novels** — *The Bishop's Sword, Ghost House, Don't Go Out After Dark, Claws of the Cougar, The Smokers of Hashish, The Secret Dancer, Don't Jump Mr. Boland!, The Footprints of Satan, Fingers for Ransom, The Three Tiers of Fantasy, The Spaniard's Thumb, The Eleventh Plague, Words Have Wings, One Thrilling Night, The Lady's in Danger, It Howls at Night, The Terror in the Fog, Oil Under the Window, Murder in the Melody, The Singing Room*

**The N. R. De Mexico Novels** — Robert Bragg presents *Marijuana Girl, Madman on a Drum, Private Chauffeur* in one volume.

**Two Hake Talbot Novels** — *Rim of the Pit, The Hangman's Handyman.* Classic locked room mysteries.

**Two Alexander Laing Novels** — *The Motives of Nicholas Holtz* and *Dr. Scarlett,* stories of medical mayhem and intrigue from the 30s.

**Two Wade Wright Novels (and counting)** — *Echo of Fear* and *Death At Nostalgia Street*, with more to come!

**Three Rupert Penny Novels** — *Policeman's Holiday, Policeman's Evidence* and *Sealed Room Murder,* classic impossible mysteries.

**Five Jack Mann Novels —** Strange murder in the English countryside. *Gees' First Case, Nightmare Farm, Grey Shapes, The Ninth Life, The Glass Too Many.*

**Four Max Afford Novels** — *Owl of Darkness, Death's Mannikins, Blood on His Hands* and *The Dead Are Blind* by One of Australia's finest novelists.

**Five Joseph Shallit Novels** — *The Case of the Billion Dollar Body, Lady Don't Die on My Doorstep, Kiss the Killer, Yell Bloody Murder, Take Your Last Look.* One of America's best 50's authors.

**The Best of 10-Story Book** — edited by Chris Mikul, over 35 stories from the literary magazine Harry Stephen Keeler edited.

**The Anthony Boucher Chronicles** — edited by Francis M. Nevins
Book reviews by Anthony Boucher written for the *San Francisco Chronicle,* 1942 - 1947. Essential and fascinating reading.

**A Young Man's Heart** — A forgotten early classic by Cornell Woolrich

**Muddled Mind:** Complete Works of Ed Wood, Jr. — David Hayes and Hayden Davis deconstruct the life and works of a mad genius.

**My First Time:** The One Experience You Never Forget — Michael Birchwood — 64 true first-person narratives of how they lost it.

**The Incredible Adventures of Rowland Hern** — Rousing 1928 impossible crimes by Nicholas Olde.

**Don Diablo: Book of a Lost Film** — Two-volume treatment of a western by Paul Landres, with diagrams. Intro by Francis M. Nevins.

**The Charlie Chaplin Murder Mystery** — Movie hijinks by Wes D. Gehring

**The Koky Comics** — A collection of all of the 1978-1981 Sunday and daily comic strips by Richard O'Brien and Mort Gerberg, in two volumes.

**Gamefinger** — Incredible 1966 sado-sleaze from Clyde Allison (William Knoles).

**Dime Novels: Ramble House's 10-Cent Books** — *Knife in the Dark* by Robert Leslie Bellem, *Hot Lead* and *Song of Death* by Ed Earl Repp, *A Hashish House in New York* by H.H. Kane, and five more.

**Stakeout on Millennium Drive** — Indianapolis Noir — Ian Woollen.

**Dope Tales #1** — Two dope-riddled classics; *Dope Runners* by Gerald Grantham and *Death Takes the Joystick* by Phillip Condé.

**Dope Tales #2** — Two more narco-classics; *The Invisible Hand* by Rex Dark and *The Smokers of Hashish* by Norman Berrow.

**Dope Tales #3** — Two enchanting novels of opium by the master, Sax Rohmer. *Dope* and *The Yellow Claw.*

**Tenebrae** — Ernest G. Henham's 1898 horror tale brought back.

**The Singular Problem of the Stygian House-Boat** — Two classic tales by John Kendrick Bangs about the denizens of Hades.

**The One After Snelling** — Kickass modern noir from Richard O'Brien.

**The Sign of the Scorpion** — 1935 Edmund Snell tale of oriental evil.

**The House of the Vampire** — 1907 thriller by George S. Viereck.

**An Angel in the Street** — Modern hardboiled noir by Peter Genovese.

**The Devil's Mistress** — Scottish gothic tale by J. W. Brodie-Innes.

**The Lord of Terror** — 1925 mystery with master-criminal, Fantômas.

**The Lady of the Terraces** — 1925 adventure by E. Charles Vivian.

**My Deadly Angel** — 1955 Cold War drama by John Chelton

**Prose Bowl** — Futuristic satire — Bill Pronzini & Barry N. Malzberg .

**Satan's Den Exposed —** True crime in TorC New Mexico — Award-winning journalism by the Desert Journal.

**The Amorous Intrigues & Adventures of Aaron Burr** — by Anonymous — Hot historical action.

**I Stole $16,000,000** — True story by cracksman Herbert E. Wilson.

**The Black Dark Murders** — Vintage 50s college murder yarn by Milt Ozaki, writing as Robert O. Saber.

**Sex Slave** — Potboiler of lust in the days of Cleopatra — Dion Leclerq.

**You'll Die Laughing** — Bruce Elliott's 1945 novel of murder at a practical joker's English countryside manor.

**The Private Journal & Diary of John H. Surratt** — The memoirs of the man who conspired to assassinate President Lincoln.

**Dead Man Talks Too Much** — Hollywood boozer by Weed Dickenson

**Red Light** — History of legal prostitution in Shreveport Louisiana by Eric Brock. Includes wonderful photos of the houses and the ladies.

**Gadsby** — A lipogram (a novel without the letter E). Ernest Vincent Wright's last work, published in 1939 right before his death.

**A Snark Selection** — Lewis Carroll's *The Hunting of the Snark* with two Snarkian chapters by Harry Stephen Keeler — Illustrated by Gavin L. O'Keefe.

**Ripped from the Headlines! —** The Jack the Ripper story as told in the newspaper articles in the *New York* and *London Times.*

**Geronimo** — S. M. Barrett's 1905 autobiography of a noble American.

**The Compleat Calhoon** — All of Fender Tucker's works: Includes *The Totah Trilogy, Weed, Women and Song* and *Tales from the Tower,* plus a CD of all of his songs.

**The Naked Trocar** with **The Best Revenge** — Two misdemeanors by Fender Tucker from 2007